Alexandra Raife has lived abroad in many countries and worked at a variety of jobs, including a six-year commission in the RAF and many years co-running a Highland hotel. She lives in Perthshire. All her previous novels, *Drumveyn*, *The Larach*, *Grianan*, *Belonging*, *Sun on Snow*, *The Wedding Gift*, *Moving On*, and *Among Friends* have been richly praised.

Praise for Alexandra Raife:

'[A] celebration of the joys of home, hearth and family . . . touchingly winsome.'

The Times

'A welcome new storyteller'

Rosamunde Pilcher

'An absorbing story with a perfectly painted back-ground'

Hilary Hale, *Financial Times*

'Scotland's answer to Rosamunde Pilcher'
South Hams Newspapers

'[a] readable love story full of emotion, pain and despair'

Coventry Evening Telegraph

Also by Alexandra Raife

Drumveyn

The Larach

Grianan

Belonging

Sun on Snow

The Wedding Gift

Moving On

Among Friends

Return to Drumveyn

ALEXANDRA RAIFE

The Way Home

CORONET BOOKS
Hodder & Stoughton

Copyright © 2002 by Alexandra Raife

First published in Great Britain in 2002 by Hodder and Stoughton
A division of Hodder Headline
First published in paperback in 2003
A Coronet paperback

The right of Alexandra Raife to be identified as the Author
of the Work has been asserted by her in accordance
with the Copyright, Designs and Patents Act 1988.

1 3 5 7 9 10 8 6 4 2

A CIP catalogue record for this title
is available from the British Library

ISBN 0 340 82237 6

Typeset in Plantin by Hewer Text Ltd, Edinburgh
Printed and bound in Great Britain by
Mackays of Chatham plc, Chatham, Kent

Hodder and Stoughton
A division of Hodder Headline
338 Euston Road
London NW1 3BH

I

Six years since they had all been together. How many more since all three of them had been here at the same time? As the car turned down the steep drive, moving at Vanessa's careful speed, the complex emotions building in Jamie made it impossible for her to try for the moment to work it out. To be back here at last, though arriving later than they had intended after the duties, formalities and discoveries of the crammed day, and after yesterday's lonely flight and all it had meant to her, was almost more than she could deal with.

Thank goodness she hadn't had to come alone. She glanced at the composed profile beside her. Was her elder sister thinking of anything beyond negotiating the tight bends as the tree-lined drive fell rapidly to the river and the waiting house? Vanessa was careful about her cars, as she was about all her possessions, and the big Rover, Cairney version of wife's shopping runaround, immaculate inside and out, must be given due respect.

Jamie found herself smiling, tension forgotten, as her mind went back to the moment of meeting this morning, and the unexpected sense of security which had warmed her at the first glimpse of Vanessa's fair head and neat figure, a sensation belonging to earliest memory.

And Phil? How was she feeling about being at Calder again? Jamie turned her head to glance at their younger sister. For Phil always sat in the back; none of them, even now, had given a thought to her sitting anywhere else. How unthinkingly they had resumed that old pecking order, and yet how amazing, now Jamie came to consider it, had been their equally unquestioning bonding to face all that had had to be faced today.

Here among the trees the last of the evening light was almost swallowed up, and Phil's face was an indistinct blur, but she turned her head, catching Jamie's movement, and Jamie knew she would be smiling.

Was either of them excited to be here, Jamie wondered. In spite of that immediate delight to see each other again, and the instinctive drawing together which had so steadied her, they had grown far apart in real terms. Letters had become rarer and less communicative, little more than a bald catching up on news, and, on her part at least, had usually been a chore.

She wanted now to share the nostalgia, apprehension and anticipation churning in her, but knew that neither of the others would feel it in the same degree. A quick frustration, belonging to faraway days, surged up at their refusal to feel as she felt, then was forgotten in the importance of the moment as the house came into sight at last, grey and quiet in the grey light.

The car rolled quietly across flattened gravel, Vanessa punctiliously making the full circuit so that it came to rest at the front door ready to be driven round to the garage, as the form had always been. How like Vanessa, even in this moment, even now that everything had changed, to observe it.

There was silence for a second as the engine died, a silence of such tense uncertainty that for once Jamie was satisfied that they were all in the grip of the same mood, subject to the same strange reluctance.

'We should have got here earlier,' Vanessa said, and though the remark was pointless, since they had had so much to do and had left Glasgow the moment they could, Jamie agreed with its sense. Sunshine, or even full daylight, would have made the moment less forbidding.

'Come on,' she said, opening her door. Instantly the air from the river was in her nostrils, mixed with the rain-fresh scents of the garden – the forgotten, indefinable, yet somehow always remembered special smell of Calder. Pale among the trees across the drive, the first to be in shadow, she saw the wisps of mist that often gathered and clung there in such chilly early summer dusks as this. Tears stung her eyes, and she blinked them away. This was not about the past; there was no time for the past now.

'I hope everything's properly aired,' Vanessa said worriedly as she too got out of the car and stared up at the blank, unlit façade of the house.

The tone and words were so prosaic, so remote from the feelings assailing Jamie, that she was able to turn tears into laughter. 'Van. I should think that's going to be the least of our worries.'

'Mr Syme said the electricity was on and everything,' Phil reminded them, hauling herself out in her turn in an awkward scramble, a scramble complicated by the fact that she dragged with her, like an anxious child warned to look after its belongings, the grubby blue plastic holdall which had drawn such a frown of disapproval from Vanessa when she saw it.

'It feels a bit strange, doesn't it? Almost as though we shouldn't go in at all.' Vanessa had come round to stand beside Jamie. Her voice sounded thin and unsure, and Jamie caught a shiver which she guessed was not solely caused by the cold touch of river air.

'Calder, ever calder, the air of evening grows,
Breathing from the shadows where swift the Affran
flows . . .'

Grandmother's voice, its soft Scots accent exaggerated, chanting on a note of cheerful irony as they came down the drive after a winter walk and met that penetrating air coiling to meet them. For years Jamie had supposed it was a real poem, not even noticing the pun. How clearly that voice sounded in her ears now, and how passionately for a shaken moment did she long to find the calm, strong, loving presence on the other side of the door, the unalterable refuge.

'Jamie, you've got the keys.'

'Oh, sorry, so I have.' Hurriedly she felt in her bag. This could only be got through by putting emotion on hold and refusing all reminders, just as that had been the only way to get through yesterday's journey.

'It seems funny that it wasn't Freda getting the house ready for us,' Phil said, and though Jamie was momentarily side-tracked by thinking that the hesitant way she offered the remark, prepared to be put down by one sister or both, was at once utterly familiar and faintly disturbing in this new adult context, she realised that for Phil too there was the painful tug of associations with the vanished past.

Then such thoughts were forgotten as excitement took over. This had to be a special moment, turning the big key in the outer door of a house which, with all it had meant to them from earliest childhood, now belonged to them.

'Seems to be stuck.' The inner door to the hall resisted Jamie's push.

'Oh, dear, damp. I knew it.' Vanessa's lugubrious tone echoing in the gloom of the porch suggested that the ultimate disaster had already befallen them.

'Are you sure you turned the key properly?' Phil asked. 'Oh, wait a minute, we can put the light on, can't we? I'd forgotten that.'

They all had, as though the fast dying gloaming light were an intrinsic part of the scene.

'Just not used for a while,' Jamie said. 'Mrs Who-ever-she-is has the back door key. Mr Syme told us that. Give it a shove, one of you, can't you?'

As Phil pressed the switches for both porch and

hall, Jamie and Vanessa, pushing together, forced the door open, and a concerted gasp of disbelief went up from all three.

The comfortable, traditionally furnished and welcoming hall of Grandmother's house had vanished. The floor was no longer covered by the muted Persian rug with its worn tracks round either side of the central table, where a big bowl of flowers was always in place above the clutter of gloves, leads and scarves, where on pain of death the car keys had to be left, where Postie laid the day's mail and picked up anything left for him. No dim paintings in heavy frames of Highland cattle meditating in bogs hung on the walls. No impossibly uncomfortable, armless, straight-backed tapestry-covered chairs, which no one ever sat on, flanked the high marble fireplace, where the jackdaws rattled down sticks every spring, and in late summer the traditional bowl of heather impaled in potatoes replaced the faded embroidery of the firescreen.

There was, in fact, no fireplace, no mirror with flanking pilasters on the chimney breast above. This, and one other major structural alteration, made it hard to believe that they were in the hall of Calder at all. The delicate wrought-iron of the curving staircase, the smooth sweep of rail polished by generations of Laidlaw hands, had been torn out. In their place the rigid regularity of stainless steel, which would have been at home in a sixties' office block, climbed coldly upwards.

On stark white walls panels of purple hessian were

decorated with reliefs of polished steel figures, their active intertwining conveying nothing, perhaps fortunately, in this first moment of shock. Black spindly furniture, vaguely Rennie Mackintosh in character, stood on a white marble floor inlaid with a central design of black and purple. The whole was glaringly lit by a chromium chandelier.

Jamie felt her throat tighten with grief and a furious helpless rejection of these horrors and all they stood for. Words would not come. She turned to Vanessa, looking upward with an astounded face, and then to Phil, who, she saw, seemed more doubtful than horrified.

For an instant Jamie let anger displace every other emotion. Surely Phil could see for herself that this was hideous and outrageous? Surely she wasn't waiting to find out how they would react before she risked an opinion? How like her. Then the flare of annoyance at something which had so often infuriated Jamie in earlier years died, recognised for what it was, a clutching at anything to deflect the realisation of what had been done here.

'My God, how dare she? How *dare* she do this?'

'The fireplace has gone. She's taken out the entire fireplace,' Vanessa said blankly, as though she had never suspected before that such a thing could be done.

'I don't like the purple,' Phil offered. She was simply choosing the chief thing that struck her, as Vanessa had done. But before Jamie's renewed irritation could burst over her at the banal comment, she

added softly, 'Thank goodness Grandmother can
never know,' reaching so precisely to what really
mattered that Jamie put an arm round her heavy
shoulders in a quick hug.

'Thank goodness indeed. That beautiful staircase,
simply destroyed.'

'And look at this horrible floor, so cold and staring.
It's like a chapel or something.'

'And what,' asked Jamie, as the chill of the outer
air crept in through the open door behind them, no
colder than the chill struck in their hearts by this
brutal metamorphosis of a place which had meant so
much to them, 'are we going to find in the rest of the
house?'

'Well, she always hated the sun. I suppose that's
what lay behind the way she planned it all.'

'You're right,' Vanessa agreed. 'It's an indoor
room. It could be anywhere, couldn't it, in a city
block of flats, in the middle of London, or New York
or Buenos Aires.'

They had come back, as though drawn against
their will, to what was clearly the focal point of
the new-style Calder Lodge, whose interior was
now wincingly at odds with its weathered walls of
dressed granite, its big sash windows and deep bays,
its crow-stepped gables and roofs of ancient graded
slates, with its wings at either side reaching back into
a hotch-potch of domestic offices of an even earlier
date.

They stood at the north end of the eastern wing

where the big kitchen had once been. Jamie had with some difficulty opened the shutters painted with *trompe l'oeil* scenes and swagged with purple silk. Across the drive a screen of half-grown conifers, far too near the house, created a denser darkness.

'Don't you remember the morning sun pouring in here, and how warm the kitchen always was?' she said, and hearing a catch in her voice, very rare from the sister who of them all was the tough and uncompromising fighter, Vanessa put a comforting hand on her arm.

Jamie gave her a tight little smile, not able to go on. In such involuntary outbursts they had released some of their shock and distress as they went round the house. Putting a hand over Vanessa's for a second Jamie acknowledged once more the sibling closeness which even after so long apart, and in spite of all differences of temperament and the divergence of their lives, seemed today as firm as it had been in the days when there had been little alternative but to depend upon each other. Though there had been as well the shifting loyalties, the treaties offensive and defensive, the siding of two against one which could in a flash become a different two against a different one. Poor Phil had generally come off worst, panting along in the wake of the others, three years younger than Jamie, seven years younger than Vanessa. She had been in turn fussed over and cuddled or callously left out, as it suited them, reduced to tears a dozen times a day, but always forgiving, always ready to adore and admire them.

'Can't you just see Freda in here, in her white apron, standing at the table with the mixing bowl in front of her,' she said now, on an unashamedly wistful note which made Jamie feel dangerously close to losing control.

'It wasn't a very practical kitchen, though, and it did need modernising,' Vanessa said, with her usual compulsion, which Jamie thought she was probably unaware of, to find some objection to what had just been said. The prosaic comment struck a jarring note.

'Vanessa, it was beautiful,' Jamie said furiously. As she spoke she could see again the wood of the long table where the grain showed orange after scrubbing, at one end of it the big basket of eggs from the hens that ranged round the yard and buildings, the morning milk still in the churn, the ladle hooked over its rim. She could see the porridge gently heaving and plopping on the stove, and the long row of Freda's cherished African violets, which loved the steamy heat, ranged along the window sill above the fireclay sinks. She could smell toast and coffee and bacon grilling. Eggs and bacon for breakfast; lost delights indeed. What had it mattered that the high old-fashioned cupboards needed painting, that the windows rattled in easterly winds, that twice a day hods of coke had to be lugged in to feed the rapacious cooker? It had been a happy, cosy refuge of good smells, treats and an unchanging order. That was what had mattered.

Now she supposed the only term that could be applied to this whole area where the kitchen had been, plus pantry, larders, storerooms and laundry, was 'living space'. The living space of a person aggressively individualistic, though even she, with all her extravagance, had not managed to keep entirely up to date. It comprised sitting-room, dining-room, study, music room and, not so much a studio, Jamie decided, though obviously Zara had painted in here, as a gallery of artefacts, most of them as recondite in intention as the panels in the hall. A striving, contentious room. A room challenging not only the glen landscape beyond its walls, but making a statement of hostility to all Laidlaws, past and present. Of whom we three represent all who now survive, and have done, though we didn't know it, for the past six years. A tremor of excitement returned as Jamie thought of all they had learned today, still barely assimilated.

'Jamie, are you listening? It's terribly late. We really should have something to eat.'

Vanessa had looked with baffled discomfort at this carefully contrived room and its elaborate contents. Even she, prosaic as her outlook was, sensed vibes here which she neither liked nor understood. Every object spoke to her of the things which made her feel most inadequate, the sort of things she dreaded being expected to discuss at one of those important dinner parties which were so much a feature of her married life. Intellectual things, she vaguely thought, contemporary art and music, clever novels with lots of dialogue, large print and short sentences, which always left her turning over the last page feeling a fool because she still hadn't worked out what was happening. And above all the technology (represented here by a mauve computer shaped like the hood of an old-fashioned hairdryer) which she blamed more than any other factor for the ever-widening gulf that distanced her from Ryan, her son. The books here, from a quick nervous glance, seemed to deal chiefly with the paranormal or with self-discovery, self-enhancement and self-assertion. As if Zara had needed to improve on that. Her eyes went to the black pedestal dining table ringed by black chairs shaped like Ss. So stark and ugly. Unhappiness reached out to engulf her.

So take refuge in the ordinary, assume the role where she could not be outshone. 'It's more than time we had dinner,' she repeated briskly.

'I'm not sure I can be bothered with food,' Jamie said, still looking around her. 'I feel as though I've got past that by now.'

'But you must eat,' Vanessa insisted automatically. Not eating was a bad thing. 'Everything's been so rushed, ever since we met this morning. You haven't had a thing since lunch, and that's not good for you. In fact it might have been better if we hadn't tried to fit everything in today. We should have stayed the night in Glasgow. I hadn't realised that it would take so long at the crematorium, waiting to arrange about the ashes and so on. I suppose we could have done it by telephone, only once they'd asked us to wait we had to, really. But we could have seen Mr Syme tomorrow, and then driven up without hurrying—'

'Vanessa.' With an effort Jamie managed to sound resigned rather than impatient. 'Vanessa, we're here. We've done everything. What's the use of rehashing it all now?' And did Vanessa really regard trundling along just on fifty as hurrying?

'But you still ought to eat, and so should Phil. I've brought enough for dinner – well, I suppose supper really – and for breakfast. I think we should bring everything in and eat as soon as it's ready, and then go to bed. We're all tired, and goodness knows how we'll cope with everything tomorrow.'

'I can hardly bear the thought of going into that ghastly new kitchen,' Jamie said.

Across the corridor behind the hall, where the gunroom and the estate office used to be, looking onto the back courtyard where the sun only briefly shone, a firm of expensive German kitchen designers had been allowed a free hand.

'Don't be silly, it's a perfectly normal kitchen, and it's beautifully equipped. I can't see anything wrong with it.'

That's the point, you idiot, it's perfectly normal. The sense of closeness dwindled abruptly. In truth they were as different in outlook, all three of them, as they had always been, Jamie thought with a new bleakness as she followed Vanessa's compact, trotting form, radiating new purpose now that she had a meal to produce.

Phil, going out to bring the hamper from the car, for she was the natural fetcher and carrier, thought wistfully of her own cosy quarters and wondered, with a doubt she would never have dared express to Jamie or Vanessa, what in fact they did have to cope with tomorrow. Cope with? What did that mean? Decide, perhaps, but what could they do to change what they had found?

Now, the flask beside the basket in the boot, a rug arranged round it so that it wouldn't fall over, was that meant to come in too? What was in it? If it was tea or coffee, the moment for either past, and she took it in Vanessa would only be scathing. On the other hand if she left it and it was something for supper she would be crosser still. But even if it had been intended for earlier in the day, it would still have to be emptied and washed out. The years fallen away, Phil, aged thirty-four, competent and responsible carer, stood biting her lip unhappily, as nervous as the fat clumsy child had ever been of inviting her sisters' scorn. Whatever she did would be wrong.

'For goodness' *sake*,' she exclaimed aloud, with uncharacteristic anger. How could she get herself into this state of anxiety, after all this time? But she knew, as she put the basket down on the step, placed the flask on it, carefully in the middle, and bent inelegantly to lift them, that no matter how many years had gone by one flash of scorn from Jamie's observant eyes, one primming of Vanessa's lips, would put her squarely back in the role of floundering, despised, plain younger sister, slow on the uptake, always in the way. She must show none of this; never show she minded.

Oblivious to its horrors she paced steadily through the hall, almost turned right from habit, and dunted gently with her foot against the door of the former estate room.

2

'It's been made into a swing door, you idiot,' Phil heard Jamie's voice faintly, for it was now also a heavily covered door. She manoeuvred herself round with the wide, well-filled basket; she was used to lifting heavy weights but with Vanessa in mind kept a careful eye on the flask. She pushed the door with her shoulder. As soon as it was open a couple of inches Jamie's fingers came round it, it was hauled back and Phil tottered.

'Do mind the flask!' Vanessa cried, looking up from the flight controls of an enormous cooker.

'Why didn't you make two journeys?' Jamie demanded, grabbing it before it fell.

'You might just as well have,' Vanessa added. 'There's a carrier bag too. Didn't you see it?'

'No, sorry. I'll go back.'

How easily they had slipped back into their old-established roles. Impatience and crushing comments had no more weight than they had had in the nursery, and for Phil, as well as the all-too-familiar sense of inadequacy, there was also reassurance to feel that her elders were in charge again. There were large matters afoot, family matters it would have been unthinkable to face without them. Ever since Vanessa's phone call last weekend telling her the news of Zara's death, she had been dogged by a vague foreboding that the safe niche she had found, where everything was comfortably within her scope, might be threatened. Even the train journey from Muirend to Glasgow this morning had been an ordeal, beset by such concerns as not knowing that everyone reserved seats nowadays, not being sure where to put her bag and, if the worst happened and no one was there to meet her, having to decode cryptic signs which other passengers seemed effortlessly to understand.

These absurd fears, which she was sure harried no one else, could never be expressed, at least not to her sisters. They inhabited the adult world of affluence and success which would always be remote to her, a world where she would have been forever aware that she didn't match up. This knowledge had been part of childhood, and had caused her much secret grief. Deep in her consciousness of herself she knew that she would never be properly grown up, in other people's terms. Beyond her own small corner, which she had been so lucky to find, the 'real' world would remain forever incomprehensible and alarming.

As she fumbled with the fastenings of the basket, and Vanessa unscrewed the flask with small, firm, well-kept hands (square-cut sapphire engagement ring in place as always), these thoughts continued to run through Phil's mind, made more disturbing tonight by her apprehension of change looming. The

altered house had filled her with unease, not anger.
This smart kitchen felt to her like a film set, nothing
to do with them, and big as it was its strong colours
seemed to close in on her. She hated black, and that
orange and fawn (the designer's burnt sienna and
sand) were horrible.

Vanessa was burying uncomfortable thoughts of
her own under a cheerful efficiency. She hadn't
phoned home, and that made her feel guilty and
on edge. As Douglas had left this morning she had
called after him that she would phone tonight, and he
had checked with one foot in the car to call back,
'God, Vanessa, you're only going to be away for a
couple of nights.' Before she could protest, 'But I
shall want to,' the car door had shut.

She shouldn't have said anything; she should have
just phoned. Now it would seem silly if she did, as he
had said, but not phoning made her feel oddly cut
adrift, and she didn't like it. When had she last been
away from home on her own? She couldn't think. She
was used to being the fixed central point around
which Douglas and Ryan revolved. She was always
there, at the end of the telephone, available by e-mail
from anywhere in the world; always there to be
summoned to airport, station or Stagecoach stop;
there to send on forgotten belongings, or tickets
and money when things went wrong. For Ryan's
adventures during his year out, which she had
worked so hard to get Douglas to agree to, had barely
taken him across the Channel. He had been the one
who chatted to someone on a bus and found his

camera had been stolen, or accepted a lift from a kind person who drove off with the rest of his kit. He had very soon run for home, and the year of promised enterprise had been frittered away. Douglas had—

She hauled her mind determinedly away from this well-worn track. Still, it felt strange to be away, and the lack of contact nagged at her as she hurried about, the feeling of guilt persisting. But she had left everything ready, done everything she could think of.

Oh, really, she caught herself up again, what are you talking about? Who else had there been to see to all the things that had had to be done since the call came from the clinic? Jamie on the other side of America, and Phil – well, there was no use expecting Phil to organise anything. Anyway, it was done, they were here, at Calder, the hardest part behind them.

And together. The feeling of being adrift lessened as she remembered that, however briefly, she was once more part of that different unit, the unit which had existed since earliest memory, where she had been leader and protector. To these two, Jamie and Phil, she was unalterably bonded by ties of blood. For a second this almost seemed the strongest bond of all, one which could never be destroyed, for they belonged to the same generation, shared the same perception of the world.

Oh yes? Perhaps that was going a bit far. She was smiling as she put the soup into the microwave. It hadn't kept very hot. Hardly surprising; it felt like a week since she had filled the flask this morning. The turkey escalopes had defrosted nicely in the cold bag, and the neat roll of lemon and herb butter she had made was still firm. Good.

'Vanessa, did you really think you had to bring plates and glasses? There must enough for fifty here.' Jamie was exploring drawers and cupboards, her look of contempt for the gadgetry and elaboration deepening as she went. And where was all Grandmother's Crown Derby? Though admittedly most of it had been showing signs of a hard life even when they were children. Where were the Worcester casseroles and soufflé dishes, the heavy silver? Packed away somewhere? After what Mr Syme had revealed today she hardly dared to hope so.

Images of the devastated house hovered, filling her with pain. The long dining-room with its ornate plasterwork and warm red walls, now sadly faded, was stripped, bare, unused; the drawing-room across the hall the same. The library shelves were empty, Grandmother's sitting-room beyond it used as a store. Her throat ached to think of it. At least the south-facing bedrooms above had remained in use, though decorated and furnished in an alien style. These rooms, she supposed, had been used by her stepmother's guests, for Zara herself had clearly stuck to those in the east wing.

Jamie winced to remember what she had done to them. 'I think we'd better have something to drink,' she said. 'Though not out of these,' slamming a cupboard door on tall glasses with angular bowls and spiral stems in different colours, and going to pull the wine glasses in Vanessa's basket from their clamps.

'Oh, but should we—?' Phil looked round as though someone in authority might appear at her shoulder.

'Phil, it's ours. All of it. Whatever's here. And what's more it has been for years. Haven't you taken that in yet?'

'No, I really don't think I have,' Phil admitted. 'Everything seems to have happened so fast . . .'

But Jamie wasn't listening. 'Question is, where's the wine kept now? I can't imagine Zara groping down to the cellar among the cobwebs, can you? Let's see.'

'Honestly, Jamie, I'm quite happy without anything to drink,' Vanessa said. 'I brought orange juice for breakfast tomorrow but we could have some of it now. That will be fine for me.' In fact, it would make a pleasant change.

Jamie took no notice. 'Ah, didn't think she'd let us down in this department. Neat.' A door at the end of the kitchen had revealed a drinks cupboard with its own refrigerator and well-stocked wine rack. 'Access from her sitting-room at the other end, look. Food could go via the corridor, but drink had to be to hand.'

'That's not very kind,' Phil protested.

'Phil, she's just died in a home for alcoholics, being dried out for the umpteenth time. I don't think we have to pretend she didn't drink.'

'I know, but—' Phil didn't attempt to explain how

she felt. It was too instinctive and formless anyway, little more than a generalised wish to be kind, and she had long ago learned that arguing with Jamie on such a point was the equivalent of standing against a wall and having knives thrown at her.

'Come on, which? Red or white?'

'I hardly ever drink wine. I don't know what I like. I'd be quite happy with orange juice too.'

'What a boring pair you are.' Jamie spoke lightly, pulling out bottles from the rack to read the labels, but she was resolved they should drink something. They had agreed as they left Glasgow, all three buffeted by memories and emotions, their heads whirling with the new and startling facts they had learned, with surmise and doubt, that serious discussion about the future should be postponed until tomorrow, and they had held to that. But now, this evening, before they attempted to sleep in the rooms prepared for them upstairs, rooms that had never been theirs, there was tension to be unwound, reserve to be shed. She turned to look at the new bright kitchen, with its rows of copper pots, its beaten copper hoods and clever lighting, its hard smooth surfaces bouncing back reflections, resistant to everything. How weird it was to see the familiar figures of her sisters against this background, as incongruous as if it had belonged to an unknown house.

Vanessa, as ever, looked almost too immaculate in her oyster silk shirt with double cuffs and pearl links, her well-fitting navy skirt, its jacket carefully hung over the back of a chair, and her expensive high-heeled shoes, enviably small. Her fair hair hugged her head in its neat unvarying shape. A memory came back of Vanessa in her teens, wailing furiously, 'I simply can't make it untidy whatever I do. It's so unfair!' and Jamie found herself grinning but at the same time wincing at the certainty that other similar memories, long-forgotten but piercing in their intimacy, hovered close.

And there by contrast was Phil, her reddish fair hair straggly round her broad face, her lumpy body shapeless in a beige, pleated terylene skirt and a short-sleeved blouse which had trouble meeting over her big breasts. Fortunately she had worn a loose brown jacket over it for the service at the crematorium. Funeral clothes; 'suitable' colours. Had she borrowed the jacket from some elderly moribund patient? Male?

How different they were and yet there was a recognisable resemblance, in the fair colouring they had inherited from their mother, in the shape of their mouths, and in the way their eyes could look so anxious. Though Vanessa was clearly still pursuing the battle against putting on weight, she would just as clearly not always succeed. Her hips were more solid than Jamie remembered, the flesh was beginning to pad out around shoulders and upper arms, her breasts were heavier.

For a moment, studying them objectively like this, Jamie had, exactly as in childhood, a treacherous conviction of not belonging to them. There had been a miserable period when she had been sure she was adopted, but the fantasies woven on this theme had had to be discarded when she had grown old enough to recognise her likeness to her father, who also had been dark, lean, and driven by an unappeasable energy. And critical and impatient, she mentally added now with a grimace.

'We should be drinking champagne, you know, to celebrate,' she said.

'Celebrate? On the day of a funeral?' Phil looked horrified.

'Jamie, that's a dreadful thing to say!' Vanessa's exclamation was as immediate as Phil's protest, but had more to do with conventional response than natural kindness.

What had she truly felt this morning, Jamie wondered. What had any of them felt as they had watched the coffin, containing the body of the woman they had so much detested and who had caused them so much pain, slide away to be consumed, in a manner Jamie had always considered at once hygienic and barbaric, by fire? Would any of them ever say, truly?

'Well, I'm celebrating.' She brought a corkscrew and a bottle of Chablis to the table, and the others glanced at her set face and argued no more.

'Let's drink to—'

As Jamie paused, and the others turned to her, waiting, gradually the hugeness of what had happened gripped them, and a strange elation could almost be felt to tighten in the room. A dark shadow which had hung in the background of their lives for

so long, and which they had assumed would be there
for years to come, had suddenly been swept away.

Jamie found herself almost breathless as she
sought for words to do justice to such a moment,
to pin it down in their minds for ever. Silence, in the
showy, absurd kitchen; silence in the big house
around them, and in the empty hollow of glen where
it lay, a silence which seemed to deepen into something tangible and significant.

'To Calder returned to us,' Jamie said. She had
thought she would speak firmly, but found her voice
roughened by emotion.

'To Calder returned,' they repeated, and each
found tears in her eyes as she raised her glass.
Different images of what the words meant might
have come to them, the tears might be nostalgia
for happy times or relief that all they had hated could
be wiped out and forgotten, but to each the toast was
apt and satisfying.

'Heavens, the escalopes! They'll be ruined,' Vanessa exclaimed, seeking refuge in the mundane from
a moment growing too serious. 'Come on, we must
eat. Phil, would you dress the salad, please.'

Jamie, jolted back to the present, thought with
exasperation that Vanessa had always been able to
reduce everything to the humdrum. Wash your
hands and brush your hair, and don't be late for
lunch. But that was Vanessa; it was part of being
together again.

'It was good of you, Nessie, to get all this ready,'
she said, in apology for that swift irritation.

'Oh, well, it was easier for me to do it.' But Vanessa didn't hide her pleasure. Compliments from Jamie were rare. 'Only I do wish you wouldn't call me Nessie.'

Jamie and Phil laughed. If Vanessa hadn't added the rider the world would have stopped turning.

Relaxing, Jamie felt unexpectedly happy – to be here, to be with the others again. It struck her that the very predictability of the routes Phil and Vanessa's lives had taken, their readiness to be satisfied with the ordinary, provided a safe base from which she could make her own ambitious or reckless flights. And to which, when disaster struck, she could return.

And I'm barely halfway down my first glass, she mocked herself, watching Phil with affection as she cautiously drizzled French dressing over the salad (where she came from it was Heinz salad cream or nothing).

Phil, glancing up, caught the look, and suddenly found herself able to say, 'It was so lovely to get that first glimpse of you this morning, Jamie. I'd hardly believed you'd come. I mean, I know it's hard for you to get away, running your own business and everything.'

'Well, there's a lot to be sorted out,' Jamie said lightly. 'Besides, it was probably time I put in an appearance.'

'Well, it's great to have you here.'

'But you will be able to stay for a while, won't you?' Vanessa asked, ladling out the soup then going to fetch the napkins Phil had ignored. 'You won't be flying off again at once, I hope.'

'No, I won't be rushing off this time.' Jamie's voice was carefully expressionless, but neither of the others, buttering the crusty brown rolls Vanessa had warmed to perfection, noticed.

'It must be jolly nice,' Phil commented (and after the years in the States Jamie's grin flickered at the expression, wondering if anyone else still used it), 'to be your own boss. And rich and successful,' she added with naive admiration. She could still be amazed at Jamie's enterprise and ambition.

'Yes, well, it all seems a bit remote for the moment.' Jamie changed the subject. 'How's your own job going?'

There had been little opportunity for catching up during the day, and driving to Glen Fallan they had been mostly silent, each affected in some way by the rites they had felt obliged to observe, each beset by memories revived, but none of them quite able to shed private preoccupations with the present either.

'Oh, I love it,' Phil said eagerly, her heavy features for the first time lit by enthusiasm. 'We've been really busy lately, but the new matron is far more efficient than Miss Busby was, and kinder too. I mean more understanding. She gives people time, you know, and that's so important . . .'

Vanessa and Jamie didn't really want to hear about Burnbrae House, but tonight all of them were prepared to be tolerant, and as the wine slipped down, Jamie taking the chance to open a second bottle while the others were loading the dishwasher, the talk, though inevitably turning back again and again to what they had just discovered, a necessary release, was mostly an exchange of news. Jamie's PR business in Seattle, Vanessa's plans and hopes for Ryan, Phil's worries about funding for the home – and far too many earthy anecdotes about its inmates – all took their turn.

Broad-brush, never going below the surface. Though they had kept in touch through the years, they were a long way from the familiarity with each other's day-to-day activities which opens the way to easy gossip and confidences. Yet as each listened to the others, in this mood of reunion and goodwill, she felt comforted, reassured that their choices had been right for them. Vanessa of course had always been happy in her home and marriage, husband and son; Jamie's career had been successful beyond all expectation; while Phil, who for a long time had been a worry, with her inability to pass a single exam or acquire a single qualification, was at least safely in a job where she seemed content, badly paid and dead-end as it might be.

3

Every time she reached the verge of sleep the too-soft, too-wide divan seemed to be swallowing her up like a mud wallow, and Jamie would jerk awake again, with a feeling of being at once stifled and disorientated. She was used to a firm mattress, and this effete softness seemed too much part of the vulgar luxury which had overtaken the dignified old house. She pulled herself up onto an elbow and switched on the light. The lemon-yellow satin quilted bedcover with its flounced valance was slung into a contemptuous heap in a corner. The lemon-yellow silk curtains were open, dragged violently back when, going to close them, she had found that they ran across the entire wall, making the room urban and unrecognisable. The wall facing her, where the fireplace had been, was filled by a range of white drawers and cupboards decorated with gold twirls. In the mirror of the recessed dressing-table she could see her scowling self, propped up on both arms, head jutting, the dainty gilt lamp beside her.

But into her anger gradually flowed awareness of the quiet voice of the river through the open windows. The first moth flittered against the yellow silk shade. Cool air deliciously stroked the bare skin of her arms and shoulders. Then with a shock that was almost physical her mind slammed against the image which had been hovering all evening, resolutely pushed away during the hours of talk. She tried to divert it again by recalling that talk, which inevitably turned more and more to the past, and equally inevitably into heated argument about long-ago incidents remembered quite differently. As tiredness, wine, and relief that the fraught day was over took their toll, it had descended to a level of mindless wrangling and helpless laughter which could never have been shared with anyone else.

Jamie relaxed a little as some of the dialogue returned, as pointless as it had ever been thirty years ago, and nearly as passionate.

'What are you talking about? That wasn't me! I never did anything of the sort.'

'It was you. You wouldn't listen. You kept saying, "This is the way *I* do it," and when you'd finished you'd sewn the whole thing to your skirt.'

'Oh, rubbish, I don't remember any of this.'

'I can still see you, with that silly piece of embroidery hanging off the front of one of those brown corduroy pinafore dresses we hated so much.'

'I liked mine.'

'Phil, you loathed it.'

'No, I didn't.'

'Then why did you kick up such a fuss when you had to wear it?'

'It was those scratchy jerseys we had to wear underneath.'

'Oh, God yes, do you remember those jerseys?'

'Do you remember throwing yours down the linen chute and thinking it would be gone for ever—?'

It had been a much-needed release, their voices rising, dredging up things none of them had thought of for years, giggling helplessly at ancient jokes, holding at bay visions of the ravaged house around them.

But remembering that torrent of talk and laughter, the sense of being safe again with people who knew her through and through, couldn't help for long. All the things waiting to be done and faced seemed to grow into a monstrous mountain, and Jamie wasn't certain she had the courage to climb it. The first step, she knew, was to confront the image which each time she had drifted close to sleep had, in distorted nightmare form, dragged her back to wakefulness again.

She threw back the infinitely light duvet and went across to her bags, from which she had taken nothing more than she needed for the night. It was almost a surprise to see her familiar chinos and sweats and loafers, as though the self she had been a couple of days ago had been left behind for good.

She dressed rapidly, then opened the heavy door with care. Vanessa might be finding it hard to sleep too. The door knob, its time-smoothed brass icy to her hand, was slightly loose, just as she remembered all the knobs at Calder were, their spindles always needing redrilled. Her mouth twisted briefly at the

Scottish usage, hearing it in a voice she was not yet ready to hear. At least Zara, surprisingly, hadn't tampered with those.

In the corridor she paused, but all was quiet. They had been exhausted when they had at last hauled themselves up to bed. Though Vanessa had thought she should put the car away.

'You know Grandmother never let anyone leave cars at the front door. She said it spoiled the view.'

'Vanessa, it's two o'clock in the morning,' even tolerant Phil had felt compelled to point out.

'But we should—'

'Forget about should. This is us.' Jamie had thought muzzily how nice it was to be back in a country where people had long ago given up worrying about the verb 'to be'. 'Haven't you got it yet? We can do whatever we like.'

'But at least we should lock up, and check the doors and windows.'

'Are you mad? It would take half the night.'

'But we're responsible now, you just said so.'

'Only to ourselves.'

'Well, I think we ought to—'

'Everything was locked when we arrived. We've only used the front door.' It had been Phil who had provided the common sense.

'Then lock it if you must and stop worrying.'

'But this is exactly the sort of place that gets burgled,' Vanessa had persisted, with all the old doggedness and certainty of right which used to drive Jamie mad. 'You may think this place is remote, but you've been abroad for a long time, and you don't realise how things have changed. Nowhere's safe nowadays. As soon as a house is empty people check it out by helicopter—'

'By helicopter? What do they see from the air, you lunatic?'

'Well, they do, and then they come and steal not only the furniture—'

'If only they would—'

'No, you don't understand. They strip out fire-places and doors—'

'So that's where the fireplaces went.'

'Oh, Jamie, must you joke about everything?'

'Listen, the door's locked and that's it. There aren't going to be any helicopters. Come on to bed.'

With Vanessa still protesting, indignant not be taken seriously, the others had pushed her up the stairs and wheeled her into the first of the rooms prepared for them.

'It's all very well for you to be so sweeping, but you simply don't realise—'

They could still hear her voice as they shut the door on her and with a quick goodnight vanished without debate into the next two rooms.

These thoughts were mere self-protection, and Jamie knew it. Moving silently on the thick carpet she went towards the west wing. Turning the corner she saw it. It was there; it hadn't been a dream.

The stunned disbelief they had shared as they rounded this corner a few hours ago seized her again. The corridor was walled off. It was as though the house ended here. That was how, for one speechless moment, it had seemed. Then reason, with a struggle, had reminded them that below this spot they had only a few minutes before been standing in Grandmother's sitting-room, dismantled it was true, but still there. The entire wing, the smaller rooms of this old part of the building with their low ceilings and deep-set windows, the nursery bathroom whose clumsy old radiator was the last to get warm in the whole house, had not been demolished, as for an appalled heartbeat had seemed to be the case. But up here it had been blocked off, and it was as though someone had wanted to wipe out their whole childhood, their younger selves, with ruthless finality. They had admitted later, when they had had the chance to assimilate what had been done, that until they came face to face with this startling barricade, each had envisaged without question sleeping tonight in her own familiar room.

The job had been skilfully done. The new wall looked as though it had always been there. Jamie put out a hand, and tapped lightly with her knuckle. Not plaster, wood. That was something, at any rate. But why? And why was the door at the foot of the narrow stairs at the end of the wing locked, the key nowhere to be found? Had Zara wanted to confine all Laidlaw ghosts here, obliterate their links with the house they had built, and loved for generations? Alone, shivering in the muffling silence of the small hours of the night, when rational thoughts are hard to summon, Jamie saw Zara's action as both calculated and malignant.

Impossible now to go back to that too-luxurious bed, to the minimalist room from which chintz and mahogany, worn rugs and tottery lamps, Chelsea figures and dim, kindly mirrors had been swept away. Jamie was shivering as much from a sense of rejection as from the temperature, as she went back along the main corridor, past the rooms where Phil and Vanessa, she hoped, were sleeping, and down the barren curve of the new staircase.

She had left her jacket in the kitchen. Not letting herself look at anything, unable to bear more reminders of the horrors that had overtaken this beloved house, she snatched it up and went through the hall. Leaving lights on and the door open, careless of what Vanessa would say, she fled away across the lawn, her shoes soaked and icy in seconds in the heavy dew.

With the lights of the house behind her, the sky ahead swiftly paled to grey. To her left the black mass of the wooded slope climbed to the glen road. To her right the starker shapes of the hills to the west stood out in an outline she knew as well as her own face in the mirror. At this time of year it never grew truly dark. She had not consciously thought of that, yet at the same time she knew she could never have forgotten it.

She wasn't running now. How forcefully it had been dinned into them as children, never to run near the end of the lawn, which jutted several feet above the rapid swirl of the River Fallan as it broke from its rocky gorge in a wide loop, before returning to it again half a mile lower down. Their mother had worried about the danger, according to Vanessa, and suggested a fence or a wall, but Grandmother had been calmly adamant. Nothing should mar the long and lovely view falling southwards to the gleam of the faraway loch. No Laidlaw child had ever fallen over the edge yet; her grandchildren surely had sufficient sense to maintain the tradition.

On the rocky promontory at the left of the lawn a paved space had long ago been laid, and here a low wall did curve round the outer rim. Towards it Jamie turned, and pulling her jacket as far under her as she could, sat sideways on the cold damp stone. It had always been a more appealing perch, for child or adult, than the chairs on the stone flags, or the bench in the shade of the giant beech tree behind them.

Dares. The past rushed back. One leg over the edge; both legs. A rite of passage. She could remember with vivid clarity the sense of emancipation of the day she had achieved that, the intoxicating feeling of space as she faced out over the drop, and she smiled in sympathy with the skinny, scruffy, ardent child she had been, always pitting herself against something or someone.

But even these memories she tried for the moment to still. She wanted, or more accurately urgently needed, after all that had happened, and at such a speed, to empty her mind, slow the teeming thoughts.

It was as though, giving them space at last, her senses woke one by one. Her eyes had already adjusted to the soft half-light of the summer night. The scents of vegetation, damp leaves and dewy grass, leaf-mould, flowers, rowan blossom, spray-soaked stone and river air filled her nostrils and could be tasted on her tongue. And there was that special, indefinable quality that belonged to the Highland night, a thinness and purity, the rich mixture of the daylight hours subtly diluted so that the most familiar scene took on a new character.

Jamie closed her eyes to absorb it, feeling its chill touch trace across her cheek, and at once the voice of the river held her, its pattern and rhythm known to her for ever. It couldn't possibly sound as it had all those years ago. A thousand changes would affect it, down to the infinitesimal wearing down of the rock walls of its course. Yet the gurgles and plucks, the run of ripples over the shingle below the further bank, the slap of the water against the dark wall below her, wove a tapestry of sound unconsciously absorbed in all the hours she had sat here, unchanged.

This was Calder. At last she was here. Without voices, without words, without shocks for the eye or mind. Though what, she wondered in fresh dread, might daylight reveal out here? No, don't even think about it. For now the light dark protected her from any devastation there might be. She could sit here – for as long as she could ignore the cold biting into her thinly padded haunches anyway – and at last let herself meet the faces which had peopled the past.

Grandmother. Large, unruffled, slow-moving, giving an appearance of indolence but always occu-

pied – with her garden and her bees, her bottling and
jam-making, her embroidery and crosswords, and
with those peaceful jobs which no one bothered
about any longer, like making lavender bags and
her own beeswax polish, dipping great branches of
copper beech in glycerine to preserve their glory for
weeks, making ice cream in her cumbersome old
machine. She was there before Jamie's eyes, in one
of the tweed suits she wore to shapeless softness, with
a pale silk blouse and boat-like lace-up shoes, beautifully polished even when they were squashed to
hideousness and had been resoled half a dozen times.
Comfort and reassurance. Grandmother had always
known how to soothe Jamie's fits of rage, even
though it was clear in retrospect that she had not
fully grasped the frustration that lay behind them, or
the way they could whirl up and take control, as
though they came from somewhere outside Jamie
herself.

It had been Jamie who had been most often left
alone at Calder with Grandmother. (Dumped at
Calder. Was that her own voice, somewhere in the
years between, bitterly making the amendment?)
Why had that been the case? And who had looked
after the others?

It was after their mother died, when Phil was born,
that the long confusing train of names and faces and
places began. Not even Vanessa could unravel it now.
Contact with their maternal grandparents, always
slight as they had lived in South Africa, had more
or less ended. There had been no question of visits to

them; Jamie couldn't remember the idea ever being mentioned. There had been nannies, housekeepers and the endless sequence of Daddy's girlfriends, from which distinctive figures emerged as Jamie grew older. Odd to think they were alive somewhere, the three Laidlaw children part of their memory store.

The houses, always big and, in her memory at least, dark and unfriendly, had been in or around Glasgow, with dull gardens where people were always ordering them to play. Play at what? She could feel her resentment at the bald instruction burn even now.

And somewhere in the background of those half-remembered houses, remote from their small concerns but dominating everything, had been the tall dark figure of her father, hurrying, busy, his attention always elsewhere, awareness of his impatience charging every exchange with a sense of pressure to say what you had to say quickly and clearly, and guilt to know you were holding him up.

Here, at Calder, it had been different. Here, in the early days at any rate, he had had time for her. Here the girlfriends had never penetrated. On Grandmother's orders, or because he had known they would be out of place? Or was it because he had spent so much time here with their mother? At the name Jamie felt her helpless envy of Vanessa pour back, Vanessa who could remember their mother properly, who could describe what she had worn and the things on her dressing-table, who could talk about things they had done together, and who had had the unfair advantage, used to the full, of being able to announce with conviction, 'Mother would never have let you do that,' or, 'I know because Mother told me.'

How fiercely Jamie had insisted that she, three when their mother died, could remember her too, inventing things she had said, consoling herself with fantasies in which she had been the favourite, admired and praised, until she no longer knew which memories were true and which were not, another layer of loss.

She would never know now. Her mother could be no more than a composite figure built up from photographs, from Vanessa's descriptions – and how reliable were those? – from stories begged for over and over again from Grandmother, grieving phrases in letters from South Africa, and a tiny handful of blurred, uncertain memories of her own. Their father had never talked of her. They had been so young at the time that they had accepted this without thought. As they grew up, his affairs and ever-changing relationships the background to their lives, to have raised the subject of their mother to him would have been unthinkable.

As difficult to pin down as these early images was the appearance of Zara in their lives. For she had come and gone at first, and even though early impressions must have been overlaid and probably distorted by later knowledge, to Jamie she had always been a threatening and unstable presence. She had been the only one, of the train of females their father had expected them to accept in the house, who had made no effort to enlist them on her side. She had ignored them; more precisely, she had disdained them, and Jamie could recall no greater sense of lightness and relief, at any time in her life, than those occasions when the rows had blazed into uncontrollable conflagrations and Zara had stormed dramatically out.

Zara Rabett. Though Jamie had come out here hoping to gather the friendly ghosts of Calder around her, and the most important of all still hovered out of reach, it was perhaps inevitable that this powerful figure would sooner or later predominate. It was her personality which had pervaded the house this evening, hanging in the offing, never quite forgotten, as they had eaten and drunk, talked and laughed. Childish humour was a paltry weapon against Zara, with her rapacious egotism, her contemptuous indifference for the feelings of others.

Her face was before Jamie now, with its olive skin and liquid dark eyes, its full lips and firm chin. Zara's exotic ancestry had been made much of, yet had somehow always remained faintly suspect. There was the great-grandfather who had been an Armenian Jew. What dubious overtones literature had given to the term, Jamie thought with a clutch at protective humour as the unwelcome associations flooded back. His wife had been the daughter of a Russian Grand Duke, conveniently untraceable. Zara's grandfather had been one of the famed Grand

Blancs plantation owners in the Seychelles, making his fortune from copra, cinnamon and patchouli leaves. (That had been a favourite joke among the sisters, doing their best to muster some defence against this new and dangerous raptor. One of them had only to whisper, as Zara was flinging these facts about to impress some newcomer, 'Don't forget the patchouli leaves!' and they would be struggling with frantic giggles. They had never had the slightest idea what they were and had never enquired.)

Zara with her gleaming black hair, her shapely hips, full breasts and firmly jutting backside, her lounging and prowling which never seemed relaxed, had radiated an aggressive physicality. A woman who wore a lot of black and looked as though she never shaved her armpits. She had small strong hands and small high-arched feet, usually shod in black or gold sandals with impossibly high heels. Dark plum-coloured lipsticks, heavy gold jewellery. Though she had never minded slopping around in a housecoat in the mornings, face sallow without make-up, stripped nails yellow and eyes small and mean, the incipient line of dark hair on her upper lip plainly visible, her temper uncertain. She had been much younger than their father. Nearer in age, they had worked out with shock when he died, to Vanessa than she was to him.

Now, with the new perspective of the years, Jamie could gauge her fierce sexuality. Remembering the way her presence had made itself felt in the house and, as reluctantly as if they were in her nostrils now, the cloying scents she wore, it wasn't hard to see the source of the attraction this woman had exerted over their father. How naive not to have recognised it before. Or, Jamie wondered, had she refused the knowledge out of an instinctive reluctance to think about a parent's sex life? She doubted if Vanessa or Phil, even now, would think of Zara and their father in such terms.

She didn't want to either. She came abruptly to her feet, chilled to the bone. How unbearable it was that Zara had spread her hated personality into every corner of even this loved place. She had been the last person Jamie had wanted to think of here, and her presence had held at bay the memories Jamie had most longed to summon.

But as she turned to go back to the house the fact that lay behind everything else, her hurried return, the events of the day, and the presence of the three of them here tonight, finally came home to her. The shadow had been removed. Before them this morning the briefest of words had been said in formal dismissal of that predatory spirit. The once sensual body was mere matter to be consigned to the flames. It had happened, it was over. They were free at last, long before they had dreamed it could happen, to eradicate anything that remained of her from this place.

And, to their astonishment, they had learned how tenuous her hold on it had been. Zara had never been their stepmother. Since their father died Calder had not been Zara's, but theirs. And they had never known.

4

'I can't seem to make this go up.'

Jamie went foggily across the kitchen, which with blinds down and lights on made her feel she had walked straight back into last night's scene, to see if she could help. The buff linen-look blind seemed to be a fixture. 'She never wanted to see out, remember. Though I suppose a view of the back yard hasn't much appeal anyway.'

'But it feels so frowsty, on such a lovely morning.' Vanessa was still searching for some catch or cord.

A lovely morning indeed. Jamie, hardly daring to look out of her window for fear of what changes she might find, had been moved almost to tears to see the lawn stretching away furred silver with dew, the tips of the trees emerging from early mist where the river wound, sun on the flank of hill where spring grass was beginning to show vivid green – all just as she remembered it. To feel shut in and oppressed minutes later by this elaborate kitchen reminded her of all that had to be faced.

'We'll take it down altogether,' she said, standing back to see how the blind was fixed.

'We mustn't damage it.'

Did any thought process take place in Vanessa's brain between receiving and transmitting? Surely she'd want every trace of Zara removed? But before Jamie could say, 'Don't tell me you're going to argue the toss over every piece of vandalism we find,' Phil came yawning in, her face crumpled with sleep.

Jamie saw Vanessa's lips tighten as she took in the crumpled T-shirt, the cheap jeans cut too generously even for Phil's hefty thighs, the pink mules edged with grubby white 'fur'. Jamie knew that not only did Vanessa find these clothes horrible in themselves, but that it upset her to see a sister of hers dressed like this – and wearing bedroom slippers *downstairs*. To Vanessa, dressing 'properly' before you came down mattered. How did Ryan react, Jamie wondered.

'Good morning. Did you sleep well?' With some effort Vanessa refrained from comment on Phil's appearance.

'Me? Like a log. Always do.'

Well, that had always been true, and the memory of a soundly slumbering younger Phil, no matter what was going on around her, made the others smile and relax.

'Any tea on the go?'

'Tea? At breakfast? Oh Phil, I'm sorry, I only brought coffee.' Vanessa sounded seriously annoyed with herself. 'I wonder if there's any here? Though I can't remember Zara ever drinking tea, can you? But if there is any I'm sure it will be all right still. She hadn't been away long—' She broke off, embarrassed. Was this a tactless thing to say when someone had died?

'I bet Mrs Whoever has a cache somewhere,' Jamie remarked, filling a black mug with black coffee and thinking how unattractive it looked, though its aroma produced a much-needed sense of wellbeing. She had slept in the end, finding the light warmth of the duvet welcome when she had come in, chilled and hollow-feeling, as dawn lightened and the birds sounded their first notes. But dreams had still beset her, and she felt tight-strung and unrefreshed, too aware of untouched aréas of pain.

'Mrs Niven,' Vanessa said.

'Well, if Mrs Niven comes in to clean, she's bound to spend half her time drinking tea.'

'Jamie, that's unfair. We don't know that. She may be very conscientious. The house is clean enough, and that enormous room of Zara's, with everything she has in it, must be very difficult to keep nice.'

'Well, didn't Mr Syme say someone comes to do the garden? Bet he drinks tea sometimes.'

Jamie, bored, sounded sharp, and Phil said, 'I'll have juice, thanks,' though without much hope of being heard. 'And how about breakfast?'

That penetrated, the suggestion diverting Vanessa's worries into a new channel. 'Goodness, look at the time. I didn't start anything because I wasn't sure what everyone would like. People's habits change, and nowadays there are so many views about what's healthy and what isn't, particularly in America I suppose, Jamie. I have wholemeal Ryvita myself,

but I did put in some bread so we can make toast if
you want it. Do you still like a cooked breakfast, Phil?
And what about you, Jamie?'

'Just toast for me, thanks.' Left to herself Jamie
would have made it, put whatever was handy on it,
and gone out to eat it on the front steps. There was
little warmth in the day as yet, but she longed to be
out in the clean sweet air, and rediscovering the
Calder that mattered most, out of doors. But Vanessa
liked toast in a toast rack, butter in a dish. The mere
idea of going outside would flurry her, particularly as
Phil was saying, indifferent to opinion, 'Yes, I'd like
a fry-up. I can do it, though. You go on with whatever you're having.'

'No, no, you sit down,' Vanessa insisted. 'I'll cook,
I'd like to. You don't get away very often, you need a
little cosseting. How would you like your eggs done?
Poached would probably be healthiest—'

'Van, just stick them in the frying pan.' Phil
thought of staff breakfast and the uncouth piles of
left-over sausages, fried bread and black pudding
that were polished off. She wished she was there.

'Are you really sure you ought to eat fried foods?'
Vanessa was frowning as she whisked into action,
happy to be in maternal, caring mode. 'You ought to
think about your fat intake, you know . . .'

Phil and Jamie, knowing offers of help would be
refused, sat down exchanging grins. The younger
ones, bossed and protected. Give her her head. Yet
what would our lives have been like without her
watchful care, Jamie found herself amending, on a

more adult note. It was easy to mock Vanessa, to groan at the way she chased down details, but no one was ever more stalwart and loyal. She couldn't help having no brains. Jamie grinned again at a conclusion she couldn't resist. Sisterly praise must be kept within bounds.

Phil drank her orange juice in satisfying gulps, feet twisted round her chair legs, shoulders rounded, capacious breasts sagging in a bra too often washed. After all it was good to be with the others, just the three of them together again, in spite of feeling shy of Jamie, sophisticated these days in a way which the untidy child, the defiant teenager, even the self-sufficient younger woman, had never promised. Now the well-cut dark hair fell into an easy shape, she wore the kind of make-up that didn't look like make-up at all, and her clothes, as casual as those Phil was wearing herself, on her looked utterly different. The high gloss of success.

It could still astonish Phil that Jamie's life had taken such a course. She was far and away the most intelligent of them, everyone accepted that, but she had always been so rebellious, so ready to shrug off the things other people thought important. Phil had admired her for it, in an alarmed way, but had always been secretly afraid that it wouldn't bring her happiness in the end.

Phil had done a lot of worrying during the year Jamie had spent in Thailand, before taking a degree in Marketing and PR at Strathclyde. She had fretted about her safety, and hated her being so far away, further all the time in terms of knowledge and experience. Then, when Jamie had unexpectedly pulled off a decent degree, by getting her head down in the final term of a highly volatile student career, she had surprised them by going straight into a conventional PR job in London and, almost before Phil had got used to thinking of her there, had been off again, to an even better job with Leadbetter Voss in New York.

PR and Leadbetter Voss had meant little to Phil, but she had realised that this was a considerable achievement on Jamie's part, and had done her best to be pleased. But in their brief meetings when Jamie reappeared it had been increasingly hard to make contact, Phil humble and awkward, ashamed of her own limitations, her failure to offer a single concrete achievement.

Then seven years ago Jamie, with the sort of courage Phil found terrifying, had launched her own business, moving to Seattle, hitting the right place at the right time and making a dazzling success of it. It could bring Phil close to panic even to think of the responsibilities involved. She had tried to form a picture of Jamie's life from the impersonal letters produced by the computer, but had felt more and more distanced by references to a culture she knew nothing about. The very words alarmed her. A duplex apartment on the hillside above the campus became a condominium (not, in Phil's opinion, a word lightly to be risked) overlooking the waterfront. Friends dropped by; Jamie did things on weekends.

It seemed the Olympics were not games but mountains. Words like trail, softbacks, elevator, though comprehensible in themselves, made Phil feel once more the baffled younger sister always left behind.

It had been much easier to accept the direction Vanessa's life had taken. Vanessa was born to marry early, to find a good-looking, socially acceptable and already successful husband a few years older than she was, to have a son, though perhaps rather soon, and to move before he went to school from their first smallish house to a much bigger and very comfortable one a few miles outside Perth.

Inevitable as it might look from a distance of twenty-one years, the period after Vanessa's marriage had been a bad time for Phil. The engagement and the run-up to the wedding had been exciting, but even she had realised later that she had been shutting out the reality behind them. At thirteen she had been very much a child. The wedding itself had been torture for her, done up in long dress and flowery wreath and agonisingly conscious of how absurd she looked, terrified of doing something wrong and spoiling Vanessa's day, gauche and miserable with smart strangers quacking away on every side.

Then, when it was over, she and Jamie had been driven back to the house in Bearsden, not by their father, who had gone on somewhere else, but by Patrick, his friend, so much part of their lives that he was almost family himself, who so often over the years had filled such gaps. Then the realisation that Vanessa had gone for good had filled her with an anguish it still hurt to remember. Vanessa's reassurances about her marriage giving them another home had meant nothing on that desolate evening. The roof had come off Phil's world, and she had hated Jamie for not caring, not even admitting that anything had changed.

Which had been Jamie's way of dealing with the terrible bleakness of the future.

After this, holidays had been divided between Bearsden, Douglas and Vanessa's house in Giffnock, and Calder. At Calder, for Phil, the days had revolved around Freda. With Freda she had shared peaceful undemanding hours, collecting eggs, hanging out the washing, tending the African violets, making beds, bringing in the washing, damping and rolling the washing (Freda thought steam irons nasty hissy things and refused to have anything to do with them), shelling peas, peeling potatoes, chopping mint and, greatest treat of all, helping to mix cakes and being allowed to run her finger round the bowl to clean up the last of the pale, fruit-studded goo. Though Jamie had been scornful of such domestic pursuits she had been too busy, out of doors most of the time, to spare much attention for Phil. Grandmother had pursued her own placid course, letting them do much as they liked so long as they were on time for meals.

Phil, wishing Vanessa hadn't made the bacon so crisp, ate in silence, shutting out awareness of her surroundings, a self-protective technique perfected long ago. There were so many things she knew she was incapable of dealing with. She knew, for example, that she was already left behind in the bemusing rush of technology, and it could make her genuinely afraid to wonder where it would lead. She hated change. Last night, finding the kitchen where she had spent so many contented hours wiped out by Zara's ruthless hand, she had felt misery almost choke her. But however she felt about what had been done to this house, she knew she would not be the one to decide what became of it next.

'Before we do anything,' Vanessa was saying, unconsciously on cue, 'we ought to buy more food. Why don't we go down to Aberfyle right away?'

'Aberfyle? What's wrong with the village shop?'

'I don't think we'll get much there.'

'It doesn't matter what we eat, does it?'

'We can't go to the village without going to see Freda.' That was Phil, looking unhappily defiant already, as if she knew opposition would be immediate.

She was right. 'Phil, you know we can't,' Vanessa cried. 'We simply haven't time. Freda likes proper visits, with proper warning.'

'She'll hear that we've been up. Everyone will know about Zara.'

'But there's so much to *do*.'

'I don't think I quite understand what,' Phil said diffidently, looking uncomfortable but dogged. 'I mean, I know there's lots to discuss, but what can we actually do, today, about anything?' She hated arguing, but no problems of their own, however complicated and unforeseen, justified hurting Freda's feelings.

'But we have to check everything, find out what's actually left. Make lists.' Douglas had told her to do that, but he hadn't known when he said it about the depradations Mr Syme had warned them to expect, Zara's reckless disposal of things they now knew had been theirs all along, or the bizarre terms of their father's will. Quailing to think of what he would say, she wished she had phoned last night after all, so that he would have had time to assimilate the situation before she saw him.

Jamie hardly heard what they were saying. With the mention of Freda, the reality of encountering the faces and figures of the past, in the altered context of today, had hit her almost like a blow. So far being at Calder had been almost surreal. They had been islanded here, shut off from all outside contact. The harried day, their arrival in the dusk, shock piled on shock as they had explored the house, the dreamlike hours outside in the spring night, had seemed outside time, filled with emotions which left no room for the present or the future.

It would be good to go to the village. It had been so much part of life at Calder, sent on errands for Grandmother. They had taken their bikes, pushing them most of the way up the steep drive and the hilly glen road, hurtling gloriously back round the scary bends. Or they had walked up by the river path.

A door slammed in her mind on the associations that crowded instantly back. She couldn't face going that way today, and she knew she couldn't meet Freda. She wasn't ready for either, with so much unresolved, so much unsaid. Not today, not with the others, caught up in a welter of trivia and practicalities.

'Phil, why don't you go and buy whatever we need and say hello to Freda for us? Explain that time's limited. She'll understand that there's masses to see to.'

'But Phil can't take the car . . .'

Did every family take so long to thrash out the simplest arrangement, Jamie wondered with a flare of impatience which, however, she managed to hide. In the end they all went, she herself going along because she longed to see the glen again. And because to go and buy a pint of milk in the village, altered as it undoubtedly would be, had a new and private significance now.

5

Though she had grown used to thinking of the third week in May as summer, Jamie was reminded as the road climbed towards the top of the glen that here a late spring was just ending. The gean trees were already towers of white, the fingers of sycamore leaves beginning to splay, birches hazed with green, but there was still blossom on the blackthorns along the river. Coming as she had from the scale and vigorous growth of America's north-west seaboard, this landscape, as the single-track road approached the cluster of houses a couple of miles below the head of the glen, with beyond them scarcely a tree to be seen, seemed fine-etched and spare, the fleeting sunlight delicate in its touch, and to her it was piercingly beautiful.

It was so good to be here again. Gripped with a churning excitement Jamie tried to take in every detail, though she knew she could never absorb enough by merely looking, and longed to be on foot.

'Gask's looking smart these days.'

The Victorian-Gothic pile, now owned by a Danish businessman, reared dazzlingly white on its hillside. A very silly castle, Jamie decided, noting without favour smart wrought-iron gates and newly tarred drive. Several of the cottages had been renovated, though, and were obviously lived in, which had to be good.

In the village not all was so spruce, but even the gardens of empty houses were still bright with daffodils, while others were a mass of flowers, overhung by lilac and bird cherry. Cushions of aubretia clung to dry-stone dykes, japonica spread rich colour against grey granite or white harling. In the hedge round the pub garden the winter brown of copper beech was beginning to catch up with the green of the hawthorns. No one was about.

At first glance little seemed to have changed, and Jamie felt thankfulness fill her, as though the discovery was reassuring in some way. But looking around her more carefully, she saw that while an unattractive new development of chalet-like houses had sprung up behind a belt of conifers, more than one of the older cottages had been abandoned, the garage was closed and the church boarded up.

However, the handle of the shop door felt familiar to her hand, and the tinkle of its bell was drowned by the screech of hinges as it always had been. The shop itself had been reorganised, as far as space allowed, on self-service lines, yet many of its offerings – the card of pink and blue plastic combs, the tottery stand of postcards of acres of violently purple heather, or of Highland cattle in the Lost Valley with 'Scotland' printed across cerulean skies – were exactly as before. The post office across the street had gone, its business now conducted here. Up-to-date as its glass cubicle might be, Jamie noted the same old box on the floor where people tossed anything too big to go in the letter-box in the former post-office wall.

The girl behind the counter gave them a nod and went on stacking her cigarette shelf. Not many tourists turned into Glen Fallan, where there was no through road, not this early in the season anyway, and in her view putting herself out for them wouldn't bring any more. As long as she sold papers and cigarettes, handled the post and paid out pensions, everyone in the glen and holiday houses would be in sooner or later.

Jamie, returning the nod, found herself wanting to be recognised and at the same time to be completely anonymous. As they got out of the car she had felt both disappointed and relieved to find the street deserted. She knew it was absurd, but she couldn't quite crush down the need to be welcomed back, to feel she had come home. But who would know her after so long? A Laidlaw of Calder. What connotations would the phrase have now, after Zara's reign?

Through a gap between the notices stuck on the window she watched Phil going down the other side of the street, well-padded body taking on a marked roll as she began to hurry towards the turning to Freda's cottage. Should she have gone too, Jamie wondered. Was she being cowardly not to? But she knew she wasn't ready for such an encounter. And for Freda Phil was the one that really mattered, and always had been.

'There's absolutely nothing here,' Vanessa hissed at her shoulder. 'I knew there wouldn't be.'

'Don't be silly, these'll do.' Jamie scooped up a packet of ham, chicken drumsticks, strangely orange and wizened, lettuce, tomatoes. 'What more do you want?'

Vanessa looked dissatisfied. 'For lunch perhaps. But for dinner I really think—'

Jamie, ignoring her, headed for the till.

'Oh, Jamie, no, you mustn't,' Vanessa protested. 'We must all pay our share. At least, not Phil perhaps, she's always hard up, poor lamb. But you and I. How much is it?' She would always do this, with punctilious absurdity, and Jamie shook her head.

'For God's sake, it's a basket of groceries.'

'But it's only fair to—'

'You brought everything yesterday. Forget it.' Jamie was annoyed by Vanessa's persistence, but was honest enough to recognise that her irritation was mixed with a new, unfamiliar apprehension.

Outside a stranger was getting out of a muddy pick-up with a couple of collies in the back, a tall skinny girl in a long tubular skirt and sagging cardigan, who gave them a shy smile as she went into the shop. Jamie found herself wondering who she was, where she lived, still with that instinctive need to reach out for contact, to find some links that tied her to this place. Ridiculous, when she was so stubbornly resisting the associations with the past that really had some meaning.

They waited in the car, not speaking, Jamie's eyes

on the well-remembered outline of the ridge which swept up to the higher peaks shutting in the glen to the north. It would have been good to go on for the last couple of miles, turning at the bridge at Nether Fallan, so that coming back they could look down the whole length of the quiet, hidden-away little glen she loved so much. But she could imagine the flurry of objections such a simple proposal would meet with.

'I feel in such a muddle,' Vanessa broke in unexpectedly on her thoughts, her voice so odd that Jamie turned, frowning, to look at her. 'I mean, the memories and so on, all the things we talked about that I haven't thought of for ages. And then those hideous rooms and wondering how ever we can deal with them. Even coming here to the village and not seeing a soul we know. I feel as though Grandmother has been somehow – wiped out. In spite of living here all her life. I feel as though we've been wiped out. Us as we were, I mean.'

'Van, I didn't know you were feeling like that.' Jamie was startled by this awkward tumble of words, so very unlike Vanessa's usual level of communication, and even more startled by the tremor in her voice. 'Hey, come on, it's OK. You're not on your own, you know.' She put an arm round Vanessa's shoulders, noting in passing how plump and cushiony they felt under the fine wool of her jacket. 'We're all feeling a bit shaken up.'

'Oh, Jamie, it was awful, last night, wasn't it? The house all dragged about like that, as though no one had loved it or respected it for such a long time.'

'I didn't think you specially cared about Calder,' Jamie said, speaking cautiously, not wanting to make Vanessa think she was arguing the point, which was how she tended to take most responses.

'Not after we'd grown up. I could hardly bear to go there after Father moved in with Zara, though of course I had to when he was ill.' Her face pinched and she made a movement with her hand as though brushing away something that mustn't be allowed to distract her now. 'But I did like it when we were small. I know it was your special place, yours and Father's, and Phil and I didn't get a look-in by comparison, but still, it was Grandmother's house, and it meant a lot to me too.'

'What do you mean, my place and Father's?' It was an entirely new viewpoint to Jamie. 'Was that how—?'

'Yoo-hoo! Coming!' Phil was hurrying round the corner, her face beaming, lumbering towards them at something close to a trot. 'Sorry to be so long,' she was calling before she reached the car, 'but Freda was so thrilled I'd popped in. I'll have to come back and see her properly very soon. I don't come up nearly often enough, as she wasn't slow to point out. She gave me some brownies, though, look. She'd just been baking. And she said to tell you she's no' best pleased with the pair of you, not so much as coming in to pass the time of day.'

Phil, out of breath as she was, effortlessly reproduced Freda's speech, and though Vanessa and Jamie were both sorry that a rare frankness between them had been interrupted, knowing it might be hard to recreate the moment which had produced it, they laughed as Phil thrust the cakes towards them, confident that they would be as delighted by the treat today as they would have been thirty years ago.

Jamie, accepting one, tucked Vanessa's comment away for later consideration. Was that how the others had seen her relationship with her father? She felt a quiver of trepidation go through her. There were altogether too many ominous things waiting in the wings at present.

Jamie got the purchase she needed with the claw hammer and wrapped both hands round the haft.

'We could ask Mrs Niven where the key to the nursery stairs is. She must know.'

'I'm sure we shouldn't do any structural damage even if the house is ours. Mr Syme won't like it at all.'

Paying no attention to Phil and Vanessa bobbing about behind her, Jamie wrenched the corner of the partition free with a satisfying rending screech.

'This is structural damage,' she said briefly. 'Putting the damn thing up in the first place.'

'Maybe we should get a man in to do it properly.'

'Whoever does the garden. He could do it.'

'What a pair of useless clucking females you are,' Jamie said, getting her fingers round the edge of the wood. 'Get a man in? Where have you been living for the last twenty years? You could give me a hand, you know. That would be more to the point than squawking and flapping.'

To her it had been the obvious first job. To be cut off from that part of the house which had most intimately belonged to them, where things they had owned and used might still be in place, was not to be tolerated. The image of this blocked-off corridor, statement-making, hostile, had hovered behind all other thoughts ever since she woke. Nothing could be done in the house, as she saw it, until this arbitrary barrier had gone.

With Phil lending her considerable weight – Vanessa was too busy crying, 'Mind the splinters!' and brushing dust from her clothes to be any use – they wrenched it back, and there before them lay their childhood.

In silence they looked along the narrow corridor, its cream walls and dark-stained wood, its whipcord runner that never ran quite straight, its watercolours of Hebridean scenes painted by a great-great-aunt, all so precisely as they remembered them that words literally would not come. Phil slipped a hand under Vanessa's arm, and that too seemed so much a part of time returned to them that Vanessa hugged it close in comfort and turned to smile at her reassuringly.

'Did she hate us that much?' Jamie asked after a moment, her voice thin. 'So much that she wanted to obliterate us? Shut us out of her sight?'

'We don't know that exactly.' But Vanessa's voice sounded uncertain too. 'Come on.'

It was a different part of the house: low ceilings; small windows deep-set in thick walls, their panes cobwebbed, their sills dotted with flies; thumb-latched doors, with steps down dangerously close inside them; wide floorboards varnished round the shapes of dust-muted rugs; white bedheads painted by Grandmother with flowers and birds. The pictures they remembered were still on the walls, studied so often that every detail remained minutely familiar – the girls with green feet who became daffodils, the sister who made the shirts of nettles, Thumbelina's house. The bookcases, with the shells and ornaments and trinket boxes along their tops, still held the well-thumbed treasures.

Emotion gripped them as, saying little, reaching out to each other with small touches of sympathy and comprehension when one or other found some special reminder move her, they drifted from room to room in turn. They sat on the low, dust-sheeted beds and stared around them, and not even Jamie felt capable of putting into words what she felt.

For Vanessa their mother was here, with her soft hair and gentle voice. For them all their father was here – from the days before Zara had appeared in their lives to exert her unwholesome power over him – tall, darkly handsome, striding in to give them perfunctory goodnight hugs with the smell of heather and tweed and gun-oil about him, always in a hurry, evading pleas and clutching hands, laughing, insisting he couldn't read to them, he'd never learned how, taking in a single stride the steps to the corridor and freedom, calling over his shoulder, 'Never keep a man from his gin and French . . .'

Freda, tight-lipped and heavy-handed, was here,

driving them into bed, laying out tomorrow's clean clothes, and in Jamie's case having a few things to say about the state of the ones she'd just taken off.

'And none of yon daft reading caper, mind, you'll have no eyes left . . .'

Grandmother, calm, unconcerned about the time, for everything at Calder moved at her pace and at her behest, was here, giving them big, enfolding hugs. Lavender, perhaps a pungent waft of the pot-pourri she'd been making or the geraniums she'd been potting, and a faint tweedy aura from her too. Her voice fading down the corridor, 'Tomorrow, my darlings, we shall think of something wonderful to do. Sleep like dormice . . .'

Jamie had not been aware of the tears on her cheeks till Vanessa's arm came round her.

'It feels as though she's here,' she said unsteadily.

'I know.'

'I'm glad we came in.' Phil came to sit at her other side, making Jamie tilt towards her as the lumpy old mattress sagged. 'You were right. It's dreadfully sad, but it will make us braver.'

To tackle the rest. Yes, Phil, normally so clumsy with words, so easily embarrassed by any attempt to express her feelings, had put it perfectly.

And to make decisions. How awful if – the thought was in all their minds – having rediscovered this untouched citadel of their past, it had to go.

'We'd better make a start,' Vanessa said, her voice bleak in spite of meaning to be brisk.

We can always come back in here if it gets too hard

to take, Jamie privately reassured herself. This won't
go away. It's survived till now, and letting in the air
won't make it crumble into dust at once. And if we
can't find the key to the stair door, she thought more
truculently, I shall break it down. This is our place,
has always been ours, and no one can shut us out of it
against our will.

'Shall we start on her room?'

They had agreed it must be done first. Though it
was the job they were all most dreading, it was an
essential exorcism. Until it was done, it was as
though no other steps could be objectively decided
upon.

'We don't need to look at anything, just shove it in
binbags,' Jamie said. 'Later we'll organise a skip.'

'There may be things of Father's among hers,' Phil
suggested diffidently, then flushed at the thought of
the intimacy this implied.

'Personally I don't care about anything of his that
was connected with Zara,' Jamie retorted. 'We'll bin
the lot.'

'But some things may be valuable,' Vanessa put in
anxiously. 'Remember what Mr Syme said about the
inventory.' Though it was not the thought of Mr
Syme's warning which had prompted the reminder.

'Vanessa.' Jamie kept her voice even. 'The object
of an inventory is that in the event of everything
being split up the total value can be fairly divided.
Among us. No one else is involved. Mr Syme also
said we could do as we liked with any small personal
possessions. That doesn't seem too difficult to grasp.'

'Let's not get cross with each other,' Phil pleaded. She had always hated that biting note in Jamie's voice. 'Everything's horrid enough without that.'

The others saw her unhappy look and smoothed their feathers. For the time being they needed each other, and they knew it.

They went back along the fusty-smelling corridor, stepped through the framework of the trashed partition, and turned towards Zara's quarters.

6

They were tired enough not to care about the pretentious kitchen tonight; tired enough for even Vanessa to admit she was glad not to have to think about cooking. What they had done had not been particularly arduous, but the emotional drain had been greater than any of them had foreseen. They had emptied cupboards and drawers, wardrobes and bathroom cabinets, their faces set, hating the subtle emanation of Zara which rose from her clothes and personal belongings.

'Most of these things have hardly been worn,' Vanessa had observed at one point, spreading across the bed yet another armload from the huge walk-in wardrobe. 'And I'm sure they were fearfully expensive. Shouldn't we take them to some nearly-new shop? It seems a crime not to find some use for them.'

They had looked at each other, then in unspoken agreement had gone on stuffing everything into bags for disposal, with a shared need to know these reminders no longer existed. Vanessa had said no more.

There had been one good discovery. Mr Syme had warned them yesterday that most objects of value in the house, things which had been in the family for

generations, had, in contravention of the terms of
their father's will, been sold off over the years by
Zara. Though the warning had not lessened the
shock of the bare rooms they had walked into last
night, it had meant that opening the door of one of
the old servants' rooms above the new kitchen and
finding it had become a dumping ground for anything which had not struck Zara as a quick source of
cash, had been correspondingly more rewarding.
Maybe she would have got around to these poor
derelicts eventually – the button-backed bedroom
chair with a broken castor, the spotted mirrors, the
dressing-table with its inlaid banding sprung with
damp, Grandmother's footstool, its needle-point
worn through where her heels had rested, discarded
rugs, lamps, curtains, and more amateur watercolours. The sad relics had been pounced on with a
pleasure out of all proportion to their worth. Even so,
there was little they could do with them. Though
each had hoped to find some small keepsake to
remind them of Grandmother, Zara had been thorough.

'There's nothing here that's really much use,'
Vanessa had said at last. Certainly it was unimaginable to think of introducing any of these dingy
objects into her own immaculate house. 'You
wouldn't have room for anything, I suppose,' she
had added, turning to Phil.

Jamie, with a sudden look of resolution which
neither of the others noticed, had opened her mouth
to speak when Vanessa had gone on in the worried

tone they were so used to, 'But if you don't mind my saying so, it doesn't seem a very good idea to go on living in as you do, you know, Phil. It may have been all right when you were younger, but you can get too used to having everything laid on for you. Perhaps you should be planning for the future a little before it's too late.'

Phil, who had also been about to speak, thinking it would be nice to have the little china lamp with the crack in it if no one else wanted it, had gaped at Vanessa, thrown by the introduction of so large a subject as the rest of her life, into this moment when so many other things were more pressing and relevant. The assumptions Vanessa and Jamie made about her were set in stone; how could she ever begin to make anything clear to them?

'I really don't see what we can do with it all, do you?' Vanessa, having put Phil's life on track, had reverted to the original problem.

Jamie, breathless with something very like panic to realise how close the moment she dreaded had come, had shaken her head mutely. With a feeling of anti-climax, almost of guilt, they had shut the door again on the finds which had seemed so promising.

Vanessa had wanted to get deeply into cleaning as soon as drawers and shelves were emptied, and had had to be restrained.

'Mrs Niven can do it. You know Mr Syme said the arrangement with her could go on as before, and with the gardener too, till plans were more definite.'

Definite. The discussion which yesterday they had

agreed to defer until they had seen what the real state of things at Calder was, but which had hung over their heads all the time, could no longer be postponed.

'All right, where do we start?' Jamie demanded, their dull supper nearly over, only the cheese Vanessa had brought still to come. And crackers, as in the UK. It was not a good moment for a reminder of cultural differences, however trivial. Jamie saw in the faces of the others a reflection of her own reluctance, and a shiver ran over her skin. This was not going to be easy. And there and then she knew she wasn't ready for the moment. She didn't have the courage. She needed more time.

She stared back at the faces turned to hers, knowing that they expected her, capable career woman, boss of her own company, to take the lead. The waiting silence thickened. But it was Vanessa, ever ready to accept her responsibilities as the eldest, who spoke in the end.

'We can't pretend any longer, can we? Unless one of us can buy the others out, there isn't really any alternative but to sell. We all know that. And as far as we're concerned, Douglas and I, I mean, things aren't terribly easy at present. Douglas says return on capital is so abysmal that we might just as well keep any money we've got in an old sock under the mattress.' There was no response to this witticism. Aware that she had muffed it as usual, though she could never see how, her voice rose defensively. 'We have Ryan to see through university, remember, and that's far more expensive than it used to be. And we couldn't think of selling up at Dunrossie and moving here. It's too far from Edinburgh for Douglas, and Ryan finds where we are cut off enough as it is. Young people have such different needs nowadays. It isn't like when we were growing up. You don't realise, since neither of you has children, but it has changed.'

Jamie took a grip on her temper. Vanessa's idea of things 'not being terribly easy' was unattainable affluence to Phil. And the patronising reference to motherhood, with its automatic assumption that anyone who was childless was a failure, was hard to take. However, there was too much at stake to be drawn by side issues. She looked at Phil, though there could be little doubt of her view as to what must be done with Calder.

'I'm sorry.' Phil's heavy jowls quivered. Never had she been so conscious of the gulf between her attainments and those of her achieving sisters. 'You know I haven't a bean.' Though, she thought, with what was close to bitterness for her, neither of them had any idea just how little carers, no matter what their experience, could earn. On duty for long hours every day, at night as well if there was an emergency, up to the elbows in poop half the time, and too often unbearably saddened to witness the decay of body and spirit which the years inflicted. Tears stung her eyes, not in self-pity, but because of the distance which had widened between the three of them.

Though it had been as much her fault as theirs. She had never let even Vanessa come to Burnbrae.

'We can't do anything but sell, can we?' she said. 'Unless we rent?'

'I wonder if anyone would want to rent a place like this nowadays,' Jamie was beginning thoughtfully, for this was a new idea, when Vanessa rushed in. 'But the house couldn't possibly be let in this state,' she exclaimed, sounding to Jamie as if she were plucking the first objection she could find out of the air. 'It would cost a small fortune to put it right, apart from someone having to organise it all. Then it would have to be repaired and maintained, and you never know what kind of tenants you'll get, though Mr Syme might—'

'For God's sake, Vanessa,' Jamie flared in an anger she didn't control this time. 'It's ridiculous to go into all that when Phil was merely making a suggestion.'

But it seemed after some argument that none of them really liked this option, and it became obvious to Jamie that, as far as the others were concerned, the decision lay with her. Would she want to buy them out? With their vague and inflated ideas of earning power in the States they imagined that she could, and Vanessa, remembering instructions, felt more and more harassed by conflicting feelings. Jamie was established in Seattle; surely she wouldn't seriously think of coming back to Glen Fallan to live? How awful not to want whole-heartedly to have her nearby, Vanessa thought with shame. Yet part of me longs for it.

Jamie, put unbearably under pressure by the expectant silence, with an abrupt movement got up and went to make the coffee they had all forgotten about. She was glad to be occupied for a few moments, but when the percolator was going she made herself turn and face them, struck by the fact that even Vanessa had said nothing.

'OK, here's what I think,' she said brusquely. 'We jointly own Calder. We know that any capital Father left has been gobbled up by Zara, though when you think of the way she lived and the rabble she entertained here, I don't suppose that's much of a surprise to any of us. It was a shock to find Father had never married her, and particularly to find this has been ours all along, but at the end of the day it doesn't change much.'

Had Hal Laidlaw insisted that these facts be suppressed until Zara died because he thought his daughters might contest her right to stay at Calder? What if they had turned her out six years ago? What if they had somehow been able to prevent her from squandering, selling and vandalising? Useless to speculate, but these thoughts, like so many others her death had brought to the surface, were hard to ignore entirely.

'Right,' said Jamie, since Phil and Vanessa still watched her mutely, their eyes anxious, their faces tight with concentration. 'Leaving property to co-heirs can lead to problems, but the last thing we want to do is fight over this. There's been a lot to take in during the last few days, and I for one don't feel we've given ourselves enough time to think things through.'

She felt in their silence that this had not been what they wanted to hear.

'But Jamie,' Vanessa said after a tense pause, diffidently for her, 'I think we need to know – would you think of buying us out? Is that even a possibility?'

Jamie's face closed, and she didn't look at either of them. 'I just think we should put things on hold for a while, that's all.'

Vanessa flushed, feeling she had pressed too hard. It was dreadful to talk about money anyway.

As no one spoke, Jamie said more sharply, 'There's no hurry, is there? Good God, it's not even a week since Zara died.'

Douglas will be furious, Vanessa thought blankly. But that could not be said. And to be fair, of the three of them only Jamie had any real thinking to do.

Phil voiced this. 'Of course you must have time to think, Jamie. Vanessa and I know where we stand, but there must be all sorts of things for you to take into account. I'll be happy to go along with whatever's decided.'

As she always had been. Jamie gave her a grateful smile.

'I suppose we felt it would be a good idea to talk over as much as we could while you were here.' It was the best Vanessa could do. She didn't imagine Douglas would think it adequate.

'This time I don't have to go back right away, as it

happens.' Jamie was afraid she had said too much, but Vanessa accepted the words at their face value.

'Oh, Jamie, that's lovely, I hadn't realised. We'll be able to see something of you at last. You'll come and stay, of course. It's ages since you saw Ryan and—'

'I want to ask you both something.' Jamie overrode her firmly, straightening from the worktop where she had been leaning, slightly surprised to find her heart-beat hurried and uncomfortable.

'What?' This sounded serious, and Vanessa looked anxious again, remembering Douglas's uncompromising orders: 'Sell and get the cash. Or if by any chance that snippy sister of yours wants to buy then make sure she knows there has to be a proper valuation. No cosy deals because it's family.'

Phil waited more phlegmatically. She had had no expectations. True, Calder had always been in the background, to be theirs one day, but she had never fully believed Zara would let it happen, no matter what their father had decreed. She had never wanted money for herself, not being interested in much that it could buy, and though she had a use for it now, should it come her way, there was no hurry. She knew from her experience at Burnbrae House, where wills and disputed inheritances regularly figured, that such matters could take years. If she was going to be lucky, then she'd be lucky. If not things would go on as before. But what could competent, inde-pendent Jamie want of them?

'Look, would either of you mind –' Jamie's voice

was less decisive now '– would you mind if I stayed on here for a bit? It's good of you to invite me to stay with you, Van, but for the moment I kind of need some space, if you can understand that. I've missed this place so much—' But there was no need to go into that. 'Would you have any objection to my staying on?'

'Stay here?' Vanessa's thoughts scrambled. Douglas would certainly find an objection. He would see it as establishing some kind of foothold. Then a rare defiance rose in her. Why should she always, immediately, see things through his eyes? Jamie was her sister; they were talking about a week or ten days at the outside. Even with Calder already belonging to them (and she dreaded to think what Douglas would have to say about that discovery), how long would it be before everything was finally sorted out? Weeks? Months? Then other concerns took over.

'But Jamie, it would seem so strange to leave you here alone, especially after you've been away so long. I mean, I'm sure Phil and I wouldn't mind you being here, of course not, but the house is hardly fit to live in, the way it is. And how would you manage without a car? Wouldn't it be more sensible to come back with me, and we could slip up for the day whenever you wanted to.'

'I didn't mean that kind of objection,' Jamie said, smiling in spite of herself. 'All that could be sorted out. I meant, would you mind my being here, in the house you both equally own? And waiting a while for a decision about it? I'd let you know soon.' Panic flickered at the words, but she gave no sign of it.

'It's fine by me,' Phil said staunchly. 'What reason could there be for you not to stay, if that's what you want?' No one, she thought sadly, had thought of Jamie staying with her. Well, of course not; but how nice if one day that could happen. 'Rather you than me, though,' she added, glancing round her.

'I don't have to be in here all the time.' Jamie's spirits rose in response to Phil's ready support.

'The whole place, I meant. I always hated it.'

'Hated Calder?' Both voices were disbelieving. 'Of course you didn't.'

'Well, perhaps not hated. But it frightened me.'

'Phil, what nonsense. With Grandmother and Freda here?'

'But you never said a word.' For a moment Vanessa felt as she often had in the past, in moments of crisis when she had been the only person the others could turn to, that the task was beyond her. Guilt filled her, even at this distance of years, to think how often she must have failed them. 'Oh, Phillie, that's awful. I can't bear to think of it.'

'But what were you afraid of?' Jamie's memories of Calder were of sun, light and freedom, of long summer evenings smelling of mown grass and blossom, of the security of her little room, and beyond it the wider security of the big quiet house. 'You used to adore being with Freda, and you cried and cried when we left.'

'Oh, well, daytime was all right, I suppose. But at night I used to think of all the enormous cupboards and the dark stairs. And I was afraid of the river.'

'The river?' But that's the spirit of the place, Jamie wanted to protest. Its voice, its life, its ever-changing mood. How could it frighten you?

'Were you afraid of falling in?' Vanessa, ever prosaic, asked. 'But we were so careful. You were always kept well away from the edge.'

'That was just it,' Phil said, with an ironic grunt. 'You made such a song and dance about it that I had nightmares about going over. And when we used to do those dares, sitting with our legs over the drop, I always felt sick. At night I wanted my window shut so that I couldn't hear the water, but Freda wouldn't hear of it. I kept my window shut last night, I can tell you.' But she didn't tell them what safety it was that she had longed for.

While Vanessa, with her usual need to rearrange even those things which had happened long ago, decided she and Phil should have shared a room, and the back stairs should have been painted white, Jamie thought, with a fresh chill, how little we know of each other, and how disturbing that is, especially now.

She was not surprised to hear a tap at her door as she was going to bed.

'Can I come in?' Vanessa, wholesome in white broderie anglaise, hair brushed, the faint sheen of nourishing cream on her cheeks, was in the doorway.

Costly and correct, Jamie thought with affection.

'Of course.'

'I wanted to ask, are you sure about staying on your own? Wouldn't it be a better plan if you came with us in the morning, and we organised everything properly? Without a car how will you even get food?'

'It's not two miles to the village.'

'That's all very well, but you know what the shop's like. And you'd have to carry everything back.'

'Not a problem. I don't need much.'

'I suppose you could always ask Mrs Niven to get you things. Or perhaps she could take you to Aber-fyle. She's bound to go quite often. But it doesn't seem—'

'I can get lifts. And there are always taxis.'

'Or you could hire a car.' Vanessa brightened up. 'Yes, that's the answer. Why didn't I think of that before? You could come with us tomorrow and pick one up. Perth might be best.'

'Not tomorrow.'

'No? But it would be more difficult if you're here alone. Or would they deliver? I expect so. Well, at least you can afford to do it the expensive way.'

'Indeed,' Jamie agreed.

'But you'll be terribly lonely,' Vanessa fretted on. 'We scarcely know anyone here now. The Dunbars still use the Toll-house, but Naomi has had trouble with her hip recently, and I think Patrick mostly comes on his own.' Jamie folded and smoothed her sweatshirt over the back of a chair with a care Freda would have applauded. 'If they were here I should feel happier about you. Now, let me think, who else is there? I heard that Hugh Erskine at Fallan has married again, though I can't imagine anyone could be as nice as Angie was. Still, she'd have to be an

improvement on his first wife. What she was called?
Was it Gabriela?'

'Don't know. They were your friends, not mine.'

'I don't think the new people at Gask are there
much, but Freda will know. At least with her in the
village you won't be quite alone.'

'Vanessa, I want to be on my own, remember?'

'But you'll see Patrick if he's up, won't you? After
all, he's practically family.'

'Of course. If he's up while I'm here I could hardly
avoid seeing him.' And I'll deal with the feelings the
prospect arouses in my own way and in my own time.

Comforted to think things were now satisfactorily
settled, Vanessa turned to go. Then turned back.

'Look, I don't want to ask about anything that's
private, but are you sure everything's all right?'

'What do you mean?' The question shook Jamie,
and she spoke sharply.

'I knew you'd snap if I said anything. It was just
that once or twice I've thought you were looking a bit
– well, fraught. Of course it was a shock to hear about
Zara, and it's been a stressful time for all of us, but I
wondered if anything was wrong. Silly of me, I
expect. I know how hard you work, and it can't have
been easy to drop everything at a moment's notice,
and then the flight and so on . . .'

'No, you're right, I am tired,' Jamie made herself
say as Vanessa's voice trailed doubtfully away.
'Things have been – difficult. That's why I need a
bit of space. Oh, and by the way, I didn't mean to
hurt your feelings by turning down your invitation,

so please don't mind. I can come another time, maybe.'

She saw by Vanessa's radiant smile that she had found the sore spot. Though to stay in Vanessa's perfect house, where comfort dripped and oozed at every turn, face to face with her enviable marriage, and her blind adoration of her far from perfect son, would have been more than she could bear at present, she knew that Vanessa was offering her the best she had.

But, hurt though Vanessa might be, Jamie had gained the breathing space she needed. Standing at the window after Vanessa had gone, till the flow of cool air drove her shivering into bed, she was swept by excitement to realise that tomorrow she would be here alone, a clean new page before her to be written on.

As she slid into sleep, happily aware of the faint murmur of the river in the background, and the even more elusive sound of the light wind moving in the fir trees beyond it, she was reminded of Phil's childhood fears. Hidden fears, hidden thoughts for all of them; it could not be otherwise.

7

Jamie felt an almost superstitious need to wait for the last glimpse of the Rover on the twists of the drive, as though if she turned away too soon Vanessa might remember something else important and come back.

But it was gone. '*Yes!*' Jamie punched the air in relief. It was a good thing Phil was on duty at twelve, or Vanessa might have gone on clucking around for ever, wondering if milk was still delivered and wanting to order it, making lists of what was in the kitchen cupboards and what she thought Jamie should buy, anxious to find out about organising a skip before she left, and telling Jamie every five minutes to be sure to let her know if there was anything she needed.

All the same, Jamie's eagerness to see her sisters gone was tinged with guilt. Being with them again had meant more to her than she had expected, and it would be a long time before she forgot the deep, primitive thankfulness which had filled her at the moment of meeting two days ago, the feeling of being safe again. The exasperation which had swiftly followed, rather than a conflicting reaction, was so much a part of being with them that it seemed almost part of the same feeling.

And yet, Jamie thought, turning towards the house, that very closeness had been a strain. Sharing the discoveries here with them, trapped by her own cowardice in the role in which they expected to see her, had meant there had been no time to absorb these changes at a deeper, more personal level, in the context of everything else which she had to assimilate. By now she needed desperately to be alone to deal with her burden of private anguish, and come to terms if she could, in silence and at her own pace, with all that had happened.

Going towards the steps, she was sharply repelled by the thought of walking into the hall. Its self-conscious ostentation had nothing to do with this moment. Instead she turned and went along the front of the house, and at once, by this simple rejection of Zara, felt optimism return. This beautiful place, deserted and still at last, was hers to savour and reclaim. Obligations and dread, calamity and pain, fell away. Around her was only sun and space, a great quietness, sweet warm air, birds still sounding their springtime calls against the background burble of the river. She was free to go where she liked, do as she liked, in a place which ten days ago had not even been available to her as a refuge. For these stolen days she could pretend it was hers alone, hers for good. It would be some form of comfort.

It was hard to believe she had been here for two nights and a day and, apart from the hours spent in the garden that first night, a memory now shadowy and unreal, had barely been outside. Even then she had been with the others, and their worries about the condition of what Vanessa kept calling 'the fabric of the house', their concern over such minor details as vanished flower-beds and overgrown shrubbery, their wrangling about where the swing had been and when the summerhouse had last been in use, had been distractingly far from her own mood of tense, half-fearful rediscovery.

She had been relieved, though, to find little trace of Zara visible outside the house. The buildings at the back of the courtyard, the workshop, the stables long ago turned into garages, the tack room piled with lumber, were much as they had always been, except for the log shed, which never in the history of Calder had been empty before. Going through the arch in the west courtyard wall they had found the cottage on the river banks where Freda and her husband had lived, now looking sad and neglected. Phil in particular had hated to see its dirty windows, half hidden by unpruned roses and self-seeded elders. Unchanged, although the path to it was grown over with speedwell and buttercups, had been the bridge below the waterfall, and the deep, smooth-slabbed pool below, a favourite if icy place to swim.

Behind the garages the slatted game larder had half collapsed. The netting of the fruit cage, greenish and rotting, gaped with holes. They had recalled long summer hours spent in there with Grandmother, supposedly picking but mostly eating raspberries and tayberries, fat warm pink gooseberries, black and red currants.

Jamie covered this ground again, wandering without plan or aim, making it hers. At last she took the path to the walled garden, glad they had not gone this far together, glad to be alone to deal with the emotions which even approaching it aroused, nostalgia, sadness at the signs of decay on every hand, yet in a way welcoming these sights because they meant that Zara's influence had not reached here, and almost unbearable delight to be back again after so long. With the memories so close and vivid, it was also rather uncanny to be completely alone, in the slumbering quiet of a summer morning. It could never have been this way in the past. Apart from Freda, who had never seemed to be absent, there would have been other help in the house and garden. In the days before most of Calder had been absorbed by Gask, there would have been estate employees as well. There had always been an awareness of people about, of work going on.

The sun was gaining warmth. Jamie could feel it on her back as she opened the old green door, noting that a new board, unpainted, had been nailed across the bottom, where doubtless rabbits had been finding a way through the rotting holes. She paused inside it, and found she was trembling. This was so much Grandmother's place.

The long beds which had held cutting flowers for the house; the strawberry patch, that alarming Tom Tiddler's ground where she had always been the one to wriggle under the nets while Phil fearfully stood guard; and the section where at this time of year rows of seedlings and the green lines of spring onions, broccoli, leeks, broad beans and lettuce grown from seed would have been showing, all had been roto-vated into one empty expanse. Better than one mass of weeds, she supposed. Looking more carefully, she saw that the paths were tidy, the box hedges border-ing them not too ragged, and the fruit trees against the walls cared for. Though Zara, who lived princi-pally on alcohol and vitamin pills, would have had no use for the produce of such a garden, and had probably never set foot in it, the jungle had been kept at bay. Jamie herself barely knew one flower from another, and had never given house room to a single plant in the Seattle apartment (she pushed that thought hastily away) but even she could see that it wouldn't be too difficult to get this garden going again. For Grandmother's sake, absurd as that might be, she was glad. Obviously in his few hours a week the gardener would have time to do little more than mow the lawns, keep paths and gravel clear, and fight back invaders like nettles, ground elder, dockens and snowberry, but it had been enough to stave off a look of total dereliction.

She set off on a slow circuit of the outer path. She used to be sent here to pick lovage, tarragon, marjor-am and fennel, so she knew what those looked like. Here they were still, spreading madly by this time. Freda had had her parsley, chives and mint nearer to hand by the kitchen door. Faces, voices, footsteps. Jamie, sinking down on the stone edging in the corner where the plum trees were, let them flow back, sometimes smiling, sometimes with a hard ache in her throat. Suddenly, without warning, tears were spilling down her cheeks.

She tried to stem them, then realised that if there were anywhere in the world where she could cry it was here. She cried for Grandmother, for the house as it had been; she cried for her father in earliest memories and, as she had never let herself do before, she cried because she had not got back in time to see him before he died. Could she have? Had she really tried? Questions she had buried, and now faced at last. She hadn't known how ill he was, she pleaded; they hadn't told her. Then she knew that whether she admitted she had been at fault or still tried to defend herself was not important. It was enough that these doubts could be brought into the light at last, and her own actions, right or wrong, accepted.

And she cried, finally, for the enormous, stunning disaster which had overtaken her own life. No, overtaken was the wrong word, a cowardly prevarication. She had willingly and heedlessly courted that disaster. Every warning had been there, but she had been so sure, so blindly confident.

She didn't cry for long. It wasn't an indulgence that suited her. Hot now, she pulled her sweatshirt over her head, dried her eyes with a sleeve and pushed back her hair. Looking about her as she followed the outer path back to its starting point, she knew that, because this place had brought cath-artic tears, she could come back to it whenever she needed comfort. Reaching the door in the wall she

paused to break off a sprig of appleringie, running
the soft, fine, frond-like leaves through her fingers to
release their scent, shutting her eyes to inhale the
evocative sweetness.

She still couldn't bear to go back to the house. She
grinned briefly to think what Vanessa would have
said about leaving the breakfast things. But this
mood of released emotion must not be wasted.
Now, she knew, she could go on, along the river
path, to confront the other waiting ghosts.

The original toll-house, half a mile up-river where
the old road had crossed to go up the west side of the
glen, had been tiny, one room like a half octagon
jutting towards the road, another behind it. Fifty
years ago Patrick Dunbar's grandfather had acquired
it as a retreat where he could escape from his over-
bearing wife, to fish, read and write his dull journals
of his dull life, during which even war had brought
little change beyond overwork, since he had remained throughout in general practice in Kirriemuir.
It was his son who had added the long room overlooking the river, put in kitchen and bathroom and
laid on water and electricity. He had used local stone
for his additions, faithfully matching the style of the
odd little house, and to Jamie, who had always known
it in this form, it made a satisfying and familiar
whole. No one had ever attempted to make a garden.
The depradations of deer and rabbits would have
made fencing essential, and fencing would have
spoiled the whole character of the place. A few

potentillas had been planted, hardy Welsh poppies had seeded themselves lavishly and stonecrop grew in the facing of the bank, but apart from that there were only wild flowers, the last daffodils on the slope behind, and the white froth of bird cherry overhanging the burn. Though the grass around the house had been mown at least once this year, to Jamie's eyes this natural look, with the arch of the bridge, the falls tumbling down the gorge and birch, alder, larch and fir on the far bank as backdrop, was and always had been perfect.

So she thought now, settling into her favourite hollow on the bridge parapet. Magical, magical place. She was glad they hadn't walked to the village yesterday; glad she had come back alone. Would the Dunbars be here this weekend? Would she be able to come up the path in the evening shadows under the trees and, emerging into this sheltered enclave, see a light in the windows of the long room? And find Patrick there alone, which from what Vanessa had said seemed most likely.

No evasion would be possible then. Before those deep-set, penetrating eyes, trained to observation, any flimsy attempt at self-justification would be useless. For as long as Jamie could remember Patrick had been a figure of authority in their lives. The two families had known each other for generations, and there had never been a time when he wasn't somewhere in the background, at Calder and in Glasgow. He had played golf, shot and fished with her father, though the two latter pursuits he had soon given up.

But even in his teens he had always had time for the three small girls, and having him play with them had been the most intoxicating treat Jamie could remember. He had been her hero and she was jealously possessive of him, resenting any attention paid to the others, sulking ferociously when he detached himself to return to the grown-up world. Sulking because it was the only way she had had to deal with the sense of being wanted by no one which so often seized her, impossible to express or communicate. She had longed for Patrick's approbation, and to please him had done her best to curb her temper and control the frustrated rages which could boil up without warning.

As they grew up he had been a supernumerary family member who could safely be confided in. It was because of him that Jamie had completed her degree course, for by that time their father took little interest in what they did. There had been monumental rows with Patrick on those occasions when she came close to being sent down, but each time her need to keep his respect swung the balance.

She had been intelligent enough, however, to recognise her dependence on him, and to see where it was leading her, and with fierce pride, in agonies of anxiety in case he would guess how she felt, she had removed herself as soon as she could. She had thrown herself headlong into her job, her new life in London and a series of relationships, but Patrick had remained unshakably her ideal, the person to whom every problem was mentally referred, with whom every joke was shared. None of her contemporaries had stood a chance.

Now, alone, free of every demand, here in Patrick's own place, too conscious of the years that had gone by since last she was here, she surveyed the past from a new perspective. Patrick, who to a child's eye had seemed unquestionably a grown-up, and a large and powerful one at that, was in fact, as Zara had been, nearer in age to Vanessa than to their father. Jamie worked out that when she was at college Patrick had been younger than she was now. But whatever the sums said, the childhood view was so entrenched that it was still hard not to regard him as a generation away in outlook – and in achievement, for she knew from Vanessa how successful he had become as a sculptor, and how much his work was in demand.

Perhaps it was partly because he was a creative artist, Jamie thought with unaccustomed bleakness, that she saw him as belonging forever to a different world. He was a balanced and well-integrated human being, who had a means of expressing himself in his work. He didn't wonder who he was or where he was going. He wasn't lost and battered and angry with himself. And he would not admire what she had done.

With a small choking sound very close to a sob, she slipped down from the parapet. The track which the old road had now become might be on Gask, but it was still a right of way and would take her to the village. She followed the zigzag up through the trees, and as she came out into the open at the top the

familiar view spread before her. She could see the
huddle of village roofs, the spire of the abandoned
church, Gask off to the left, starkly white, and below
the hills to the north she could pick out the much
older house of Fallan, as dark and unadorned as a
lump of natural granite on its high perch. All there,
waiting for rediscovery and new acquaintance.

But unexpectedly she found she didn't want to go
on. She needed nothing from the village; she could
manage with what food she had. But Freda was there.
For an instant Jamie craved mindless, certain, nursery comfort. Then she thought of the questioning
which would go with it. She had only just achieved
this marvellous solitude; why relinquish it so soon?

But as she went down the track again she was
perturbed by her own vacillation. Normally she
was decisive, sure of what she wanted, her approach
positive and upbeat. As she crossed the bridge she
barely glanced at the Toll-house. It too reminded her
that decisions waited. She would come back to it
again, while it still slept undisturbed, and try to get
into some kind of order the emotions it awoke, so that
when it was occupied she could go up the grassy path
to knock at the door with some semblance of com-
posure.

'I mustn't chat too long . . .'

'Why, what are you doing?'

'Nothing in particular.' Vanessa sounded flus-
tered. Had the virile and passionate Douglas hauled
her off to bed without delay, Jamie idly wondered. 'I

just wanted to make sure you're all right. I thought afterwards, I should have given you Mrs Niven's number. And I've been looking up car hire firms for you. Do you want to take the details down? Have you got a pen?'

'Vanessa, there's a *Yellow Pages* here too. I'm not living in a tent.'

'Yes, I know, but after living abroad for so long I thought you might need help. Everything seems to change so fast these days. Did you manage to do any shopping? I felt awful rushing off and leaving you without making sure you had everything. I should have run up to the village and got some things before we left, only with Phil having to get back—'

'I'm fine.'

'What did you have for dinner? I still can't believe there was nothing in the freezer. It's terribly bad for them to run empty. You should always fill them with blankets or newspapers or something.'

'Vanessa, I've eaten. I shall eat tomorrow. Please, please stop panicking.'

'I suppose you're right. But I still don't like to think of you alone there. Which reminds me, I was telling Naomi that you're staying on for a while . . .'

Damn you, Vanessa, why can't you ever resist meddling? Jamie felt a terrible sense of invasion, of choices being removed, of enormous demands rushing upon her for which she was by no means ready.

'. . . well, actually she phoned me, to ask how the service had gone, and to apologise for not being there. But she's much less active nowadays, in quite a lot of pain, though she doesn't admit it, and she never could stand Zara anyway, so she would only have come out of kindness to us. She apologised for Patrick too, but I assured her we hadn't expected him to appear. Anyway, he may be at the Toll-house in a few days' time. He hasn't been up much recently, she said, as he's been so busy, away in Japan at some symposium or other. But if he's there I shall feel happier about you, though I'm – oh, Jamie, sorry, I'll have to go. Douglas wants me.'

'You're talking to me. Tell him he can wait.'

'No, really, I can't. Sorry, Jamie, talk to you soon. Must go. Lots of love. Look after yourself.'

The receiver clicked down, and Jamie raised her eyebrows. Couldn't Douglas have waited a couple of minutes for whatever he wanted? And why did Vanessa sound so odd? Almost furtive. It struck Jamie that she had kept her voice low all the time they had been talking, as though she hadn't wanted to be overheard. But that was absurd. What had they discussed that was in any way private? With a feeling of unease, so slight as to be forgotten at once, she turned back to the table.

Vanessa hadn't enquired if she had enough to drink, she reflected sardonically, holding up her third glass of St Emilion to the light to enjoy its colour. It had gone surprisingly well with herb omelette.

8

Not even a lot more red wine than she was used to had helped Jamie to get a good night's sleep. In fact, she thought, not much enjoying what happened to her head as she swung her legs out of bed, it had had the opposite effect. But she knew it wasn't only the wine. With Vanessa's phone call yesterday's sense of dreamy isolation, and the feeling that no eyes, no contact, could penetrate it except by her choice, had gone. Mrs Niven and the gardener would doubtless put in an appearance before long and, though she might mock Vanessa for fussing, she would need to go to the village for supplies. There was the visit to Freda as well, with all its associations. The happy anticipation of seeing her was still tinged with apprehension, but she knew Freda would be mortally offended if she delayed too long.

Is that all that's bothering you? Jamie pulled a face at herself in the mirror. What were these contacts compared with having soon to meet Patrick's discerning eyes, and come face to face once more with Patrick's uncompromising standards? But she felt better as she splashed water over her face, the soft, clean-smelling, cold glen water which was one of the minor pleasures of being back.

As she dressed with her usual speed she turned over plans for the day. First and foremost she wanted to create a space for herself which had no connection with Zara and the unsavoury friends with whom she had surrounded herself. How fortunate it was that, however desperate Zara had been in the end for cash, and though she had stripped Calder virtually to the bone, she had not found a way to dispose of it. Father had seen to that, though Jamie still had to come to terms with his way of doing it.

Carrying coffee and toast down to the river wall, she delighted in the sparkling air, the spear-like shadows across dewy grass, the promise of warmth in a sun already high, the birds singing as though the place belonged to them and the glimpse of vibrant red as a squirrel darted up a beech tree, then peered round the trunk to watch her. Colder air coiled off the water. Oystercatchers flashed across the pools, their fluting calls bringing back a hundred memories.

She was truly, actually here. And there was no need to hide her feelings or tailor them to someone else's mood. How could she ever have reached that point anyway, she who despised such a lack of moral independence?

Concentrate on something else – her intention to move into her own old room. She could never make the room she was using look as if it belonged to the house again. Who would want to buy Calder, her thoughts moved on, its principal rooms with their heavy cornices, cavernous fireplaces and huge sash windows looking sad and bare, at odds with the modern sophistication and bizarre colours Zara had introduced into the sunless room she had used? Whoever bought the house would have to choose one look or the other, and the cost of recreating a harmonious whole would be considerable. What, for a start, could be done with the hall?

Jamie was putting her mug and plate into the dishwasher when she heard a car. Steps came across the courtyard and a key turned in the back door. Irrational relief filled her to have that door open at last. No searches, even by Vanessa, had turned up the house keys, and their absence had left a niggling feeling of being still not entirely in control. The sound of that key turning seemed to promise that many things would be resolved.

In came a tall gaunt woman wearing fawn slacks and a fawn anorak, a look of deep suspicion on her face. She must have seen the light in the window, and certainly wasn't startled, but she looked far from pleased.

'Good morning,' said Jamie. 'Mrs Niven? I'm Jamie Laidlaw.'

'I wasn't told anyone was to be here.'

It was not the friendliest of greetings. With lips pinched she came to dump a capacious bag on the table, her eyes darting jealously round the kitchen as her bony shoulders writhed her anorak free. Her skin was so colourless that Jamie thought she could see what went on underneath it. Not attractive. Her nose was long and pink-tipped, the sort of nose that did a lot of sniffing. She hung up her jacket and pulled a nylon overall from her bag. Of fine brown and white check, at three paces it looked fawn.

'I shall be living here for the time being,' Jamie said, seeing no reason to explain further, much less to apologise for her presence. Saying it brought one of those moments of realisation that could still take her breath away, and she hugged it to herself exultantly.

'Living here?' Mrs Niven looked not only unenthusiastic but disbelieving. 'Mr Syme said nothing about that. Just for the two nights, he said. So I did three rooms and—'

'Yes, thank you. We were very comfortable.' Whatever they might have thought of their present style, the rooms had been meticulously prepared. 'Why don't we sit down and have coffee, and discuss what's to be done?'

'I'm no' one for sitting down.' Mrs Niven glanced pointedly at the clock. 'I've my rooms to do.'

'Well, that's what I'd like to talk about. What is the present arrangement?' Jamie persisted, feeling Mrs Niven might launch herself at any moment into some ironclad routine and all possibility of communication would be gone. 'I don't even know how often you come in, or what hours you do.'

Mrs Niven stared at her, as though finding it hard to believe such time-wasting discussion of the obvious was being asked of her. 'I do my three mornings, the same as I always have.'

'Which mornings are they? And for – what – three hours, four hours?'

The bloodless face took on the vivid hue of the

nose tip. 'If I'm in at the back of nine then I'm away at the back of twelve. I'm not one for short-changing anyone. I've my man to get off to work, and the children to take down to the school bus and—'

'No, please, I hadn't even looked at the time,' Jamie broke in hastily. 'I'm only trying to get a picture of what happens.'

'Yes, well, it's not me that comes and goes as it suits me,' Mrs Niven muttered, with a malevolent glance towards the window which meant nothing to Jamie. 'I do my three hours and very often more, though I never put in for any extra if I'm kept back, and there's been times when I've had some clearing up to do, I can tell you.'

'I'm sure there must have been.' The thin skin was more than a physical feature, it seemed. 'Look, do sit down. I'd like to decide how we're going to tackle—'

'First off I tidy up in here.' Mrs Niven's pursed lips as she looked around suggested that she resented finding nothing to tidy this morning. In what state had she found the kitchen in the past after some of Zara's parties? 'Then I do my rooms.'

'But which rooms?'

'The bedroom and the front room, of course.' Mrs Niven clearly thought Jamie not very bright. 'There's not much call to do more than pass a duster over the rest when there's no visitors.'

The front room. What a lovely language we have, Jamie thought with passing pleasure. Zara's sitting-room. Nothing to do with where it was located.

'That's what Mrs Laidlaw wanted,' Mrs Niven took the chance to put in. 'That's my routine.'

The name shook Jamie. Grandmother's name. She had been too young when her mother died ever to think of it as hers. She had fiercely resisted associating it with Zara, and it was still new and incredible to know it had never in fact belonged to her. Though she had used it, of course, and would be known by it here.

Jamie couldn't bring herself to say it.

'You'll have heard from Mr Syme that my—' she began, but stopped short. The title of stepmother, loathed and avoided even in her thoughts, had never existed either, another fact she had hardly had time to take in. 'There won't be any need to clean those rooms now,' she wound up firmly. 'They won't be used.'

It occurred to her, unlikely as it seemed, that Mrs Niven might be distressed by Zara's death, or at the very least would expect some reference to it, some respect paid, some solemn tone assumed. Then Mrs Niven was going to be disappointed.

'Not used?' Mrs Niven sounded more indignant than afflicted by grief. 'If you're to be staying here there's no other place to sit.'

'Look, please sit down.' Jamie's patience was dwindling. She drew out a chair and Mrs Niven, after a moment's resistance, perched on the edge of it, every line of her proclaiming that this was a load of nonsense, she'd never get through her work at this rate.

'How about coffee? Or tea?' Jamie reached for the kettle.

'I've had ma' breakfast,' Mrs Niven said shortly.

'All right.' Jamie came to sit opposite her. 'Now, my sisters and I have already dealt with most of the personal belongings –' Jamie saw Mrs Niven's mouth turn down ominously, and wondered if they had forestalled depredations regarded as a right '– though there's still a good deal of packing up to do, of ornaments and so on. However, none of that's urgent. What I'd really like to do today is to sort out the old nursery wing, the rooms we used when we stayed here as children.'

'Oh, no, you'll not get in there. Those rooms are closed off.' The tone was full of patronising satisfaction, and for the first time Mrs Niven looked almost cheerful. 'They have been for years.'

'The corridor's been opened.' Jamie kept her voice matter-of-fact. Appearing to score points would achieve nothing. 'Which reminds me, you don't know where I can find the key to the nursery stairs, do you? And the spare back door key. There must be more than one, and it's a nuisance having to use the front door all the time.'

'They're put by safe enough,' Mrs Niven assured her flatly. 'Don't worry about that.'

'But I'd like to know where they are.'

'I have them away with me.'

'At home?'

'Aye, no one can touch them there.'

'Mrs Niven,' Jamie said gently, 'this house belongs to my sisters and to me. I'm living here. I'm grateful to you for taking care of everything, but now I should like all the keys returned to their proper places.'

Mrs Niven tightened her lips, lifted her chin and studied the wall.

'So please bring them when you next come,' Jamie continued smoothly. 'And for today, I should like you to begin by cleaning the nursery bathroom.'

'The bathroom in the back wing?' Mrs Niven abandoned the attempt to convey that she knew better than Jamie what was right and proper. 'But that bathroom's never been touched for years. The Lord knows what state it's in.'

'Exactly.'

Jamie's dark eyes, the most striking feature of her thin face, which could be very daunting when they flashed with temper, met the pale-lashed ones with a look of calm authority. It cloaked an anger which Mrs Niven would not at all have cared to discover. What an irritating legacy from Zara to have to pussyfoot around this dismal woman, Jamie thought, longing to tell her here and now that she was out of a job. Fresh from a cut-throat world where a few days ago she would have had no hesitation in dealing with the problem with swift ruthlessness, to Jamie it was a tempting solution. But a sense of obligation, very much bound up with Calder, restrained her. That sort of high-handedness wouldn't do in a place where jobs were so scarce. This unprepossessing creature had worked here for some time, her husband was probably in some low-paid local job and they had a family.

'It's not what I'm paid to do,' Mrs Niven was objecting.

Perhaps those beige pants weren't up to anything more demanding than pushing a vacuum cleaner around, Jamie thought. But exactly who did the woman think was paying her now?

She waited.

'It's not what Mrs Laidlaw—'

Jamie came to her feet. 'There is no Mrs Laidlaw.' Zara might have used the name, but that single phrase denied her claim to it for ever.

'Oh, dear, what am I thinking of? I haven't got used to – it just slipped out.' Mrs Niven didn't precisely apologise, but she did look embarrassed, assuming that Jamie minded her loss. 'I didn't mean—'

'That's all right. So, let's make a start on the nursery wing, shall we? I want to sleep there tonight.'

'Sleep there? But is something wrong with the rooms I did for you? They were all turned out and aired, let me assure you, which is more than can be said for the rooms in the old part. If you don't mind my saying—'

'Come along.'

As they went up the front stairs Mrs Niven's face was pink again. No sniffs could be heard, but they were there.

Disapproving as Mrs Niven had been, she had worked hard and efficiently. Jamie, working with her, had done her best to shut out both the memories brought to life as long-forgotten objects surfaced, and the uncertainties of the present. But now, going back alone after lunch, she let the thoughts flow as they would.

The shabby little room looked fresh and bright and exactly as it used to. The afternoon sun was already coming round to it, and its windows shone after Mrs Niven's ministrations. How hard it had been to go to sleep in here on golden summer evenings, Jamie remembered, when she had longed so passionately to be outside still, every sense alert, energy filling her.

She had waited till she was alone to move her things, and it gave her great, uncomplicated happiness to stow them away in the white wardrobe and the shallow drawers, still lined with their Tinkerbell paper and sticking more than ever after the years of damp. A vision of the streamlined Seattle apartment rose before her but, safe in this refuge, she could raise a brief smile at the contrast. The duvet from the guest room she brought with her. No sentimental clutching at the past would make her revert to blankets and eiderdown. How uncomfortable was the bed going to be? It didn't matter. It utterly changed the feeling of the house to have established herself here. She almost longed for bedtime.

Then suddenly she had had enough of domestic concerns. What was she doing indoors? The afternoon was warm and bright, summer had definitely overtaken spring. She longed to sluice off dust, forget change and decay, and get out there.

In the old bathroom, gleaming and welcoming, she surveyed its battered Victorian splendour with real affection. Time – and Zara – could never erase the deep comfort and pleasure associated with bath-time memories here. There had been an anxious moment this morning when she had wondered whether the plumbing would still be connected, but when she had tried the taps, though there was some monstrous clanking and rumbling, though the first gout of water was dark brown and it took as long as ever to run hot, everything had still worked.

No tub in that efficient land where she had spent the last ten years could match the sturdy old bath at Calder, with its gaping taps, its claw feet spread on the cracked green lino, and the throaty voracity with which the wastepipe sucked it empty. It did more to raise Jamie's spirits than anything else had yet done, and she felt something close to her normal ebullience as she pulled on a clean shirt and chinos, and pushing some money into her pocket went out via the back door.

She grinned, closing it behind her, to remember how fiercely Mrs Niven had tried to hold on to 'her' key.

A shabby blue van was parked in front of the garage. The tool-shed door was open, and squatting outside it, doing something to a mower, was a girl in olive-green T-shirt and trousers, the sun striking coppery lights from her head of short, red-brown curls. The gardener?

'Hi.'

The girl jumped and dropped her spanner. 'God,' she exclaimed, scrambling to her feet, 'you gave me a fright! I wasn't expecting anyone to be about. I thought you'd all gone. I didn't hear a car.'

'I don't have a car.' Not here, not anywhere. 'Sorry to startle you. Though I was surprised to see you too, come to that.'

'Didn't Mr Syme tell you I worked here? At least,' the girl looked amused, 'I suppose I still do?'

'Definitely.' Jamie liked her big cheerful grin. 'Only no one had ever said when you appeared. Also, somewhere along the line I seem to have missed the fact that the gardener was female. I'm Jamie, by the way, the middle sister.'

Smiling, she held out her hand, and the girl shook it with a firm grip, not bothering to apologise for the state of her own. She was stockily built, with generous breasts and hips, and exuded a look of muscular good health, her arms, face and neck already deeply tanned. She had an engagingly relaxed air which Jamie took to at once.

'I'm Maeve – Maeve Quinn. Great to meet you. Look, I've a flask of tea in the shed and I was going to have a cuppie before starting mowing. I was shifting the blade to low cut, though that may be a bit optimistic. Want some?'

'I'd love some, but we don't have to drink yours. Why not come into the house?'

'Ach, I've plenty. And who wants to be inside, weather like this?' Certainly Maeve didn't have the look of someone who spent much time indoors.

'Right, thanks.' Jamie felt consciously willing for events to bowl her in any direction they chose.

Maeve gestured hospitably to a plank set across two logs against the sun-warmed wall, and disappeared into the shed to reappear with a filthy old canvas bag and a mug. She polished the rim of the latter with her fingers, but poured tea for Jamie into the cap of the flask.

'This is properly washed,' she said. 'Honest.' Side by side they sipped in friendly silence. Jamie found it immensely peaceful, and somehow unsurprising to find herself here.

'You're staying on on your own?' Maeve asked eventually.

'I am.'

Maeve nodded. Another tranquil pause stretched in the drowsy warmth. 'Look, I should have said – I'm sorry about your – stepmother, wasn't it?'

'Thanks. But it's all right. We weren't close.' It seemed important to make that clear, though Maeve only nodded again, making no comment.

'There'll be plenty to do in the house,' she offered next, without emphasis.

Jamie twisted her head to smile at the temperate phrase, and met the glint of a grin in Maeve's hazel eyes. 'I spent the morning working with Mrs Niven,' she returned obliquely.

'Ah,' said Maeve. 'Did you now?'

Jamie laughed and Maeve's grin widened.

Without hurry, they filled in a few facts as they occurred to them. The heat of the sun, trapped in the windless shelter of the courtyard, pinned them against the stone wall, and Jamie let herself relax and drift in abandonment to sensation.

'Am I holding you up?' she presently felt she

should enquire, though not anxious to disturb their shared ease.

'Ah, the grass can wait,' Maeve said, flattening her shoulders against the wall, spreading her arms and tilting back her head. She looked as though the sun would have to set before she would feel impelled to move.

Jamie, amused, asked no more.

'It occurs to me,' Maeve next interrupted their baking somnolence to say, 'that you're my boss.'

'One third of your boss anyway.'

Maeve laughed. 'You'll maybe be glad to hear, then, that I don't charge for sitting in the sun.'

'I hadn't given it a thought,' Jamie told her truthfully. 'What does occur to me, however, is that I was on my way to the village, and now I shan't get there before the shop shuts. Ah well.'

'I can run you up,' Maeve at once offered. 'In fact, I'll tell you what, why don't I put this lot away and leave the mowing till tomorrow? We'll not get rain tonight. That would be the sensible thing.'

As the blue van coughed its way round the potholes of the back drive, the shortest way to the village but not the one Vanessa had taken, Jamie reflected that there could hardly have been a greater contrast between her companions of the morning and the afternoon. She was also aware of the satisfied if unspecific conviction – this is going to be good.

9

With cold shock, Jamie thought, she doesn't like me, she never has. It was a shattering discovery.

She and Maeve had been just in time to catch the shop. More accurately, the Closed sign had already been turned round, but Maeve had thumped on the door and shouted, 'Hey, Dorrie, open up a sec, will you?' and the unforthcoming girl of yesterday had good-naturedly obliged. Maeve had introduced Jamie, grabbed a couple of tins of baked beans and a moment later the blue van was to be seen – and heard – heading raucously towards the top end of the village. Did it have an exhaust?

There, Jamie had learned, Maeve lived in the small wooden building at the top of the garden at Craigard, which in the past had been used as family accommodation while its owners let their more substantial stone-built house to summer residents, moving back in each winter.

Braced by Maeve's laid-back but direct style, Jamie had walked round to Freda's in pleasant anticipation, deciding it shouldn't be too hard to fend off difficult questions, certain of her welcome and expecting to be made much of. Freda, after all, was one of the rocks of childhood, second only to Grandmother as a source of unquestioned affection. Her sharp voice and her standard reaction to any attempted caress – 'Away with you, none of that daft carry-on with me' – had been simply part of who she was. Only Phil, motherless from birth and very much Freda's baby, had managed to break through that thorny barricade to be given cuddles and endearments.

Jamie had arrived at the worst possible moment, that much had immediately been clear. But, more chilling, she had been made to realise she had come to the wrong door. It hadn't for a moment occurred to her to go round to the front. That was the sort of inconvenience inflicted by strangers, to make Freda go through the house to answer it. Traipse through the house, as she herself would have put it. Front doors as inaccessible as hers were usually kept locked, bolted and with draught excluders in place for months on end.

She had been hustled through the kitchen, where the old brown teapot and a plate of fish fingers and chips on the scored Formica table announced that Freda had been about to sit down to her tea. It was suffocatingly hot in there, the television was on, and on the back of a dingy armchair a black and white cat arched itself into a croquet hoop of indignation at the intrusion.

Jamie had been taken, after greetings which were far from an effusive reception for the returned traveller, into the dim, overcrowded sitting-room, where a clematis covered half the window, and where the mandatory three-piece suite formed an almost impenetrable laager around the fire. The heavy air, smelling faintly of soot, spoke of long disuse.

Angry with herself for not having planned this more considerately, Jamie had suggested coming back at a better time. But that, with its inference that Freda's housekeeping might be found wanting, had given almost as much offence as appearing without warning in the first place. Well, the housekeeping wasn't up to much, Jamie had thought defiantly, left alone while Freda vanished to make more fitting dispositions. That kitchen had looked downright squalid, Freda was wearing a grubby overall and stained, down-at-heel slippers, and the meal she had been about to sit down to had looked highly uninviting.

'I'll put it in the oven,' she had said sharply, when Jamie had begged her to have her tea, saying she would be quite happy to sit in the kitchen.

Freda had reappeared after some delay, overall gone, hair combed, shoes replacing slippers. 'I'll put a match to the fire,' she had said, sounding as if she had no desire to do any such thing, going down clumsily on one knee, matches in hand, before Jamie could stop her.

'Freda, please don't bother, not for me. There's really no need. It's been so hot this afternoon.'

But Freda had ignored her. It was not for Jamie to say what hospitality she would offer in her own house. She had accepted help in getting up, but had offered no thanks beyond a grunt, creaking off at once to the kitchen. The fire must have been laid for some time, as thick yellow-white smoke poured up from damp paper and kindling, escaping in acrid trails round the cast-iron hood.

'Oh, *damn*.' Jamie had prowled restlessly, trapped in the situation she had so thoughtlessly created. She should have known that at this distance of time she could not run in here as and when it suited her, the child whose appearance would always give pleasure. Too many years had gone by for that. She was not only an adult now, she was one of the family to whom, of all people, Freda would have wished to present an impeccable front.

And to have spoiled her tea, most sacrosanct of meals. How often, Jamie had thought, trying to divert her thoughts as she waited, had she tried to explain high tea to American friends. They had clung to the idea, no matter what she said, that it was afternoon tea on a grander scale, unable to believe it was a cooked supper where you drank tea and finished up with scones and cake.

It was not high tea, naturally, which Freda had presently borne in. High tea was not for Laidlaws. Tray with snowy cloth, its resistant creases suggesting it had been a long time in the drawer, fluted bone-china tea-set, but – and red patches in Freda's cheeks showed all too clearly her feelings on this score – only a few custard creams on the cake plate.

'This is no' my baking day,' Freda had said, not

looking at her, and Jamie had flushed in her turn to have put her in this position.

They had managed a stilted exchange of family news, though Jamie had been unable to forget the supper in the oven, getting drier and nastier by the minute. How had she imagined it would be simple to talk about her own life without going into details? What exactly had she envisaged? An instant resumption of a cosy nursery relationship? Approbation of everything she said and did because she was who she was?

Venturing reminiscences which she had thought could be depended upon as a shared source of pleasure, she had been jolted to find Freda's view of them very different from her own. They had elicited not friendly laughter or some reciprocal memory, but such comments as, 'Aye, and who did you think had to clear up after you?' or, 'You always were a determined little madam, I'll say that for you.' Comments which had contained no humour at all.

There had been something very like disdain, or at best a complete want of interest, when Jamie told her what she had been doing today.

'Damp, those rooms will be by now,' Freda had said dismissively.

'They are, a bit, but it's so lovely to be back in my own room again.'

'Not much sense sleeping there when you've the whole of the house to choose from.'

When Jamie, without revealing that Zara had never owned Calder, had expressed relief that it was safely back in Laidlaw hands (for the time being at least, though this rider too she kept to herself), she had been startled to find that Freda saw it as some kind of crowing.

'Aye well, very nice, I'm sure, for those that can get it,' she had said grimly. 'There's plenty would be glad of a hundredth part of it.'

With growing dismay Jamie had been forced to realise that to Freda she was nothing more than one of those resented people who live on the other side of the social divide – the people Freda had spent her life working for. A stranger, with whom no contact existed. So had Freda's loyalty to the family, her affection for Grandmother, been a pretence entered into and maintained by both sides, cloaking an arrangement which was never anything but basic supply and demand?

And yet, though Jamie had detected a difference in Freda's attitude towards each, Vanessa and Phil still seemed to be in favour. Vanessa had never failed to keep in touch, to send a present at Christmas and to remember Freda's birthday, and this, evidently, was not seen as patronising. It had soon emerged that Freda knew more about Douglas's business achievements and Ryan's activities than Jamie did. This, putting Jamie at fault and Freda in a strong position, had mollified the latter slightly, though she didn't miss the chance to point out Jamie's own deficiencies as a correspondent.

So the atmosphere had appeared to be warming slightly, until the moment when Jamie, confident that references to Freda's favourite, Phil, would be well received, found she had walked into a minefield. Every opening was met with tightened lips and resentful looks.

Searching for some remark that could not be controversial in any way, Jamie had said, 'I suppose she must have been at Burnbrae for about twelve years now. Looking after old people obviously suits her better than nursery nursing did. She was miserable at that children's home in Paisley. But it's more than I could do, I—'

'Fourteen,' Freda had cut in sharply. 'Fourteen years this July she's been there. And she doesn't always enjoy it, as you should know, though things are better for her now.'

She had paused, watching Jamie closely, as if waiting for some response, but when Jamie floundered, 'Better? Has the job changed? She didn't say,' she had rapped out, as though gratified to find she'd been right, 'No, you'll no' ken about that. And no,' she had added, hauling herself to her feet and picking up the teapot, 'you couldn't do it, you're right about that. You couldn't begin to look at doing what she does. I'll fetch more hot water.'

'Freda, please don't bother. I've had enough tea. Or let me get it, if you'd like more yourself.'

Wrong-footed, Jamie had felt as though she was reaching back through the years to the behaviour expected of her, while at the same time her shock at what had finally been made clear waited to be faced and somehow absorbed.

'You stay where you are.' Freda wasn't having any truck with this attempt at appeasement. She had gone out again, movements stiff, back rigid with offence.

Shaken, Jamie tried to gather her wits. This was about more than arriving at a bad time, more than the meagre meal and messy kitchen being exposed to view. It was about more, even, than the uncrossable gulf between where they came from. This was personal dislike, brought into the open by her reference to Phil, though why that should be was beyond her; but dislike, Jamie realised with certainty, long-standing and deep.

How shattering it was to look back and see that the affection so confidingly trusted in had never existed. But what arrogance to have assumed that Freda, officially employed as cook-housekeeper, but obliged to double as nanny whether she liked it or not when the grandchildren came to stay, should have welcomed their arrival. Although she had always been provided with extra help, most of which it was true she had despised, she must have resented the invasion. More work, extra meals, noise, mess, her comfortable routine disrupted. But the role had been played out; the children had seen what they were meant to see, had believed what it had been reassuring to believe.

There was nothing surprising about that, Jamie conceded. Any servant with sense could project the convenient – and rewarding – faithful retainer image. What was disturbing was that she herself had gone on accepting the fabrication without ever examining it; had come here this evening naively confident that she would be bestowing pleasure. She cringed to think of it, seeing herself for the first time through Freda's eyes – the difficult, hot-tempered child, always at the root of any nursery dramas, the kind of child no nanny could warm to. And she saw too the woman who had turned into the lane half an hour ago, without a thought for Freda's convenience, expecting to be met with open arms.

Hot with shame, shaken by the new light in which the past had been revealed, and beginning to be conscious of a yawning sense of loss which there was no time to examine now, Jamie, hearing Freda's heavy tread returning, pulled herself together to get through the remainder of this disastrous visit.

How shall I ever be able to go back, was the question that beset her as she headed for the ford and the rickety footbridge below the village. Turning the corner, she saw a new bridge, wide enough for vehicles, all ugly girders and concrete. Whoever allowed that, she thought furiously, not ready to look kindly on any change.

More distressing than to think she could never go back, was realising there was no need to. Freda, though she might like her due of attention (were those Christmas presents from Vanessa accompanied by generous cheques?), patently didn't find any pleasure in Jamie's company. It was time to forget the cosy image of doting nanny longing for a visit,

ready to hang on her every word, admire achievements and condone shortcomings. But it hurt to
realise that affection she had taken for granted all
her life had never existed at all.

These unwelcome thoughts, the discovery that
treasured memories must be reviewed in a new light,
disgust at her own naivety, but above all the puzzling
question of what Freda had thought she should know
about Phil, made her blind to her surroundings as she
followed the track down-river. But gradually the
calm beauty of the evening caught at her senses.

Nearly midsummer as it was, the sun was still well
above the western ridge. Ahead of her its light drew a
glowing green from the young foliage of the trees which
followed the descent of the river to the distant glinting
waters of the loch. The track crossed open ground here,
though huge boulders, deposited by long-ago glaciers,
dotted the slopes of sheep-grazed turf.

Knowing that if she pounded on in this frame of
mind she would never sort out her thoughts, Jamie
turned aside and found a comfortable seat on one,
dumping her bag of shopping at its foot. In her
distress she had forgotten to pick it up, when at last
she had felt the formalities had been served and she
could leave.

'Don't forget your messages,' Freda had said. The
dry tone had seemed to Jamie to hold a taunt that she,
the supposedly clever one, could be so incompetent.

All right, she said to herself, you've found out that
someone dislikes you. Are you pretending it's the
first time that's ever happened?

But it was more than that, and she knew it. It felt as though a cornerstone of her life had been knocked away. For a dreadful moment in that smoky, crammed, ill-lit room not only had Freda's affection been revealed as spurious, but Grandmother's had been in question too. It was obvious, looked at calmly, that there was no foundation for this doubt, but its brief stirring had unnerved her. She was too vulnerable at present to be able to deal with such things with her usual good sense.

Suddenly there seemed too much to cope with. The moments of tranquillity shared with Maeve this afternoon, the surge of optimism about the future as they had headed up the glen together, seemed far away, but Jamie did her best to concentrate on them as something positive. How extraordinary that immediate sense of ease with Maeve had been. There was undeniable appeal too in the way she lived, surviving on gardening and other odd jobs, and apparently working to a timetable dictated by the seasons and the weather.

In spite of the aching sense of rejection as she had walked away from Freda's cottage, Jamie saw that there could be, if she wished it, a way to a new acquaintance with the glen through Maeve. Yesterday's feeling of being an outsider had been exaggerated by awareness of her own situation. Yet how tenuously, she saw, they had in reality belonged here in the past – the grandchildren visiting one of the big houses for the holidays, toted back and forth to tea or parties at other big houses, included in the equivalent adult gatherings as they grew up. She had never been much interested in any of it. Calder was what had mattered, especially Calder when shared with her father.

Remembering Vanessa scraping round to think whom they would still know, Jamie grinned. No doubt Vanessa's idea of renewing contact would be to throw a dinner party. How else would one set about it? But Jamie felt no inclination to get to know the new owner of Gask, nor was she particularly keen to re-establish contact with the Erskines at Fallan, especially as Hugh had recently remarried. Who among the other inhabitants of the glen, a population doubtless more fluid than it had been in the past, would remember or care about them? And Zara would hardly have done much to conciliate local opinion.

Oh, come on, don't sink into doom and gloom. Zara's gone, you can forget her.

Jamie slid down from her rock. There had been more good things today than meeting Maeve. There was her room awaiting her, for one thing. And supper was another attractive prospect. She was starving in spite of Freda's yukky biscuits. All she had to do was walk down this familiar path, which she had thought of so many times in the years away, and let the quietness soak into her, listen to the evening music of the birds, watch the river tip itself down its rocky falls or slide dark through alder-fringed pools. She would not evade what she had learned, but a peaceful evening of supper, early bed and reading herself to sleep with some old favourite should provide some solace.

She came down the zigzag at a run, and was onto the crown of the bridge before she saw the car tucked in below the slope of mown grass, and realised that the door of the Toll-house was standing open.

IO

I am absolutely not ready for this. Jamie checked on
the bridge, seized by a crazy desire to run. Had she
been seen? Could she get to the river path and,
vanishing into the trees, fly for the safety of Calder?
Then shame overtook panic. It would be like trying
to dodge Phil or Vanessa, unthinkable, cowardly and
unkind. Unnecessary too. Whatever state of mind she
was in, with guilt and bruised self-confidence upper-
most; whatever the feelings which would be reawoken; whatever alarm bells were ringing to find herself
faced with this encounter unprepared, surely she
could deal with them.

Heart bumping, legs oddly shaky, she left the
bridge and went up the path. Who was here? It
would be easier, no question of that, if Naomi were
with him.

Patrick had seen her. He seemed to fill the doorway, coming to greet her. And at the sight of his
familiar figure, the stoop of the heavy shoulders, the
jut of the big head, everything fled from Jamie's
mind but pure, intense relief. In that first instant
he seemed primarily an image of safety, an adult on
whom she could depend without question, whatever

she had done. Time reeled back – not the six years since seeing him after her father's death, but far back into childhood, when what she had felt for him had been the uncomplicated, ardent love of a child who had had nowhere else to pin her affections.

'Jamie! What a wonderful surprise!' Patrick's booming exclamation, the smile that lit his often dour features, also came straight from that faraway time. For him the pleasure of seeing her had never changed. 'I've only this minute arrived. I was going to get the fire going and then come and roust you out.'

'Hello, Patrick.' Impossible to keep her voice under control, or to do anything about the radiant delight which must show in her face.

'Come in, come in.' He stood aside and with a wide gesture of his arm swept her into the long room, taking her carrier bag and slinging it onto a chair.

'How are you? Let's have a look at you.' He hadn't hugged her. That wasn't what they did. But he caught her shoulders, turning her towards the glowing evening light pouring in through the long windows, and though Jamie knew that firm grasp was nothing more than affectionate welcome, she wondered whether the veneer of calm she had summoned to walk up the grassy slope would survive his penetrating scrutiny.

'I'm fine, thanks. I was on my way back from the village. What a surprise to find you here. I hadn't thought you'd be up so soon.' Conflicting feelings were rushing through her: the absolute, instinctive conviction that everything in the world was all right now, that he would take care of everything, and panic because she wasn't ready to face him. She resisted a temptation to duck her head to avoid his eyes; it had never helped her before to hide from Patrick anything he intended to know. But he asked no questions for the moment, merely giving her a little growling shake of pleasure and releasing her, reminding her piercingly of the casual handling the teenage Patrick had dealt out, though only to her, since she had always been the one to respond joyfully to the thrills and spills.

'Ah, girl, it does me good to see you. I was sure you'd have gone back at once. I could hardly believe my ears when I heard you were staying on at Calder.'

'It's lovely to see you as well.' How lovely it was indeed. Jamie's eyes stung, and she turned hastily away to look round the room. 'It's such ages since I was in here. It looks exactly the same. I'm glad you haven't changed anything.'

She had always liked the robust but sure touch Patrick had with colour and design – the warm sand colour of the walls, the beamed ceiling, solid woodwork and open stone fireplace, the whipcord floor covering and the thickly lined velvet curtains, their rich tan streaked and muted by sunlight. It was a room masculine, workmanlike and generous in scope.

'Naomi isn't with you?' But the place was too small for her arrival not to have been heard, and Naomi would have appeared at once to add her welcome. So there would be no shielding presence of a third person between herself and Patrick's observant attention.

'No.' His face settled into its habitual sombre expression, and Jamie saw that he looked much older, the thick hair which had so early been flecked with grey (the joke had been that he never washed the stone dust out of it) now much greyer.

He's no oil painting, she thought, with a rush of intense affection. The pronounced cheekbones, deep hollows of the eyes and strong jaw looked more than ever as though they could have been carved from one of his own blocks of the iron-hard black granite which, purist (and masochist) that he was, he favoured for much of his work. He was a formidable man and, in the way Jamie well remembered, he still seemed to dominate the space around him with no conscious effort. It had always been an enjoyable challenge to defend her own space from him, but she felt scarcely capable of it today.

'She hasn't been very active for some time now,' Patrick was saying, and he looked around him in his turn. 'I'm not sure she'll ever see this place again, to be honest with you.'

'Oh, Patrick, no! I hadn't realised it was as serious as that.'

'It's difficult for her to get about and she's constantly in pain, though she'll rarely admit it. In her own house we can adapt things to make life easier for her. Here everything's a struggle, and she finds it heartbreaking not to be able to enjoy the place as she used to. Which I find heartbreaking to see, as you may guess.'

He allowed himself a harsh grimace. He had never made any secret of how much his mother meant to him, and Jamie had always envied them their enjoyment in each other's company. Although they didn't live together, it struck her that when Naomi died, and she must be well over eighty by now, Patrick would be very much alone. It had never occurred to her before; and not for the first time today she saw how, involved in her own concerns, she had failed to move forward in her perceptions of what was happening to the people closest to her.

'Food? Drink? Talk?' Patrick offered. 'I was just about to bring in some logs. The evenings are still nippy, up here anyway, and you need a fire when the place hasn't been used for a while.'

He took it for granted that she would stay, and Jamie, relieved that the first moments of meeting had passed so harmlessly, was happy to do so. Why had she imagined that he would probe and question as he used to, forcing her to face unpleasant truths for her own good? Now they were two adults whose lives were barely in touch, and then only through others. It should be simple enough to have a drink, make supper and eat it by the fire as they used to, talking with the ease of people who have known each other all their lives and can dip at will into a fund of shared references.

Had she seriously hesitated about coming in? This, of all things, was what she most needed, to be welcomed without question or reserve. And she had had plenty of practice in the past in keeping hidden those feelings which had no part in friendly companionship.

'Let me help. What first? The fire?'

'Yep. Dry kindling there. The portion of today's *Times* which I shall never look at here . . .'

It was good to set to work together and, as they moved about bringing the little house to life, to exchange a tumble of news, jumping from one thing to another, but not minding about loose ends left dangling, knowing they had time to weave them in at their leisure. Agreeing that it would be a sin to waste the beautiful evening, they went to sit for a while on the rough knowe behind the cottage which caught the last of the sun, then, chilled the moment the shadows stretched across the gorge, came back to the welcome fire.

It was a long time before they thought about dinner, and that too was part of long-established tradition.

'Have you got enough for two?' Jamie belatedly thought of asking, when they finally made a move. 'Though come to think of it, my shopping's here somewhere. Nothing inspired, mind you – village shop. A couple of those chicken and mushroom things in pastry—'

'And I've got a couple of steaks.'

Jamie laughed. 'Why didn't I know that? When do you not have an enormous steak somewhere in the offing? But wasn't the other one meant for tomor-

row?' So he wasn't going straight back. How good it
will be to have him here, was her first reaction. Her
second, how on earth will I be able to go on pretending?

'Typical woman's response,' Patrick rebuked her.
'You sound like Vanessa.'

'Oh, please! Steak it is then. What else can I kick in
with? Tomatoes? Peppers?'

'Sounds good. And you may be pleased to know
that I brought fresh pasta, mounds of it.'

Patrick, while insisting he was no cook, had always
done rather well for himself, Jamie recalled, smiling.
Then, aware of the broadness of the smile, realised
she was happy, crippling worries for the moment
pushed aside.

The compact, well-equipped kitchen was unchanged, and it felt astonishingly normal to be in
it again with Patrick, wine within reach, talk centring
on the work in hand, or on trivia that was part of their
shared background. For Jamie time had stopped.
Everything beyond these walls ceased to exist, except
a generalised, contented awareness of the insubstan-
tial scented darkness of the summer night quiet
around them. Even the thought of Calder, maimed
and altered, had receded. This, the moment, was
enough, and Jamie felt alive and fully functioning
again in a way she hadn't done since before she had
even heard the news of Zara's death.

'So what happened this afternoon?'

Jamie's head jerked up. They had dined well,

taking their time, and she was leaning down to set the coffee pot on the hearth after refilling their cups.

'This afternoon?'

'This evening, then, if you wish to be pedantic.' That was the authentic Patrick note, faintly ironic, but signalling that however she might writhe on the hook he would reel her in and have an answer.

'I don't know what you mean.'

'Jamie.' Scarcely reproof, more resignation that she should waste time on useless prevarication.

Jamie looked at the fire, her mouth pinching in spite of her intention to give nothing away, as the misery of what she had learned at Freda's returned. But it wasn't important, she reminded herself. It affected no one but her and need never be revealed. It was simply a fact she should have grasped long ago but had been too arrogant and complacent to recognise.

'Freda hates me.' Was that really her voice, blurting out in raw distress the words she had never meant to say?

Patrick waited, deep in his old leather chair. Reading lamps stood on either side of the fireplace, the only lights on in the room, but his face was partly in shadow, and unreadable.

Jamie held on for one second more to the pain, and then out it spilled. 'She's always hated me. I never knew. Never even imagined it. It was awful. I bounced in, full of myself, return of beloved nurseling and all that, ready for hugs and kisses, tears of joy—' Her voice wavered and she broke off, making a fierce effort to get it under control.

Patrick waited, very still.

'It doesn't really matter. In itself, I mean,' Jamie went on after a moment. 'God knows, at my age, why should it? But it took me by surprise. Freda had always been part of – well, childhood, Calder, everything I loved about Calder. But that wasn't the worst part. What shook me most was that I'd never questioned it. I'd just gone on believing nothing had changed, like a child. I'd never taken the trouble to look, to think about any of it.'

She fell miserably silent, and with a movement she wasn't aware of huddled deeper into her chair, wrapping her arms round her chest protectively.

Patrick pulled himself to the edge of his seat to stir the fire and add a couple of logs.

'Freda always was a self-serving, two-faced old fraud,' he said conversationally, propping up the poker and sitting well back again so that Jamie should feel free to talk at her own inclination and in her own time.

'Freda?' Even after the afternoon's revelations the description was startling, and Patrick laughed.

'You saw her with a child's eyes, as someone who looked after you. I never did. And your grandmother had plenty to say about her to my mother, believe me. But by and large she was a hard worker, didn't mind living in an isolated place like Calder, had no family of her own to divide her loyalties and, grumble as she might, was prepared to look after you lot as well as do her real job. One puts up with quite a lot from employees like that.'

'And she could cook.'

'And she could cook.'

'And she did love Phil. Vanessa too, I think.'

Patrick smiled, though his eyes, in the shadows, were not smiling. How often he had seen the eager child rebuffed. It hurt him still. 'Yes, she did love Phil. Phil was more her baby than anyone's. Vanessa she accepted as the useful and conscientious eldest, always ready to look after you two. In Freda's terms she couldn't be faulted, though I'm not sure what degree of affection existed. But you, scruffy little tearaway—'

He shook his head, reaching for his whisky glass, not choosing for the moment to go on. Memories poured back of the skinny, passionate, resolute child, always in trouble, swinging from wild despair over one disaster to blazing enthusiasm for a new enterprise which would inevitably lead to the next. He could still see so clearly the bright face, the clothes that never seemed to belong to her, the stick-like arms and legs. A child longing for affection, shut out by temperament from the bond between the more placid Vanessa and Phil, alternatively spoiled and neglected by her father, too young to remember her mother and too old to find a way into Freda's grudging affections.

'My God, Jamie, how you battered yourself against life,' he said, the memory of it almost unbearable. 'You never chose the easy way to do anything, did you?'

Her eyebrows went up in resigned agreement.

'How did you know something had happened today?' she asked.

He gave a grunt of amusement. 'The bright tone in which you said, "I've just been to see Freda, as a matter of fact", when I asked what you'd been doing.'

'Yes, well, you always did know me far too well,' she said with sudden sharpness, defensive again.

Also I saw in your eyes that something had hurt you, and though we've dealt with Freda I see it still. I hear a great many things that you are not telling me. And I mind seeing your vividness quenched, your face too thin and drawn, your eyes dark and hollow as though it's been a long time since you've had a good night's sleep. And a long time since you laughed, you to whom laughter is as essential as breathing. But one bludgeoning question is enough for now. If I'm to arrive at what's troubling you I must give you time and exercise some care. But arrive at it I shall, because you, my Jamie, are in a parlous state, and that I will not have.

'How about,' he suggested, having allowed some quiet moments to diffuse the tension, 'going on talking as I walk you home? Or even, since we are now staid elderly folk, as I drive you home?'

'Speak for yourself,' Jamie retorted, waking up at once. 'Drive to Calder? I don't think I've reached quite that state of decrepitude yet. But if you feel that you have I can always walk home on my own.'

'You can not,' said Patrick, getting to his feet and setting the guard over the fire.

Jamie grinned, putting their coffee cups on the tray. She knew to the finest margin when it was useless to argue with him. He would see her home as he always had, but she also knew from his tone that he had let the subject of Freda go, and she was glad of that.

'Here, you'd better borrow a jacket. The air from the water can be chilly.' He began to look through the possibilities on a row of wooden pegs. 'It must be rather thrilling to think of a Calder waiting for you which is properly in the family again.'

They had already spoken of the discoveries which Zara's death and the full disclosure of their father's will had brought but, noting Jamie's reluctance to refer to future plans, Patrick had not asked what the implications might be. Now it seemed natural to ask, 'How long do you think you'll stay?'

Jamie looked at him with sudden alertness. 'Did Vanessa tell you to ask me that?'

'Vanessa?' He was taken aback by the question. What had Jamie been hiding? 'What's it got to do with Vanessa? It was a perfectly ordinary question.'

'Sorry to snap,' Jamie apologised hastily. 'It was just that I'd had the impression that for some reason she didn't want me to stay on, and I thought she might have said something to you.'

'Why should she feel that? The place belongs to the three of you. She and Phil have their own homes. Why shouldn't you be there?'

'We're supposed to be deciding what's to become of it.' Jamie wished she hadn't set this hare running.

'So?'

'I'm supposed to be deciding, I mean. The others want to sell. I just wanted a bit of time before a decision was reached, that was all. I'm not squatting or trying to stake a claim.'

'Jamie, what are you talking about? Even if Calder's to be sold there's no reason that you, any or all of you, shouldn't live there till the deal's completed. It's not like you to be so woolly-minded. In fact, it's a good thing to have it occupied. Remote empty houses known to be on the market are a prime target these days.'

Jamie wasn't listening. She stood with the coat he had given her clutched in both hands. A wave of misery seemed ready to curl and break over her head.

'Jamie?'

She made one final attempt to maintain the pretence. 'I'm supposed to be making up my mind whether to buy the others out or not,' she said, but failed to strike the businesslike note she had aimed for.

'It must be nice to be the success story of the family.' Patrick, feeling the tension almost tangibly building, and at a loss to account for it, did his best. 'Fresh home from the land of opportunity—'

'Don't!' Jamie's voice cracked out, and she swung round on him with a desperate honesty. 'It's all a sham. Phil and Vanessa don't know. No one knows. It's all gone, everything.'

'Jamie, what do you mean?'

She rushed on wildly, 'Don't you understand, I had to sell my car and anything from the apartment that was mine to pay for the flight and to have something to live on when I got here.'

'Good God, Jamie, whatever—?' Patrick began, but he abandoned the question and, gripping her arms, lowered his head as though willing her to lift hers to look at him. 'Jamie, whatever's happened, we'll deal with it. Everything's going to be all right. You're safe, you're here. It will be all right, I promise you.'

The reassurance of the past, unequivocal and all-embracing. Jamie's head was still bent, but Patrick could feel the tremor in her muscles as she struggled to keep her feelings in hand.

'How like you,' she managed to say, though he could barely hear her through the tears she was forcing down. 'How like you to go straight to the core of things, and not even need to know what's happened. You're right. I'm here. The rest doesn't matter. I've blown everything through my own blindness and idiocy, but what the hell?'

Patrick thought he had rarely heard such self-condemnation in any voice. Gently he freed the jacket from her taut grip and tossed it aside. 'Come on.' With an arm round her shoulders he drew her back towards the fire. Whatever was going to be revealed or withheld, they could not go into it while threading their way over the rocks and tree roots of the river path.

It didn't matter what hour of the night it was.

Whatever had happened to her, whatever disaster she had brought upon herself, and his face was grim at what she had already revealed, he had every intention of hearing about it.

11

She had met Bryden Campbell in the most conventional way. It had been at a dinner winding up a hectic but successful day which had seen the opening of an up-market travel and sportswear company, part of a new leisure centre which had received a lot of publicity. It had been her biggest challenge to date, and for the whole day, unbelievably, there had been no serious blips to contend with. The weather and conditions had been perfect, the timings had worked like a dream, and every part of the jigsaw had slotted into place in a way which, she had learned the hard way, almost never happened. Praise had been lavish, praise as fulsome and meaningless as the criticism would have been savage if there had been some foul-up. It was money talking and she knew it, but all the same relief that the distinctive brand of marketing for which she had held out had proved itself so triumphantly, combined with exhaustion, for sleep had been way down her list of priorities lately, had produced a heady euphoria.

Bryden owned the helicopter hire firm she had used for the first time for this event, after much hassle with a previous company. Though his was

the name on the guest list her dealings up till now had
been with his operations manager, as Bryden had
been absent on some quite different business in, she
gathered, Greenland.

At first glance he had not stood out from the well-
heeled, well-set-up throng, mostly male, with powerful confident voices, faces flushed with the bonhomie
induced by good food, good wine and self-satisfac-
tion, but with eyes that never ceased to track the
room for more useful prey. These people were not
part of the computer-orientated nerd-world which
had overtaken Boeing's long-established predomi-
nance, but they did represent the commercial developments it had brought in its wake.

Jamie had long ago learned the rules of this hard-
nosed environment, and could bend them to her
needs as smilingly as anyone. She had early discovered, while still working for Leadbetter Voss in New
York, that in PR her accent was an unexpected asset,
and she had taken care not to lose it. A tendency
towards a courteous rather than an aggressive tone
had also been useful. When she started up on her own
she had deliberately put as British a stamp on any
commissions she undertook as was compatible with
market demands and the culture in which she operated. She had put her emphasis on style and quality,
keeping the usual glitz and razzmatazz to a minimum.
Holding her breath, she had pitched her fees accord-
ingly, and had sold herself with a speed that still
astonished her.

After dinner, moving dutifully round the overheated Mount Rainier Room, a private function suite in Seattle's most exclusive hotel, listening smiling as one pompous voice after another ground through convolutions of gratified polysyllables, she had wondered how soon she could slip away. The job was done and dusted. Time to go home and fall into bed, in happy contemplation of the cheques winging in, and the spin-off commissions waiting to fall into her hands.

Groaning inwardly to be caught as she threaded a way towards her client, she had responded with dredged-up warmth to the introduction to Bryden, steeling herself for another bout of male complacency while the smile flashed on and off and the eyes ranged over her head, for with her part done she knew she had become a faceless person.

Instead, she had found herself talking to someone who seemed, in that clamorous crowd of cardboard cutouts with whom she had nothing in common and never would have, someone so much on her wavelength that in seconds they were planning a joint escape. It was like running into one of her own friends and sinking with relief into normality. It was like having already reached the stage of kicking off her shoes and taking off her earrings, yet afterwards she was never able to pin down what exactly it was that had created this feeling.

She remembered that Bryden, who was tall and good-looking in the well-toned American way, had to her pleasure been wearing a conventional stiff shirt with his dinner jacket (and was she tired of mirthful questions about what happened to the pants), scorning the frills and fancy variations which abounded. She remembered that he had bent his head to hers and spoken quietly, creating a small private enclave of their own, and that he had made her laugh.

'Can we get out of here? Are you through with everything you have to do?'

Though there must have been some dialogue before that, none had survived in her memory, nothing beyond the sensation of not being alone at the party any more. What had happened to the man who had introduced them? She couldn't remember that either.

She had felt energy re-charging as she replied, 'Through in every sense. My stint's done. Anything over and above would be expending my life's blood.'

'I can't believe they've paid for that.'

'You're right.' She had glanced round the room. 'I'll need to say a couple of goodbyes.' It had been a good day, after all – and offending clients made no sense.

'I'll be at the scenic elevator.'

'Three minutes.'

She couldn't recall any further discussion, or any doubts. Bryden had seemed someone with whom it was natural to take flight, with whom plans could be made in the tersest of words, as though they already knew each other well.

They had walked to a wine bar a block away, and had talked for hours. They had sketched in their backgrounds with broad establishing strokes, but at this first encounter what they had enjoyed most was real and instant communication. And they had made each other laugh. Of all the things Jamie had liked about Bryden that first night the most important had been that he laughed, not only at the things she laughed at but in the way in which she laughed at them. By this time she had come across many shades of American humour, from the dry and pawky to the stunningly banal, but here was the savour she most relished, here was someone for whom her jokes did not have to be translated.

The evening hadn't ended with Bryden taking her home, tearing off each other's clothes the moment they were inside the door and leaping into bed. Bryden did go back with her in the cab, but only walked her to the main door, fingers linked in hers. He had turned her to him as she was about to let herself in, and drawn her into a quiet, almost restful hug, sending no urgent or explicit sexual message. For Jamie, punch-drunk on tiredness and the elation of a job successfully completed, and stunned to find such an attractive man attracted to her, that enfolding embrace had been more satisfying than any ardent kisses could have been, and more reassuring.

Her phone had rung before she was awake, and twenty minutes later Bryden had arrived. That day he had flown her to a cabin on Priest Lake which belonged to a friend of his (friend absent) and they had picnicked, hiked a little, lazed and talked. It had been the first of other similar days. Seattle and the mountains, the sound and the islands, made the perfect playground. They were young, fit, had energy and money to burn, and both liked to pack their time to the full.

Then, while Jamie was still dizzily trying to take in what had happened to her life, Bryden had told her he was married. He explained that he hadn't lived with his wife for over a year but that they were not divorced or officially separated, because his wife wouldn't agree to either. They had a daughter of six who was with her mother, now based in Fort Collins.

This news had shattered Jamie's dazzling happiness, and she had a bad few days while she digested it. Not that she was interested in marriage, with Bryden or anyone else. That had never figured as a goal for her, nor had she ever been able to imagine anyone wanting to marry her. Men married the Vanessas of this world, if they valued their self-esteem, which in her experience most of them did. But this was serious baggage, changing the scenario completely, and she had to adjust to its existence.

Her initial reaction had been anger. Bryden should have told her at once; he shouldn't have given feelings the chance to develop without making his situation clear. She had decided that was it; it was over. Getting involved with him would only lead to someone getting hurt, and it wouldn't be Bryden. The whole business was sure to get messy, and in the past Jamie had had no difficulty in walking away from such entanglements. But she had been rejected too often in her life to take this particular revelation lightly. Full of resentment and self-righteous indig-

nation, for several days she had wanted nothing more
to do with Bryden.

But she was too honest to stay angry for long.
Bryden had come clean as soon as it was obvious that
they wanted to go on seeing each other. He had at no
point misled her. What more could she have asked?
The thought of him had gnawed away at her no
matter what else she was doing, and his absence
had created an empty space in her life that was
disconcerting after knowing him for so short a time.

Although well into her thirties, Jamie had up to
this point only had two relationships which could
have been described as long-term, and each had
ended when she refused to make them permanent.
Although she got on well with men, better than with
women on the whole, she had a regrettable tendency,
when they showed signs of becoming amorous, to fall
back on her native irony, too close to mockery for the
average male ego to enjoy. And she had been too
independent for most of them, too visibly capable of
going it alone.

The real problem had been that no one had ever
come close to the ideal she had grown up with.
Beneath the readiness to grapple with the world
and establish her own toehold in it, there was a need,
barely recognised, for a maturity and strength more
solid than her own – and for someone to see past the
success story and recognise her fundamental insecurity. It had been asking too much, she could see
that for herself. She had been taken as read, and most
relationships had been short-lived and fiery. Also

Jamie had instinctively resisted casual sex. She saw herself as naive, out of date, absurd even but, for her, sex had to be an expression of something more than itself.

Bryden, recognising that Jamie was not a woman to dismiss lightly the facts he had revealed, had liked her all the more for it, particularly as her reaction indicated a level of feeling for him which he had hardly hoped for by this stage. He had therefore removed himself temporarily from the scene, to enjoy a little marlin fishing off the Florida Keys.

In his absence Jamie had gone haplessly through the hoops she had so despised others for going through in the past, amazed at their abject readiness to do so. First she had told herself that no one of Bryden's looks, personality, and ability could have failed to have someone in the background, and that the best thing she could do would be to write off the whole episode and get on with her life. Then she had reminded herself that, after all, he and his wife were no longer together and, as Bryden had explained, would have been divorced months ago if it had been down to him. So if she, Jamie, and Bryden spent time together technically it would hurt no one. She had not been looking for a committed, long-term relationship anyway, and with the work she currently had on hand she barely had time for one, so what was all the fuss about? What, in effect, had changed?

Bryden had not made contact during the time he was away, and when he reappeared, calling first to check if he could drop by, he had been understanding and compliant, ready to walk away again at a word, respecting Jamie's right to make her own choices, exerting no pressure.

'Say the word and I'm out the door. I mean it. This is your call.'

Seeing him again, the emptiness of the days without him still raw in her mind, Jamie had found she was more than willing to accept the situation as it was. They enjoyed being together, in fact the need and desire to be with him overrode every other consideration at present. This was about fun and sharing; there was no need to look any further. Why burden something so good by worrying about the future? Keep it light, go into it with eyes open and the facts clear.

At this point, now that Jamie had got past the first glitch, Bryden had thought it beneficial, over a long, softly lit, expensive and soul-baring dinner, to spell out a couple more things. His faults, in short. He didn't want her to make any more unfortunate discoveries. She should know, up front, that he was a lightweight. No woman with any sense would get mixed up with him. He had never been a stayer, and good intentions were so much dross he scattered in his wake. Although with Jamie he had found a – something, she was never quite clear afterwards which word he had settled on – he had never experienced before, he still didn't have a lot of faith in himself, it was only fair to warn her. But, he'd insisted, this thing with her *was* different, and never again did he want to go through such hell as these past few days had been, when he had known that the only thing to do was give her enough space that she could be sure of how she felt.

He had also taken the chance to tell her that, as in love, so in business. 'I guess you should know, as regards sticking to anything, I have the worst track record in the world. The thing that turns me on is a challenge. I am one all-time dabbler, believe me.' His wide grin had said he was happy with that.

Honest and meaningful disclosures indeed, but by this stage Jamie could no more have taken his warnings seriously than she could have concealed how she felt about him. That night they had made love for the first time, and it was startlingly good and satisfying. Jamie, had she been honest with herself, would have admitted that till now she had thought sex a much overrated pastime. Exciting in prospect, and she had always enjoyed the preliminaries, and often the act itself, but she had never been swept away, and the part of her brain which had remained aloofly observing had not found it even close to the thrill it was cracked up to be.

It had been amazing and marvellous to find that she and Bryden were physically as well suited as in every other way. Jamie's secret fears that she was not as attractive as the sort of women he would normally date were forgotten. What happened between them, the way their bodies woke to swift awareness, the consciousness of being carried into a shared world of sensation oblivious to everything else around them, and above all the conviction that this was the same for them both, left no room for doubt.

This discovery changed Jamie's life. She had had no conception that such happiness could exist, and with her usual whole-heartedness she tossed hard-won independence overboard. Who needed it? That had been a half life; this was reality.

During the first weeks of their affair Bryden was away a good deal, which kept feelings at a high pitch. His various enterprises, never discussed with Jamie, for they both preferred to keep their business lives separate, took him to Alaska, Newfoundland, Hawaii and Sacramento in rapid succession, but when he was free he devoted all his time to her.

At first when he was away Jamie was anxious and insecure, a state of mind she had believed left far behind her. But she was still far from confident of her power to hold a man like Bryden. It was impossible not to wonder if he played the field – she had seen the way women reacted to him, and found it hard to deal with – or even if he sometimes saw his wife on these trips. Or his daughter, who was likely to be a more compelling magnet, as Jamie could guess from the tone of his voice in his occasional references to her. But there was nothing to suggest that Bryden ever went near Fort Collins, and gradually she stopped worrying about it. In practical terms it was hard to see how Bryden could have fitted such visits into his packed schedule anyway.

He would turn up at any hour of the day or night,

once with a couple of live lobsters he tipped out onto the kitchen floor, which had to be dealt with without delay, once with a marmoset he was transporting – illegally, Jamie presumed – for a friend, but always with champagne, flowers, presents, laughter and loving.

From the moment he drew her to him in bed, and the magic began to flow between them once more, all Jamie's doubts would vanish, and as the weeks passed she slowly began to trust in his love. Apart from the friend with the Priest Lake cabin, he had few close contacts in Seattle, and when he was free he wanted Jamie with him. Originally he had planned to be there only for as long as it took to get the heli-copter business going. He had rented a tiny apart-ment and, although he talked about finding something bigger, he never found the time to do anything about it. Although it would have seemed natural for Jamie's much larger apartment to become their base, he clung to his inconvenient little pad, and they continued to shuttle uncomfortably between the two. Jamie had hoped he might suggest moving in with her but, still shy of taking such a major initiative in her personal life, she had said nothing and this step had not been discussed.

Among Jamie's friends they were accepted as a couple, and to her surprise Jamie enjoyed this, proud to be seen with Bryden, but she could still be terrified when she saw how in any group the women gravi-tated inevitably towards him. Though deeply com-mitted to her business, which continued to flourish, she was less prepared now to put in the killing hours she had previously taken in her stride. She had an excellent assistant, Gail, with whom a personal as well as a working relationship had developed, mostly over hurried lunches together, or a drink when they left the office. Jamie was much more willing these days to delegate to Gail, and for the first time since coming to the States work no longer took precedence over everything else.

The pace was strenuous all the same, partly because the unpredictability of Bryden's appearances made any routine impossible. Just as Jamie reached the point where it began to seem too exhausting to roll yet again out of Bryden's bed after far too little sleep, and drive home to get herself together to face another gruelling day; or alternatively drag herself to the kitchen to make coffee before Bryden left, having just rolled grumbling out of hers, he proposed buying somewhere to live together.

They discussed the options and went to look at a few possibilities, but in the end found nothing to equal for location and convenience the condo Jamie already had. Bryden wasn't comfortable, however, with the idea of living there while she owned it. He wanted his full share of costs and responsibility. Jamie was happy – in fact overjoyed, though she did her best to sound businesslike – to transfer the apartment to shared ownership. The new footing suited them both, and for Jamie a reassuring element of permanence seemed at last to have entered her life.

12

For the first weeks of that year it rained and rained, grey day after grey day, and when the rain let up the high-rise city on its jutting peninsula was raked by fierce winds for days more. Jamie hadn't minded, deep in her new happiness, and enjoying the atmosphere of enterprise and development which was sweeping away the rather staid and homely mood of the place.

When at last winter relented and spring warmed from its cool, pastel-coloured first arrival to full-blooded colour and fragrance, Bryden took Jamie across to Vashon Island, promising her a surprise. The hilly wooded islands were densely green against the blue waters of the Sound, sunlight was brilliant on the snowy magnificence of the Olympic Mountains and turned the city back to gleaming white.

He took her to a cedar-log cabin, surrounded by cherry trees in flower and rhododendrons thick with cerise buds, its sun-baked, weathered deck facing the immaculate symmetry of Mount Rainier. This small slice of paradise, it seemed, belonged to them.

Paradise. Idyllic. The clichés were theirs for that long, wonderful summer. Bryden seemed to be away less and they used the cabin, whose interior was by no means as homespun as its exterior suggested, more often than Jamie had dared to hope. They found increasing pleasure in each other's company, and Bryden began to make noises about offloading some of his scattered enterprises and concentrating his interests in Seattle. Though Jamie asked no direct questions, she gathered that he had something specific in his sights, and for the first time she let herself consider seriously the idea of their making a life together. By autumn Bryden told her that he had a company in line for takeover, though still not saying what it was. He also began to talk about looking for a larger apartment.

Jamie was so used by now to knowing nothing about his activities, that she resigned herself to waiting to hear what he'd decided. Meantime he was here, spending more time with her than ever before, and at last talking openly of putting pressure on his wife to agree to a divorce. Though he never spoke of it as affecting his relationship with Jamie, for her a thread of speculation inevitably ran through thoughts of the future, and there was always a small thrill when it surfaced unexpectedly.

The company Bryden took over handled advertising, to Jamie's surprise, for she hadn't known he had any interest in this field. But to him one business was very like another, and the same successful operating technique could be applied.

Jamie's voice, which had recounted the substance of this tale sometimes with a defensive fluency, sometimes with such halting painfulness that Patrick had longed to stop her, to assure her that the rest would keep, and that she need tell no one things which hurt too much, faltered into silence.

It had been obvious as she talked that this rough outpouring was a therapy she had desperately needed. Patrick guessed that his unexpected appearance this evening had jolted her into an unburdening which otherwise, with more time to muster her defences, she might have resisted. But there had been no chance to adjust to any new footing between them. She could, once the floodgates had opened, tell her story as though time had stood still, and he was nothing more than a trusted but indistinct adult figure, always there in the background, part of the remote world of the grown-ups, a listener whose feelings there was no need to take into account.

The fire had died to a bed of soft white wood ash. There were no more logs on the hearth, but Patrick had not wished to make a move to fetch some, fearing that the merest touch of the present would check the flow. But the room was warm, holding at bay the cool of the night, the faint chill breath of river air.

Jamie, Patrick was certain, would not be aware of the fire, the temperature, where she was or even in any real sense who she was talking to. He waited, motionless. Would she go on, or was whatever she had arrived at too painful? He guessed that, if she went on talking, she would be putting into words for the first time, even to herself, some recent and barely grasped disaster. Was it Zara's death that had brought her home, he wondered, or would she have come anyway, driven to seek sanctuary? Though she could never have turned to Calder if Zara had still been there.

'For ages nothing seemed to change,' Jamie said, after a pause which had seemed to stretch beyond the point where she would resume.

Patrick found he was letting his breath out carefully. He had not been aware he was so tense.

'Yet it was all happening, it was all in train, it was rushing towards me. And I had no idea . . .'

She had both elbows tight in against her, hands balled into fists, knuckles pressed against her jaw. She looked very small and drawn in on herself, and Patrick thought again, with savage anger at whoever had done this to her, that she was far too thin and gaunt.

'Of course I should have known. I can't imagine how I was taken in for a second.' But how to put into words the trust she had placed in love and happiness, her growing confidence in a shared future, her readiness, for the first time in her life, to relinquish control, gladly and gratefully? Someone had wanted her; someone was going to look after her. It had been a magical experience and, being Jamie, she had gone for it with her whole heart.

'He asked me if I'd marry him when the divorce was through. Even then I was amazed that he was prepared to take on the commitment again. And with me! I'd always seen myself as hopeless as a wife. Not my scene. I only had to think of Vanessa and her lifestyle to know that.' She missed Patrick's quick frowning look, as if he were checking for something underlying the words. 'But I wanted it. God, how I wanted it. And we had so many other things going for us. It was then that – he –' she seemed unable now to use Bryden's name '– began to push for me to be less involved at work. I wasn't putting in anything like the hours I had at the start, but I was still very much hands-on, and we were busy and doing well. I couldn't leave the whole thing to Gail. I found it more and more a balancing act to spend the time at home that he expected. My God, he meant me to . . . That's exactly what he wanted . . .'

Her tone of blank discovery strengthened Patrick's impression that this shock was very new. She was still fumbling to put the pieces together. 'Of course he did,' she repeated. 'He *wanted* me to find it impossible to meet all the demands. It was part of the process, and I never realised. Anyway,' putting that aside as though this wasn't the moment to deal with it, and going doggedly on, 'he suggested quite soon that the two companies should amalgamate. Or rather that his should take over mine. Obvious, wasn't it?'

She looked at Patrick this time, but even so he wasn't sure she was aware of who he was, other than some dependable and well-disposed listener, the necessary recipient of all that had to be told.

'What happened?' he asked quietly, to keep the words coming.

'Oh, nothing original.' The bitterness in her voice

made him wince. 'America, as you know, is a land of lawyers, lawyers who will do practically anything if you pay them enough. Though I'd learned the hard way not to move hand or foot without taking advice, though I'd learned to protect my back with every job I took on, with leases, employees, insurance, everything, I didn't bother to have my lawyer cut the deal with his lawyer. I let his lawyer handle the whole thing. Wild. I didn't even go through the paperwork properly. I was madly busy—'

She broke off, and Patrick saw the realisation in her face, and would have sworn, had it not been impossible for her to look more wan and drained, that it became paler.

'Of course I was busy.' He saw her mind racking up the pointers ignored at the time. 'Of course those papers appeared precisely when I literally hadn't an hour to spend on them. Nothing was left to chance. So what else was choreographed in the same way, things I still haven't woken up to? God, oh *God*!'

At the bleakness of that exclamation it was all Patrick could do not to go to her and gather her up and tell her not to think of this ever again, to let it be over, behind her, and not hurt herself any more. But if anyone had ever needed the release of words it was Jamie tonight, and he stayed where he was, his muscles tight with anger and resistance, his face dark and grim.

'Well, there you are,' said Jamie, stirring at last, pushing herself back in her chair, her arms flat along its arms. In a rapid, defeated voice, full of self-contempt, she polished off the story. 'The whole thing was a scam. From beginning to end. A beautiful, minutely planned and perfectly executed scam. He was getting pretty expert by the time he decided to hit on me. Each one pays for the next, it seems, and the next is sure to be bigger yet. The advertising company didn't exist, of course, but now he has a nice little PR agency to throw into the scales. He'd acquired the helicopter company in the same way. The widow of the previous owner had fallen into his arms and – bingo. With each deal he had more cash up-front to make the next play. Any extra running costs he met by long-haul trucking. That was what he'd been doing on those "business trips" away. It was the exact opposite of how he sold himself, and yet I can see him fitting into that scene too, enjoying it even, getting right inside it. Pulling off another con. That was how he got his kicks. Plus there were the opportunities for wheeling and dealing, an extra bonus. Irresistible. So, nothing was as it seemed, and I'll probably never unravel all of it.'

She paused, and the silence was taut with pain. When she went on she seemed to be speaking to herself, and Patrick could hardly hear her. 'Every word he said, everything we did together, has to be looked at and looked at again, and a new twist will always be there.'

Silence again, as though she was absorbing this, then, in a different tone, self-mocking now, almost harder for Patrick to bear than that desolate bleakness, 'You have to hand it to him, he's very, very good at what he does. It's a career like any other, and he brings to it a first-class brain, imagination, flair and enterprise. He started out by reading law – good, isn't it? – but never took his degree because too many openings turned up too soon, and he couldn't resist them. But he learned to wait, later on. Learned to take his time, making sure every last detail was in place. Perhaps that was the real secret of his success. Also he had a useful network of chums who would, say, set up a phantom office for a day, lend a property, front a company. As he explained to me.'

'He explained how he worked it all?'

'He was proud of it. I think he thought I'd be impressed. As someone close to him, you understand.' She hurried on. 'As one good business brain to another, except he forgot he'd just proved his had the edge on mine, and as a result I'd been wiped off the board. But yes, he seemed to think I'd relish the finer points. For instance, he hadn't known the owner of the place on Priest Lake, our first trip together. And the Vashon Island cabin belonged to another buddy. No money changed hands because Bryden had put some business his way, I dread to think what.'

The cabin supposedly given as a surprise present. Generous, substantial, but, unlike a car, a piece of jewellery or a round-the-world trip, it had been something smacking of permanence and domestic stability, adding another dimension to their life together. Patrick began to glimpse the scale of the rethinking facing Jamie.

As though finding the whole thing suddenly unbearable, she came to her feet, startling him.

'Patrick. I'm sorry, I can't believe I've wasted your time with all this stuff. I've been talking for hours. You must be bored to death. And look at the time, it's after two. I do apologise. You must—'

'Jamie, it's all right.' Getting to his feet in turn and finding himself, so tense had he been, so determined to make no move to distract her, surprisingly stiff, Patrick couldn't bear to descend to polite social nothings. He felt raked and abraded by what he had learned, and by an aching perception of what Jamie was struggling to come to terms with.

'No, I must go,' she insisted. 'It'll be light soon. You should have given me a kick hours ago. Thank goodness you're a night bird, and don't have to be up early in the morning. Well, it's morning now—'

'Jamie, you're not going down to Calder tonight.'

'Of course I am. There's no need for you to come though. I've torn down that path a hundred times on nights darker than this. I'll be there in less than—'

'No.' That was the Patrick of the past, brusque and immovable. How could he let her go in alone to that deserted house, thronged with its uneasy ghosts, alone with all this grief so freshly churned up? 'You'll sleep here. Mother's room is always ready. You're not going to spend tonight by yourself in that empty house, and that's all there is to it.'

Looking into her face, seeking eye contact so that he could impose his will, he saw sadness fill it as fresh realisation returned.

'Oh, Patrick, for a moment I'd forgotten Calder had changed. I was imagining it as it used to be, warm and safe and comfortable, with Grandmother there, and the others, everything still in place. I don't think I can bear it . . .'

Her face crumpled and tears filled her eyes. She looked exhausted, beaten down. Patrick saw the tremor of her shoulders as the new images overwhelmed her and, his own throat hard, his eyes wet, he pulled her roughly against him, longing to envelop her and keep her safe from every threat.

She had always brought disaster on herself by her own recklessness, but beneath the determination and defiance he had known that what she had needed, whether she recognised it or not, was stability and the assurance of affection. Of the sisters, she had suffered most from the unsettled family background, the changes and insecurities of childhood. She had pinned her faith on her father, but Hal had let her down without compunction. This time, it seemed, Jamie had had grounds for trust. The relationship with Bryden must have seemed to her sound and sure and full of promise. It was easy with hindsight to see everything as suspect, but what reason had Jamie had to doubt him at the time?

That she should have met with disaster on such a scale in her personal life, in this way of all ways, and at the same time have the success for which she had worked so hard ripped out of her hands, was bad luck of the cruellest kind. Patrick could hardly endure it for her.

★   ★   ★

Jamie's room was empty, and Patrick went outside to look for her. It had rained in the night and the morning was soft and dreich, trails of mist clinging in the larches on the opposite slope. The figure hunched on the bridge looked desperately forlorn, and as Patrick went down the slope towards her he knew it was going to be hard to find the right words and the right tone.

In fact he failed, and in silence leaned beside her. She turned to give him a fleeting smile, and woebegone was the only word he could find for her this morning.

'Did you sleep at all?'

Her mouth twisted. 'Not much.'

Words of comfort, the endearments he longed to use, would be treacherous offerings at present. Stick to the practical.

'Could you face breakfast?'

'Do you know, I'm not sure that I could.'

Silence. The brisk run of the water below them, cold stone dew-dank under their elbows, birdsong muted in the still air, the blanketing quiet of the hills.

'Come on. Hot coffee at the very least.'

Patrick took her hand in his, a gesture unusual between them, and, aware of the lifelessness of the thin, icy fingers in his, felt compassion overtaken by fierce anger towards the man who had done this to her. Accustomed to seeing her bounce back from every crisis, he was appalled to see her so quenched and defeated.

They were in the kitchen, going through the motions of preparing breakfast in silence, when behind him, in a voice he barely caught, he heard her say, 'It did seem real, you know.'

He put down the bread knife and turned, his face almost as drawn as hers. 'Oh, Jamie, I know. I know it did.'

She stared at him wanly, forgetting the coffee filters she had in her hand. 'He said he had cared too. It had been real for him. While it was happening.'

Patrick did his best to deal with the anger that would help no one, and waited without speaking.

'You see, for him, it could be like that. I mean, he had that capacity, to be deeply into something for as long as it was important to him, and then to switch off. It was as close as he could come to genuine feeling, I think. He said it – our relationship – was something special for him, and that was why he had let it go on for so long. He'd had everything in place in the autumn, but he said things were so good between us he'd held off. God,' she exclaimed in sudden disbelief, 'am I saying this?' She slammed down the packet of filters, scattering them. 'Am I actually grateful that he did that?'

She closed her eyes, gathering up control, then with unsteady hands began to fit a filter into the basket. Patrick longed to take it away from her, chuck the whole lot aside, shout at her to forget it, but he knew there was no room for his own anger yet.

'I don't think it could have been – the way it was,' Jamie went on in a muffled voice, her back to him, 'if there hadn't been some element of reality. I would have known. I'd surely have known.' A pause, her hands still. 'How could it have been so happy if it was all a pretence?'

'Jamie.' Patrick stepped across the small space between them, in his brain an urgent warning to remember that this was about her, and only her. Instead of crushing her in his arms as he longed to do he turned her gently to face him. 'You're right to hold on to that. It must have meant something to him. From what you say, he knew he wasn't a stayer, and that's his loss, but it doesn't mean he wasn't capable of some true feeling.'

And that, may God forgive me, is as far as I can go.

Jamie's face had lit up gratefully. 'That's what he said. And I think he did believe that, because he'd laid everything on the line at the beginning, I would have understood there'd never be any kind of permanence.'

Patrick watched the bleak look deepen as the thoughts turned.

'Oh, I'm just putting sticking plaster over the wound,' she cried with sudden violence. 'I haven't even told you the best part. You see, there was no wife, no daughter, no ties of any kind. He just found that a handy form of protection, should anyone be silly enough to expect too much. What he felt for me might have been real while we were together, but only because it was part of the set-up, an essential element in pulling off another coup. I'm sure he "genuinely" felt as much for the widow of the helicopter pilot, or anyone else he'd used along the way. I drew the line at hearing the details, though he was keen to tell me, confident I'd admire his skill and enterprise, I suppose. That was the thing, you see. He was amazed that I minded so much. He kept saying, "Hey, lighten up, we're two of a kind. We're in it for the kicks, remember." But do you know,' she leaned her head for a moment against Patrick's chest, as though this was getting too difficult, 'even then I couldn't hate him. I still can't. When I try to, the attraction's there again; everything in me protests. He was – such good company.' The simple, helpless little phrase told so much. 'Even when I knew the whole thing had gone, the business, the apartment – the house on Vashon Island had never existed – I still couldn't hate him. But I'll have to learn to, or I don't know what I'm going to do.'

That was the question burning in Patrick's brain, but he knew he couldn't ask it. What would she do?

13

Though she protested, Jamie was glad when Patrick insisted on going down to Calder with her. She couldn't shake off the irrational expectation that, after the familiar surroundings of the Toll-house and the lulling sense they had given her of being carried back in time, she would find the big house as it used to be, serene, peopled, flower-filled and cared for.

But the impact of the new reality was lessened by Patrick's fury at what Zara had done, and sharing the horrors with him removed some of their power to hurt.

'It's hard to know how to live in it,' she remarked, when they had made the circuit of the house. 'It was some comfort to find those bits and pieces of Grandmother's, but I'm not sure that I'd achieve much by lugging them down, even if I could shift them.'

'Well, there's no problem with that.'

'No, I know, thanks – but the empty rooms are so huge. I end up in the kitchen more or less by default, doing my best not to look at it.'

Patrick nodded. 'There's certainly an uneasy feel to the place,' he said, looking around him with renewed disbelief as they came back to the disfigured hall. 'Almost as though Zara did what she did not because she wanted to create a new style, more that she wanted to destroy the old one. Arrogant and vindictive seem the appropriate words.' He eyed with disgust the stark angularity of the steel banisters. Structurally, there was nothing that couldn't be made good, but the cost of returning the house to a harmonious whole would be formidable. How much of the Laidlaw money had been squandered by Zara since Hal died? He was thankful that Jamie had at least found her old bedroom as it used to be, and had one corner where she could feel at home.

He had taken some care to hide the feelings which had assailed him to be back once more in those simple little rooms along the nursery corridor, rooms well-remembered from the days when he had been in eager demand for piggy-backs upstairs, and as many bedtime stories as he could be cajoled into reading.

Nostalgia had gripped him. High-pitched laughter and squabbling voices; the smells of soap and bath-water and damp towels; small scudding figures still charged with energy; Freda, mouth clamped repressively, putting out the orderly piles of tomorrow's clothes; golden summer-evening light fingering round drawn curtains; and the agreeable prospect, when he could get away, of sitting outside the French window of the drawing-room for before-dinner drinks in the scented lingering warmth. Wellbeing.

And now the travesty that lay beyond this undisturbed enclave. It concerned him to think of Jamie rattling around here alone, with so much pain to work through and so little to comfort her. In a way it was the worst of places for her to be just now, yet where else could she go? He hesitated to urge the obvious answers on her, to suggest that she went to Vanessa or came back with him, to Blackdykes or to stay with his mother. He understood her need for solitude in which to lick her wounds, and he understood too her fierce independence, battered though it might at present be.

'Are there things you had planned to do?' he asked. 'Anything you'd like a hand with?'

'It's kind of you, Patrick, but I'm not sure I can think about it yet,' Jamie replied restlessly. The question marks over the future were too big. Everything which had so recently happened, now put into words, made yesterday's sense of progress appear childish and trivial.

'I can understand that,' Patrick said. 'Then how do you feel about going up the hill for a couple of hours? Forget all this. The rain looks as though it might hold off. The sky even seems to be brightening.'

Jamie's face brightened too, he presumed at the idea of postponing any attempt to improve her situation by domestic activity.

In fact for the moment Jamie wanted more than anything to go on being with him. Now that everything was told, now that the pretence, which from some obscure form of cowardice she had almost needed to believe in herself, of being able to hold on to Calder, had been shattered by the harsh facts, there were many things to face and she knew she wasn't ready for them. The protective numbness in which, stitch by stitch, she had unpicked her life during the past few days – was it really only days? – had cracked apart.

'You're sure you wouldn't rather do your rediscovering alone?' Patrick asked as she turned to the door. Growing up, her passion for this place had been, as he remembered only too well, proprietary, shared only with her father. But Hal Laidlaw, after the early years of wanting her to be a son, had become bored with the game, and as the children got older he had spent little time with any of them. That absurd business of giving her a name that could be made masculine, Patrick thought with quick anger, an anger whipped up by the welter of emotions set milling by being with Jamie again, learning what had happened to her, seeing the house, and above all walking once more the knife-edge between his true feelings and accepted friendship. Jemima, for God's sake. Family name or not, it hardly belonged to the twenty-first century. Phillida was slightly better, though it too, whether deliberately or not, could be shortened into a boy's name. Then, illogically, Patrick found himself hotly resenting the idea that Jamie could be anyone but Jamie.

Time to get out of here, and clear this rubbish out of his head with fresh air and exercise.

'No, really, I'd rather you came,' Jamie was saying. 'Unless you have things you want to do?' She looked suddenly uncertain, like a dog with tail drooping in doubt when the walk seems to be off again.

Patrick laughed, amused to find so much of the child in the mature and ambitious career woman he had barely seen in ten years. Or he laughed because he was delighted that she wanted him with her. 'Come on then.'

Without debate, they went past Freda's cottage and down to the footbridge below the falls.

'Needs a bit of attention,' Jamie shouted above the thunder of the water, coming down fast after last night's rain, pointing with her foot to rotting holes in the planking.

'The wood never dries out properly.'

Who would have the means or the will to take Calder in hand? What would become of it? The questions rose in both their minds, and in silence they left the bridge and took the path along the side of the gorge, while the river swung away to curve below the lawn.

Soon the path began to climb, and presently took them clear of the trees onto the open hill. They paused when they reached a small crag, from which the wide spread of hills to the west could be seen. Here, again without discussion, they settled on a convenient ledge, where so many shooting lunches had been shared. For a while they didn't speak, each needing time to absorb the fact that the long separation was over, and satisfied for the moment with that.

'I hardly know where to begin thinking,' Jamie confessed eventually, with a half-laugh that sounded actually shy. 'Let alone talking.'

'I know.'

'I feel sort of – washed clean – to have told you everything. But empty. I can't describe it.'

Patrick put his hand over hers for an instant, where it gripped the edge of their stone perch, but only for an instant, not trusting himself to let the contact prolong itself. The discipline of the past held good, and he was thankful for it.

'The rest is time,' he said.

'Yes.'

They watched the sky to the south gradually warm and lighten, the distant loch take on a reflected gleam. It was not quite warm enough to sit for long in comfort, but neither wanted to move.

'It will have to go, of course. Calder. I know that. I just didn't have the courage to face it right away. I needed to believe it was there. I let myself think there might be enough left of Father's money, or something in Zara's will perhaps. Oh, I don't know that I was even thinking as clearly as that. It was all one big, dark muddle.' She fell silent, then began again more awkwardly, 'I didn't deliberately mislead Vanessa and Phil, you know. I just let them go on thinking whatever they thought.' Another pause. 'I did mislead them, though, didn't I? Because I was afraid.'

Wincing at the bleakness of that, Patrick knew he couldn't deal with it yet. 'I don't think their believing you can buy them out matters,' he said instead. 'The outcome won't be affected, apart from any decision being delayed a bit. You'll be able to explain, when you're ready. They'll understand.'

Explain. Go through the agonising story again. If only Patrick could tell them for her. Jamie closed her eyes for a second, overwhelmed by a longing to turn and burrow into his arms, hide herself in his hard strength, be protected by his uncompromising good sense.

'Vanessa was a bit odd about it,' she said, clutching at the first thing she could find to distract her thoughts. 'She was really anxious for a decision, and she didn't seem a bit happy about my staying on. I couldn't see why.'

Douglas wanting the whole thing cut and dried, no doubt. Patrick's mouth hardened. 'It would be difficult for Vanessa to imagine anyone wanting to be in the house as it is,' he said, keeping his voice neutral.

'She did a bit of squawking, I must admit, though I think in her heart she rather fancied the kitchen.' Swinging in her volatile way from despair to amusement, Jamie laughed at the memory, bringing back so vividly the lively girl he had loved that Patrick's heart turned over. 'She got very excited when I bashed down the corridor partition. As law-abiding as ever, my big sister, though I'm never sure who it is she's so anxious to please.'

Patrick gave her a sharp look which she missed, but all he said was, 'Don't knock it. She's a giver, and you've done your share of taking from her.'

'How nice to be ticked off again,' Jamie remarked, leaning her head against the rock wall behind her, an unrepentant smile curling her mouth.

'And much good it does,' Patrick grunted, but for

them both there was a pleasure in slipping back to a
status quo long relinquished. 'Look,' he went on,
'Vanessa is right in a way about your being here
alone. Though the house is a bit barren, you can
easily survive in it, but you will need a car.'

I know I need a car, but I can't afford one, much
less hire one as Vanessa gaily suggested. 'I can
manage for the time being,' Jamie said shortly.

'As long as you don't need to leave the glen. But
won't you find that restricting after a while?'

'Maybe. To be honest I feel too punch-drunk for
the moment to be able to gauge anything realistically.
The transition from the way I was living, the city, the
pace, the demands, the whole—' He saw the memories hit her, saw her resist them. 'Well, you know all
that. Then to be back in Glasgow, in the hotel, jet-
lagged but unable to sleep. Horrible dreams. Being
with Van and Phil again after such ages, and having
to be the person they thought I was, because no way
could I tell them what had happened. Then the
cremation, which seems like another dream now,
confused and unreal. I can't remember a thing about
it, except trying to take in the fact that Zara had gone,
that it was her actual body in the coffin, her actual
body about to be burned. It was impossible to grasp
that the cloud hanging over Calder had finally been
lifted. Hearing from Mr Syme that we'd owned it all
along was like seeing something through the wrong
end of a telescope, bright, clear, but far away and
inaccessible. Then on the same day to be back in this
amazing silence, which I'd almost forgotten. To be

here, with all the memories – it was like jet-lag intensified a hundred times over.'

He could feel it as she had felt it, but he didn't interrupt.

'It was all of it,' she pursued almost dreamily. 'Finding our rooms unchanged, going to the village, walking along the river path – it was like walking back into childhood. Yet inside me something cold and panicky insists that it can't be real, that none of it has anything to do with me any more.'

Patrick could hardly bear to think of her here, struggling to adjust to these new circumstances, without resources and, as far as he could see, without any clear objective. Before he spoke he made certain that his voice would not reveal his fears.

'Fortunately, there are answers to hand,' he reminded her. 'You're home. You're not on your own. And a solution to your immediate problem is that my mother's car is sitting idle in the garage, I'm sure never to be driven by her again. Why not have that? It's still insured and so on. I haven't wanted to point up the fact that her driving days are over by selling it.'

'But Patrick, I can't accept such a—'

'Don't give me that crap,' he exclaimed, getting to his feet and taking a couple of steps away and back, releasing some of the ready anger which made people so wary of him. He had a few close friends, mostly artists in various fields, but he had no wider social circle of casual acquaintances such as most people take for granted. He was too forthright, too easily bored, too impatient of the superficial. Now he said sharply, 'Either you don't need a car because you want to cut yourself off from everything for a while, which I should fully understand, or you do need a car – and without one you won't get very far with organising whatever you decide to do next – in which case I expect you to have the sense to take one that's available. I'm not interested in polite protests.'

'Well, I'm protesting now,' Jamie retorted, firing up exactly as she used to. 'Good God, I'd barely opened my mouth! Surely I can at least make sure that Naomi really doesn't need—'

'I've told you she doesn't.'

'The years haven't done much to mellow you, I must say,' Jamie observed. 'Don't even try to bully me. I shall make up my own mind.'

'Good, then make it up.'

She looked at him glowering down at her, the big shoulders hunched in the familiar way, the rough head jutting aggressively. What a craggy chunk of humanity he was, she thought with a rush of grateful affection.

'I shall talk to Naomi. It's her car.'

In time Patrick realised that, in the way he should have had enough experience to guard against, she was winding him up, and a grin briefly lit the heavy features.

'I can't think why, but it's quite nice to have you back,' he remarked. 'Come on, let's get walking.'

With objective interest, as they left the track and went on up the steep hill face, he noted his relief to know she would at least be mobile and in that sense independent. It changed her seeking sanctuary here into something more normal, less blind and desperate, and he was glad of it. It also made it possible to put forward a suggestion which had occurred to him as they went through the despoiled wastes of the house.

'Jamie, there's another possibility,' he said casually, as they came out onto the sweep of bent patterned with heather, which rose to the ridge above Gask. 'If you find the house too sad, you know you could always use the Toll-house. Would that appeal to you?'

'Oh, Patrick.' She stopped and turned to him, and this time there was no mistaking the gratitude in her face. 'That's kind of you. Really kind. You know how much I'd love it. And yet—' She broke off, giving him a little rueful smile, and he knew she wasn't going to accept. 'In a funny way, showing you all that Zara has done made it seem more bearable. It's a fact, it's happened. The images of the past belong in the past, with Father and Grandmother and all that's vanished. And if you look at it another way,' she added more lightly, 'what more could a person who's fallen on hard times ask for than a big house to swan around in, everything laid on, cleaner and gardener thrown in, and all in the loveliest glen in Scotland? What have I got to whinge about?'

'Put like that,' he conceded. How good it was to see the thin face alive and mocking. He thrust his hands deep into his pockets.

Jamie didn't add that for her the mere fact that she had found the Toll-house lit and occupied, that it was once more in place, as it were, an essential part of the scene, was almost as good as moving in. Better, for moving in would alter a delicate balance. What mattered was for Patrick to come and go as it suited him, without warning, and be discovered there, exactly as before.

'Mind you,' said Jamie, reverting to what she had just said, keeping to the mundane, 'not that I want much more to do with the cleaner. Efficient but dire. Besides, I'm not really sure what she's *for*, now that we've packed up most of the stuff she used to dust. Only I suppose I shouldn't deprive her of her income.'

'She can still be paid, even if you don't want her to come in,' Patrick pointed out.

'What would Mr Syme say?'

'Vanessa-speak,' Patrick protested. 'What's become of the incisive executive brain?' He regretted the words the moment they were out, but Jamie didn't appear to notice his tactlessness.

'I'll have a word with her. It won't make any difference to Vanessa or Phil. But the *gardener*,' she sounded suddenly cheerful, 'that's another matter entirely. Have you met Maeve?'

'I have.'

'And?'

But as an appreciative smile creased Patrick's face, Jamie was startled by a pang of jealousy. It gave her a frightening glimpse of the harm which trust betrayed had done. She saw Bryden's smiling, self-possessed face; smiling, refusing to be touched by her shock and pain. 'Take it easy, Jamie, we both know where we're coming from.' Moving on, untouched, still smiling, out of her life.

Jamie hastily caught at a sense of proportion. Patrick and Maeve, in their different ways and at their different levels, both represented enjoyment and reassurance. No memories of Bryden could mar that straightforward pleasure. Of course Patrick would know Maeve, and Maeve was exactly the sort of person he would like, easy, smiling, colourful, unfettered by time and rules. Had Maeve been to the Toll-house? Had Patrick been to the garden house at Craigard? Why not?

Although she saw the absurdity of that unexpected flash of jealousy, nevertheless the fact that life had rolled on here while she had been away, would roll on again without her, made Jamie feel strangely bereft for a moment. Just as yesterday she had had to accept that Freda had moved on from time-serving toler-ance to an indifference bordering on hostility, she must accept that she had no part in anything that happened here.

Right, she'd got that straight. She plunged into telling Patrick about the meeting with Maeve yester-day, and he responded by telling her about Maeve's first appearance in the glen, camping by the river with a stunning-looking Japanese girl. He was amus-ing about the impact the pair had made on the local scene, and as they laughed together Jamie's momen-

tary feeling of exclusion was forgotten. It was Patrick
who brought it back.

'Are old associations strong enough to counteract
yesterday's bad vibes, I wonder,' he said, as they
crossed the bridge again an hour or so later, and came
to Freda's cottage.

Jamie paused, head tilted, frowning, as though
making sure of the honest answer. 'I think they
are,' she said slowly. 'I can only see this house as
the cosy, friendly place where we used to run in and
out whenever we felt like it. Always good things on
offer, always sure of our welcome. Though I don't
know why Freda put up with us, in what was supposed to be her time off.'

'I don't think I remember her as ever having time
off, especially when you lot were up here,' Patrick
commented drily.

Jamie shook her head. 'It is strange, you know.
That surly old woman I called on yesterday seems
someone quite separate. A rather disagreeable stranger. Freda, the real Freda, is tucked away somewhere
with Grandmother, and with – oh, I don't know,
things like warm scones, Dettol stinging on grazed
knees, the smell of ironing and the taste of porridge
and a lot of grumbling – and a pretty heavy hand at
times too,' she wound up, smiling. She looked at the
shuttered cottage. 'That Freda's still here. She'll
never go away.'

Patrick waited for a moment more. 'It might be a
more practical place to live. Had you thought of
that?'

14

The four rooms of the cottage, two up, two down, faced west towards the river. Its back adjoined the steading buildings and the high wall of the yard. Inside its central door a narrow staircase rose steeply; at the north end a scullery had been tacked on, with a bathroom above it.

'My American self is having a bit of a battle with my Calder self,' Jamie admitted, wrinkling her nose at the spartan black and white fittings of the latter, the stained loo bowl and blue marks below every tap.

'I can well believe it. This isn't too attractive,' Patrick assented. Nothing that couldn't be dealt with, but he was careful to make no suggestions at this stage. It was hard for anyone else to imagine just how anchorless and vulnerable Jamie must be feeling. All he could do was let her see that options were open to her, and if possible give her the confidence to believe that pieces of the shattered pattern could be picked up and re-shaped in a different form.

'Isn't it odd, I'd never realised how hideous it was,' Jamie remarked, though she sounded cheerful about it. 'I suppose I didn't come in here much when

I was older, and of course as children we never looked. It was just "Freda's", accepted as it was.'

They had always taken it for granted that in the cottage life was not quite the same as it was in the big house. It had been understood that things which Freda would never have done there, or allowed them to do, were perfectly in order here. Things like the little clutch of tomato ketchup and HP sauce bottles, forbidden joys to them, left standing in the middle of the table, alongside the salt and pepper and the bowl of sugar with brown lumps in it where people had used wet spoons. Things like Freda washing her hair in the scullery sink, and the comb with the black teeth which was kept on the shelf above it and used impartially by Freda and her husband.

Jamie tried to chase down a name for him, but couldn't remember him ever being referred to as anything but 'Freda's husband'. He used to pad about in stocking feet and collarless shirt, sour-faced and silent, except for sniffing and hawking as he tipped his chair dangerously back, varying the entertainment by picking his teeth. He would sit noisily sucking in tea from a huge mug, ignoring Freda's nagging about getting back to work, a red mark dividing the tanned skin of his forehead from the white skin of his skull, where strands of dark hair lay flat and sweaty.

There had been antimacassars draped over plush chair backs, crocheted doilies under brass candlesticks on the sideboard, lace curtains at every window. In very early days there had been a range for cooking, a pulley above it perpetually draped with yellowing woollen underwear which Jamie had avoided looking at, but these had long ago been superseded by electric cooker, washing machine and spin dryer. Once Jamie had been shocked to see Freda sweep the carpet with the dirty broom she used for the back kitchen floor, but even then there had been the acceptance that things were done differently when Freda was in her own house.

She had certainly never noticed the dark wallpaper, the gloss paint which covered every inch of woodwork in a bilious shade of milk-chocolate, or the mean dimensions of the sixties tiled fireplace in the sitting-room. Nor had she ever noticed that, in the south gable-end, windows upstairs and down had at some time been filled in.

'They'd have overlooked part of the lawn,' Patrick said, coming to look. 'Couldn't have the servants catching a glimpse of the family at play, that would never do. Shame, they'd have had the best view. The house smells surprisingly dry, doesn't it, considering how long it's been empty.'

'I always remember Freda having the fires going full blast, winter or summer.'

'She wouldn't have seen any reason not to. Any amount of free Calder fuel on hand.'

'It's odd, I really do find it hard to believe that that grumpy old woman I saw yesterday is the same person.'

'Good,' said Patrick. 'Keep it that way.' He didn't want the memories marred for her. She had enough to contend with. Watching her face as she went from room to room, he had seen in it something of the peaceful pleasure that had been there the previous evening as they prepared supper together at the Toll-house, before she had begun to talk. It was just the sort of comfort she needed.

'Well, what do you think?' He came to stand at her shoulder in the recess of the sitting-room window, as she gazed across the gorge to the tree-clad slope beyond, where the strengthening sun brought out the varied shades of early summer green. He was conscious of a need to be close to her, physically close, if this was to be a moment of decision. His mouth twisted ironically as he acknowledged the feeling.

'I hardly dare think about this, you know,' Jamie said, still gazing out.

'Because?'

She stood for a moment more, very still, then turned her back to the window, propped her skinny haunches on the narrow sill, and met his eyes with honesty.

'Because,' she said, 'in a way it's too perfect. And it brings me slamming up against all kinds of decisions. And I haven't the slightest idea what I'm going to do about any of them.'

'OK.' Patrick kept his voice deliberate. 'We can look at the issues in turn, if that would help.'

She gave him a quick smile, grateful, but so wry that it wrenched him to see the pain behind it. For a moment she said nothing, was not, indeed, capable of saying anything, in the grip of a wild longing to turn the clock back, to have still in place the fabric of her life as it had been two short weeks ago, hectic, involving, intact and complete. Even if that meant Zara still in control of Calder; even if it meant having missed that startling rediscovery of closeness with Vanessa and Phil, still rock solid below the surface differences, to be tapped into at need; even if it meant forgoing the moment of shaken anticipation when she saw that the Toll-house was occupied, and walked with thudding heart up the grassy slope to the door.

'Too perfect?' Patrick was saying. 'Then let's start with that. Why too perfect?'

Jamie dragged herself back to the present with an effort. That whole packed, hurtling year, so full of hopes and promise, had had no more substance than the flash of sunlight on the waters of the Sound. Here at least there was the immediate comfort of Patrick's big, hard-muscled body close to her own, and the certainty that, in spite of the years, his support and concern were still there for her. Jamie allowed herself the luxury of drawing on that comfort for a second before she spoke. She would have made nothing of her life, she knew, without this man. He had dragged her back again and again from the brink of disaster, had made her face her responsibilities and stick to what she had set out to do.

No one else had ever taken such trouble over her. Vanessa had worried about her, it was true, but her solicitude had taken the shape of anxious nagging, so far from grasping what lay behind Jamie's defiance

that she had done more harm than good. In any case
by that time she had been immersed in her marriage,
husband and son.

But Patrick had been determined to drum some
sense into her, whether Jamie wanted to listen or not,
and she was in no doubt that anything she had
achieved she owed to him. And now she had thrown
it all away. No, don't think of that. There were other
things to focus on now. She collected up some
coherent thoughts.

'It seems almost too simple. Like trying to dive
back into the past without facing up to what a fool
I've been. I know I could tackle this.' She nodded
past his shoulder to the ugly room. 'I could create a
little haven here rather like my own room in the
house, but without the horrors hovering in the
wings.' She could find a sort of peace here, she knew,
with that miraculous silence, which was never absolute silence, around her, and the beauty of the landscape she had always loved at her door. 'It could only
be a temporary breathing space, though, couldn't it?
And anyway, before I can even consider it as a
possibility, I have to tell Vanessa and Phil the truth.
I must get that over with. I can't believe I let them go
away not knowing, but there just seemed too much
to . . .'

She couldn't go on. It was going to be a long time,
she knew, before these waves of loss and realisation
would stop sweeping over her.

Hearing the desolate note creep back, Patrick
tested his own voice in his mind to make sure that

he could safely speak. 'It was too soon. There were too many other things to deal with. Don't worry about it. It won't make any difference in the long run, and Phil and Vanessa will understand. Why don't we stick to the practical objections for the moment, if there really are any.'

He saw the restless twist of her thin shoulders and, finding his hands lift involuntarily to take them in a steadying grip, checked the movement firmly. He thought, as detachedly as he could, that there had been a lot less wear and tear on the emotions when she had been on the other side of the Atlantic. That's my Jamie, an ironic inner voice commented.

'Practical things. Oh, I don't know, water, electricity, does the chimney work.'

'Don't be silly.'

'Patrick, you know perfectly well what I mean,' Jamie exclaimed, suddenly angry. 'Calder has to go. It's as good as on the market. How can I settle in here, knowing that? I already feel I'm holding up the process for my own selfish needs, and that's not fair to the others. To think of moving in here is a dream, clutching at straws. Calder is over for us. Phil and Vanessa recognise that, and I must too.'

Knowing her habit of direct dealing, Patrick could understand how much she disliked the false position she had put herself into by concealing the true facts behind her return. How must it feel to know that, if she couldn't stay here, she had nowhere else in the world to go? And how must it feel to be so abruptly without means after the high-flying years? It was obviously disorientating, for she seemed blind to much that was obvious.

'Right,' he said. 'Calder has to go on the market. But not necessarily the whole kit and caboodle. It could be sold in lots, remember. This house, for instance, could be taken out of the sale.'

Jamie stared at him, obviously struggling to read-just her thoughts. 'Goodness, I hadn't thought of that. It never occurred to me. I suppose I've always seen the place as an entity. Wouldn't splitting it up lessen its value though? And would anyone buy it if the cottage were – but what are we talking about? It couldn't happen anyway. You appear to have forgotten that I don't have a cent to my name.'

'Jamie, get your brain into gear. Admittedly the value of the house has been reduced by Zara's de-predations, but it's still highly desirable – substantial, well designed, in a magnificent position and with twenty acres or so of ground still belonging to it. The main rooms downstairs, in spite of looking a bit sad and tatty, are basically unspoiled, and it wouldn't be too difficult for someone to get the place into shape again. It will certainly sell, and I should think sell well. Have you entirely overlooked the fact that you will come in for a third of whatever it fetches? That you could, just for the sake of argument, buy this cottage from the others with your share of the pro-ceeds? It lends itself very conveniently to being a separate lot, since it faces away from everything, even the courtyard. As another option, you might sell the steading buildings separately too, for conversion. But even if you decide to live somewhere else,' he hoped he had kept out of his voice his dread of her vanishing again, 'at least you'll have some capital to start you off.'

Jamie was staring at him, her face pinched, its bones too prominent. 'I've been almost afraid to think of that,' she confessed. 'I know it sounds crazy, but right now I feel as though I can't count on anything. I've been having awful dreams, dreams where the house is in ruins, literally crumbling away. Finding that Zara has run through everything Father left, and even sold things which never belonged to her at all – I don't know, it made the whole lot seem like fool's gold, as though it would vanish at a touch.'

'I think I can understand that.'

'But it goes even deeper, Patrick.' She straightened up and turned to the window again, and he waited, not allowing himself to touch her. 'Don't you see, because I've messed up so badly myself, because I got everything so terribly wrong, I don't feel that I can trust in myself either.' She bowed her forehead against the dirty window-pane, hiding her face from him.

She didn't deserve this, Patrick thought, looking at the defeated curve of her shoulders. Whatever her faults, and he knew them all, she didn't deserve this.

But even as he thought it, she straightened her back with decisive firmness. 'God, how melodramatic I'm being.' She was even smiling as she swung round to face him again. 'Who could be luckier, really? To have everything I owned wiped out one week, and a chunk of a place like this tossed at my feet the next. Lucky, but dim with it, it has to be said, because it hadn't crossed my mind that any of it could be kept.'

'It's certainly a thought,' Patrick managed to say pragmatically, though he was almost more moved by her determination to be positive than he had been by the moment of bowed defeat. 'Why don't you talk to Vanessa and Phil as soon as you can, and see how they feel about it?' But not how Douglas feels, a warning bell rang. 'Even short-term, though, I can't see any reason why you shouldn't move in. You can collect up whatever you need from the house. And if there's anything I can't shift we'll call in Maeve, she's got muscles for six.'

Jamie laughed, as he had meant her to. The fun of making the move with Patrick and Maeve to help sent her spirits rocketing. 'What an idiot I am. Why didn't I think of all this for myself? I've been walking round in a fog. How could I have let anything Zara did get to me so badly? But to be honest, I'm still having trouble taking in the fact that that part of our lives, knowing she was here and hating the thought of it, is over.'

It was hardly surprising, Patrick thought, stringently keeping the compassion he felt out of his face. 'So, knowing you, you want it all to happen *now*, I suppose?'

'I do.' Jamie laughed, the sparkle back in her eyes. 'But I suppose before I actually move in it might be reasonable to consult the others.'

'Consult them? Tell them what you intend to do, I presume you mean.'

'Won't Vanessa flap?' Jamie said happily.

The years rolled back. For Patrick she was in an instant the provocative child who had the measure of both sisters to the finest degree, winding them up with an ease and joyous lack of compunction he had found hard to resist. He could see her now, dark hair hanging over her face, her clothes dragged on anyhow, her whip-thin body charged with vibrant energy. He had loved her courage, her reckless, no-holds-barred response to a challenge; he loved them still.

Turning his attention to a less personal aspect, he thought of warning her to go easy on Vanessa, but he could see no way to do so without provoking questions he was in no position to answer. Instead he said, 'Look, why not come down with me when I go back? I know Mother would love to see you. You could stay as long as you liked, either at Longmuir with her or with me, and then take the car and go on to see the others.'

He saw panic instantly rise, and saw her resist it. He hated to see this evidence of her new sense of insecurity, and once more anger at what Bryden Campbell had done to her burned in him.

'That sounds good. It's so kind of you, Patrick.'

Though he could have wished for a little less formality and a little more warmth, he was glad that she had agreed to his proposal.

'And I'm really grateful for the offer of the car.

You know that, don't you? But how soon do you need to go back? Are you very busy at present?'

'There's no hurry,' he said. The fact was, he shouldn't have been up at the Toll-house at all. The commission for the City Council was behindhand already, and the problems he had had in setting up the Inverness exhibition, where the space allocated to it in the library had been far from appropriate to its needs, had taken up far too much of his time.

But he knew he was ready to work night and day if necessary to catch up, if it meant giving Jamie the time she needed to muster her resources to face the world again.

15

It was extraordinary how, almost in a single step, the new Calder, suddenly alive with possibilities, overtook the old. The house Jamie remembered seemed nearly as remote as the other houses she had lived in as a child, and now she could accept that. Her eye was already getting used to the changes, and it was easier all the time to ignore them. Stairs were stairs; they couldn't be disguised with a slap of paint, or improved by a different carpet, so don't look. The kitchen, when all was said and done, was very much like the kitchens she had been accustomed to in recent years. The sense of a rescue operation being urgently needed, and one which she had no means of undertaking, faded, as did the less specific sense of uncomfortable presences hovering.

Doing the ordinary things that were part of life here, like going down with Patrick to shop in Aberfyle, helped to put things back into perspective. Jamie found the little town more huddled and shabby than she had remembered, its air of small-country-town prosperity lost in tacky propitiation to tourism, its resources unbelievably limited. But that, she accepted, was partly the contrast with the lifestyle she had so recently left behind. The more agreeable aspect was to find an unchanged, easy friendliness, so that a tenuous feeling of homecoming soothed the deep sense of disorientation which at present underlay everything.

On the way back they stopped at Mrs Niven's and, though the recollection of her reception at Freda's hands almost made Jamie turn tail at the door and fly for the safety of Patrick and the car, she was reassured to find that the courage to face a potential confrontation had not entirely deserted her. Though it was slightly chilling to be kept standing on the step, and Mrs Niven's pale eyes were watchful, she began by making it clear at once that there would be no change in existing arrangements over pay. With that out of the way, in spite of Mrs Niven's wariness turning to resentful hostility under her eyes (was she a chum of Freda's?), it had been easy to say that, since she would be at Calder herself for the time being, no caretaking was necessary, but that she would be in touch when Mrs Niven was needed again. She went into no details, but smiled serenely, as though taking it for granted that the good sense of this was obvious.

Mrs Niven, indignant and offended, was clearly searching for objections, but couldn't find any offhand. As Jamie picked her way along the concrete path, however, round rabbit hutch, abandoned garden hose, plant pots full of moss-covered mould and an old car seat with foam padding bulging from its cracked, sun-weathered plastic, she could feel the eyes on her back, watching through the crack of the door as if to make sure she left.

'I'm not always in, mind,' Mrs Niven rallied herself to shout after her, dimly feeling she shouldn't be picked up and put down just as this stepdaughter or whoever she was thought fit. Any day now she'd be off back to America anyway, so what business was it of hers?

'That's fine,' Jamie called back cheerfully. Mrs Niven slammed the door.

'Took the huff, as she would say,' Jamie reported to Patrick. 'I wasn't asked in. There's a surprise.'

Might there have been too many damning objects to be seen in the house, Patrick wondered, having spotted while he was waiting a handsome stone bird-bath he recognised, half-buried in the grass and nettles by the shed. He thought he wouldn't start that hare running – Jamie was all too likely to whip out of the car and launch into battle – but he might take up the matter with Eric Niven in his own time.

'Goodness, what a relief to know she won't be bringing that sniffy nose of hers into the house any more,' Jamie was saying. 'At least not when I'm there.' It felt as though one more piece of Zara had been satisfyingly eliminated.

'No doubt she'll take the money and find herself another job as well,' Patrick remarked.

'She's welcome.' Jamie dismissed the subject.

Back at Calder, they enjoyed a thorough trawl through the rejected furniture stored upstairs. With a use in view for it, and with Patrick there to heave aside wardrobes and armchairs and rolls of mice-chewed carpet, they could open drawers and get at cupboards, and several more relics were brought to light. To Jamie, in her new positive mood, every one was a treasure.

'It's a load of junk, Jamie,' Patrick protested, though in fact rather pleased to see that she was still capable of the well-remembered enthusiasm.

'How lofty and damning. Don't you know that bagatelle boards are fetching a huge price nowadays? And that pouffes are very much in fashion? Oh, and look, this is the rug that used to be in front of Grandmother's desk with the dog baskets on it.' She had begun to unroll a rug so faded that no pattern was discernible, and a smell which clearly told that it had been rolled up and tossed in here uncleaned rose on the dusty air.

Patrick, seeing her face alight with pleasure at this find, was besieged by memories so sharp that he had to turn away. How often in the past had Jamie's readiness to be swept away by enthusiasm been crushed by the indifference of others. How often he had seen the eagerness fade, to be replaced by a defiant determination to like what she liked and feel what she felt. Fortunately she had been too inherently optimistic to have learned the lesson, and here she was, still laying herself open to being put down, still ready to fight back from the most damaging disillusionment of all. Patrick smiled, though at the same time it made him wince to think of the contrast between this roomful of has-beens and the style in which he imagined she had been living in recent years.

'You think you'll be able to furnish your cottage, then?' he teased, more to lighten his mood than hers.

'Patrick, can't you just see it? Dear old battered friends like this will fit in so perfectly. All right, laugh if you like, but I think it's pretty lucky I'm happy with them, considering the state of my finances.'

She spoke matter-of-factly, and Patrick recognised with admiration that on this score at least she had already accepted the facts. The disintegration of a way of life which lay behind her bankrupt state would, no doubt, take a long, long time to come to terms with, if that were ever wholly possible, but this aspect she had faced and put aside. The only way from here was up, and up she would assuredly go.

They cooked dinner together once more, this time at Calder, but Patrick made sure that, whatever his own inclination, there was no talking into the small hours. He suggested again that Jamie slept at the Toll-house, not entirely happy to leave her on her own, but he wasn't surprised when she turned the invitation down.

'You'll be all right?' he couldn't help asking, when she came out to the car to say goodnight. I don't want to leave you, I want you under my wing. But perhaps she would sleep more soundly in the big house tonight.

And so she did, lulled by the promise of new prospects to turn to. But she barely had time to assemble them, or to worry about a stir of apprehension at the thought of telling Vanessa the truth, before tiredness caught up with her, and in the low, narrow and, to be truthful, lumpy bed, the windows open to the sound of the river and the call of a tawny owl hunting on the hill beyond, she slid into sleep.

'I hardly thought you'd be hustling me away so soon,' Patrick commented in mock protest. He spoke to break the silence between them, for Jamie had not said a word since they had left Calder after lunch.

'You said you had work waiting.' Jamie's voice was unexpectedly crisp, and he took a quick look at her. He knew her response was not prevarication; that was not her style. They were on their way to Longmuir because that was what she had chosen. But what fears, he wondered, were surfacing as she was carried further and further away from the place where she had begun to find, though perhaps not in the form she had foreseen, a safe base from which to make some new beginning.

'I do, yes,' he said without emphasis.

She said nothing, but gave a little nod, as though acknowledging her sharpness as out of order. It was clear that it was not a point engaging her mind, however. Patrick had guessed correctly. She was in the grip of fears whose strength had startled her. She felt as if she were right back at the beginning again, stunned and bruised, trying to bring her mind to bear on urgent practical issues, such as realising any financial resources left to her and organising her journey, while at the same time struggling to take in the news of Zara's death, with all its implications,

and the fact that she would find herself face to face
with Phil and Vanessa long before she was ready for
such a meeting. Now it seemed as though the shelter
she had found at Calder was being knocked away
before she could begin to trust in it. Well, it was her
own fault, she reminded herself angrily. She had
been, as usual, too impatient, unable to wait a day
longer to take the next step.

Her conversation with Maeve this morning didn't
make it any easier to leave Calder either. Maeve had
appeared at about eleven intending to mow, but
finding that the half-hearted sun still hadn't fully
burned off the dew, had gone instead to weed between the flagstones in the sitting-out place at the
end of the lawn. Seeing her there Jamie had taken out
coffee for them both, and had been unable to resist
sharing the idea of living in the cottage.

Maeve, as laid-back as ever about leaving work till
a better moment, had been happy to go with her and
have a look. It had been clear that, to her, no shortcomings were apparent. Jamie had had the impression that, water off and the dust of years
notwithstanding, if Maeve had been in her place
she would have moved in last night.

'Of course it may not happen,' Jamie had kept
reminding her – or reminding herself. 'The others
may not agree. There may be problems I haven't
thought of. And anyway, it wouldn't be for long.'

'It's a gem of a place, no question of that,' Maeve
had said warmly. 'There's a whole lot you could do to
it.' Her ideas went further than Jamie's, and were

infinitely tempting. 'It would be no trouble at all to take out that fireplace. Look, it's barely holding to the wall as it is.' She had whipped the screwdriver from the back pocket of her moleskins and begun to prise the tiles away from the wall there and then, very much in the manner of a workman whose investigations leave no alternative but to proceed with the job whether that had been the intention or not.

Jamie, laughing, had pulled her hand away. 'Don't tempt me! We can't do anything until I know whether the idea's feasible. Anyway, all I'd thought of doing was camping in here rather than staying in the house, which feels so – so ill at ease at present, neither one thing nor the other.'

'And there's far too much of it besides,' Maeve had said, not a person to let atmosphere or bad vibes worry her, and transferring her attention to the wall-paper. 'I didn't touch it, I swear to you! It was coming off by itself. It would be no trouble at all to have it down, though,' she had added longingly. 'And do you not see how easy it would be to knock those windows through again. They're only filled in with small stuff.'

'I suppose I should be thankful you only had a screwdriver with you and not a crowbar,' Jamie had mocked. But how enticing the images had been.

'Well, if it works out you'll be snug enough in here, that's for sure,' Maeve had commented with frank envy. 'Anything you want a hand with, let me know. It would be a nice change from gardens.'

'Maeve, would you really help? It would be such

fun.' Jamie, hearing the yearning note in her own voice, had there and then decided that she couldn't let another day go by without tackling the obstacles which lay between her and this desirable solution.

But to face people, to be asked questions, to find answers which struck the right compromise between honesty and searing revelations. More than that, to come to terms with her own new standing, to take on, almost, a new persona. Which led with scary swiftness to the question of who, in fact, she now was. It was too soon to be doing this, she protested violently. There had been too little time. She sat tense and rigid beside Patrick, longing to ask him to turn round and take her back.

Patrick had thoughts of his own to deal with. It had been a jolt to his settled and largely reclusive life to hear that Zara had died, and to know that Jamie would soon be back in the country. He had steeled himself to seeing her at Vanessa's or at his mother's, in glimpses which would necessarily be brief and at the social level he considered a waste of time. When he had learned that she was still at Calder, and planning to stay for some days, there had been no decision to make. While he let himself believe that he was making a realistic estimate of how he could make up time lost on what was after all a major commission, his limbs had ignored whatever his brain was saying.

He had been at the house for lunch, which was the time he generally phoned Naomi, and he had found himself without conscious decision going back across

the yard to the workshop, switching off the extractors, unplugging the air tools, not even pausing to
assess the work he had done that morning. He had
collected up some food and overnight things, phoned
his mother again to say that he would be away for a
couple of days (that had been the difficult part, for he
felt all the questions and surmise, unspoken as they
were, as an intrusion on his fiercely guarded privacy),
had shut up the house and headed north.

All he had hoped for was a few hours with Jamie, a
day or two, if he was lucky, with the easy coming and
going between the two houses back in place. He had
needed to seize this opportunity, after the depriva-
tion of the years, to re-establish if he could the
affectionate footing which was part of the shared
past, unmarred by the quarrels which had flared
every time they met before Jamie had left for the
States. He wanted, too, to discover whether the
feelings which had provoked those quarrels, on his
part at least, had been metamorphosed by time and
maturity to something less violent and painful.

They had not; that much had been clear the moment he saw Jamie coming up the path to the Toll-
house towards him. Patrick's heavy features tightened in a grimace of self-ridicule as he drove. Better
accept that those feelings would never change. But
apart from this discovery, which in his heart of hearts
he had known was inescapable, there was the new fact
that Jamie's life in America had fallen apart, and that
she was still in the process of crawling out of the
wreckage. Every atom of him wanted to help and

protect her. A powerful sexual and emotional need for her, too long suppressed, made him long to snatch the moment, move in when she was without defences, and let the future take its course.

But this was Jamie. This was the child, the girl, whom he had always tried to look after. This attitude towards her was too ingrained for him to think seriously of trading on any vulnerability. She saw him, it was only too clear, in precisely the same role as before – the family friend, the older brother or the father figure, it hardly mattered which, to be trusted and confided in, but never to be seen as a man, a mate, a lover.

And now even the couple of days he had envisaged, of mixed torture and delight, in the place they both loved so much, had been cut short. Just as well perhaps, he told himself, then swore silently, Oh, Christ, you don't have to be so fucking sensible about it.

Making a last-minute decision he turned to go through Pitlochry instead of taking the bypass.

Jamie stirred, coming out of her absorption as she realised he was heading into the town.

'Thought you might enjoy the road over the moor,' he said.

'Oh, Patrick, how lovely,' she exclaimed with pleasure. 'I much prefer coming this way, and it's such ages since I've been over here.' And taking this slower route would give her a little longer before she had to gather up her resolution to meet what lay ahead.

16

Jamie wasn't prepared for the piercing clarity of the memories of her grandmother which walking into Naomi's sitting-room brought back. The return to Calder, she supposed, had produced too many different sensations to call up the images with quite this intensity. Though the house at Longmuir was nothing like Calder, being a careful conversion of a pair of stone cottages into a comfortable modern dwelling, this room was so much of the style of Grandmother's generation – the well-cared-for furniture, the worn but beautiful rugs, the chintzy sofas with soft, fat cushions – that for a second it felt as though Grandmother might walk in on their heels.

She and Patrick's mother had been friends all their lives, had gone to the same parties as children, moved in the same circle when they came out and had, as they would remind each other occasionally when enjoying a bout of frivolous reminiscence, arranged between them who should have which husband.

Feeling oddly trembly, Jamie went to greet Naomi, the sight of her, shrunk and huddled in her straight-backed chair, not attempting to rise, adding another layer of poignancy to the moment.

'How lovely to see you.' The flaccid skin offered for her kiss, the faint scent of face powder and verbena, the touch of the silver hair, short now but still thick and densely wavy, against her cheek, added up to a brief, intimate and nostalgic contact which dangerously rocked Jamie's self-control. She could only smile, and fold the poor gnarled hands in hers for an instant,

'Darling Jamie, I had so much hoped I should see you before you left.' Smiling affectionately, Naomi was nevertheless scrutinising her with eyes that had lost none of their alertness. 'Though I don't suppose any of us feel much inclined to mourn Zara, I'm sorry it had to be such an event that brought you back.'

Was there a hint of reproach there? Naomi had always been the more outspoken of the two friends. Grandmother had been calm and placid, slow-moving and largely tolerant; Patrick's mother shrewder, expecting a little more of one, not slow to criticise.

These thoughts had to be pushed aside in the immediate need to sidestep questions with as much truth and as little detectable evasion as possible. Until she had had the chance to talk to Vanessa and Phil, Jamie had no intention of discussing her affairs with anyone but Patrick. There had been no need to say this to him. Close as he was to his mother, he had never allowed her to probe too deeply into his concerns, though Jamie suspected that she knew a lot more than her son intended her to see.

'I hope you'll be able to spare more time for us than merely coming to tea,' Naomi remarked, when

the trolley had been wheeled in, and Patrick was
pouring out. He filled three cups, though he knew his
mother would not risk the humiliation of struggling
to hold one, or to eat anything, while they were there.

'Of course I will,' Jamie said, and hurried on,
hating the feeling that so much had to be concealed,
'I'm sorry to turn up like this without giving you
proper warning, but I do hope to be back for a while
this time, so it would be lovely to come and see you
again. And I can't thank you enough for letting me
borrow the car. Are you sure—' She broke off, colour
rising in her cheeks. How could she say to this
woman so twisted with pain, who had once been
upright and brisk and active, gardening, walking her
dogs every day, playing golf twice a week, Are you
sure you won't be needing it?

'I'm delighted that the car will be used,' Naomi
said crisply, and it was clear that was all that she
wished to be said on the subject. 'You are to stay at
Vanessa's tonight, I gather.'

She had invited Jamie to stay with her when
Patrick had phoned to say they were coming. She
might not be very mobile, but she prided herself that
guests could still be looked after as before. In fact,
this pride had not been put to the test for some time,
and when Patrick had said that Jamie had already
arranged to go to Vanessa she had known in her heart
it was a relief. She had a small circle of friends within
easy reach, who gave each other light lunches
adapted to failing digestive systems, or tea in the
tradition of their generation, though most of the

baking and home-made jams remained untouched.
With these friends she would occasionally attend a
lecture on archaeology or local history, or appear at
some local charity event. More and more, however,
worries about getting in and out of cars, about steps
and stairs and disgracing herself in front of strangers,
would spoil these pleasures, though the pain of the
unaccustomed demands on mobility was endured in
silence.

Patrick had also assured Jamie that she was welcome to stay with him – sardonically noting the
conflicting emotions which flurried up in him at
the thought – but he hadn't been surprised when
she refused.

Jamie knew she had to get to Vanessa's with the
least possible delay, and seize her first chance to get
the difficult confession over.

Vanessa, when phoned at lunch-time, had as usual
hurried into a welter of plan and counter-plan.

'Oh, Jamie, of course I'd be delighted to have you
here. I didn't think you'd last very long up there on
your own. But what a nuisance this is the very
evening I'd promised Debbie I'd go round with some
cold-dye fix. She didn't realise she'd need it as well
when she bought the dye, though you might have
thought they'd tell her in the shop, it's no use without
it, but everything's so impersonal these days, nobody
cares about anything like that. She needs it for some
curtains, though I think they're fine as they are, to be
honest – I didn't say so, naturally – and I know she's
keen to get on with them because she has some

friends coming to – I know, I could call in on my way back from – no, no good, she won't be back by then. Never mind, look, I'll think of something. And please don't think it's any trouble to have you, you know I don't mean that. We're all looking forward to seeing you, and it's especially nice that Ryan's at home, it's ages since you saw him.'

What a drag, Jamie had thought. Her chief memory of her nephew was of a sullen thirteen-year-old at the time of his grandfather's funeral, resisting with glowering resentment his mother's constant prodding towards good manners and communication.

'He's nearly as tall as his father now. You'll hardly recognise him.' Vanessa had still been rattling on. 'Goodness knows what time Douglas will be in. He can hardly ever say, and to be fair I do see that if he commits to a time and then can't make it it's really worse. Anyway, don't worry about any of that, I can fly around this afternoon and see to everything. I always keep the guest rooms ready, because I never know when Douglas will bring people back. There's loads of stuff in the freezer, I always make sure of that. What time do you expect to be here? Though if you leave Longmuir just after tea you'll hit the very worst of the traffic, and that road is a nightmare these days . . .'

She was never going to say no, so why do we have to go through all this, Jamie had thought, but she had resisted cutting in. Other people went through the same process, revising plans, reviewing the options for feeding the unexpected guest, totting up the things to be done – but mostly they didn't do it aloud.

Do I want to go, she had wondered, with a sudden panicky idea that she might need the safety of Calder after braving Naomi's sharp appraisal. I'll have the car by then. I could come back and go down to Dunrossie another day. But until she had talked to Vanessa nothing could move forward; the momentary panic had died down.

Now, not enjoying being in an unfamiliar car on the busy road, once she had managed to get onto it, she was conscious of a faint unease which had nothing to do with what lay ahead. Naomi had been welcoming, there was no question of that. The interrogation Jamie had feared had in fact been little more than courteous questions about her general welfare, easily parried. It was clear that little outside the bounds of her own life, daily more circumscribed, held much interest for Naomi now, and though there was some relief in being let off, Jamie felt sad too.

It was Patrick, though he disliked small talk, who had kept the conversation going, deflecting any enquiries which he thought Jamie might not want to answer. Yet there had been something, a feeling in the air, a hint almost of disapproval. Jamie hoped she had imagined it. Perhaps it was nothing more than her own consciousness of concealing the truth. But the impression remained that Naomi had for some reason not been entirely pleased with her.

The thought of her visit to Freda came uncomfortably back, and Jamie was angry with herself for allowing the comparison to present itself. She felt rattled by driving on the left, and by the unexpected speed and volume of the traffic on a road she hadn't remembered as so busy, or so narrow. She tried to take in something of the landscape, but the dull sweep of farmland running down from featureless small hills to the firth had never appealed to her.

She minded parting from Patrick, she finally acknowledged. It had been so wonderful to have him appear at the Toll-house, to have him close at hand, to fall into their old companionable ease together. It had been so normal, in fact, that she had assumed, without thinking it out, that for as long as she was here contact with him would be as much part of everyday life as it used to be. Of course that was absurd. She was angry with herself for making the assumption. It was quite possible that Patrick wouldn't be in the glen again for weeks. She knew how busy he was, and he had told her that he was often away, either involved in setting up travelling exhibitions, or even attending symposia abroad, which not only sounded rather grand but suggested an impressive degree of success.

Passing the side road which ran as though laid down by a ruler up the swell of arable land to her right, she looked for the glimpse of the old steading of Blackdykes where he had his workshop. That was his world, in which he was absorbed, fulfilled and self-sufficient. He and she were two separate adults now, with separate lives. She pictured him turning, any time now, into that narrow road, plunging back into his own activities, all thoughts of her forgotten.

She felt very lonely suddenly, and it was a relief to be forced to concentrate on getting onto the right road for Dunrossie, since the traffic system around Perth had altered considerably since she had last come this way.

To her dismay, resistance built up at the mere sight of Vanessa's house. She really didn't need that just now, she thought with an attempt at humour. But the house spoke so clearly of Douglas, of Douglas's taste, Douglas's need to make a statement, Douglas's insistence on perfection, that it irritated her before she even turned into the drive. Perched on the south-facing slope overlooking the wide, and to her very dull, valley of the Earn, it seemed to have nothing to do with the traditional stone dwellings of the hamlet below it.

Its harling was cream and looked, as ever, as though it had been recently repainted. It was roofed with red pantiles, and its design, with two wings flanking a higher central block, was unScottish in a way that had always offended her. In your face, she thought with a curl of her lip as she headed up the hill. Once in the drive she found herself resenting the ordered colour of the garden, the perfection of the lawns, the white cast-iron tables and chairs on the terrace. Pulling herself together, she reminded herself that this was not a good frame of mind in which to approach this visit, which was an important one for her. But as she got out of the car she hoped very much that Douglas wouldn't be home yet.

She had forgotten Ryan. His smouldering presence hung like a miasma over the effusions of arrival and greeting. He was wearing baggy cargo trousers, a black T-shirt down to mid-thigh, and enormous orange logger boots.

'I thought you'd be off having a look at the world,' Jamie said, driven to a challenging and aunt-like greeting in response to his silent stare.

He grunted something unintelligible, and his eyes slid away from hers.

Vanessa rushed in, as she had always done when he was a child, at once trying to propitiate him and fend off Jamie. He had had such a marvellous plan, but at the last moment some wretched friend had let him down . . . really not wise to go alone, you never knew what might happen, nowhere's safe nowadays . . . he's looking for a job, and really no one could try harder . . .

Jamie didn't listen, feeling stifled already in the shining wastes of the well-tended house, choking on waves of polish and pot-pourri, at odds with the pale colours, the safe 'good taste'.

'Not that I don't want you here, darling,' Vanessa wound up gaily. Ryan, not me, Jamie concluded, seeing the tiny movement Vanessa's hand made as though it longed to touch his arm but didn't quite dare, her face smiling, her eyes anxious. Ryan, mouth turned down in contempt, turned his back on her and walked out.

'Poor boy, it's so frustrating for him. I do sympathise. All his plans fallen through. He's done his level best this year to get something organised, but there are so many restrictions and criteria, no one realises until they've actually tried.'

Jamie, following her up the smooth curve of the stairs (white paint and willow-green carpet), let the babbling wash over her. Light poured in from the big window facing across the strath, and gleamed back from the parquet floor of the wide landing, with its Chinese rugs, button-backed chairs covered in cream brocade, its cloisonné jars and overblown Coleman garden scenes. The 'guest wing' corridor was muffled in thick soft carpets and long velvet curtains. In the too-warm bedroom, and the luxurious bath-room with its champagne-coloured fittings, no detail had been overlooked. Satin-covered hangers in the wardrobe, lavender sachets dangling from each one, embroidered Victorian housewife ready for urgent running repairs, coloured balls of cotton-wool (Jamie had to think for a moment to recall the word) in a cut-glass jar, fluffy towels scaled to every need, scented soap for shower, basin, bath and bidet – Jamie felt as though she'd arrived in a hotel where the house-keeper had just finished making her inspection.

Oh, Vanessa, what's happened to you?

But on the talk flowed, sister welcoming sister, and Jamie, oppressed by these surroundings as she was, was grateful for that welcome, conscious of an ache that could be a growing awareness of being adrift and alone, or even a rare longing to cry.

'Goodness, look at the time. I must run down and give Ryan something to eat,' Vanessa interrupted herself to say, looking at her watch. 'And then I promised I'd take him down to catch the bus. It's so awkward for him stuck away out here. He hates the bus, and I do agree that the times aren't at all convenient, but it would mean leaving you on your own for too long if I ran him into Perth.'

Which clearly Ryan had demanded, and was just as clearly a service he normally received. Jamie didn't pick up her cue to say, Don't worry about me. What was wrong with a bus?

But Vanessa, it appeared, hadn't been worrying about leaving Jamie alone. 'I don't think Douglas could possibly be back yet,' she said, as if to herself, looking at her watch again, and then out of the window.

Jamie looked at her quickly, caught by something in the tone she didn't like. Had there been rows about Vanessa doing too much chauffering for Ryan? If so, Jamie felt Douglas probably had some right on his side.

'It's only down to the end of the road. No distance at all.' Vanessa seemed to be reassuring herself. Jamie thought if it was no distance at all Ryan could walk, but outspoken sister had not yet overtaken well-behaved guest.

It was good to feel the silence spread through the house when the car had left, giving Jamie a brief breathing space which she felt she needed. Going downstairs, she prowled the quiet rooms with the objective interest of a stranger, finding that, exactly as she remembered, they held her at a distance with their self-conscious perfection. No sign that Ryan had just had supper was visible in the kitchen. Unsympathetic to him as she was, Jamie hoped for his sake that he had some retreat where he could put his feet on the furniture and strew his gear around.

A car came round to the three garages with automatic up-and-over doors at the end of the house. Vanessa, guilt and defensiveness fighting it out as she hurried back? Or Douglas?

Jamie was slightly surprised to find herself squaring up to the prospect of meeting her brother-in-law, her affable, sociable, good-looking and popular brother-in-law.

17

It was Vanessa who came hurrying in. Her spirits had noticeably lifted now that she didn't have Ryan to worry about, and she seemed to have decided she had not been giving Jamie the attention due to a guest, and especially due to a sister who had been absent for so long.

'How nice to have a little time to ourselves,' she said, though with an involuntary glance at the clock. 'Have you been making yourself at home? Is everything all right in your room? You will say if there's anything you need, won't you?'

Yes, some unscented air, and perhaps a paw-mark or two on the carpet. 'Everything's perfect, thanks. You know it is.'

Vanessa flushed with pleasure and Jamie, who had only just resisted speaking impatiently, wondered how often she received any praise. If your life work was rubbing up your house to a high polish, you might like an occasional acknowledgement of your efforts. How many people came here? There was an odd sense of isolation about the house, not just because of its position on the open hillside, or the fact that architecturally it blended with nothing around it, but because it seemed to give no sign of human life being lived inside it. Jamie had always had the impression that Vanessa had a busy social life, and knew she did a lot of entertaining but, thinking back over their conversations while they were at Calder, she thought there had been few references to friends.

'I'll get the trout and the potatoes into the oven,' Vanessa said, again with that glance at the clock which seemed to be compulsive. 'They can take care of themselves, and we can sit down and have a drink.'

Jamie, who had thought for a moment she was going to say 'a nice little chat', asked if there was anything she could do to help.

'Absolutely not, I won't hear of it, you're here to be looked after. It's time you had a holiday. You're not looking well at all, you know, Jamie, and if you don't mind my saying so, in my opinion you're far too thin, although I know you'll insist you're not. I'm not going to let you do a single thing while you're here. In any case, everything's more or less ready. I shall only have to put the vegetables on when Douglas arrives, and do the sauce at the last minute. The fish –' a hefty salmon trout, which lay neatly parcelled in foil on a baking tray, with four large potatoes, lightly greased and pricked, waiting beside it '– is supposed to have twenty minutes to the pound, but wrapped up like this the timing isn't too critical. I always try to plan something that can hang about without getting spoiled. I've made a cold pud, so there won't be too much bobbing up and down. Douglas always hates that when we have a guest.'

'No, thanks,' would have done, Jamie thought, but without malice. She hadn't been here long enough for Vanessa's burbling to have got to her yet. Anyway, it looked as though whatever talking they did until Douglas appeared would remain on a domestic level. Until dinner was safely over Vanessa's mind would be more occupied by what was happening in the kitchen than by any news Jamie could offer. Well, that was fine by her.

It struck her, watching Vanessa arrange the potatoes to her satisfaction on the oven shelf (one originally intended for Ryan, or two for Douglas because he was a man?), that the feeling of closeness, of the bond of the past being indestructible, which had been so much in evidence when the three of them met on the day of the funeral, would not return here.

Did she feel that because the atmosphere of the house seemed so unrelaxed, or because her motive for having come, and all that lay behind it, was as yet undisclosed and weighing on her uncomfortably? Or was it that here, in her own house, Vanessa's primary role was not that of elder sister, but of wife and mother? Jamie could still remember the bleak, disbelieving moment when she had first recognised that shift of focus, and her anger at herself for having allowed such a natural piece of moving on, of growing up, to take her by surprise.

But, studying Vanessa as they settled in the sitting-room with its windows opening onto the terrace, its empty stretches of light carpet, its flowers and Chelsea pieces and well-placed lamps, sipping dry sherry from fragile engraved glasses, Jamie realised there was more to this feeling of constraint. There was a tension in Vanessa which she had not noticed before, even during the stressful day in Glasgow. There was a drawn look about her mouth, something in her eyes which Jamie couldn't define but didn't like, and an incapacity to sit still for two minutes together which soon became maddening. Strange too that she hadn't noticed before how much older Vanessa was looking, as though she relied too much on make-up and careful grooming. Did she colour her hair, Jamie wondered, rather jolted to think any of them could have reached that stage. It looked just as it always had, but perhaps by now it should have faded a little. She felt a quick protectiveness for her elder sister, whose preoccupation with appearances and endless worrying made her too easy a target for teasing.

Douglas appeared at ten to nine. No suggestion had been made that they should start dinner without him or, Jamie felt sure, would have been made if he hadn't turned up for another hour. She was left in no doubt that the whole production was for him, because of him, and planned with the desire to please him.

He came in with his firm step, stooping to brush Vanessa's cheek with his lips as she hurried to greet him, allowing her to take his briefcase and dispose of it while he strode across the room with arms wide to take Jamie's shoulders in a firm grip, kissing her warmly on both cheeks. The same old charm, she registered with interest, worked on her at once, as smoothly and effectively as it always had. He looked and sounded genuinely pleased to see her, and it was hard to resist. He was a big man who carried himself well. He had a look of positive enjoyment in life, and a determination for others to share that enjoyment which swept one along. Whatever reservations Jamie might have about him when he wasn't there, his presence produced a real and instant warmth. He was heavier than she remembered, his firm cheeks, with the scraped look of having been recently shaved which some men seem to preserve all day, noticeably more fleshy. He was immaculately dressed, as always, in the expensive and well-cut uniform of those men who drive the world along by means of their power, energy, money and never-appeased appetite for success.

There was no reference to having kept Jamie and Vanessa waiting, and no suggestion that Douglas would do anything but take as much time as he liked when he disappeared to wash up. Tidy up, Jamie corrected herself. Did that mean have a shower, change? If that suited him, it clearly would. And it was equally clear that to Vanessa waiting for Douglas was right and fitting. Jamie felt, almost, as if the house itself had been waiting, its real function on hold until he was there to take charge again. For the first time, as Douglas returned, a red cashmere sweater in which he looked very good indeed replacing jacket and tie, she could feel it was a home.

There was one moment when bonhomie seemed to slip, as she became aware of a tense low-voiced exchange between Douglas and Vanessa, together by the drinks table at the far side of the room. Vanessa seemed to be explaining, placating. Douglas questioning Ryan's absence, Jamie surmised, not paying much attention. But there was unmistakable anger in the jut of Douglas's head, even in the pitch of his voice, controlled as it was, and Vanessa's cheeks were pink as she stood for a moment longer by the well-furnished table, while he turned away, the drink she had mixed for him in his hand, and came to sit down, his smile back in place for Jamie.

The atmosphere relaxed again at once, Douglas settling into a big chair which comfortably accommodated his big body, while his big voice flowed easily from a couple of token questions about Jamie's affairs into the joke about yet another government U-turn which had been going the rounds today, his dominating presence giving the room a focus it had lacked till now. There was a sense of things falling into place, things happening. Vanessa trotted back and forth, refilling Jamie's glass, bringing in warm cheese straws (which she had made), vanishing to put the broccoli on, returning to ask the right questions about Douglas's day. Ministering, Jamie thought, her lip faintly curling. But she knew that disparaging her sister's officious care was a way to suppress the pang of remembering – remembering herself and Bryden, such an incredibly short time ago, together in the apartment at just this moment of the day, unwinding, off-loading frustrations, sharing jokes, moving easily around each other in an accustomed pattern. A pattern she had imagined would . . .

Douglas, Jamie observed, wresting her thoughts forcibly away, allowed Vanessa's questions to flitter past him like moths, harmless, not worth his attention. Vanessa, on the other hand, apparently accepted that none of them would be answered or that, if on this occasion they were, then the replies would be directed towards Jamie, and seemed content to busy herself in little-wife-waiting-all-day-at-home mode.

Why does that still infuriate me so much, Jamie wondered, watching the performance unroll. It must suit them both or they wouldn't do it. Vanessa had never made any bones about the fact that she was grateful never to have to work, never to have to think about money, or hesitate about what she spent on Ryan, the house and herself. She saw it as natural and reasonable that if Douglas was prepared to provide this, then her job was to run his house, keep the domestic wheels efficiently turning, and nurture him in any way he required.

And yet, if this was what they both chose, and after all it was the way they had lived for over twenty years, why was there this brittleness in the air, as though at any moment one or other might forget their lines and the whole thing would fall apart? There was nothing that Jamie could put her finger on but, in spite of protests from both host and hostess, she insisted on going to help Vanessa as Douglas sank his second enormous gin-and-tonic, and crunch time arrived in

the kitchen. It was the second impulse of protectiveness she had felt for Vanessa today, and she mocked
herself for being silly enough to get caught up in the
hassle, as Vanessa got tense about opening up the
packet of trout, pouring off the juices to make the
sauce, removing the skin and slicing along the bone in
the correct manner to lift away the moist, delicately
lemon-flavoured flesh. At the same time vegetables
had to be strained, a cross cut in each baked potato
(only one knife was right for the job), the sides
squeezed and ready-cut chunks of butter added,
and the perfectly chilled Sauvignon had to be opened.
Jamie thought Douglas could have done that.

As they sat at the oval dining table, food hot and
beautifully served, silver polished, glasses gleaming,
flowers arranged in what could only be called a table
decoration, conversation was effortlessly resumed. It
was, to be honest, unlikely to dry up with Douglas
and Jamie present, and though there were moments
when his questions about her business affairs were
too searching, and she wasn't sure that her generalised remarks on a subject in which, until only days
ago, she had been closely involved, satisfied him, he
gave no sign of noticing anything unusual. Neither,
which was even more of a relief, did he make any
direct reference to plans for Calder. They talked
about the house, naturally, about Zara's depredations
and the revelations about Hal Laidlaw's will, but
though Vanessa's eyes more than once went anxiously to Douglas's face, and she gave little attention
to what she was eating, the question of what Jamie

intended to do was not raised. She had the impression that some agreement had been reached that it shouldn't be, as though this first evening was set aside for a reunion with a long-absent family member, and she was grateful for that.

There was little, later, that she could identify as the source of the unease which she carried with her to bed. There had been the brief exchange when Douglas came down to join them for drinks, but surely that had been no more than a standard marital spat, almost certainly about Ryan – who, now Jamie came to think of it, had never reappeared. How would he get back, how late would he be? Would that cause trouble? He hadn't been mentioned much during the evening, except for Vanessa rehearsing once more the list of universities waiting to welcome him with open arms, though she seemed to keep a doubtful eye on Douglas as she did so, as if ready to stop at the first warning sign. Jamie hadn't listened with much interest. It sounded pretty much pie in the sky to her. It occurred to her now that if there were any family rows when Ryan got back she was unlikely to hear them, for the family rooms were in the other wing.

But there had been one disturbing moment which she had been trying not to think about, and as it surfaced in her mind she felt once more the discomfort she had experienced at witnessing it. It had happened during dinner. Vanessa, rather than ask Jamie to pass the shrimp sauce to Douglas, who had wanted more, had jumped up and taken it to him, standing at his shoulder to serve him.

Idiot, Jamie had thought with lazy tolerance, savouring her wine with pleasure. Typical Vanessa, always over-egging everything.

A tiny exclamation had made her glance up. Not even an exclamation: a breath indrawn. A fleck of sauce had landed on Douglas's trousers. It was unlike careful, neat-handed Vanessa to be so clumsy, and after a moment of dismay she had rushed into apologies. She had rattled the sauce boat down on the table so hastily that Jamie had thought it lucky the ladle didn't bounce out and spatter sauce far and wide, and with incoherent apologies had rushed off to fetch a damp cloth.

What had been strange, however, and Jamie still couldn't decide precisely why it had struck her like that, had been Douglas's reaction. He had leaned back from the table, arms raised out of harm's way, and had looked up at Vanessa's horrified face with a strange intensity, his own flushing darkly. He had said nothing, and it was that silence, that waiting stillness, combined with his evident anger, which had made Jamie feel so oddly uncomfortable. That, and the way in which he had stayed as he was, not moving, until Vanessa hurried back and with small contrite sounds began carefully to wipe the sauce away. Was it this waiting to be tended, making no effort to deal with the trivial accident himself, or the humility of Vanessa's pose, bending over him, dabbing at his thigh, dismayed, that had left this feeling of distaste? Or was it Douglas's smile to Jamie herself, as he got his anger under control, eyebrows raised in exaggerated resignation, suggesting the stock joke, You just can't get the staff nowadays.

Then the moment had passed and dinner had proceeded. One tiny hiatus in an otherwise efficient operation, yet Jamie found she couldn't get it out of her mind.

She didn't know how long she had been asleep when some sound woke her. After a struggling moment as she worked out where she was, she listened to it again in her mind. A car? It must have been. Had someone had to fetch Ryan?

She pushed the question away; none of her business. But as she began to slip back into sleep the image that persisted, a muddled image which seemed more like part of a disturbed dream from which she had barely emerged than an actual memory, was the picture of Vanessa dabbing so anxiously at Douglas's thigh. And now the sexual connotation which had lurked there all along, but which Jamie had refused to recognise, was clear. The male leaning back, passive, to receive the attentions of the subservient female. Vanessa's bright, bent head, lower now in this distorted image of half-dream, and in Douglas's face, smiling above her at Jamie, a complacent, sated arrogance.

'That's horrible!' Jamie flumped over onto her other side to dislodge the ugly inference, trying to focus her mind on relaxing each limb in turn, hoping that if she could hold thought at bay, dismissing this as part of her dreams and therefore harmless, she

would drift off again into sleep. Other impressions of
the evening swam back, however, refusing to be
ignored, all clouded with that same sense of unease,
merging into a strong dislike of being in this house,
feeling its elaborate comfort closing in on her, warm,
scented and smothering.

Suddenly Jamie couldn't bear to be alone in the
strange bed. She passionately wanted Bryden's hard
fit body beside her. Her body ached for his, for his
arms, his hands, his lips. She wanted wanting, release
and assuagement.

Then confusedly she found herself longing to spill
out to Patrick this agony of loneliness which could
rush upon her so unbearably. She needed to tell
Patrick too about that small, disturbing incident this
evening. It was a fundamental need to tell, not to feel
so absolutely alone, and Patrick was the only person
in the world to whom anything and everything could
be told.

The thoughts ebbed and flowed, formless, sliding
away from her. Bryden, pain and rejection, longing
and desire. Douglas, smiling, watching. Vanessa
contrite and hurrying. Patrick, her rock . . .

When Jamie woke to find Vanessa beside her bed,
crisp and fresh in a soft blue-and-white striped skirt
and white top, a tray in her hands with teapot, milk
and lemon, cup and saucer, the images of the night
hovered in one dissolving memory and were gone.
They were unthinkable in the bright light as Vanessa
drew back the curtains, unthinkable at the sight of

Vanessa, brisk and wholesome, in the sense of well-being she brought with her, in the scent of herbs which the warmth of the teapot released from the quilted tea cosy (who else in the world still used a tea cosy?), in the fragrance of Earl Grey.

'I just crept in. I'd have let you go on sleeping if you hadn't heard me.'

And made fresh tea half an hour later and tried again, tireless in her wish to tend and cosset.

'Did you sleep well?'

It seemed to Jamie now that she had, those blurred moments more part of sleep than waking. 'Very well, thanks. Though did I hear a car at some point?'

'Oh, only a taxi. Ryan coming home.'

Vanessa turned away, automatically starting to tidy the clothes Jamie had tossed across a chair last night. Pretty pointless, Jamie thought, but said nothing, because for one second as Vanessa turned away something in her face revealed that for some reason the taxi had been bad news. The unforgiving morning light showed lines in her face and a strained look about her eyes which Jamie would rather not have seen.

'So, where's the morning up to?' she enquired, deliberately casual, closing her eyes to honour the first sip of scalding tea, then putting the cup down so that she could dispose her pillows more comfortably behind her. 'Who's up, who's down? Got any plans?'

Vanessa clutched at these enquiries gratefully. 'Well, Douglas has gone, of course. I gave him his breakfast at six-thirty. He's generally off early, and this morning he had an important meeting.'

When would he have an unimportant meeting?

'Ryan hasn't surfaced yet –' also of course '– so I was thinking, how would you like to have a tray up here, and be really lazy for once? Then when I've given Ryan his breakfast, though goodness knows what time he'll appear, because he was quite late last night – he thought a friend would bring him back, that had been the plan. I knew that when I took him to the bus, but then the friend let him down and he had trouble finding a taxi. It really is impossible at that time of night. Well, anyway,' Vanessa started again, having lost the thread, 'I thought we could go into Perth and have a little prowl round and then have lunch somewhere. It's probably changed a lot since you were last there. Ryan may want to go in, in which case he could come with us, but he'll have to make his own way back, I'd be quite adamant about that. Or we could walk this morning, and have lunch here, if you'd prefer it, only then I might just have to pop into Perth with Ryan anyway. Pauline, who helps in the house, doesn't come today so there are one or two things I have to do, but after that I've no plans at all, so you can decide. Whatever you like.'

Jamie, conscious that she had landed on Vanessa at short notice to suit her own needs, and remembering of old how seriously the morning chores were taken, every day, no matter what, decided that the most helpful thing was to keep out of the way. She disliked breakfast in bed. In fact breakfast was pretty much of a non-event for her, and she usually grabbed something at the office if she bothered at all. But she knew

Vanessa's need to feel that she was looking after her guest (in this case her overworked sister, who had never known how to take care of herself properly), so breakfast in bed it would be. And after that whatever was asked of her in the way of working round Ryan's needs, and if possible keeping her mouth shut about it.

Then, at some point in the day, when there was time and opportunity before some demand of husband or son absorbed Vanessa's attention, she must tackle the subject of the future, and the explanations indivisible from it, about what she must now accept as the past.

18

'Move into Freda's old cottage? But Jamie, you can't possibly do that.'

Vanessa's voice was startled, but there was more than surprise in the way she received the idea. There was a dismay so strong that it sounded almost like fear.

Jamie frowned in quick exasperation. What on earth was there to get so excited about? What was the big deal? Vanessa's capacity to find a drawback in everything was getting to be an obsession. But she knew the impatience merely cloaked her own reluctance to embark on the disclosures which could no longer be avoided.

'Why do you always rush to say no to everything? Why don't you give yourself time to think?' she demanded, her good intentions about taking this slowly forgotten in the face of Vanessa's instant objection. 'Whatever's going to happen about Calder, how can it make any difference whether I'm in the big house or in the cottage?'

'But it hasn't been lived in for years, it will be damp and dirty and horrible. There'll be no water, the pipes might have burst . . .' Vanessa was so clearly clutching at straws that Jamie's irritation blazed up, and she conveniently forgot that she had raised identical objections to Patrick.

'Vanessa, if we're going to talk about this, at least let it be on a sensible level. None of those things matter. They can all be sorted out. Can't you ever think of anything but goddam cleaning?' Seeing the hurt look in Vanessa's eyes she made a sound of wordless vexation and, closing her eyes, laid her head for a moment on her arms, folded along the top of the gate where they had paused in their walk to lean. Getting her anger in hand with an effort, she straightened up to look with disfavour across a dull field to an equally dull hill, as she searched for a way to start again which would not have Vanessa leaping down her throat before five words were out. She knew that her dislike for this placid landscape, which was in fact looking its best in fresh spring colours under pleasant sunshine, was exaggerated. Certainly road and railway dominated the broad valley at their backs, and the hamlet of Dunrossie was little more than a single characterless street of Scottish domestic architecture at its worst, but she knew her rejection of the scene had more to do with associations and atmosphere than with any special lack of beauty. And on this visit, perhaps because she hadn't been here for some time, these negative feelings seemed intensified.

Bad conscience was probably at the bottom of it, she was honest enough to recognise. For though she had got as far as introducing the subject of the cottage, she was still evading the bigger and more painful issues which had to be addressed.

'Look, Vanessa, I'm sorry. I shouldn't have bitten your head off like that. Forget about Freda's cottage for the moment—'

'I expect it would be all right really,' Vanessa rushed in, appeased at once by the apology and ready to abandon protests if this was what Jamie really wanted. 'We could probably make it habitable. I mean, if you're there for a few days while you're making up your mind it can't make any difference to anything, as you say. Only it does seem a lot of work, if it's not to be for long, and I don't see quite why you want to do it. But I expect I could manage to come up and help you with the cleaning and so on, if that would be any use, though perhaps it would be better if I didn't stay the night. I wonder if any furniture was left in it? I can't remember. But we could easily take things across from the house. The gardener could help with anything heavy.'

For a second the image of Maeve warmed Jamie, a source of pleasure still private to her, but this was not the moment to share it with Vanessa, accurate as her comment had been.

'Or if Phil came up as well,' Vanessa was pursuing, 'we'd probably be able to manage between the three of us. She's so used to lifting, in her job. I wonder if she could get some time off, that can be a problem for—'

'Vanessa, *please*.' Jamie made a fierce effort to hold down her temper. 'Please, please be quiet for a second. All that can be sorted out in due course. But first there's something you have to know. I should have told you before, only – well, it was just too difficult to talk about.'

She knew she wasn't prepared for it even now, her brain refusing to shape the sentences to recount the débâcle. This isn't the place to talk, she thought almost wildly, here in this narrow road with cars and farm vehicles passing at our heels, in this featureless landscape, so different from Glen Fallan, which gives no comfort. She had thought that away from the house they would be safe from interruptions, from the telephone, from Ryan's needs, from Vanessa's compulsive activity. Now she saw that she should have waited till they were back, having tea, anchored in one spot however briefly.

'But Jamie, whatever it is, I'm sure—' Vanessa began from sheer habit. 'No, no, sorry, I won't say another word, I promise,' she promised hastily, quelled by the look of anger which Jamie turned on her. She waited anxiously, alarmed at what might be coming, not knowing how to offer comfort without words.

There was one tense second while she against every instinct kept silent, and Jamie struggled with a desperate reluctance to begin, knowing that to do so would open the sluice-gates to torrents of concern, questions and, ultimately, decisions. It was like taking a step into the next phase of her life, with no going back possible; and very bleak and uninviting the prospect looked.

'I should have told you before,' she said at last, her voice hurried and muffled. 'You and Phil both, when we were at Calder. But to be perfectly honest, I didn't have the guts.' Her eyes travelled over the empty rectangle of grass before them; nothing there to catch the attention; nothing to help her. 'I'm broke, washed up, the business has gone bust. Everything's sold, the apartment, the lot. And Calder will have to go too. I'm no more able to buy you and Phil out than fly to the moon.'

She would be grateful to Vanessa forever afterwards that, now the agonising moment of confession had come, there was no outburst of consternation and questioning, not even a breath of recrimination about having concealed all this till now. There was only, the years swinging back, instant and loving comfort, Vanessa's arms going round her, Vanessa's voice soothing, 'Oh, Jamie, no! Poor baby, how dreadful for you. How truly dreadful. Everything you've worked so hard for. I'm not surprised you couldn't talk about it. Of course we had no idea. But it will be all right. Everything will be all right . . .'

In her bath before dinner, choosing that rather than her customary shower in a deliberate effort to relax, Jamie was thankful that, in accordance with a habit going back to student days, she had told Phil and Vanessa almost nothing about Bryden. At least today she had been spared the necessity of telling once more the shaming tale of her blind gullibility. Patrick knew, and that comforted her, but no one else need know. She could cope with being seen to have failed in her business enterprise; it was something she didn't have to explain or defend. She had flown too high and she'd crashed. It happened. But the pain of naïve loving, of happiness and trust betrayed, that she could keep to herself.

They had fallen inevitably into a welter of question and explanation as Vanessa began to take in the implications of Jamie's news. They had walked and talked – Jamie almost amused to find that soon she was the one trying to tone down the drama – and had come home for tea and talked some more. Then Vanessa, who for once had forgotten to keep an eye on the clock, had begun an anxious scramble to get dinner going. Though before long, with some half-heard excuses and a defiant air, neither of which Jamie felt had anything to do with her, she had abandoned her preparations to go and collect Ryan from some point unspecified. It appeared that an ultimatum had been delivered by Douglas, and that Ryan was on parade for dinner tonight. Had Vanessa also received orders about not ferrying him about so much, and was she risking Douglas's wrath by disobeying them?

The next question which would have to be discussed, Jamie knew, was what must be done about Calder. It would have to be sold, there was no way round that, but should it be put in order first? A few thousand spent on it now would unquestionably mean a better selling price; and would delay the day when it would vanish from Laidlaw hands for ever. Moreover it would give her a valid excuse to stay there, overseeing the work. But she mustn't let that sway her, and the views of the others must be taken into account. But, thinking of Calder, the reality of it, the beloved place, Jamie found it hard to keep her mind on cold financial considerations. Its image rose before her, slumbering through quiet afternoons with the sun on its face, the great beeches and sycamores standing well back from the lawn which swept down to the little bluff, the shining coil of the river below. She felt a violent longing to be there, now, away from the subtly cloying atmosphere of this house. She let her thoughts drift, seeing the cottage on the river bank, the straggle of untrimmed roses nearly obliterating its lower windows, the peeling paint of its green door. How good it would be to let in some light. She lay, her eyes closed, on the edge of sleep, sunlit images of contented solitary days there flickering behind her lids, the roses reduced to order and loaded with blooms, the door standing open, the rooms freshly decorated and furnished with old friends, the steady rush of the waterfall soothing music in the background.

Then a less soothing thought surfaced. Vanessa seemed too ready to take it for granted that Douglas would have a say in what was decided. Or, indeed, would have the final word. Several times as they had talked this afternoon she had said, 'Of course I'll have to see what Douglas thinks,' or, 'I'm sure Douglas will want to get things moving as quickly as possible . . .'

When Jamie had asked what it had to do with him, Vanessa had said quickly, flushing, 'But of course it concerns him. Anything that's mine is his as well. I couldn't make any decision without consulting him. I wouldn't dream of it.'

'Your share of Calder belongs to you,' Jamie had argued sharply, partly out of a jealous sense of family ownership for a place that meant so much to her, but also with a little stir of foreboding.

'Well, not really. Everything we own we own jointly. That's how we like it to be. You've never been married, Jamie, so you don't understand that, but it's the usual way that things are done, I assure you.'

Typical Vanessa comment, earnest, reasonable, and totally unaware that anyone might mind anything she said, Jamie thought resignedly, hauling herself up and leaning forward to let the water run out. She had let it get too cool to be comfortable, and she felt ruffled and apprehensive about the evening ahead. If Douglas, as Vanessa said, thought the only answer to the question of Calder was a swift sale, take the cash and forget it, she foresaw a fight on her hands if she wanted to hang onto her retreat even for a few weeks. And then what?

As she padded through to the bedroom her face was grim. Last night Douglas had been all charm towards her. There had even been a sneaking flattery in the inference, which she remembered of old, that it was a pleasure to have a woman in the house with whom it was possible to hold an intelligent conversation, share a joke without being snared in laborious explanations, and generally meet him on his own level. Now she saw how unkind to Vanessa it was, on her part too, to have responded, and she resolved that this evening she wouldn't let him play that game.

She wouldn't let him decide the fate of Calder either. It wasn't up to him. It wasn't only up to her and Vanessa either, come to that. How easy it was to forget poor old Phil, or at least assume she would be ready to fall in with whatever they decided. In the past it had been a case of the two elders dragging along in their wake the bumbling under-confident sibling. Perhaps now, Jamie thought with irony, since Phil was thirty-four years old, they should regard her as a responsible adult with views of her own. Hold on, no, not Phil! Sisterly habit was too strong. Jamie was grinning as she began to dress.

But when Douglas came in, earlier tonight, so that Vanessa, hearing the car, flew into a panic about dinner, and when the ritual of greeting and taking his briefcase to put in the study for him had been enacted and Douglas had gone upstairs, Vanessa came back to the kitchen with a strained look on her face which, for all her flapping about not having everything ready, had not been there before.

'Jamie, I was just thinking,' she began, with such a false note of cheerfulness in her voice that Jamie looked up in surprise from the courgettes she was slicing.

'What?'

'Would you mind very much – I mean, I know it

must seem rather strange when I've been saying how much Douglas wants the whole thing about Calder sorted out – but I think he's had rather a difficult day, so perhaps it would be better after all if we talked about it another time. Would you mind very much? And especially this idea of your staying in the cottage. Not that it can make any difference, I do see that, but he may think . . . And then this news about your business and everything, it may not be the best time. Tomorrow evening might be better. In any case, now I come to think of it, it wouldn't be a good idea to have any serious discussions tonight, would it, with Ryan here?'

Ryan's presence off was marked by the sounds of an electric keyboard, sounds which had become markedly less intrusive since Douglas's return.

'It would be quite awkward, in fact,' Vanessa fretted on. 'I know Douglas insisted he should be in for once, and I do see that it's more courteous to you, but at the moment they are so much on each other's nerves that I can hardly—' She pulled herself up. 'Oh, well, it's natural, isn't it? Father and son. It will resolve itself once Ryan's at university, I'm sure. Or if he got a job this summer, though there really isn't anything for him round here, he's not making it up—'

'Hey, what's all this about?' Jamie abandoned the courgettes and went across to where Vanessa had come to a halt in front of the double ovens, apparently at random, since she was doing nothing. Jamie's voice was gentle, but Vanessa swung round with quick defensiveness.

'What do you mean? It's not about anything. I'm just trying to suggest that we give Douglas a bit of space this evening. That's not unreasonable, surely? You don't realise, he's been under a lot of pressure lately.'

She seemed to become aware that she was speaking too forcefully, and took some trouble to make her voice calmer as she ended. But Jamie had the impression even so that her attention was elsewhere. She almost seemed to be listening, as dogs are capable of doing, to something beyond the immediate sounds around her.

Had Douglas told her about a new crisis? Had today's meeting had some outcome which would adversely affect them?

In fact, Douglas was drunk. Jamie didn't spot it at first. His manner was as affable and expansive as ever, his voice and movements betrayed nothing. Jamie had lived for so long in a country where people monitored every mouthful of food and drink they swallowed, obsessed with safety and health, that she had almost forgotten anyone could drink to excess. Even business associates had been more likely to drink mineral water than wine at lunch, and a proposal to have a drink after leaving the office usually meant exactly that, one drink. Also, knowing Douglas had just had to drive up from Edinburgh, it didn't occur to her that he might have been drinking before he set out.

What alerted her was the speed with which he downed his first drink, and the over-emphatic click with which he put down the empty glass on the table beside him. Nothing more, yet at once she was conscious that his face was too flushed, too openly complacent. And then, as he watched Vanessa come, unasked, to take his glass to refill it, Jamie caught something in his eyes, a waiting, measuring look. A look she didn't like at all.

She could see why Vanessa had begged her not to introduce a topic which was almost certain to prove inflammatory. Now that she was aware of it, Jamie could feel the coil of tension tightening in the elegant tended room. Suddenly every topic seemed to conceal pitfalls. Vanessa, tight-lipped, vanished frequently to the kitchen with an air of seeking refuge, but always reappeared quite soon, as though afraid her absence might be correctly construed and resented.

Jamie told herself she was exaggerating, and did her best to relax. Then, finding Vanessa turning her attention to her like a conscientious hostess, making an obvious effort to introduce some topic which would include her, but unable to keep her attention on what she was saying herself, let alone on any replies, she decided she wasn't imagining it.

Ryan, who had slouched in in silence and disposed himself in an uncouth sprawl on a sofa at the far end of the room, was his father's principal target, however, and Jamie could feel her own apprehension building as confrontation seemed inevitable. If she felt that, how must it be for poor Van? And how often did this atmosphere prevail?

Ryan, fortunately, was doing nothing to provoke his father. Presumably he knew the danger signs as well as his mother. But his very uncommunicativeness, the ducked head, the deliberate blankness of his dark eyes, so like his father's, clearly goaded Douglas, and Jamie was thankful when they moved to the dining-room, and the tension slackened with the change of scene and the small activity and exchanges as they began dinner.

Douglas put away a startling quantity of wine. Vanessa, her face increasingly pinched, drank none, and barely touched her food. Jamie, resenting having family dissension so blatantly paraded before her, did her best to keep some kind of conversation going, if only for Vanessa's sake. Soon, however, she found she didn't have to bother. Douglas was ready now to talk, and talk he did, his voice gathering power, propounding his views on Europe, the welfare benefits system, the cretinous failings of the captain of his golf club over the plans for new locker rooms, and other large subjects.

Jamie's principal reaction was anger. Anger that he had driven his car when he was in this state, anger that he should impose this sort of scene on Vanessa, who had a hard enough time as it was trying to balance the demands of husband and son, and anger that because of his selfish indulgence it looked as if she herself would have to stay at Dunrossie for a third night.

She longed to phone Patrick, but knew he would probably be in his workshop, where he couldn't be disturbed. Knowing he was out of reach increased her feeling of being isolated here, with no one's thoughts in tune with hers. The three members of the Cairney family were locked into some scenario of their own, in which she had no part, and it was hard not to let her feeling of being excluded swell into a sense of being altogether alone. For years she had kept those closest to her by blood at a distance, and now some distinctly chilly draughts were swirling around her.

It was a relief when the meal ended. Ryan disappeared the moment he could, having hardly uttered a word from start to finish. Jamie noted in passing that he never, as far as she could see, lifted a finger to help his mother, not so much as handing her his plate as she cleared away. Nor did his father, of course. Had Vanessa fought that battle and lost, or did she genuinely see her role as serving these two indolent males, neither of whom ever appeared to thank her? This evening Douglas had almost ignored Vanessa. Or was that a good thing, in his present state? Vanessa, with her inability to accept the simplest remark without question or obstruction, could be infuriating, and Jamie could imagine that living with her for twenty years could not have been easy.

It was a considerable relief, though neither she nor Vanessa made any comment, when Douglas also disappeared after dinner, saying he had work to do.

19

For a second night Jamie didn't sleep well. Each time she stirred and woke she had yet again the befuddled feeling of escaping from some disagreeable dream, of which no details could be chased down. There was only the silence, though gradually the distant sound of traffic would penetrate as she listened; nothing more. But the feeling of something being wrong persisted, and she realised that the bad vibes of the evening had left their impression. How unattractive the prospect was of another evening here, even if Douglas hadn't been drinking. Why did it all have to hinge on him? Why couldn't she and Vanessa discuss what to do about Calder, getting hold of Phil as well of course, little as she would have to say. It was no distance to Muirend, and it would be convenient for Jamie to go straight on to Calder from there.

But she knew it was hopeless. Vanessa wouldn't voice an opinion without Douglas present, let alone make a decision, and all they had touched on so far was the problem of selling the house as it was. The part that mattered to Jamie, the possibility of keeping the cottage out of the sale, hadn't even been mooted.

But when she came down the next morning she

found that, though Douglas had already left as before, and Ryan was still in bed, today the routine was different. Breakfast was set in the dining-room. This was one of Pauline's 'mornings' and apparently her needs were paramount.

'I would have given you breakfast in the kitchen,' Vanessa began apologetically as Jamie sat down. 'It's much nicer in there in the morning because it's so sunny – not that it's particularly sunny today, though the forecast did say it might improve later – only Pauline likes to start in there. Then I'm afraid we mustn't be too long as she'll want to come in here. She does this next. I wondered, though, could we talk? After breakfast, I mean, if you don't mind, only we'll have to move somewhere else. I let Pauline have downstairs to herself on Tuesdays and Fridays, because she prefers to hoover everywhere in one go, then dust and then polish and so on. I do any tidying upstairs, and then on her other days we do it the other way round.'

And how would you prefer to have it done, Jamie longed to ask. Did Vanessa have no say about it? Was she perpetually at the bidding of son, husband and cleaner? Lucky there were no cats and dogs to add their voices. But Jamie suppressed comment. There was a fine-strung look about Vanessa this morning which she didn't care for, as though last night's tension had not been shaken off. Her face was pale, in spite of the make-up which did her no favours in the morning light, and her eyes looked red and oddly smaller, her mouth vulnerable. Also tiredness seemed to be making her clumsy, since she splashed coffee over the hot-plate as she picked up the pot.

'Oh, how I hate making a mess,' she cried, really angry with herself.

'Have you hurt your hand?' Jamie asked, seeing her wrap her right hand in her left for a second. She began to get up to help, but sank back into her seat as Vanessa, on her way to fetch a cloth, made a little flapping gesture telling her to sit down again.

'I staved my thumb yesterday,' Vanessa said dismissively over her shoulder. 'It twinges a bit if I pick up something the wrong way. Please don't fuss.'

That was rich, coming from Vanessa. But no fuss suited Jamie fine, just so long as she could fortify herself with hot coffee before this damned Pauline rousted them out. Concern stirred once more, however, as Vanessa sat down again. How haggard she looked, almost diminished somehow.

'How are you feeling apart from the staved thumb?' Jamie enquired. 'You don't look to me as though you'd slept much.'

'What do you mean?' To her surprise Vanessa's face reddened.

'Just what I said,' Jamie protested. 'Are you sure you're not sick or anything?'

'No, no, I'm fine. But you're right, I didn't sleep very well. It's such a strain when Douglas and Ryan are at loggerheads all the time. I was sorry you had to see that last night—' She looked as though she was going to say more, then veered away to another topic. 'I do worry about what Ryan will do. In the future, I mean. Oh, I know he'll be fine, of course he will,' without that certainty there was nothing, 'but jobs are impossible to find these days. It was all right for us. If you had a degree or a training or something then a career was there for you. You didn't have to worry about it.'

I don't think so, Jamie demurred silently. And when did you ever concern yourself about a training or a career, Vanessa, or anything except that potty little job in the gallery, selling fancy wrapping paper and pot-pourri and picture frames, marking time till some guy came along? A guy; Douglas. And now . . .

'I know it wasn't what was planned when we agreed to let him have his year out,' Vanessa was running on in her troubled way. 'Being at home, that is. But he did have plans and he was badly let down. I wouldn't have wanted him to go off round the world alone. And if he can't get a job I don't see any alternative to his living here. How is he expected to survive? What's he supposed to live on? This is his home, after all. It's no trouble to have him here, and what are mothers for, if not to look after their offspring?'

She asked this on a note of false cheerfulness which made Jamie wince as much as the premise did.

'I'm glad of the chance to see something of him, to be honest,' Vanessa went on. 'Goodness knows, they leave home soon enough. I know you can't understand that, having no children of your own, but if you think how much they're away from you once they go to school, it's actually quite nice to spend some time with them.'

Ryan spend time with his mother? Doing what, Jamie wondered. Did Vanessa believe in the clichés? Did she truly feel she was close to the surly Ryan, who responded to any conversational offering with a grunt just short of contempt, and a downward movement of his head which suggested nothing more than a strong desire to escape. The reference to her own childlessness Jamie set aside, not allowing herself to feel anything about it either way. Poor old Van had to have something to hold onto as a form of achievement.

'I know lots of fathers and sons clash at this age. There's nothing unusual in it.' By now Vanessa seemed to be talking to herself, and Jamie had the impression that all this guff about Ryan was a verbal form of protective colouring. So what was wrong?

'Oh, Pauline!' Vanessa sounded actually relieved at the interruption, as the door was dunted open by the hoover, and a small dark woman in black leggings and a billowing Aloha shirt came tramping in. 'This is my sister, Jamie. Jamie, this is Pauline, who looks after us so well. My absolute mainstay.'

Don't, Jamie begged, her teeth on edge, nodding a greeting to Pauline, who took no notice of her, but stooped to plug in her cleaner, sticking out her flowery behind in a marked manner. Presumably she would clear the table before she began to vacuum? Or was plugging it in a form of haka, the threat of warfare to come?

'I'm not sure where we—' Vanessa began, oddly at

a loss as they decamped, Jamie taking a last cup of coffee with her.

There must be a dozen rooms in this house. Sad.

'Your bedroom? Mine?' Jamie was half joking.

'Oh, not my room!' Vanessa exclaimed, and then must have realised how strange this sounded, for she added hastily, looking embarrassed, 'It's horribly untidy, that's all. Douglas always strews his things about, he's hopeless.'

'Oh, come on, this is getting silly. My room's untidy too. Who cares?' Jamie was beginning to feel rattled. Why the need for privacy? What was going on?

She thought she understood, when Vanessa at last embarked on her explanation, why she had allowed such trivia to delay the moment, consciously or not.

'Jamie, I hardly know how to say this. It's an awful thing to do to a guest, especially to my sister and when I've hardly seen you for years. Though you may not realise it, I do miss you terribly, and I think about you a lot more than you—'

'Vanessa, get on with it.' Jamie was frowning, but she made an effort to keep her impatience in check. Anxiety had begun to curl, more serious than the familiar irritation with each other which they were so used to that they hardly noticed it was there.

'I hate to ask this,' Vanessa's eyes, meeting Jamie's with difficulty, were full of distress, 'but would you terribly mind leaving today?' The moment she got the words out she was horrified to have said such a thing to anyone, let alone to one of her own family. It went totally against the grain of her giving, caring nature. 'Oh, Jamie, I'm sorry. How appalling that sounds. Do forgive me. Only you see, I think it really would be best. I'm not sure I can explain.'

'I think I'd like you to try.' Jamie meant to sound matter-of-fact, but instead her voice was clipped and almost hostile. Even so, though she was taken aback, and this was not a particularly good time to find herself not wanted, her concern was not primarily for herself but for Vanessa. It was hard to imagine what could have driven her to make such a request.

'Oh, Jamie, please don't be hurt,' Vanessa begged, dreading to think that yet another person would be estranged from her, and yearning for help and support. 'I realise how terribly unkind it must sound. You know I'd love to have you here for as long as you want to stay. You do know that, don't you? But it's just that—'

Her eyes went round the bedroom, lighting on nothing. She was obviously searching for some explanation that would be palatable.

'Look, don't start fudging, whatever you do,' Jamie begged. 'Of course I don't mind going.' She decided that to say how much she had been longing to do just that would hardly help. 'I came without giving you any warning, and I knew it wasn't necessarily convenient for you.'

'Oh, no, no, it's not that.' Vanessa minded having the ready hospitality on which she prided herself called in doubt. 'It's nothing like that.'

'Then what the hell is it?' Jamie demanded, still with restraint, but with the unmistakable intention of getting to the bottom of this. 'Has there been some row about my being here?'

Vanessa gazed at her in pleading silence, her mouth trembling.

'Tell me,' Jamie insisted. 'What's Douglas been saying? I've a good mind to phone him and find out.'

'Jamie, *no!*' That sounded nothing short of terrified, as Vanessa jumped up out of the chair Jamie had pushed her into. 'You can't, you mustn't. You don't understand.'

Jamie put her coffee cup on the bedside-table and came to her feet too. Going to Vanessa she took her arm and made her look at her. 'What don't I understand?'

To her dismay, Vanessa's face crumpled, her eyes filled with tears, and her mouth, its muscles out of control, was dragged square and ugly as wrenching sobs overtook her.

'Oh, Van, honey, don't!' Jamie put her arms round her and hugged her tightly. 'I can't bear for you to cry like this.' Contact was not part of their relationship, but then she had never seen Vanessa in such a state before. It shook her, in the way that a child is shaken by seeing its mother cry. To Jamie, Vanessa had always been that mother figure, stable and competent, setting the standards of behaviour for them all.

'Hey, come on, don't cry this way. Tell me what's wrong. You can tell me. We'll sort something out.'

She could feel in the softly fleshed shoulders the effort Vanessa was making to claw back calm.

'It's OK, it's OK,' she said, still holding her close. 'We can talk, you can tell me.'

'It's this business of Calder,' Vanessa said at last, her voice unsteady, when she had got through several tissues from their lace-covered box and gulped herself quiet, and they were sitting side by side on the unmade bed. 'Douglas is so angry about it.'

It was the last thing Jamie had expected. 'Calder? But we haven't even discussed it with Douglas.' And what in God's name does he think it has to do with him anyway? But that she didn't say.

'He knew we would have been talking about it,' Vanessa explained, scrubbing at her eyes. 'He made me tell him last night.'

'But tell him what?' Jamie demanded, baffled. 'We haven't decided anything. We can't till we talk to Phil in any case. There's nothing to tell.'

'Well, there was that stuff about your business and everything,' Vanessa said, and Jamie realised that even in this moment automatic defence for Douglas was still in place. 'We hadn't told him about that, and of course it does mean you're not in a position now to keep Calder.'

'But Vanessa, I don't see what any decision we make has to do with him,' Jamie said, exasperation getting the upper hand in spite of her good intentions. 'And what's all the urgency about? Do you realise it's only a week ago yesterday that I got back? A week ago today that Zara was cremated?' Even as she spoke Jamie was working it out again. It seemed impossible, but it was true.

'I'll have to tell you,' Vanessa said, her voice nervous and hurried. Thank the Lord for that, Jamie thought ironically. 'You see, Douglas needs – that is, we need – the money rather urgently. I can't explain exactly, but it seems that several of our investments have gone wrong lately. You've been abroad, so you won't realise what's been happening, but I assure you things have been very difficult here. It's vital to get an injection of cash. I think that's what Douglas said. Then everything will be all right.'

Jamie didn't smile at this naïve speech. Anger was filling her, an anger she knew it was important not to release. Her long experience of dealing with people and handling tricky situations came to her aid – though a detached part of her mind reflected that she had never expected to have to call on these skills while perched on a bed with Vanessa at Dunrossie, having just been asked to leave the house.

'OK,' she said. 'Let's pick the bones out of that. Is it one of Douglas's business ventures that needs the boost, or your private funds?'

Vanessa turned to gaze at her blankly. 'But won't that be the same? If Douglas has business difficulties won't that mean we have less money?'

Jamie saw she would have to put this into terms Vanessa could relate to. 'Are you struggling, on an actual day-to-day basis? Are you saying you can't keep this house, for example? That you won't be able to afford to put Ryan through college? That you're having to cut back on entertaining, clothes, vacations?'

Vanessa was looking alarmed. 'Douglas didn't mention any of that. I didn't ask either, to be truthful, because I didn't even imagine such a – but of course Ryan must go to university. That's never been in question. Goodness . . .' Her voice trailed away as she contemplated this ultimate disaster.

'All I'm trying to establish is whether you need to get your hands on some instant cash to survive. I hardly think that's the case, do you?'

'But when we heard about Zara, it was the first thing Douglas said.'

I bet it was.

'And when I came up to Calder, he wanted me to come back with a definite answer about whether we would be selling or whether you wanted to buy. He guessed you might, but either way he wanted things put in train right away. When I told him the state the house was in he—' Vanessa checked, shook her head as if to clear it and went on, 'well, he was very angry. He said that if work was essential to make it fit to sell, then all the more reason not to hang about.'

Jamie had the impression that a certain amount of paraphrasing was going on here. 'And he wasn't happy about me swanning about there, putting the whole plot on hold,' she added helpfully.

'No, he was livid about that,' Vanessa agreed, her blind habit of accepting all Douglas said as right and fitting back in place. Jamie wanted to shake her. But who could shake this sad little doll, with its neat fair hair, its neat fresh clothes, and its pretty painted face smeared with mascara and tears?

'So you want me to go because you think there'll be more rows tonight if I stay?'

'Oh, Jamie, do you mind awfully? The last thing I want to do is hurt you. But Douglas seems to think you're delaying things deliberately. He said something about it before, but now that he knows about you losing everything he's convinced of it, and I think it might get too difficult if you were still here when he got back.'

So that was what lay behind the affectionate welcome her brother-in-law had given her, Jamie thought. Plausible bastard. Whatever Vanessa said, it did hurt. She was too anchorless at present not to mind this feeling of rejection, whatever its source. How angry Patrick would be. The thought of being able to tell him about it brought brief comfort.

'OK, I know it's difficult for you,' she said, taking Vanessa's hand for a second. Feeling Vanessa wince involuntarily, she released it hastily. 'Sorry, that's the hand you hurt, I'd forgotten. Look, don't worry, I'll clear out. Of course I will, it's no big deal. It will be good to get back to Calder anyway.' That much she felt she could allow herself to say. 'But as to deciding what's to be done about it, or anything else concerning it, I have to remind you that it isn't up to Douglas. Yes, I know you're a couple and all that, but Father meant it to come to us. It's Laidlaw property. We don't have a lot of choice, I know, but it's up to you and Phil and me to agree on how to handle it.'

It was not the moment to mention her more specific plan. The three of them must be together when she poked a stick into that hornets' nest.

Turning to look at Vanessa she was startled by the expression on her face. It looked almost like fear, but it was quickly concealed.

'How about deciding who we get to sell the house, and asking them to send someone up to have a look? They'll be able to advise us as to the best course.'

'That's what Douglas said we should do.' Vanessa spoke with such patent relief that Jamie let this pass. 'Shall I ask him who we should contact?'

'I'll deal with it,' Jamie said. Do I actually not trust Douglas? That's rather awful; I shall have to think about it later. 'When we've talked to Phil.'

'So I can say that things are moving?' Vanessa sounded happier. 'I think Douglas really prefers it that you won't be buying,' she added candidly. 'He was afraid Phil and I wouldn't insist on the market price.'

Heading up the A9 an hour later, this remark came back to Jamie, and she laughed aloud. It was so outrageous, and it was so like Vanessa to repeat it in all good faith.

Phil had not been able to meet them today, and had resisted with great stubbornness, indeed almost with alarm, the idea of Jamie calling in on her way north.

'She's never let me go to Burnbrae House either,' Vanessa had said, when Jamie reported this. 'I think it's pretty grim and she's ashamed of it.'

Thinking this over with perceptions made more

sensitive by the emotional drubbing of the past few days, Jamie saw how they, she and Vanessa, had created this defensiveness in Phil. Whatever the shortcomings of Burnbrae House, it was her place of work, and her home as well, and unfavourable comments from family members could not be welcome.

So for the moment everything was on hold, and suddenly that seemed good to Jamie, who felt that recent events had been altogether too much of a roller-coaster ride. She needed time to draw breath, to deal with reawoken feelings, to review the encounters with the past and the hints of promise for the future.

So you find the future promising, she mocked herself. Optimistic all of a sudden, aren't you? But it was comforting to realise that, as ever, her spirits refused to be quenched, and that somewhere in the last few days a rough-and-ready acceptance of what had happened had already begun to take shape.

20

The three of them met in Muirend the following week, to have lunch in the garden of a hotel by the river. Phil was clearly ill at ease in its pretentious atmosphere.

'I've never been here before,' she said when they were seated on the terrace, and the food had finally arrived. 'It's horribly expensive, and look at these tiny portions.'

Portions? Was that Burnbrae speak? 'It was you who chose the place,' Jamie pointed out.

'I thought you'd want somewhere posh.' Said without rancour, but it reminded Jamie that while she and Vanessa had taken for granted a considerable degree of affluence and comfort Phil had been living at a very different level. Today her heavy body was clad in a green T-shirt and creased cotton skirt; on her feet she wore enormous sandals of squashy brown leather; her bag was cumbersome, scuffed and not leather. But, looking at her in despair, it occurred to Jamie that whatever style or quality her own clothes might possess, they would now probably have to last her a long time. It was a timely and salutary reminder.

'Well, I think it was an excellent choice.' Vanessa rushed in as always to deflect argument. 'We'll be able to sit in the garden and talk for as long as we like.'

'Anyway, Phil, you'll have a bit more spending power before long, and you might come to like posh places too,' Jamie said. As an attempt to make amends for her criticism, unspoken as it had been, it was clumsy. Phil received the comment with a look which said that no matter how much money she had she wouldn't waste it on eating here.

Not much sisterly bonding today, Jamie thought, half rueful, half amused. On her return to Calder – and there had been a relief to get back which had exceeded even the thrill of last week's arrival – she had decided that the best course would be to write to Phil and explain what had happened, giving her the chance to assimilate the news before they met.

Phil had phoned the moment she could, fortunately catching Jamie in having lunch, and though confused sounds in the background suggested that she hadn't found a very private place to call from, they had got the first round of dismay and concern out of the way. So now Phil knew that Calder had to go, and the ground was cleared for discussion of how and when.

Jamie plunged into the subject as soon as coffee was in front of them. Most of the other tables were empty by now, and the peace of a warm afternoon had settled on the sheltered terrace.

'OK, here's where we're up to. I've talked to Mr

Syme and he's definite that a certain amount of refurbishing is essential, but he says the selling agents will be the best people to advise us.'

'Will it be that firm in Aberfyle? I used to like looking at the photos in their window,' Phil said.

'For Pete's sake, Phil, we're not going to some tinpot local firm.'

'We could redo the bathrooms,' Vanessa was off on quite a different tack. 'I saw some heavenly catalogues not long ago when Debbie was doing her alterations. Absolutely mouth-watering Victorian stuff, all back in fashion and perfect for a house like Calder.'

'But isn't that rather silly, when the new bathrooms work?' Phil asked. 'What's the point of putting old stuff in? A new person might want to rip it all out again.'

'Look, the important thing is to get rid of Zara's wild in-your-face stuff,' Jamie cut in. 'What we're aiming for is to recreate some kind of unified whole.'

As they all set off busily on their own tracks she was objective enough to realise that they must sound pretty much as they used to thirty years ago.

'Anyway,' she said, breaking across a wrangle about what the flower pattern had been in one of the antique loos Zara must have sold, 'I have made one marvellous find, one which will make the biggest difference of all. I was rootling around in the stable loft with Maeve—'

'Who's Maeve?'

'The gardener. And guess what we—'

'But I thought Maeve was a girl's name,' Vanessa argued. 'Or is it short for something else?'

'It's Irish, isn't it?' Phil asked.

'Yes, it's Irish. Yes, she's a girl. But never mind that for now. I'll tell you about her presently.'

'But has she been doing the garden all along? Then what about the odd-job man?' Vanessa couldn't let this go. 'Does Mr Syme know? When he talked about a gardener-handyman, I assumed—'

'She's the handyman as well. Just skip all that for a minute, can't you?' How these two could bog one down. And how Jamie hated being held up when she had something to say. 'She said she thought she'd seen—'

'But when was this? Does she come in at the weekend?' Vanessa was not to be deflected. 'That means paying her double time. I'm sure that can't be right. Shouldn't we check with Mr Syme?'

'Vanessa, can we keep on track here?' But an uncomfortable memory made Jamie swallow down her irritation – Vanessa's tear-stained face as she talked about Douglas's insistence on realising the funds tied up in Calder. Was she seriously worried about money? Were things that tight? 'Let's stick to discussing plans for the house, yes?'

'So what did you find?' Phil asked.

'The old banisters for the front stairs! They're still there, in the loft. They haven't been very carefully stored and some are damaged, but I'm sure they could be matched if necessary. We didn't turn up much else that will be any use, but wasn't that incredible?'

To her it had been a magical moment; almost a vision of Calder restored.

'Well, I suppose so.' Vanessa sounded far from sure. 'Won't it cost a fortune to put them back? I mean, stairs are rather basic, aren't they? Part of the structure. How are we to pay for everything? The house won't have been sold by then, and none of us have that kind of money.' In her anxiety she forgot to be tactful.

'Vanessa, are you crazy?' Jamie demanded. 'We borrow, of course.'

'I don't like the idea of that.'

Hadn't Douglas taught her anything?

Phil wanted to ask if the new stairs were really that bad, but held her tongue. She had learned long ago that in aesthetic matters she would be wrong every time. She shifted her broad haunches a little on the bench she was sharing with Jamie, and put up a hand between her eyes and the sun. She hoped she hadn't got sweat patches showing under her arms. Vanessa would hate that. She knew her forehead must be pink and shiny. She had never liked the heat, but she didn't suggest moving inside. Vanessa and Jamie had always enjoyed the sun.

So much for her thrilling discovery, Jamie thought resignedly. Well, Calder had never meant as much to the others as it did to her; she should have remembered that. They could never have come close to the excitement of that moment, or the dread that the roughly piled heap might after all prove to be beyond rescue, which had filled her as she and Maeve had started to drag aside the intervening lumber.

Maeve had turned up without warning on Sunday

morning. Jamie had come across her looking like a voyager in space, togged up in protective clothing and with a plastic container strapped to her back, setting out to spray the docks and nettles in the lost patch of ground between the walled garden and the back drive.

'It's always a toss-up trying to decide how much to do,' Maeve had said by way of greeting, pushing up her visor. 'One person's idea of keeping things under control isn't necessarily another's. I could go on for ever, only you'll not be wanting to spend a fortune, I suppose.'

'How kind of you to take that into consideration,' Jamie had mocked, delighted to see her. 'You do happen to know it's Sunday?' Unlike Vanessa, she had not been thinking of rates of pay.

'Sunday. You don't tell me! When the weeds stop growing, I suppose you mean? No,' Maeve had squinted up at the sun, 'with conditions like this, so still and all, I'm not about to take the day off because a few bossy old men several hundred years ago invented some handy rule about the seventh day to suit themselves.'

So much for the faith of her fathers. Jamie had felt once again the happy certainty that a wealth of things waited to be discussed and shared with Maeve. For the moment, however, she had talked about plans for the house, and Maeve had exclaimed with an enthusiasm that matched her own, 'But I'm sure a whole load of that stuff's still around. I don't know what state it will be in, mind you. Let's have a look.' And with the greatest alacrity she had shed the spraying equipment and led the way to the yard.

Apart from entering into the search with gusto she had been spectacularly useful, slinging bulky objects aside with casual ease, heaving at rails buried under piles of cumbersome dross with a vigour that had brought several unexpected finds to light.

'Nothing here that can't be sorted,' she had pronounced, when it began to look as if most of the original staircase was still extant, and Jamie had believed her.

I wanted to believe her, she warned herself, looking down the hotel lawn to where, presumably since the public couldn't be relied upon to tell the difference between water and dry land, ugly safety fencing disfigured the river bank. And I'm glad I went looking with her and not these two. How stifling it could feel, this sense that their minds never marched with hers. She was suddenly bored by the whole scene, longing to be on her way back up the glen, longing to talk to Patrick. But those were pleasures which must wait. They hadn't even reached the main issue yet.

'Look, there was something else I wanted to float past you,' she began, as lightly as she could. 'Well, a couple of things. Now we've agreed in principle that we have to sort the house out before trying to sell, how would you feel about my staying on while that's being done?'

She saw from Vanessa's face that Douglas's warnings about gaining a foothold at Calder had rushed back, and anger flared that he should imagine she would try to take advantage of her own sisters in any way. If that was an indication of how he operated himself, she thought with distaste . . . And couldn't Vanessa ever do any thinking on her own behalf?

She was fluttering now, uncertain but placating. 'I really don't know. I expect it would be—'

'Of course you must stay,' Phil interrupted flatly, in a way rare for her. 'There's no question about it, is there? In fact, it couldn't have worked out better, the place being there for you exactly when you need it. I don't mean I'd have wanted Zara to die or anything, but if that was going to happen anyway, wasn't it lucky it came about just when you'd lost everything? Anyway, someone will have to oversee the work and keep an eye on the place. If you'd had to rush back to America, one of us would have had to go up and down, and it would have been terribly awkward. Oh, Jamie, sorry, I know it's awful for you.' She caught herself up, reddening. 'I only meant—'

'It's OK,' Jamie assured her quickly. 'Of course I know what you meant.'

There had been nothing but the most earnest kindness in this speech, an unusually long one for Phil, but what had struck Jamie most, before Phil saw she had been insensitive and had floundered to a halt, had been a new confidence and authority in her manner. Had it been there before and she hadn't noticed it?

'But nothing's settled yet,' Vanessa was saying. 'I mean, we haven't decided what needs to be done, or can be done, and we've no idea how long the work would take.' She was sure none of this would find favour with Douglas, and dread of facing him with any but the news he wanted to hear made it difficult to produce a coherent argument.

God, not back to the beginning again, Jamie groaned silently. 'Sure,' she made herself say calmly, 'I know that depends on the verdict of whoever comes to look over the place. We've got that far. But *if* work has to be done, how would you feel about my being there?' It was hard to maintain the even tone. And the important part still lay ahead.

'What problem can there be?' Phil asked, before Vanessa could speak. 'It's Grandmother's house. Well, our house, but you know what I mean. Why shouldn't Jamie be there? She's got nowhere else to go. Why does she have to ask? I don't see what we're talking about.'

She sounded so baffled that Vanessa flushed.

'Of course I want to help Jamie,' she insisted. 'How can you imagine I wouldn't? But there's a lot to think over.' She almost added, 'You wouldn't understand,' the patronising rider which had so easily crushed the humble younger sister who struggled with any new idea.

'Well, here's something else to think over.' Jamie spoke brusquely, finding it surprisingly hard, now it came to the point, to launch her plan into the stormy seas of family discussion. She noted with interest that her heartbeat had quickened. So that was how much it meant to her. 'I was wondering about the possibility of keeping Freda's cottage out of the sale, and then buying it from you with my part of the proceeds from the house.'

There was a moment of startled silence as Phil and Vanessa took this in, their heads coming round to Jamie with an identical jerk of surprise. Then Phil, as could clearly be seen in her face, began to turn over the implications, getting her thoughts in order before risking speech.

Vanessa, on the other hand, after that first blank moment, rushed in appalled. 'Jamie, I'm sure that would never be allowed! How can you think of splitting up the property? No buyer would be interested in having someone living on the doorstep, not the sort of people who'd want a house like Calder anyway. And it would drastically reduce the price. I'm positive Doug—'

She bit back the name, aware in spite of her consternation that Jamie would not be receptive to Douglas's views at the moment. But the thought of his anger made her quail.

Phil surprised them by asking, 'But has this got anything to do with Douglas?' There was no aggression in the question. 'This is just up to us, isn't it?'

Good for you, Phil, Jamie applauded gratefully.

'Yes, but, you see, Phil, you don't understand about being part of a couple.' As she had done with Jamie, Vanessa clutched with relief at this irrefutable fact to support her, but Jamie, not waiting to see how Phil would respond, cut her short.

'Don't let's get dragged into that. Let me finish what I was saying. I agree that selling as two lots might mean the house fetches less, but I could make up the difference to you. No, Van, *wait*. It would be a purely business deal. You, both of you, would end up with whatever would have been your share. Though I don't see that excluding the cottage would necessarily be too detrimental. It's quite separate, outside the courtyard, not overlooking anything –' I don't think I'll mention those south-facing windows I've got my eye on '– and access could be via the back drive.'

'But anyone wanting to walk up the river from the garden would have to pass it,' Vanessa said, deeply alarmed by this new development and doing her best to put forward the objections she knew Douglas would expect her to make. 'Or wanting to go over the bridge,' she added, clutching at any straw she could find.

Jamie, fighting down her frustration, took the trouble to answer the absurd point. There was a good deal at stake here.

'It's Gask ground on the other side of the bridge now, remember, so they'd be leaving Calder anyway.' As she spoke she recalled that neither sister had been very interested in the changes which had overtaken the estate, and had certainly never shared her grief when most of the land had been sold off. A memory came back, too vivid to be comfortable, of her sense of isolation at the time, and her fury at their indifference. The fact was they still saw Calder, as

Phil had referred to it just now, simply as Grand-mother's house.

She pushed that aside and went doggedly on. 'Anyway, that's my suggestion, and all I'm asking is that you consider it. It would mean we wouldn't lose Calder altogether, and you'd still be able to come there too, of course. However, the chief thing I want to say is this. I don't want you to feel you have to agree because suddenly I don't have a roof over my head. Forget that. I can easily find somewhere to live, and I'll have to look for a job of some sort pretty soon anyway. Just consider the proposition, that's all I ask.'

'I don't see that there's anything to consider.' Again Phil got in first. 'I think it's a great idea. Only I don't see why you should pay us back just because of some imaginary figure the house might have made. I think we should keep the cottage out of the sale, sell the rest and split whatever we get three ways. Have the cottage. I don't want any money for it.'

'Oh, but—' Vanessa looked horrified, but couldn't find a way to protest which wouldn't sound unge-nerous after this. But her dismay could be read in her face.

'You're a doll, do you know that?' Jamie was saying to Phil, grateful and impressed, with a choki-ness in her voice that surprised her. She had never heard Phil sound so positive, and felt a real contrition that in the past she and Vanessa had ridden over her so carelessly. 'Thanks for that, but of course we'll do the thing equitably. I won't hear of anything else.'

That was some relief, Vanessa thought, feeling she was rocking back from some perilous brink. But it still left the original idea in place.

'Two to one, then,' she said, her voice tight.

This reduced the matter to something like a nursery squabble, and Jamie frowned in annoyance. Then she saw Vanessa reach down for her bag, open it, stare into it for a moment, taking nothing out, and close it again, having trouble with the fastener. Her hands were shaking, and Jamie guessed that the action had reflected an instinctive need to touch some familiar comforter.

She felt a pang of concern for her, mixed with guilt, and frustration that they didn't seem able to discuss anything rationally and straightforwardly.

'Vanessa, why are you getting so steamed up about this?' she asked. 'Even if you don't agree, it's not a question of taking sides. I've made a suggestion, that's all. Surely it can be kicked around among the three of us without getting into a fight?'

'It's an idiotic idea,' Vanessa burst out, her voice barely under control. 'The place would never sell. I don't believe Mr Syme would agree for a second.'

For Mr Syme read Douglas. What had Vanessa's instructions been today? Sell with all speed; no delays, no options. Would it really come to two against one? Jamie felt distaste at the mere thought. Surely they could come to some workable agreement, especially as she was determined the others shouldn't lose out? But to act according to Douglas's wishes – or orders – that she was not prepared to do.

'Whatever happens, I don't think it should make us miserable,' Phil was saying, with that new firmness Jamie still wasn't used to. 'It's our family home. Father meant us to have it. Zara's gone and now it belongs to us. It's supposed to be a *good* thing. And Jamie's the one who needs it and can benefit from it. You and I are fine as we are, Vanessa, so why shouldn't we do all we can for her?'

Jamie felt her throat tighten again at this generosity. In the heady climb to success she had given little thought to Phil's circumstances. If she had remembered them at all she had at best been thankful that Phil had found some slot where she seemed settled, and she had pushed out of her mind a faint distaste for what she actually did. Yet who was the first to reach a helping hand now? Whatever Calder brought was Phil's inheritance, the only real money she was ever likely to acquire in her life.

'Of course I want to help Jamie, you know I do,' Vanessa protested, but she was ignored.

Jamie turned to Phil and, in a gesture quite alien to them, reached out to hug her big, yielding, soft-fleshed body with gratitude, too moved to put into words what she felt.

21

Jamie turned on her back to float for a moment or two more. They had always used this pool at this time of day, rather than the deeper one below the bluff, by now in shadow. The water was lit to amber by the late afternoon sun, but having spilled down the deep-cut, tree-hung gorge on its way here was tinglingly cold. How good that felt after the dust and heat of a strenuous day, and its satin-softness was still one of the minor pleasures of being back. Jamie looked up through slitted eyes at the blue sky, hazing to milky paleness now that the afternoon was slipping away. It would be light for hours yet. She felt one of those surges of formless gratitude which so often overtook her these days, gratitude to have emerged from disaster without irrevocable damage, and found a safety she had hardly dared to hope for.

Thoughts of Bryden were still difficult to deal with, especially at night, when she would wake longing helplessly for him, and hate herself for it. The sudden shift from being part of a couple, focused on a future full of promise, to being alone, with no real occupation and nothing ahead of her, was not easy to adjust to. But, though she would have found it hard to define the process, as the days passed the thoughts of Bryden were becoming so well-worn that there was no fresh emotion to be wrung from them. As sharp as ever, however, was the stab of wounded pride. That could still bite deep. And shame, always shame, that she had been so blind. These she kept to herself, not returning to this area of pain even with Patrick, only touching on it in generalised terms with Maeve in their occasional enjoyable, take-no-prisoners discussions about men, and never letting Phil know the relationship had existed. With Vanessa, there wasn't much discussion about anything at present.

Frowning, her mood of lazy peace fragmenting, Jamie brought her feet down, found bottom and made her way to the bank, twitching her towel from the low branch of a birch tree which the cattle had rubbed smooth, for the gorge widened here to give a few acres of grazing.

She dried herself vigorously, aware that she had stayed in too long. The sun wasn't strong enough by now to warm her, and she shivered and grumbled as she dragged on her clothes. But she knew physical discomfort wasn't the source of her ill-humour; she rarely took much notice of that. The truth was she felt wretchedly at odds with Vanessa these days, and she didn't like it. Apart from minding it for herself, the suspicion nagged that Vanessa needed some support from her which she wasn't giving.

But why did she feel that, she asked herself as she crossed the sunny field to the gate which led into

what was left of the Calder demesne, and went up the
steep path between the trees to the lawn. Although
Vanessa had made such an issue about Douglas
wanting her to get her hands on the proceeds of
the sale as soon as possible, there was still no real
evidence of straitened circumstances affecting the
lifestyle of Dunrossie, where Jamie had been back
for lunch, not to stay.

As absorbed in domestic preoccupations as ever,
Vanessa maintained the flawless standards which
meant so much to her, put a huge amount of effort
into whatever entertaining Douglas chose to offer,
and cherished her admirable possessions. God, she
even enjoys washing and ironing, Jamie thought, but
she knew what lay behind the spurt of irritation.
Unchanged as all this appeared to be, and it was hard
to imagine Vanessa in any other setting, each time
they met Jamie was struck by the tension in her, and
her look of strained tiredness. A lot of strife centred
on Ryan, and that no doubt was part of the problem,
but at a deeper level Douglas and Vanessa had
reached the classic crux of modern times, husband
at the height of involvement in his career, offspring
leaving the nest (supposing Ryan ever got round to
it), and wife left at home with less to do, no independent interests and, more seriously, no concept of
employing her time to suit her own needs.

I'm not sure I could live with Vanessa on a daily
basis myself though, Jamie conceded, going up the
front steps. What am I talking about, she instantly
corrected herself, she'd drive me crazy in a week.

She liked coming in this way now. There had been in the end little disagreement about what should be done to the house. The selling agent's estimate of how much the expenditure of a few thousand pounds would recoup had silenced even Douglas.

Mr Syme had made sure, however, that a balance was kept. Here in the hall, for instance, he had ruled that there was no point in re-opening the chimney and then having to hunt down a fireplace which would be 'in keeping' (a phrase which had become part of everyone's vocabulary). If a buyer wanted to do that for himself he could. He could also carpet or otherwise cover the floor. Similarly in the kitchen, and the bedrooms and bathrooms at the front of the house, Mr Syme felt that to get rid of Zara's innovations, which no one could deny created a high degree of luxury, would be a pointless exercise.

But here Jamie could look around her with pleasure. The bizarre panels had been stripped away, the walls were waiting to be redecorated, and the solid, handsome staircase was back in place. Extraordinary how that single factor made such a difference. To me anyway, Jamie conceded, for she had had to accept that for Vanessa and Phil no deep feelings were involved.

The other big job had been the gutting of Zara's rooms in the east wing. Her collection of artefacts had realised more than any of them had expected, and that too had been useful in modifying Douglas's complaints.

It had also removed immediate worries for Jamie

about what to live on, though Mr Syme had done his best to make her accept some recompense not only for supervising the alterations, but for tackling many jobs herself.

'It's only reasonable that the estate should pay,' he had argued. 'I can't imagine either of your sisters contesting that. It would have been much more complicated to put everything in hand with no one there to keep an eye on what was being done.'

But Jamie had disliked the idea intensely. For one thing it would have sent Vanessa (read Douglas) into orbit, and for another it would have seemed strange to accept payment when she was living here expenses paid. Even a car, taxed and insured, had fallen into her lap. All she had to do was put petrol in it and feed herself. And buy the odd pint for Maeve, of course.

But she knew her reasons for refusing went beyond these considerations. She had destroyed everything she had achieved through her own egotism. She had been flattered and impressed by a professional con man, exactly as every other woman Bryden had hit on in the course of his career had been. In spite of her success in the cut-throat world of business, and her pride in what she had done, when it came down to it she had shown no more judgement than the dimmest little housewife stuck at home with her man to look after her and no experience of the world behind her. It was hard to come to terms with. Jamie felt, though she couldn't have said so even to Patrick, that she should take the rap for her stupidity. Almost she didn't want to find her way made too smooth.

Well, you've got that wrong as well, haven't you, she mocked herself, exuberance rising irresistibly as she gazed round the half-finished hall which, if truth be told, looked a lot worse than it had in Zara's day. If she was trying to do penance she wasn't making much of a fist of it. Things had worked out better than she could ever have imagined.

Water and power were now on in the cottage, and she had cleaned it from top to bottom, with some assistance from Maeve. This had not been achieved entirely without altercation. Maeve found it hard to operate on a purely domestic level. She was always ready to whip out her screwdriver and probe damp wood or bulging plaster, disappointed if no real disaster was revealed and leaving a gaping hole behind her, or to pick away at a fireplace surround to see what the tiles underneath looked like (dull and cracked, which was why they'd been covered up in the first place), then finding that the paper wouldn't stick back after her attentions. It was the same with the furniture, when Jamie shifted a few bits across from the house. Maeve couldn't resist investigating veneer lifting with damp, or varnish starting to look streaky, and glaring bare patches would be left in her wake.

'You know, it would be no trouble at all to strip this down,' Jamie would hear her call. 'A bit of linseed and turps and a nice rub up with wax polish, and it would look like new.'

'What have you done?' Jamie would wail, coming to look. 'Maeve, if you have to do all this poking and scraping, why do you always do it in the *middle*? Now I'll have to do something about it.'

'Oh good,' Maeve would grin, unrepentant. 'Nice little job. Won't take you five minutes.'

But it had been great fun to have her help, and Patrick had also briefly appeared, back at the Toll-house for a couple of days when Jamie had thought there was little hope of seeing him for some time. Putting her plan into action, and sharing the work with these two, secure in the knowledge that she was safe at Calder for a few weeks at least, Jamie had been aware of a feeling of steadying down, of having some firm base beneath her feet again, and that had brought a peace she hadn't known since the day Bryden had broken his shattering news.

At the root of this feeling of security, she was ready to admit, was not only Patrick's presence, but the knowledge that, even if he wasn't at the Toll-house, he was there in the background, in her life again, bringing a stability she badly needed just now.

Patrick, for his part, working away obligingly at any job he was given, providing large picnics to lure Jamie and Maeve outside at every chance, didn't reveal that he had had no more than three hours' sleep per night since Jamie's visit to Longmuir, determined to get his current commission out of the way and spend as much time as he could in the glen before she vanished again.

Settling into the cottage had been for Jamie a very different thing even from sleeping in her room in the nursery wing. No Zara vibes here. No reminders either of the changes which had overtaken her once-adored father as Zara gradually took control of his life. Whatever associations with Freda lingered, they remained the uncomplicated images of childhood. Her encounter with Freda in the present, though from time to time she would recall it uncomfortably, might have been a shock to her ego but couldn't mar her pleasure in the new arrangement.

And today she had had the most marvellous news, news she was looking forward to sharing with Maeve this evening. Worries about Vanessa pushed aside, Jamie felt nothing but heady anticipation as she went through the house, out by the back door and, beginning to run from sheer exuberance, raced through the shady courtyard and out through the archway into the sun.

'She's agreed? Just like that?'

'Mr Syme phoned this afternoon. Isn't it great?'

'It certainly is, and I'm thrilled for you. But Vanessa didn't phone to tell you herself? That seems odd. You've talked to her since, though?'

They were sitting on the rickety verandah of Maeve's hut, a mammoth packet of crisps raggedly open between them, Jamie drinking the wine she had brought with her, Maeve with a can of lager clasped on her stomach, firm-muscled legs in combat trousers outstretched, booted ankles crossed on the verandah rail. She was dressed for the evening. During the day, through this spell of fine weather, she had been wearing nothing but shorts and singlet, and the

workmen at Calder had shown a marked tendency to
stray off course, to be encountered almost anywhere
outside, ostensibly in search of just a wee length of
pipe or a handy bit of wood.

'Not yet.' Jamie's brows drew down. Mr Syme had
added the message that Vanessa wouldn't be available this evening, but would phone tomorrow. A
dinner party, or attending some function, Jamie
had supposed. Douglas did a lot of business entertaining, in Edinburgh as well as at Dunrossie, and
Vanessa had always been expected to toe the line.
Why am I putting it like that, Jamie wondered,
annoyed with herself. Vanessa loved the whole shooting match, enjoyed dressing up, wearing expensive
clothes and jewellery, elaborate food and smart surroundings.

'I've hardly taken it in yet,' she admitted to Maeve,
dismissing this small stir of doubt and letting excitement seize her again. 'Can you believe it? Owning the
cottage! Really and actually owning it! I hadn't dared
let myself hope it could work out. I feel as if I've
rushed from everything to nothing and back to everything again in one crazy whirl. Could anyone have
been luckier?'

Maeve turned to grin at her. Not everyone would
see it quite like that, but Jamie seemed to have an
amazing capacity to survive catastrophe on a scale
that would knock most people out cold, and come out
the other side bursting with fresh optimism. Her life
had fallen apart, she had absorbed the blow and, with
head still ringing, had staggered to her feet again.

Without visible means of support, or any specific plans that Maeve had heard of, her mood was already upbeat. This must have been the quality which had taken her so far in the first place, Maeve surmised, and would enable her to make a fresh start when the moment came.

For the time being, it seemed, she was to be in the glen. Maeve would drink to that. They had spent a lot of time together by this time. One job they had tackled had been 'deZarring', their new word, the rooms in the east wing, transforming them with fresh light paint. It had been decided to dub the lower room a studio, and let it take its chance with potential purchasers. They had worked together outside too. Maeve normally preferred to get on with jobs on her own, but she found Jamie's company a bonus. She also liked having a definite aim. Presentation was all, the agent had warned, and it was far more rewarding to work with that in mind than to be restricted to merely keeping the garden under control.

'Though it will probably end up putting me out of a job,' she would point out, without rancour, as she and Jamie cleared run-offs from the drive, cut back seedling trees and dragged away fallen branches.

'Not necessarily,' Jamie argued. 'The new people may want a gardener, and you'll come highly recommended.'

'Huh, part of the package.' But Maeve never worried much about events which were out of her hands anyway, and never looked too far ahead. For the moment, she still had her other jobs in the glen, not prepared to let people down just because there were extra hours suddenly available at Calder. Work of one kind or another always turned up; she had learned that long ago. She had every intention of enjoying any benefits which came her way, and Jamie's company was definitely one of them. In the nearer term a pile of scampi and chips and a couple of beers also figured, when they got themselves together sufficiently to go along to the pub.

They lingered peacefully, idling and gossiping, discussing plans for the cottage, which in Jamie's case might be altering a curtain rail or putting up a few shelves, and in Maeve's stripping every inch of wood, gutting the kitchen and bashing through the filled-in windows. The western sky was warm with soft orange light, and Maeve's face and arms glowed with the golden tan Jamie so much admired. Then suddenly, from one minute to the next, bars of grey cloud were spreading across the bright expanse, the air turned chill and, shivery and goose-pimpled, they couldn't bear to be outside another second.

'Leave this lot,' Maeve ordered, pausing only to tip down the last drops of lager. 'Come on, grub.'

It was sybaritic pleasure to pull on a big soft sweater and, hunching her shoulders up to her ears and pulling the sleeves over her hands, Jamie hurried after Maeve down the mossy path to the lane, as eager as she was for hot food and warmth.

She had been to the pub with Maeve several times by now, and knew they would be welcomed into its inner circle. Maeve seemed to know everyone in the glen, but usually gravitated to whichever group included Fraser Kerr, the manager of the Gask sawmill. He was a big, quiet man, born and bred in the glen, who had, rashly as he was the first to admit, left it for a while for life in foreign parts (Aberfyle), and returned vowing never to move again. Now in middle-age, he had a comfortable air of having found what he wanted in life, of being his own man, and Jamie guessed that Maeve was drawn to him, whether consciously or not, as a refuge from the unsubtle attentions of the younger males.

Tonight Fraser was one of a group round a big table and as he raised a hand in greeting Jamie, with surprise, recognised the man sitting opposite him. It was Hugh Erskine from Fallan, a figure from the past whom she would not have expected to find in the bar of the local. But he had recognised her too, after a moment's hesitation, and was coming to his feet.

'It's Jamie Laidlaw, isn't it? I'd heard you were at Calder. How very nice to see you. I'm sorry we haven't been in touch before this. Hello, Maeve, how are you? Won't you both join us? I see you know Fraser. My wife, Louise. Cass Scott, who's staying with us.'

Louise the fair, smiling woman beside him, Cass the much taller one at the end of the table, and next being introduced was the very girl Jamie had seen on the first morning when she and Vanessa and Phil had come to the shop, the untidy, skinny girl driving the muddy pick-up with the dogs in the back.

'This is Abby, who used to be at Fallan with us.

Her husband, Geordie Macduff, who works with
Fraser at the sawmill . . .'

Tucking away names and facts, Jamie nevertheless experienced a moment of disorientation. Hugh
Erskine belonged to the faraway days when the
young of the scattered big houses had been rounded
up for any party going. Older than Jamie, he had
been very much part of Vanessa's scene, and they
had known him well, also his elder brother Roder-
ick, who had died in his early twenties, and Hugh's
second wife Angie – though no one had known
much about his disastrous and tempestuous first
marriage.

The self of those days and her present self, coming
in for a few drinks with Maeve, the events of the past
few weeks barely assimilated, still hardly believing
that the cottage (*Freda's* cottage) was to be hers,
seemed for a moment impossible to reconcile. Who
could have imagined, in Grandmother's day, this
gathering in this place? Jamie, attuning herself, let
the talk flow round her.

'So lovely, walking down by the river. We thought
we should take our chances before the children
descend.'

Jamie tried to work out who the children were.
Angie had had two boys, she thought, but hadn't
there been a daughter of the first marriage? She
couldn't remember. Were there younger children
now? She would find out in time. That was a pleasant
thought.

They were talking about the sunset, and the good

weather they'd been having, but Jamie felt most at home when the inevitable note of caution was struck. 'Aye, but that late spring will mean poor feeding. There'll not be many birds this year.'

'Have you sorted everyone out?' Louise asked Jamie kindly. 'Cass is over to organise my cook for the summer, as well as being a friend. She runs an agency, and was my boss once upon a time. I came to Fallan originally as a temp cook.' Her eyes, smiling, went to Hugh who, smiling in reply, turned to talk to them.

'So Calder's to be sold, I hear,' he said. 'Is that sad for you, or have you been away so much that you don't mind? I remember it well in your grandmother's day.'

'Did you ever see it in Zara's?'

He grinned. 'Not personally, but there were rumours. I'm sorry, by the way, to hear—' he remembered to add formally.

Jamie shook her head. 'No. No one's sorry.'

He nodded, accepting that. 'Are you over for long this time?'

The new, exciting answer to that rushed back, but before she could speak she was startled to see Patrick come in. She wouldn't have expected to see him here any more than she would have expected to run into Hugh Erskine. Time had moved on. Pleasure at seeing him added another layer of feeling, for Jamie had not dared to hope he would be back in the glen so soon. She liked the way his presence brought cohesion to the scene, for he belonged to both past and present and knew everyone here except the Erskines' guest, Cass.

'Thought it might be worth looking for you here,' he said to Jamie, drawing up a chair beside her, his dour face relaxing a little, as the flurry of greetings died down. 'Now that you've fallen into bad company.'

'Me, he means,' Maeve said, raising her glass to him.

'We assumed he meant you.'

'What are you drinking, man? A dram, is it?' Fraser asked.

The mood was so easy and natural that suddenly the different elements and time-scales seemed effortlessly to meld, and Jamie found herself luxuriating in the feeling of not having to face the world alone, which Patrick's company could always bring. Gratitude to be here almost overwhelmed her. Links within links, and she was part of them. In her present footloose state it seemed almost too good to take in.

She turned to look at Patrick, and he returned the look, one eyelid dropping briefly, sending the message that he guessed what she was feeling. But he couldn't know entirely, because he hadn't heard today's news. What better moment to share it?

The evening turned into a celebration, and as they toasted Jamie and the cottage, the future of Calder, and the incredibly rich buyer who would put it back exactly as it had been before, spend a fortune on the garden and be away most of the time, Jamie felt her elation almost getting out of hand.

The party became general, no one called time that she heard, and in a state of alcoholic beatitude she abandoned her car (Naomi's car) and, somewhere in the small hours, with dawn already past, let Patrick drive her home.

22

The screws in the hinges of the floor-to-ceiling cupboard were embedded in rust and flaking paint, but Jamie, hot and swearing, persisted till she had loosened them all. When she was down to the last one, however, she wished she'd waited for Patrick or Maeve to help her, for the door was unexpectedly heavy, and clearly had every intention of slewing round and flattening her as soon as the bottom hinge was freed. With a resolute effort she held it steady and got the final screw out. Then, with the door propped against the wall, she paused to hook her hair behind her ears and get her breath back.

The rain drove against the window in spattering gusts, and the ill-lit scullery was gloomy and dank on such a dull morning, but Jamie didn't care about the weather. In spite of having gone to bed so late, and the amount of wine she'd drunk last night, she was still on such a high that she felt nothing could ever depress her again.

How tolerant Patrick had been of her mood as they came home, knowing how impossible she was finding it to wind down. She thought of arriving back in the cool, rainy, sweet-smelling dawn, and the way they

had walked on, without discussion, and gone down to
the bridge. She thought of those moments leaning on
its rail, watching the falls, when Patrick had gathered
her up close against him, and they had stood in
dreaming silence with the infinitely delicate touch
of the cold spray on their faces, the rush and tumble
of the water in their ears, and all of life had seemed to
pause in a moment of great simplicity and peace.

They had come in and made coffee, more to warm
their icy hands than anything and then, suddenly
overtaken by tiredness and the hollow dawn feeling,
her teeth had begun to rattle against the mug and all
at once she had been yawning and shivering. Patrick
had shoved her unceremoniously up the stairs and
departed, and she could barely remember anything
after that. She only knew that she had been asleep the
moment her head touched the pillow, plummeting
into the depths of oblivion.

But she had woken after only a few hours, her first
thought the miraculous fact that she was going to
own this house. It had been enough to whirl her out
of bed and into action, and she had only paused for
coffee before starting work. Now she could think on
Maeve's level – well, somewhere closer to it at least –
and could do anything she liked to the place. Dab-
bling about with the emulsion or turning up curtains
was not enough today, and she had set about the first
structural job she could find within her means –
hanging this door the other way round, so that it
no longer opened into the face of anyone coming
from the kitchen. Now that it was off, she rather liked

the look of the open shelves. What was the wall like behind them? Damp. Oh, well, who cared? It might dry out with the door off. But the great thing was, there was no one to tell her to do something different, no one who had a say. Absorbed, happy, all other preoccupations put on hold, she rubbed down the varnished wood, filled a few of the more obvious cracks and holes, and began slapping on the undercoat.

The whole aspect of life was changed. She had a base. She had adapted to the new Calder. Its memories were still there, safely tucked away, but it had become its new self, belonging to none of them, a big unwieldy building in the hands of the workmen, which would presently re-emerge as a pleasant, comfortable house once more. Speculation as to who might live there revolved idly and optimistically in Jamie's mind as she worked.

Mingling with these thoughts were images of last night's party, of Hugh Erskine, so much more relaxed and approachable than she remembered him, of his smiling, gentle wife Louise, and of scatty, friendly Abby and her inarticulate but plainly adoring husband.

And Maeve and Fraser. Now there was a thought. It was clear there was an excellent understanding between them, a reciprocal appreciation which was probably unstated. But presumably that was all. Maeve was so self-sufficient and independent, her life so busy and well-rounded, it had to be all. Among the many women living alone whom Jamie had met, she saw Maeve as the one who had most emphatically made the choice for herself, and who found the greatest contentment in her way of life. One telling sign was that she never harped on about how well it suited her; in fact never talked about it, as though it wasn't a point that ever occurred to her.

Jamie had known where her thoughts would bring her; where her thoughts had started; where they so often ran, deep below everything else that she was thinking or doing. Did Maeve find with Fraser even a glimmering or shadow of the sense of absolute rightness which she herself found when she was with Patrick? Or did Maeve not need such reassurance? But was there any human being who didn't, at some time or in some degree?

Jamie knew that if Calder – this cottage – was to be her base, then for her own peace of mind she must examine her feelings for Patrick with honesty. Last night, when he had so unexpectedly appeared, there had been the instant, unfailing conviction of everything now being all right, which nothing seemed to change or diminish. All right. A phrase from childhood. What did it mean now?

Jamie paused, remembering to hold the paint brush over the can, but oblivious to everything else around her. She had felt no longer alone in relation to the group she was with. She had felt that someone who knew her, understood her and was always and for ever 'on her side', without question, had, by simply coming to sit next to her, subtly changed the whole tone of the evening. Enjoyment, awareness, confidence in herself, had all moved up a notch. It was so much part of her life that it was easy to take it for granted, but such a response had to be re-assessed if she were to remain in any place where she would see Patrick on a regular basis.

A flutter of trepidation stirred at the thought of altering the established footing between them, but was instantly threaded with the temptation to see what would happen if she did. She knew this temptation only too well. It had hurtled her into more than one disaster in the past, and now she made up her mind that it must never endanger her relationship with Patrick.

But what precisely was that relationship?

Scarcely aware of what she was doing, but needing to give this her full attention, Jamie put down the paint can, laid her brush across it, and went through to the kitchen, to take up a position at its window where she could stare out across the gorge.

Simplest to say that Patrick was like a member of the family, part of their lives for ever. But for Jamie the word family had no happy associations. Patrick had, indeed, been the one stable element outside it, always there to turn to when members of her actual family, in their various ways, had failed her. How vividly she could recall, so vividly that she felt shaken by it even now, her joy whenever he had turned up, the soaring delight. She also recalled, less comfortably, how bitterly she had resisted his assumption of authority as she grew older, furious at his interference and forthright criticism. But she had long ago put that into perspective, acknowledging that Patrick and Patrick alone was to thank for keeping her on some productive – and lawful – track, refusing to let her waste whatever talents she had.

Father figure. That was the obvious cliché. She had adored her own father but he had let her down. Patrick had moved naturally from the big brother role to fill the gap. He had provided the safety net, however unflattering and outspoken he might be, which for most people was provided by their families. And, in spite of the flouting and the fights, she had admired, respected and trusted him.

She still did, and that lay at the heart of her problem. Always, inescapably, as childhood hero-worship and adult appreciation of what he had done for her coalesced into the feelings she had never had the courage to define, she had known how inaccessible he was. To him she was still the thrawn child rushing head-on into yet another catastrophe, always doing everything the hard way. To her he was the grown-up. The gap of age between them was not twelve years but a generation. Patrick's dour character and tendency towards reclusiveness had always reinforced this feeling. Like Maeve, he had a life that was balanced, fulfilling and complete.

No other man could ever take the place Patrick held in her life, that was certain. Other relationships were quite distinct from this closeness and acceptance. Even with Bryden this had been the case. Yet none of this, Jamie knew, approached the truth of what she felt about him – that to be with him was to be home.

What a lunatic word to choose, she told herself, trying to shake off the morbid mood which had overtaken her. She had hated home and couldn't wait to get away from it. Muddled memories swarmed back – her father promising to take her on the hill and leaving her behind; the desperate jealousy she suffered when Vanessa talked so confidently about 'Mummy'; the waiting – waiting at windows, waiting in the dark rooms of tall houses, waiting for the end of term and then waiting to be allowed to go to Calder; the horror of realising that Zara was never going to go away; and the ache of emptiness, of chances lost for ever, when she had stood six years ago at her father's funeral service and accepted that he had long ago stopped caring, perhaps had never cared.

As Bryden had never really cared. And here you are standing at a window again.

Anger sprang up to have let herself reach this point. '*Don't!*' she said sharply aloud. 'Just *don't!*'

Ten minutes ago she had been bursting with joy, she reminded herself in exasperation, going back to finish her painting. But the thoughts about Patrick had to be faced. He had said he didn't come to the Toll-house very often now, but she would be living within his orbit nevertheless, something which hadn't happened before in their adult lives, and at a time when she knew she was intensely vulnerable. The responsibility for preserving a friendship which meant more to her than any other lay with her, and she must find a way to meet it.

How astonished Patrick would be at this mish-mash of sentiment, she reflected, her mouth twisting, as she squatted down to finish the last bit of shelf.

When he appeared after lunch, ready to help with whatever job was on hand or enter into any amount of discussion about other improvements, the normality of being with him brought that home to her once more. But he need never know about such thoughts. He was there, close at hand for brief interludes, or busy at Blackdykes with his own life; but he was there, and on that foundation the rest could, in time, be rebuilt.

The day, Jamie decided, rolling into bed a good deal earlier than she had last night, or this morning, had been good. Put the temporary emotional storm down to lack of sleep and forget it. It had soon been overtaken by a larger contentment.

It had been good to work away with Patrick there, the fire lit, the rain never relenting, the voice of the river taking on a deeper note as it foamed down. And it had been good to hear pounding feet coming along the path, and to see Maeve burst in, drenched herself, but carefully shielding from the rain a battered but pretty pie-crust table.

'Wow, it's coming down in stair-rods. Hi, Patrick. This any good to you, Jamie? There are a couple of gouges here and there, but they'd fill in no bother at all.'

'Maeve, it's perfect. Where did you get it?'

'Abby spotted it. Been chucked out at Gask. She

thought you might like it. Geordie brought it down
in the pick-up because he knew I was doing a job at
one of the chalets.'

Apart from her pleasure in the acquisition, there
had been for Jamie a deeper pleasure in the thought
that Abby had remembered her, had taken the trouble to rescue this treasure for her, sure she would like
it, and had got it to Maeve. Just one shabby little
table, but for a second Jamie was warmed by a vision
of being woven into the network of glen lives, and by
recognising that Abby, Maeve, herself, and Patrick,
who had picked it up to examine it and was com-
menting, 'What a beauty,' all viewed it in the same
light.

After tea, for which Patrick had produced a bag of
doughnuts from his poacher's pocket, they had gone
across to the house where the work, after seeming to
be suspended at exactly the same point for days, had
suddenly taken a leap forward – possibly because the
rain had kept Maeve away – and where with every job
completed it was easier to accept its new future. The
past was almost forgotten. Not visually, since elements of it were in fact being reinstated, but, Jamie
knew, because her mind no longer clung to it or
needed it.

The only thing bothering her as she went to bed
was that she hadn't made contact with Vanessa. That
seemed rather churlish in view of her delight that
Vanessa had finally agreed about the cottage. The
message via Mr Syme had been that Vanessa would
phone today, and Jamie knew the workmen would

have fetched her if there had been a call. Obviously Vanessa hadn't tried to get hold of her, but she could have called herself.

This evening she had gone to the Toll-house for supper, and to her shame hadn't given the matter a thought. Now it was too late to try. Tomorrow would have to do, but she felt guilty all the same. Her slight surprise of yesterday, when Mr Syme had passed on the message from Vanessa, returned bringing a vague unease. Had there been a major battle with Douglas about the decision? Well of course there would have been trouble. He had been flatly against the idea from the start. But presumably Vanessa had been able to convince him that it wouldn't mean any serious financial loss.

I should have contacted Phil too, Jamie thought belatedly. Had Vanessa talked to her? It would have been friendly, at the very least, to make sure she was still happy about the plan. Well, she would be; there was no real doubt of that, but she should be made to feel included. Perhaps the best thing would be to go down and see her, breaking through this resistance she put up against them visiting her at Burnbrae House. If Jamie were to be living here, within easy driving distance, she wouldn't want to feel permanently debarred. Surely the place couldn't be that bad?

Tomorrow she would put all this right. Tomorrow there would be more jobs to get at, more light to let in, more of herself to stamp upon this refuge she had found. Maeve might appear. Patrick would still be around . . . With images hovering of his deep-set, direct and uncompromising eyes, his lined face and broad work-hardened hands, her thoughts began to blur and blend. Through the open window the roar of the river, thundering down after the day's rain among the rocks its own passage had smoothed to glass, seemed to grow louder, overtaking coherent awareness. Sleep engulfed her, and down she went into that soothing ceaseless sound and movement.

Some sudden, violent noise cracked through this steady flow. Jerking awake Jamie was for a moment back in Seattle, in the city environment of security systems and double locks and the never-quite-forgotten consciousness, however remote, of a hostile sub-culture in the background. It was a huge relief to realise, even as her heart thumped and adrenalin shot up, that she was here, at Calder.

And that sound was not someone smashing their way in, it was someone hammering on the door, which on the whole burglars, rapists or whatever were unlikely to do. Trembling from that sudden jolt out of sleep, but not afraid, Jamie grabbed a sweater and tumbled down the stairs.

'I'm coming, stop banging like that.'

Maeve, waving a bottle, looking for a party? Some local crisis, accident, fire or flood? But wasn't Calder too far from the road for anyone to come here for help?

There was no outside light, so it was by the unshaded bulb above her head in the tiny square of hall that she recognised Vanessa standing on the step, a Vanessa wrapped in a dark coat, its collar up, her hair on end and untidy as Jamie had never seen it.

'Vanessa, for God's sake, whatever's happened?' Had she run her car off the road? But what would she be doing in the glen in the first place? And at this time of night? Drawing her in Jamie felt the tremble, grimly controlled, of the arm she took, and then, startlingly, in response to her touch, felt that fierce control splinter and a wild shaking overtake Vanessa's whole body. Her teeth began to chatter audibly, and it was evident that she could hardly stand.

'Vanessa, what *is* it?' Jamie cried, but more to release her own confused shock than in expectation of an answer, as she struggled to get Vanessa to the nearest chair. It was hard to take in that she could possibly be in such a state. Jamie found her brain would barely work and that her mouth was trembling with distress.

Getting Vanessa into one of the high-backed wing chairs, Jamie went back to switch on the light, and turned to find Vanessa, blinking and dazed, gazing up at her with what looked like desperate pleading, all pretences swept away in a new and terrible vulnerability. Her jaw was grazed, her cheekbone swollen and bruised, and a deep discoloration was spreading round her half-closed eye.

'My God,' Jamie whispered, going to kneel in front of her, taking her hands with the utmost gentleness, as though to touch any part of her would cause more pain.

Their eyes locked. Vanessa tried to speak, but her

lips quivered uncontrollably. Bending forward to hide that battered face for a moment, her tangled hair gleaming under the light, with a desperate effort she gathered words together.

'This is the last time. The very last time. I shall never go back.'

23

Who would have imagined, Jamie reflected with a certain grim humour, that one of Zara's tarted-up guest rooms would have proved such an ideal and welcome refuge?

She thought from Vanessa's breathing that she was at last asleep. Certainly those dry, racking sobs were over, sounds revealing an abandonment to grief which she had found almost unbearable. To see Vanessa, so contained and competent, always so carefully turned out, reduced to this heedless despair had shaken Jamie almost more than anything she could remember. It was like seeing the rule book thrown away, opening the gates to a terrifying anarchy. She had longed wildly to fetch Patrick, the only 'grown-up' who could help them.

She had hugged and soothed Vanessa, barely holding back tears herself. She had made tea, banal but obvious recourse. She had hastily lit a fire and pulled Vanessa's chair close up to it. But Vanessa had not let her touch or even examine that beaten face. And with an aching resolve to do whatever was required of her, Jamie had held her tongue as the incoherent, disjointed gouts of pain and humiliation spilled out.

'He gets so angry. He watches me and watches me till I don't know what I'm doing. He despises everything I say. I know I make him angry, I know I'm stupid and can't grasp things and get everything wrong, but I've tried and tried. I promise you I have. Only this really wasn't anything to do with him, was it? You said that yourself. It was our decision, ours, not his. But he gets so—' Shuddering, her voice wavering, Vanessa had closed her eyes, bowing her head, huddling into her navy cashmere car coat, rain still lightly misting it. 'He comes so close to me, his voice is so loud, and he gets so angry . . .' Tears had oozed out of the tightly shut lids, one now puffy and dark, and had found their way down her wincing, contorted face.

Jamie could imagine how threatening Douglas could be, his breadth and height daunting in themselves in comparison to Vanessa's essentially soft and feminine build, his voice powerful and overriding, his contempt and certainty, and his easy command of words, beating down all opposition. In a flash of revulsion Jamie could imagine how, having demolished any resistance Vanessa might put up, having reduced her to tears or pleading or apology or whatever he had looked for, he would get a buzz from this display of domination, walking buoyantly away, ego gratified by his reassertion of control.

But to think that such confrontations could lead to actual physical harm to Vanessa. The thought had sickened Jamie, and it had been hard to keep her shock and anger in hand. The awful thing was that, now the evidence was before her, it was an easy step to realising that this could have happened before. She had not needed Vanessa's desperate, 'This is the last time,' to believe that. It was as if part of her had known all along, burying the idea so deeply that it had had no chance to take shape.

'It's never been like this before though,' Vanessa had said presently, as though for all her distress she had caught Jamie's thought, and in her voice there had been something oddly like appeal. Appeal to whom? Was it important that she held on to this fact? 'He's been angry so often lately,' she had hurried on. 'About Ryan, and money, and things at work, and I'm so hopeless at understanding those. Then he was furious about Calder, of course. When he found out it had been ours all along, and what Zara had done with the valuable stuff, he went on and on about it. It wasn't about this cottage, not at first, but the house, selling it quickly and so on. Then he was so on edge, flaring up about any little thing, dinner being late, or a suit he wanted to wear being at the cleaners. Of course I know lots of husbands get impatient about things like that . . .'

The tremor in her voice as she tried to reduce this to some kind of normality had been more distressing to Jamie even than seeing the poor bruised cheek and swollen eye. Husbands might indeed get angry about petty domestic shortcomings, especially if other problems were bugging them, and Vanessa's ability to made a production out of the smallest issue was enough to drive anyone mad, that had to be conceded, but few husbands were driven to strike out like this, and it was a violation of every rule of decency to do so. Jamie had had to get up and deal with the fire to conceal her anger that Vanessa, even now, seemed actually to want to believe that there was some excuse for what Douglas had done.

'It was as though – when he got really impatient with me, I mean – as though he just couldn't keep hold of himself. He'd simply boil over. Only, in a way . . .' Vanessa's voice had trailed into silence, and with a hand to her cheek, though not touching it, she had appeared to be making an effort to establish the exact truth of what she was saying, looking back to assess with scrupulous fairness scenes Jamie hated to visualise. 'He didn't exactly boil over,' Vanessa had amended, her voice so thin that Jamie had to lean close to hear her. 'It wasn't like losing his temper. It was almost as though he made a decision. His eyes would change. I'd see them change. Then I'd know . . .'

It was a whisper so bleak that it had sounded as if it were meant for her alone.

'Oh, darling Van!' Jamie had drawn her close, rage and compassion stifling her. Yet not incredulity. The step of believing that Douglas was capable of this had already been taken, and the questions in her mind were on another level. How long had it been going on? Why had Vanessa allowed it to go on? What exactly had Douglas done to her? Did Phil know? But this Jamie had instantly dismissed. This was not the kind of thing one would let Phil even guess at. She was the last person Vanessa would have told.

'Sometimes it would be when we were getting ready to go out somewhere,' Vanessa had still sounded as if she were talking to herself, tentatively putting into words for the first time things she had become adept at burying. 'So that I'd have to make the effort to pretend nothing had happened. It was so awful, trying to be bright and normal and say the right things to people, and knowing he was watching me, and that if I didn't behave in the way he wanted me to he would . . .'

The sick feeling swelling in her, Jamie had tried to resist this picture. That kind, neat, well-meaning Vanessa, who spent her whole life doing her best for everyone around her, vulnerable through her very good intentions, should meet with such treatment whipped up an anger far more violent than anything in her own life had produced. For the immaculate house at Dunrossie, with its pastel perfection and faintly scented air, to be the scene where violence, whether verbal or actual, had been done to this gentle girl seemed a total outrage. And Douglas, smiling, affable, good host, decent chap . . .

She had let Vanessa talk until she had no more to say, hunched slack and uncaring in the dim old chair – a telling sight indeed, for Vanessa was obsessed about posture and was frequently highly irritating on the subject to others. Her look of defeat had roused in Jamie a furious protectiveness, but she had disciplined herself to suppress all demands as to why

Vanessa had let matters reach this point. With guilt she had seen again how inaccessible she herself had been.

Apart from it not being the moment to embark on such questions, practical decisions had had to be made. So far there was only one bed in the cottage. Vanessa would have been welcome to it but, even in this crisis, Jamie had known it would be useless to suggest that she slept in it while Jamie took the chair. Vanessa, she had been certain, would have fretted so much about the arrangement that neither of them would have got any sleep. On the other hand it had been unthinkable to take Vanessa across to the house, make up a bed for her and leave her there alone, a prey to doubts and fears, and the ugly memories of angry words and the moment when the blows had come.

For an anxious second Jamie hadn't been able to remember whether electricity was on in the house or not. At various stages of the work it had been turned off. Then she had remembered, calming down, that she and Maeve and Patrick had gone round the house after the men had left, and everything had been working.

Thank goodness Patrick was up at the Toll-house. She had longed to fetch him there and then, for her own comfort as much as for Vanessa's. But tomorrow he would come down. And then everything would be all right. Jamie had smiled at herself for clutching at the reassuring mantra once more. What she thought Patrick could do, or how much Vanessa would want him to know, were not what mattered. Simply it was good to know he was close by, and the thought had steadied her as she had hastily collected a few things and come back to persuade Vanessa to set off with her through the garden.

Vanessa had brought nothing with her, and that in itself said so much. Hers had been a desperate flight, and Jamie hated to think of the brutality which had finally driven her to it. But did this rushing into the night, just as she was, more subtly suggest that this was a gesture, a plea for help, and not something which had been thought out over time, or was meant to be for good?

It had been a relief to remember that the rooms they had used on their first return to Calder were waiting, not affected by the rehabilitation process. It had seemed almost bizarre to Jamie, as her mind turned to details, to realise that hot water could be swiftly produced, that linen was waiting in the linen cupboard, and everything they needed was to hand.

Lying now in one of Zara's luxurious beds, Jamie recalled with a wince of distress their walk across to the house. Vanessa had barely seemed to know where she was going, moving uncertainly like an old woman, clinging to Jamie's arm. Her indifference to whatever Jamie decided to do with her, the absence of her usual meddling instinct to improve on the plot, had been another poignant aspect of the night.

Vanessa looked dreadful in the light of a sunless but clear morning. She had no make-up with her other than a lipstick which had been in her bag, and Jamie could have wished she hadn't had that, observing how her skin, paler than Jamie's, which in any case had already acquired a tan, looked an almost transparent white in contrast to the angry bruising produced by Douglas's fist. The skin was pouched even round the good eye, a violet-blue circle below it. It was clear that she had barely slept and, exhausted and distracted, she seemed unable to bring her mind to bear on anything approaching a decision, or even to remember what had been in her mind when she had fled here.

'I feel so awful,' she said tremulously, as Jamie brought toast and coffee to the table where, against all custom, Vanessa had sat down obediently when ordered, making no move to help. She plucked at her sleeve as she spoke, and Jamie realised that her statement had nothing to do with apprehension or tiredness, but for the moment was concerned with the fact that Vanessa was wearing what she had had on last night, a silk shirt and skirt and high heels. She had rejected all offerings from Jamie's wardrobe, but the fact that she had had to put on yesterday's clothes clearly distressed her.

Jamie, ever keen on action, wanted to dive at once into plans for going down to Dunrossie to fetch what was needed. Even she could see, however, that there was a good deal of ground to be covered before they reached that point. Glancing at Vanessa's disfigured face she felt a lurch of concern to think of all that had to be resolved, mixed with doubt about Vanessa's capacity to deal with any far-reaching decisions in her present state.

'Does Douglas know where you are?' she asked carefully, filling Vanessa's cup and pushing the toast rack towards her. Vanessa seemed oblivious of either action, sitting hunched and motionless, her lips tightly compressed.

'He'll guess that you came here, won't he?' Jamie tried again, but even as she said it realised that it wasn't necessarily true. She had been away for so long, no one could pretend that she had made much effort to keep in close touch. She might very easily not be the first person Douglas would think of.

'I can't go back,' Vanessa said with sudden violence, clutching the edge of the table with both hands like a child determined to resist being lifted away.

Jamie let a moment pass, to make sure her own voice was under control before she spoke. It seemed vital to keep this discussion on the calmest level she could achieve. 'There's no question of your going back unless you want to,' she said definitely. 'And there's no need to decide anything right away either. We have this place. It's ours, yours as much as mine. You can be here for as long as you need or want to be.'

For a second the image of the cottage as her inviolable and precious retreat rose before Jamie's eyes, and she was immediately furious with herself for the selfishness of the reaction. But the image was at once superseded by a different one – the cottage as a shared and safe place for Vanessa, which they could defend together. For ever afterwards Jamie was thankful to know that the second vision had had more reality than the first.

'I think, though, that we ought to let them know where you are,' she persisted, though speaking with caution. 'It would probably save a lot of trouble in the long run and—'

'Them?' Vanessa broke in, her head jerking up, her face startled. 'Who?'

'Well, Douglas and Ryan, of course,' Jamie said blankly. 'I expect—'

'I thought you meant the police.' Vanessa shook her head as though to clear the thought from it. 'Ryan's not at home. It's just Douglas. You don't think I could have left like that if Ryan had been there, do you? I always like to be there for him, you know that. I wouldn't have dreamt of—' She broke off, confused and upset. 'Jamie, didn't I tell you he'd gone? I thought I had.'

'Gone? Gone where?' Jamie had a feeling of being close to the source of some frightening explosion, without any idea of how to prevent it.

'Oh – to stay with a friend.' The answer was so hurried and dismissive, as though Vanessa had thought better of revealing this news after all, that Jamie let it go. What kind of row had there been to make Ryan quit his comfortable nest?

'I still think we should tell Douglas that you are here, though,' she said gently.

'Oh, Jamie, no! We can't do that, we can't,' Vanessa rushed into panic. 'You don't understand.

He'll come up here, it will be dreadful. You've no idea how—'

'Vanessa, he's quite likely to come looking anyway.' Jamie hated to press the point, but it was no use evading it. 'If you tell him first it may keep things on a more civilised level. Or he may be satisfied with that and stay away until you're ready to talk.' Jamie had never felt on a less certain footing, quite unable to judge how Douglas would react or what he would want.

Vanessa reinforced Jamie's feeling of being out of her depth by saying worriedly, 'I do hope he got away all right this morning, and managed some sort of breakfast.'

Jamie's mouth opened and closed again as Vanessa went on, 'It's not good to start out so early with nothing to eat. I left things ready, but he may not have bothered. And I know today is really busy for him. That was partly why he was angry, because I'd chosen to tell him that I'd phoned Mr Syme when he had such a big day ahead.'

Her voice, confident for a moment as she found herself back on the familiar track of everyday concerns, became unsure again. For a second Jamie wondered if she remembered where she was, or why she had come.

'You got breakfast stuff out for him?' she asked in disbelief. After a scene of such proportions that her husband had punched her in the face, Vanessa had – what? – laid the table, put bread by the toaster, coffee ready beside the percolator? It was totally bizarre, yet in an appalling way believable, that Vanessa, conditioned before all else to caring for her husband and son, had been unable to walk away without performing these services.

But this had carried them way off track. 'Vanessa, wait a minute.' Her throat tight and her voice husky, Jamie went round the table and put an arm round Vanessa's slumped shoulders. 'Look, forget all that for the moment. It doesn't matter now. We should try to concentrate on what you want to do. Yes? Don't you think so?'

Vanessa rubbed a hand across her forehead. 'Yes, I suppose so. You're right.' She didn't sound convinced.

'Then I think you should stay here for a couple of days at least, till things have simmered down. We – or I, if you prefer it – can go down and fetch whatever you need from Dunrossie. I think we should contact Douglas and let him know you're here and that you'll be in touch again soon. I can phone him for you, or we can leave a message at the office. You don't need to speak to him.' She had felt the tremor of Vanessa's body at the idea of talking to Douglas, and rage at what he had done flared again. She knew that for Vanessa's sake she must contain it.

'It seems so awful to abandon everything.'

For a second Jamie thought Vanessa meant that she saw herself as having left Douglas for good, and she felt relief and admiration rise, but Vanessa's next words showed that she was still inescapably preoccupied by domestic trivia.

'I'd taken a pheasant out for dinner, so it should be thawed, but it ought to go into the oven by—'

'Vanessa. Stop. Look at me.' Very tenderly Jamie drew that sad face round to hers. 'None of that matters. Truly. Douglas will find something to eat. If he knows you're not there he'll eat on the way home, or stay in Edinburgh.' It galled her to have to produce such answers on his behalf, but she understood that for Vanessa they had to be cleared out of the way before she could apply her mind to any larger issue. Though on the one hand she had made the dramatic and extreme gesture of driving off into the night to come hammering on Jamie's door, on the other she was still deeply enmeshed in the role that had given her life its only meaning for so many years. Jamie wondered with foreboding how much time and patience it would take to free her from the ingrained need to care for and serve.

'But if he comes here!' Vanessa exclaimed, forgetting practical matters for the moment, and swinging back to the more terrifying reality of what she had set in motion. 'If he comes tonight! Jamie, I shouldn't have come. I can't drag you into all this. I'd better go back, it's the only thing to do. I must have been mad.' But in the act of starting up from the table, pushing Jamie aside, looking as if she were ready to head off at once, she stumbled, almost incapable of standing, and began to sob helplessly. 'But I can't go back. I can't, not to that.'

'Van darling, it's all right. I promise you it will be all right. He shan't hurt you, ever again. I won't let him. You're safe here. I'll look after you.'

And Patrick will look after you. Because the very first moment that I think it's all right to leave you I'm going over to the house to phone him. And he'll come at once and see to everything, and we'll both be safe.

24

'Vanessa, you poor, poor dear.' Patrick took one look at the bruised face she turned up to him, with its attempt at a smile, lop-sided and self-conscious, and folded his arms around her.

Patrick's hugging Vanessa, Jamie thought with a moment's blank surprise, the kind of surprise a child feels when adults do something out of the ordinary and excessive. Don't be so silly, why shouldn't he hug her? It's the most natural thing in the world for him to do. But the consciousness stirred again of time having moved on while she was away, leaving her behind – and there also sparked a fierce longing for Patrick to wrap *her* in his arms like that. She wanted to feel their hard strength, his big hard body against hers, needed and ached to be for a moment absorbed and encompassed by maleness. It was an unsettling reaction, and one she really didn't need right now. She was ashamed as well that it could have intruded at a moment when Vanessa was in such straits, needing all their help and sympathy.

Patrick didn't settle down to get the whole story out of Vanessa, as Jamie half thought he might do, still unconsciously reverting to childhood days when for them all he had been part of the hierarchy of authority. She could feel his anger, and no one looking at the grim lines of his face could doubt it, but she had the feeling that this development was not altogether a surprise to him. In practical terms, however, his chief concern was to establish what Vanessa wanted to do next.

'Give yourself time to think,' was his immediate advice to her. 'You've come away, you've taken the step, that's the main thing. Stay at Calder for a day or two. It's quiet here, and you needn't see anyone. But I do think you ought to let Douglas know where you are, as Jamie says. That keeps things on a sensible level.'

He didn't elaborate the point, but when Jamie went to the back kitchen to make coffee, leaving Vanessa still sitting at the table where they had had breakfast, deep in her thoughts, gazing unseeingly at the fresh green of the birches in the still, faintly misty air, he followed.

'You can cope with her being here, Jamie?' he asked in a low voice, coming close so that he could look into her face. 'You're sure this is all right with you?'

'Of course it is.' But Jamie was grateful for the understanding which lay behind the question. She knew he wasn't asking it because there was any real decision to be made, but because he had not forgotten that she had her own problems to work through.

'She could have the Toll-house if she wanted it,' he offered. 'You know it's there for her.'

'Patrick, that's kind, but she couldn't really be there, for all kinds of reasons.'

'I know.' Patrick had suggested it more to assure Jamie that support was there for her, than with any hope of changing the plan. It had been a delight for him to watch her pleasure in acquiring the cottage, her evident feeling of sanctuary there, and he had been glad that she had found a place to lick her wounds and find her feet again. He had also recognised her need, not unlike Vanessa's though in her case the signs of violence were not visible, for time and space. There was no question of her not wanting to give Vanessa refuge, but Patrick thought the timing could hardly have been worse.

'Good girl. She does need you,' was all he said, but he took Jamie's arm for a moment, his grip warm and emphatic, and it pleased her very much. She sensed, however, that the focus of his attention had remained on the still figure in the room behind them.

'That anyone should do this to Vanessa, of all people,' he said savagely, his voice still carefully suppressed, but full of a disgust which Jamie found comforting. 'That bastard Cairney.' He had always disliked his plausible glibness and unshakable complacency. But Douglas would have to wait.

'I shall take you down to Dunrossie,' he told Vanessa with finality, when Jamie raised the question of clothes. 'No, no argument, of course I shall. I'd intended to stay up at the Toll-house for a couple of days more anyway.' Work could take its turn. In fact at present he wouldn't care very much if he never worked again. The self-contained solitary years looked very barren now.

'But should we say to Douglas if we're going to the house?' Vanessa asked anxiously, apparently with a confused idea that she had created some kind of official separation by walking out. Patrick would have been interested to know exactly how she saw her action, but knew that any useful discussion on that score must still be some way off.

Jamie, however, had leapt in with indignation. 'What are you talking about? It's your home, just as much as his.' Even now this willingness on Vanessa's part to see Douglas as boss, arbiter, the man who must be placated. It infuriated her.

Patrick quelled her with a look. 'Vanessa,' he said gently, 'it might be better to wait to contact Douglas until after you've been to the house.' Or did she secretly long, he momentarily wondered, beneath the surface fear, to see Douglas and renew the confrontation. Had it become in some degree compulsive? Was fighting with him better than being away from him?

'You think he might come back if he knew I was there?' Vanessa asked, looking startled. Then she said, so much in her normal manner that Patrick almost smiled, 'Oh, no, I don't think so, Patrick, I don't see how he could. He's got such a lot on today. He said so last night—' She broke off abruptly, her face changing. It was one of the factors he had used to fuel his anger. For Christ's sake, didn't he have enough on his plate without her going behind his back to make such a bloody stupid decision, getting involved in things she knew nothing about . . . ?

She shivered, hearing again the furious tide of words. The decision about this cottage where she now was. With an effort she pushed the memory away. 'I do know he's very busy,' she said, her voice wavery, but doing her best to give Patrick a practical answer.

'Then we won't worry about him,' Patrick said easily. 'We'll just collect what you need, and you can sort out anything you have to in the house and then we'll come back.'

Jamie, seeing the grateful smile Vanessa gave him, felt deeply thankful that he had been on hand today.

'You'll come too, of course,' he said to her, when Vanessa, from habit, had gone upstairs to 'tidy up'. She would never think of going anywhere without checking her make-up and brushing her hair. No consciousness of absurdity interfered with the ritual today, even with so few aids to hand.

'Will you need me?' Jamie was uncertain. It seemed rather a gang of them, just to fetch a few clothes. But she knew that behind the question lay a reluctance to go back into that house, with its deceptive air of serene comfort, now that she knew what ugly things had been going on beneath the surface. Then she was ashamed of being influenced by that distaste. How could what she felt matter?

'In spite of what Vanessa says about Douglas being so busy, we can't be certain that he won't be there,

waiting for her,' Patrick warned. 'That's why I want
to take her down. But she'll need you there too, for
company and moral support. And more importantly
you might be able to prevent her from being railroaded into staying, if by any chance Douglas is
there. I wouldn't feel very happy about leaving
her, now that things have reached this point. I think
the time has come for some good hard thinking about
the future, on both sides, and if possible for a few
ground rules to be laid down.'

'But did you know or suspect something?' Jamie
asked. How long had this sort of thing been going
on? Had Vanessa talked to Patrick? Then why had
he said nothing? And what had she herself missed
that she should have seen, in Vanessa's letters and
while she was staying at Dunrossie? The uneasy
atmosphere, Vanessa's nervous fussing, Douglas's
air of self-satisfied control – how simple to interpret
them now, and how inconceivable to have missed
them before.

'I'd begun to be concerned,' Patrick said briefly.
'But, as you can imagine, I had no idea matters had
come to this. I hardly ever see Douglas and Vanessa
together. I used to think that Douglas put her down
far too much, and was destroying her self-confidence, but I came to the conclusion that she'd grown
so used to it she hardly noticed it any more. That was
bad enough. But this!'

His face was so dark with anger and contempt that
Jamie wondered whether a confrontation with Douglas would be wise. Then she found she rather

relished the prospect. Her money would certainly be on Patrick.

'It's so good of you to help us,' she took the chance to say hurriedly before Vanessa came back.

Patrick shot her a strange look, frowning as though this annoyed him, began to say something but changed his mind, turning brusquely away. It happened so quickly, his expression becoming impenetrable again at once, that Jamie was left jolted and puzzled, feeling she had been clumsy in trying to thank him, but not understanding why he should object.

Vanessa reappeared, her coat in her hands. 'I know it's June, but it's quite chilly this morning. I wonder if I should put this on. I think perhaps I shall, though I don't expect I'll need it in the car. It's not easy to tell in here – this really isn't the warmest of houses, you know, Jamie.'

The familiar debate about a trivial decision, conducted out loud; the mock-teasing tone which Vanessa appeared to believe softened the criticism she was sure no one minded, made Jamie decide wryly that she must be feeling better. But it would have been hard to mind anything Vanessa said at present.

Douglas was not at Dunrossie, but the house itself seemed for Vanessa to exert almost as powerful an influence as his presence would have done. As she went in its quiet, composed air seemed alien, as though entering it now was subtly different from hurrying in after shopping or ferrying Ryan or calling on a neighbour, with her mind already on the first job to be done. Now she felt as if she shouldn't be here at all.

But after the strange, suspended moment of uncertainty, normality returned. This was her home; her life was here. What had she been thinking of, rushing off in the middle of the night like a hysterical teenager? Here things waited to be seen to, the ordinary familiar things, comfortably within her scope, which she did every day of her life. Thank goodness this wasn't one of Pauline's mornings. Whatever would she have thought if she had arrived to find – what would she have found?

Suddenly for Vanessa the most urgent thing was to hide or put to rights anything which might hint at what had happened here last night. Shame and a fierce instinct for privacy brought hot colour into her face.

'I'll go up. By myself. Don't come, I must just—' She had difficulty in framing a coherent sentence.

She turned to the stairs and Jamie checked a movement to follow in support. Her face anxious, not sure what Vanessa most needed from her, she watched her go up.

Patrick, a dark protective shape, remained near the door, watchful, concealing the compassion which filled him to see Vanessa's distress.

She took three steps, then paused, looking upwards in sudden tension.

Had she heard something? Was Douglas there after all, sleeping off who knew what excesses? The others strained their ears, but there was nothing but the unnatural waiting stillness of an empty house with, emerging into sudden prominence, faint sounds from the kitchen of fridge and freezer, and closer at hand the ordered, mellow tick of the long-case clock.

Vanessa turned, a look of helpless disintegration rather than fear in her face. 'Oh, Jamie, I can't. I can't do this.'

'It's all right.' Jamie leapt up the stairs to throw her arms round her in fierce reassurance. 'You don't have to. You don't have to do anything you don't want to. We're here. It's OK.'

'You'll have to come with me.'

'Of course I will. Or I'll fetch the things for you if you prefer. Just tell me which. Or we can forget the whole idea and just go away. We'll buy what you need. You don't ever have to come here again if it's—'

If it was what? Impossible to go on.

'No, no.' The suggestion of not completing a job she had set out to do steadied Vanessa at once. She had always thought it wrong not to do things because you didn't feel like it. Far too many people let themselves do that nowadays. She had always clung to rules without examining them, and it helped her to pull herself together now.

But after all there was nothing to show anyone what had taken place, so few hours ago, in the wide light bedroom with its soft and feminine style. There was only the unmade bed, and Douglas's clothes tossed down. Without thought, almost as though welcoming the sight of something which needed to

be done, Vanessa went forward and stooped to pick
up his shirt.

'What are you *doing*?' Jamie couldn't keep back the
exclamation. To her Vanessa's action screamed male
dominance and willing female subservience, and she
was horrified to see anyone so conditioned that
simple untidiness could set her in motion, without
any memory intervening of actions so monstrous that
they had driven her from the house.

Vanessa turned with the shirt in her hands, ar-
rested by the disbelief in Jamie's voice. Then she
stared down at it, this expensively crafted piece of
fabric which she had so painstakingly chosen in the
first place, and so often washed, dried and ironed
with care and satisfaction. What to do with it now?
Drop it on the floor again, and in that single action
abdicate her role, her entire function? Walk out of
this room and leave the bed unmade, nothing
touched or tidied? On the one hand there was the
appalled note in Jamie's voice, reminding her that to
do anything else would be inconsistent, nullifying the
step she had already taken. On the other weighed the
habit of years, the ready, unthinking service, her
innate love of order, and something else, the importance of which she had never realised till now – her
need to be valued.

Jamie, with an effort keeping quiet after that one
involuntary exclamation, saw something of this
struggle. It seemed to her as if in the next second
of their lives Vanessa must step off the fence on one
side or the other. So loaded was the moment that it

seemed quite credible that the future course of her life would hinge on this decision.

With a small choking sound Vanessa let the shirt slip from her hands and, going blindly to her dressing-table, began to gather up at random objects lying there. In the end it was Jamie who did most of the packing, crushing into the first bag that came to hand anything Vanessa seemed to want. Vanessa herself seemed numb, nodding at suggestions then worriedly changing her mind, her attention concentrated mainly on holding back tears. From time to time she would light on something essential and give it to Jamie, for it didn't seem to occur to her to fill a second case herself, but on the whole she seemed to have no definite purpose. She neither selected what it would be practical and appropriate to take, nor made sure of special treasures she couldn't bear to leave behind. It was so unlike her usual positive efficiency – she was one of those women whose way of packing a suitcase or wrapping a parcel is the only way – that Jamie would almost have welcomed some protest at her own summary methods.

Downstairs once more, Vanessa appeared to have forgotten that they must leave. She went at once, with what looked like happy purpose, along the wide central corridor to the kitchen.

Jamie looked questioningly at Patrick.

'No hurry,' he said.

'So long as she doesn't settle in.'

'You go and help her. I'll put this lot in the car.'

As Jamie stood in the kitchen doorway she had an

uncomfortable feeling that she was witnessing something which no one should see.

Here there was no sign that Douglas had paused so much as to make coffee before leaving. Jamie watched as Vanessa glanced at the untouched table and then, still with that benumbed air, went to the freezer, touching the handle but not lifting the lid, then to open first a cupboard and then the fridge. She looked in, apparently failed to focus on what she saw there and shut the door again. Then she pulled open the dishwasher, which she herself had put on last night after dinner, and stared at the gleaming ranks. She lifted out a cutlery basket, and Jamie stifled a protest. But Vanessa only put it down uncertainly on the worktop and turned away, as though not sure what one did with it next.

'I should water the plants while we're here,' she said, but she sounded doubtful.

'If you want to, but Van, there's really no need.' Jamie spoke softly, coming to stand half facing her to gain her attention. How could she say that one more day of loving attention would make no difference to the plants now?

'I left a pheasant out . . .' Vanessa let the sentence die away.

In the drama and emotional release of her arrival at the cottage she had talked to Jamie with a frankness she had probably never approached in her life before, and as the details of the night's events returned in all their horror, she had vowed again and again that she would never go back to Douglas. Yet here, in this prosaic morning scene, the thought of turning her back on every object and activity which had filled her days for so long seemed exaggerated, outlandish, nothing to do with her or the way she did things.

'What if Ryan phones?' she asked, swinging round on Jamie with renewed energy, as though in this question duty and care found a legitimate purpose. The switch from the apparently trivial to the crucially important momentarily winded Jamie.

'You'll be able to tell him where you are,' she said, pulling herself together. 'You can phone from Calder, any time you like.' Did Ryan know or guess what went on between his parents? Had anything he had seen or heard had anything to do with his departure?

Vanessa looked at her. 'I've no idea where he is,' she said tonelessly.

Jamie gazed back, stunned. Vanessa had said that Ryan was staying with a friend, and she had assumed he was in Perth, nearby, on hand. Before she could take in this new fact – or wonder what anger Vanessa had had to face from Douglas over it – Vanessa went on, still in that expressionless voice. 'He won't come back, I know that.'

'Vanessa –' Jamie cleared her throat and started again. 'You know that can't be true. But let's talk about it later. All you need to think about at the moment is that you're coming to stay with me. You don't have to look any further than that.'

After a pause which seemed to Jamie to stretch endlessly, Vanessa nodded. 'I know.' She looked around her. 'How odd,' she said, almost under her breath. How odd to walk away from this kitchen which had been at the heart of her life, where, hour upon hour, bustling and content, she had always done her best. Without another word or glance she went past Jamie, along the corridor, through the hall, and out of the door to the car.

Patrick looked interrogatively at Jamie, seeing the muscles of her face tight with the effort to hold back tears, but she could only shake her head at him mutely. As he drove away Vanessa turned her head to look at the bright, well-tended summer garden with a stony face.

When Patrick left them at the cottage, he drew Jamie out for a quiet word, and she walked with him through the archway to the courtyard. 'If Douglas turns up don't hesitate to call if you need me.'

'Do you think he will come?'

'Well, I can't see him accepting this very readily, can you? The service was too good, for one thing.' His mouth turned down in an expression which Jamie had never seen before. 'But I'm sure he won't be violent,' he added. 'He's far too clever. Hectoring, applying pressure, certainly, but he won't touch Vanessa again. You needn't worry about that and nor need she, but you may want help in getting rid of him.'

'Thank goodness you were here, Patrick,' Jamie said fervently. 'I hardly know how to thank you.'

He looked at her, making no comment, and she had the impression that he was waiting for something more.

'I know Vanessa's grateful too. I'm sure she'll thank you herself when she's more—'

'What about Phil?' Patrick interrupted brusquely.

'Phil?'

He made an exasperated sound at her blank tone. 'Phil. Your sister. It hadn't occurred to you to contact her and tell her what's going on?'

'But Phil isn't – I mean, this isn't the sort of thing that—'

'The sort of thing that what?' he demanded, releasing some of his anger at last. 'That you would think of telling your dim younger sister, who now, may I remind you, is in her mid-thirties, and holding down a demanding job which you couldn't begin to look at.'

He turned away and Jamie had the impression that he had been on the brink of saying more. She was baffled by the sudden attack. 'But she'd be so upset,' she protested, clinging to the accepted view. 'Wouldn't it be better to tell her later, when the picture's a bit clearer? After all, what could she offer in this—?'

'A good deal more than you may think,' Patrick said shortly. 'Let me know if you need me.'

Watching him head towards the back drive, Jamie was reminded of how she had felt in rebellious student days, when he had left her in no doubt of his disapproval. What could it mean? She needed his support right now, and not just over Vanessa, or to get her through the next couple of days.

Telling Phil. What had Patrick started to say? What were the words he had held back?

25

When Douglas came it was impossible to believe that he was the man who had dealt Vanessa such vicious blows. Jamie found herself looking again and again, deliberately, at the spreading bruises, in an effort to keep the facts before her. He appeared so concerned, entering so totally into their own feelings, that it seemed some separate person must have performed this act. He charmed not only Vanessa but for a moment he almost charmed Jamie, and it was the most insidious, helpless sensation to realise it was happening and to be unable to resist it.

Douglas was absolutely up-front about the whole episode, insisting that he didn't blame Vanessa in the least for coming to Jamie. He avoided loaded phrases like 'running here' or 'walking out'. He was affectionate, protective, and gave every appearance of being ready to listen to whatever she said, and agree to whatever she wanted. All the excuses were there – pressure of work first and foremost, something which could not be contested or even fully gauged by little wife at home; then his concern over Ryan's future, the ongoing rows and tension with Ryan, the shock of his departure, and the very natural worry over his present whereabouts; and finally this decision to let Jamie buy the cottage, which Vanessa had for some inexplicable reason made without consulting him.

Yet, most cleverly, as Jamie realised, he wasn't presenting these factors *as* excuses. He wasn't actually apologising. He was taking the position that his anger had been understandable and justifiable, and that they were both adult enough and sensible enough to see that. He had merely let his feelings get out of hand for once. It was quite unforgivable, and such a thing would never happen again.

And now, surely, passing smoothly on from that, comfortably settled into the largest chair, his well-dressed, well-groomed presence making the little room look inescapably tatty and makeshift, Vanessa wasn't going to leave him to fend for himself? She knew how hopeless he was at that sort of thing, always had been . . .

How dare he blatantly use such an appeal, Jamie thought furiously, astounded by his nerve. And he didn't even add that he needed Vanessa for herself, or missed her in any way. Patrick's words, 'the service was too good', came back. Yes, but not many men would play on that angle so outrageously and imagine they could get away with it. How well he knew Vanessa, for of course it was this very aspect which would most readily move her, playing on her guilt and at the same allowing her to believe that he wanted her, giving her by implication the essential assurance that she was needed.

But you should be needed for you, Jamie cried to

her silently. Don't you see that? Not to cook his dinner and iron his shirts and see that his suits are cleaned. How impermeable was the shell which any couple built around their marriage, she reflected, praying that Vanessa would see what he was doing. But wasn't this what Vanessa, in her deepest heart, had wanted? To be followed, cajoled and persuaded, as she saw it; offered the simplest route back into her citadel which, whatever its shortcomings, was known and safe. Where she knew who she was and what was expected of her, and she could fulfil her given role with at least a measure of confidence.

How passionately Jamie longed to leap in with reminders of the reality beneath. But though Vanessa had insisted that she remain in the room, and Douglas had had the sense to accept the proviso, making it plain (to Jamie at least) that he disdained wasting time or energy on arguing such a minor point, nevertheless ordinary courtesy and discretion meant that her presence was no more than support for Vanessa and a check on anger exploding. She was not there to make an input.

Finding it hard to resist Douglas's approach herself, in the sense that it was impossible to be openly rude to him when he was putting his hands up to what he'd done and apparently contrite, it wasn't difficult to guess the effect it would have on Vanessa. And weighing the balance in his favour were the incalculable factors of more than twenty shared years, Vanessa's dislike of quarrelling in any form, and the long conditioning of accepting Douglas as her superior in every way, and of placing her needs far behind his and Ryan's.

The very fact of having offered Douglas a drink – Zara's drinks cupboard, it was by now agreed, had been her most acceptable legacy – had reinforced his 'well, we're all grown-ups after all, aren't we?' approach, and had set the tone of the visit as one of good sense and good behaviour. Jamie could feel Vanessa's resolution ebbing as though it were running out through her own fingers. The anguished cry of last night, 'I shall never go back!', seemed remote indeed now.

Jamie longed to drag Vanessa to her feet and make her look in the nearest mirror, or to touch a finger to that damaged face, to make her feel the pain again.

However, she found to her surprise, Vanessa had not let the smooth flow of Douglas's words blind her to his first mistake. With a look of gathering herself together, having trouble with a nervous trembling of her mouth, she said, 'But it didn't happen just once, did it?'

Tension crackled in the room. Admiration leapt in Jamie, but she scrupulously concealed it, knowing that nothing must interfere with the moment of challenge. But though the words had been brave, and Vanessa had signalled her refusal to be railroaded, the tone had wavered somewhere between defensiveness and a terrified apology for clinging to the truth.

Douglas, his eyes narrowing, his face changing in a way that gave Jamie her first flicker of doubt about not having gone at once to phone Patrick, decided at the ultimate second to treat this as a protest for form's sake, a last-ditch feeble attempt to resist the inevitable. All the same, he didn't appreciate his time being wasted.

'What are you talking about?' Even to him that sounded too hostile. That damned sister of hers, with her observant eyes and sharp perceptiveness, and ten times Vanessa's guts too, it had to be said – he could do without her. It was none of her bloody business. He summoned a smile, deliberately relaxing. 'Come on, darling, you know as well as I do that this was a one-off. You can appreciate the strain I've been under lately. Nothing of the sort will ever occur again.'

'It wasn't a one-off.' Vanessa's voice, though scarcely audible, was steadier, and she continued to face up to him, her hands tightly locked to hide their trembling.

She's going to stick to it, Jamie thought, amazed and shaken at Vanessa's unexpected courage. She's really going to stand up to him. Her eyes went to Douglas's face, where the fresh colour of his slabby cheeks had darkened ominously.

'What are you talking about?' he demanded angrily, but Jamie saw from the quick tightening of his mouth that he had immediately regretted opening the doors to Vanessa's possible reply.

All she said was, 'You know what I'm talking about,' still in that faint but resolute tone.

Jamie, not even aware that she had moved, came

closer to her and, aware of her own heart beating faster, winced to imagine what Vanessa must be going through. If only Patrick were here. If this turned nasty, as it had every appearance of doing, how angry he was going to be that she hadn't summoned him. Impossible to do so now. She daren't leave Vanessa alone here with Douglas even for the few minutes it would take to race across to the house.

'For God's sake, Vanessa, this is private stuff.'

Jamie had been afraid that Douglas would bluster and raise his voice, browbeating Vanessa into giving in by sheer pressure. But this restrained, intimate tone, excluding Jamie as she moved closer to Vanessa, was infinitely more scary, and Jamie felt a shiver of actual physical apprehension run through her.

'But it did happen.' Vanessa kept to that single fact, as though to try to reason or refute Douglas's arguments with specific instances was beyond her, but this she would cling to like a drowning man a spar.

'Look, all right, we can talk about this if you want to. But I'm damned if I'm going to discuss our affairs in front of your sister or anyone else. Get your stuff together, and come on.'

'I can't.' It was little more than a whisper.

Douglas's mouth was a thin ugly line, all affability and confidence that he would get his way forgotten. 'For God's sake, Vanessa, can you honestly say I've ever done anything of the kind to you before? Can you? Can you? Answer me. You can't, and you know it. And didn't you come running here –' not caring now what words he used '– because you were shocked at what I'd done? So what does that prove? That it was the first time. I've told you, it won't happen again, so let's forget all this nonsense and be on our way. It'll be midnight before we get back, and I've got an early start again tomorrow. If you had any idea of the pressures I'm under . . .'

The tried and proven stratagem. No truck with an appeal to the emotions, no 'I love you, I want you.' Just 'Come to heel, damn you, get back to the sink.'

You total bastard, Jamie thought, shaking now with anger, an anger chiefly produced by the fear, the certainty, that Vanessa would never resist this.

'Come on, Vanessa, I've never known you behave like this before,' Douglas said impatiently, and actually looked at his watch. It was a fatal mistake. He was being inconvenienced, unforgivably held up. He had sacrificed his entire evening to this ridiculous game, and now he was barely going to get a decent night's sleep before more important matters claimed his attention.

Vanessa gathered her forces. 'I'm not coming back.' The words hung in the air, loaded with their different levels of meaning. I am not coming home with you now, tonight. I am not coming back to you.

Jamie, rigid with sudden hope, made a conscious effort to subdue any facial expression or body language which would announce it. For the first time she felt that she really shouldn't he here.

'What do you mean?' Douglas's anger exploded, an

unnerving force in a space which abruptly seemed too cluttered and constricted. 'You'll do as I say.'

Vanessa, her face chalk-white around the areas of discolouration, reached a hand to Jamie, and as Jamie took it in both hers she could feel its violent quivering. 'Really. I'm staying. I can't come back with you. I'm staying here with Jamie.'

'I've never heard anything so ridiculous. Do you think I'll lay a finger on you? And if you don't come home, now, how can we sort anything out? This is pure melodrama. You've been reading too many of those damned female magazines, that's your trouble.'

They faced him in silence, standing close to each other, and for one breathless second he stared back at them, his face suffused with fury. Then the decision to let it go was discernible in his eyes, and a look of scathing contempt overtook the anger. 'You'll see sense,' was all he said, and turned to the door.

'Don't go. Don't leave me alone,' Vanessa whispered, clutching at Jamie's arm as she made a move to follow him.

'I'll be right back.' Jamie felt an indefinable but strong instinct to go with Douglas, to see him off the premises in effect. Part of it was a wish not to let him think of the pair of them cowering in relief to have been let off the hook.

'What the hell do you want?' Douglas demanded, as he heard her behind him. In spite of his openly hostile tone, one part of her brain relished the sweetness of the night air, and the sense of space and openness after the shut-in feeling of the cottage room, vibrant with clashing emotions.

'I thought I'd better see you off,' she told him bluntly. She felt no trepidation now, as though out here normality had overtaken high drama.

'There's really no need, I assure you,' he said, but the heavy sarcasm had no effect.

'Surely one can see off a guest,' Jamie replied silkily, and grinned at his grunt of anger.

He didn't go without firing a shot, however.

'This matter of the cottage,' he said, turning with the car door open, about to get in. 'You're not going to get away with it, you know.'

'What are you talking about?' Jamie, taken unawares, snapped out the question unguardedly, and at once wished she had kept her mouth shut.

'It's not Vanessa's decision. Though so far all the men in your life have shown their great good sense by declining to marry you –' Jamie was thankful that he couldn't guess the pain of that knife turning '– the fact is that no property can belong exclusively to one partner and nothing that Vanessa has arranged with Mr Syme has any validity without my agreement. So I suggest you make your plans to leave Calder without delay.'

The smooth tone was back, the patronising certainty of power. It wasn't hard to see how, when he had first arrived this evening, he had briefly made Vanessa's account of what had taken place last night seem exaggerated and improbable. It wasn't merely a question of exerting charm. Douglas, by his looks,

his build, his manner, the way he dressed, proclaimed himself as one of those men who order
affairs, make decisions, who would follow whatever
path he chose and expect others to fit in with his
decisions.

Jamie wanted to say, 'I think you'll find my father
tied things up so that even you couldn't swing them
to suit yourself', but she saw in time how unwise it
would be to enter into a wrangle on such a point. She
told herself that Mr Syme wouldn't have commu-
nicated Vanessa's decision to her if there had been
any doubt about it, and if that was the case then there
was no need even to reply to Douglas. But he had
succeeded in at least one of his attempts to wound.
The barb about her not being married had bitten
deep. The pain and shock of learning what Bryden
had done flooded back with fresh intensity. In effect,
she had been alone all the time.

'You don't believe me, do you?' Douglas was
saying, his voice soft now, which seemed to Jamie,
shivering in the chilly air, to be infinitely more
menacing than all his bluster. Her eyes were accustomed to the dusk by now, and in the half light his
fleshy features looked more emphatic in their lines,
and cruel.

Jamie wasn't prepared to play his games. 'Good
night, Douglas,' she said, and was glad to find she
had managed to keep her voice impersonal. 'Please
don't come here again without phoning first to see if
it's acceptable.'

He laughed at her, getting into the car and slamming the door without another word, driving smoothly away as though no part of their exchange or of the evening had rattled him.

Jamie stood for a moment, eyes closed, getting her feelings under control. Douglas seemed to have left so many things for her to deal with, not least the conviction that nothing she or Vanessa could say or do would ever prick his thick hide of well-nurtured self-esteem.

She longed intensely for Patrick's balanced outlook, his blunt integrity, the never-failing comfort of his presence. He never let her off lightly, it was true, and he was certain to think she had put Vanessa's safety in jeopardy tonight by not doing as he had told her and contacting him as soon as Douglas showed up, but even Patrick's disapproval was better than his absence. How used she had always been, even through the years away from him, to measuring her behaviour by the yardstick of his opinion, and feeling guilty towards him when she saw herself failing to meet his exacting standards.

Like family in the background, I suppose, she thought now, scrubbing her hands wearily over her face and turning back towards the cottage, slightly startled to find what a demand on her resources the confrontation with Douglas had been, even though she had been a mere bystander. How much more taxing it must have been for Vanessa, and how in need of support she must be feeling right now.

Much as she longed to phone Patrick, visualising him reading in front of the fire in the comfortable long room of the Toll-house, and assailed by a sharp sense of loss not to be there with him, there was no question of leaving Vanessa alone for a moment longer. She must be wondering what was going on, panicking about some ugly head-to-head taking place, and wondering if she should come to find Jamie. And she must be shaken to the core of her being to realise that she had faced up to Douglas at last. It was probably coming home to her too, Jamie thought as she ran back through the semi-darkness, that as one consequence she was stuck here, in this half-furnished, half-decorated cottage, her home and all she owned left behind.

For the first time it struck Jamie that there was some parallel between her situation and Vanessa's. There had barely been time to think of it till now. Not only in the way their lives had been suddenly wrested out of shape, flinging them into space with all firm footing lost, but in the way that each had presented a façade to the others.

Opening the door, and calling, 'It's me,' in reassurance, Jamie knew she was still struggling to reconcile the image she had had of Vanessa's perfect and desirable life with the grim reality. And she guessed she had been given only a glimpse of what truly went on beneath the glossy veneer.

26

Gradually, hearing nothing more from Douglas, and with the first sense of emergency and drama fading a little, they began to adjust to the new situation, and to talk. There had been no period in their adult lives when there had been the opportunity, or the inclination, for such closeness, and at first they were shy of it, needing time to get used to the frankness which the heightened emotional level between them had engendered.

It was also hard for Vanessa to reconcile herself to her new surroundings, far harder than it had been for Jamie, even though she too had been used till very recently to a high degree of comfort and convenience. But Vanessa cared, that was the difference. She liked things to be 'done properly'. She liked having attractive objects around her. They gratified her but they also reassured her; almost they established who she was. To find herself suddenly in a spartan little cottage, furnished with a few sad old remnants which to her eyes had barely even been cleaned, with none of her familiar props about her, forced questions upon her of a scale and gravity that appalled her.

Yet every time she longed for home and her normal

ordered existence, her 'routine', wishing passionately that she had never fled, memories would flood back which would swing her to the opposite extreme, vowing that she would never again put herself into the situation of dreading every moment the threat of violence.

In her dreams too the images would come, distorted and terrifying – Douglas's eyes at that instant of changing, the instant of decision, when she would know with sick dread what was coming; Douglas's face, cold, threatening, calculating the level of her fear with a cynical watchfulness, as he waited his moment.

Although they were no longer sharing a room in the big house, having with Maeve's help brought another bed over to the cottage for Vanessa, the cries of terror with which she would wake from these dreams, her muffled sobbing when she couldn't sleep and was faced with the blank reality of what had happened, could not be hidden from Jamie, who would come in to comfort her in mingled thankfulness that she was on hand, and black rage against Douglas for what he had done to her gentle sister.

It was in these shared moments of the night, with pretences stripped away, that Vanessa was able at last to spill out some of the truth. She would describe an isolated incident, a dinner party perhaps, when Douglas had either not succeeded in eliciting the response he wanted from a guest concerning some vital project (for he regarded social occasions as mere padding for pushing through business deals in comfort), or where he had felt some other male had paid her too much attention.

Jamie, tucked up on the bed beside her, doing her best to keep silent and let the sad, uncertain words stumble on without interruption, would be horrified not merely at the specific incidents which Vanessa described – the tension of the drive home with anger as tangible as a third presence in the car, the attempts to deflect what was coming, the anxious search for any means to placate and soothe – but at how long ago this had been the background to her daily life.

It was this thought that stayed with Jamie, behind all she did. It had been going on for years. This was what had lurked beneath the enviable veneer of social correctness and material success. And she had never had the faintest idea of it, had accepted what was presented to her, and been alternately bored by and impatient with Vanessa's preoccupation with trivia, her endless striving for perfection. Because perfection, she now saw, was what Douglas had demanded. And if he decided it hadn't been delivered he meted out punishment. To Vanessa. Even now it was hard to believe.

But as, defences down in these conversations through the already lengthening nights, Vanessa became more used to the idea that Jamie now understood what her life had really been, she gradually found herself able to talk on a different level, exploring, in a way she had never had the courage to do before, the underlying motives for Douglas's behaviour.

'It began to seem almost as if he planned it,' she said once, and Jamie felt a terrible coldness spread through her at what might be coming. 'As though he – well, liked hurting me. Enjoyed it. Oh, what am I saying, that sounds so exaggerated and impossible . . .'

Vanessa put her hands up to her head, as though wishing physically to suppress these thoughts. 'It can't really have been like that.'

'Go on,' Jamie said quietly. The only light in the bare room was from the tiny square of landing between their doors. Jamie had learned by now that Vanessa hated to have her put on the light beside her bed, and part of her memory ever afterwards of these scenes of agonising soul-searching was that dimness, their voices hollow and disembodied, as voices in the dark can sound, their faces hidden from each other.

'It was as though whatever I did, however hard I tried, he would find something wrong, something to be angry about. As though he watched for things. I began to think he wanted something to be wrong. It was sort of – necessary – necessary for him to be angry. Like needing a drink or something. I don't know how to describe it. Sometimes I had the feeling that he had waited all day for the moment when he could—'

With a sob she turned to push her face against Jamie's shoulder, clinging to her.

Another time she said, 'He didn't always touch me, you know, or even very often. Sometimes he would just come very close, with that look in his eyes. And then do nothing. But it was almost as bad. He was wanting me to plead with him, of course.' She paused for a moment and then said, as though it hurt to bring the words out. 'I always did.'

The hopeless, shamed tone of that confession gave Jamie a terrible insight into how those scenes must have been played – Douglas with the power, the mastery, getting his kicks from whipping up her fear, Vanessa from her very nature unable to face up to him, hoping against hope that by placating she would avert the inevitable.

'He never hurt me in any way that could be seen,' she said once. 'Or very badly. Not until now. He was careful, I suppose, though I didn't think about it at the time. Or afterwards.'

With shame to realise how long it had taken her to make the connection, Jamie asked, a flush of distaste and anger rising in her cheeks, thankful that Vanessa couldn't see it, 'That time when I was there, at Dunrossie, when you told me you'd staved your thumb? Vanessa, was that—?'

In an odd way, the fact that she had been in the house when actual violence had taken place brought home to her the reality of what Vanessa had had to live with more starkly than anything she had hinted at or described. A normal morning, having breakfast, Pauline furbishing up the sunny, tranquil rooms of a house where well-brought-up people enjoyed a civilised affluence.

Jamie thought back to the preceding evening, remembering Douglas's charm, his well-honed performance as affable host. And she thought of how Vanessa had hurried to be in the right place at the right moment to take his briefcase, pour his drink. Not the actions, then, of the devoted wife who wishes to cosset her weary husband after his arduous day forwarding the affairs of the world, but the anxious and conciliatory submissiveness of someone actually afraid.

Jamie recalled Douglas's expansiveness to her, his welcome, his apparent good humour, but, yes, there had also been his watchfulness of Vanessa, and back with fresh, sharper revulsion came the incident when Vanessa had spilled the sauce, and Douglas had leaned back in his chair, smiling, letting her mop it up for him, his eyes on her face. And for that he had – what? – twisted her arm?

It made Jamie shiver to think that these incidents, related by Vanessa so disjointedly and with such painful embarrassment, didn't belong to some vague time in the past, but that one had been enacted while she was staying with them, and that she had suspected nothing. There seemed to her no question that Douglas got his kicks in this way. That, in fact, was something which Vanessa herself, in the new perspective which being at Calder forced upon her, could finally accept beyond doubt.

'It's become almost like an addiction, I suppose,' she said, allowing herself to use the word for the first time. 'He can't live without the buzz it gives him to frighten and hurt me.'

'Did he ever harm Ryan?'

'Oh, no, I'm absolutely sure he didn't!'

Was that just instinctive rejection of an idea she couldn't bear to contemplate, Jamie wondered; but she didn't pursue the point.

'He used to roar at him and bully him, and I know that's what drove the poor boy to leave, but he never touched him. I'm beginning to wonder, though, if his anger with Ryan, his frustration about Ryan never getting himself together to do any of the things Douglas expected of him, wasn't just one more way of finding fault with me. Or do you think I'm imagining that?'

Finding fault. What a restrained and humble little phrase to choose.

'No, I don't think you're imagining it.' Jamie resisted asking whether Vanessa thought Ryan had known what went on between his parents. If she preferred to believe that he hadn't guessed, then nothing would be gained by putting the possibility into her head.

But Jamie shuddered to think of all that had gone on in the smiling house of Dunrossie.

Patrick was Jamie's lifeline during these first, dislocated days, when everything in her own life seemed to be on hold, and she watched in distress as Vanessa was buffeted from one decision to another by guilt, doubt, fear and tears. He had remained on hand at the Toll-house, and though he had been forthright in his comments on the risk Jamie had taken by not letting him know when Douglas had come, a risk she

was more acutely aware of now than she had been at
the time, he made it clear that any support and help
he could give were there for her.

'What I need most of all is to get out of the house,'
Jamie confessed on the third morning after Vanessa's
arrival. 'I know it sounds unkind, but this heavy
emotional stuff is desperately claustrophobic, I can
tell you. Even with poor old Van in this state I could
shake her sometimes. She spent yesterday afternoon
agitating about new curtains, cleaning dust out of the
buttoning of the chairs with a pin and—'

'Jamie,' Patrick interrupted her.

'What?'

He waited.

'Oh, all right, I know, it's doubtless good therapy.
Is that what you want me to say? I do see that, of
course I do, and I promise you I didn't say a thing,
but you know it isn't exactly my scene.'

And your own troubles are still raw and huge, and
you've had to put them on the back burner just
when you thought you had a chance to work through
them and begin to get them behind you. Patrick said
none of this, but his eyes read the tiredness in her
face, and he understood only too well the frustration
she must feel to have to stand back and allow
Vanessa to make her decisions in her own time
and in her own way, muddled and vacillating, and
to be unable to take the situation by the throat as she
was accustomed to do.

'What you need is a dose of fresh air and exercise,'
he said, not without a flicker of ironic humour that

his own feelings must remain even further down the list of priorities.

'But I can't leave her, can I?' Jamie said, though with evident longing.

'Why not? Douglas won't let anything interfere with his business interests, so he's not likely to appear during the day. And in fact I should doubt, now that he's tried coming up to haul Vanessa back and failed, that he'll try that approach again. Not his style to risk another rebuff. Anyway, isn't Maeve about? I saw her van in the courtyard. Couldn't she do something in the cottage? I'd back her against a posse of Douglases any day.'

'So would I! Well, I suppose she could get on with stripping the sitting-room wallpaper.' As she spoke Jamie had a beguiling vision of Maeve and herself working amicably side by side, falling readily into the special brand of talk and laughter they enjoyed. Now, both that easy companionship and the precious solitude of the cottage which had meant so much to her had been wrested away. Then shame at her own selfishness made Jamie feel even worse. Nothing she had suffered could be compared with the nightmare Vanessa had endured, and to hanker even for a moment for the dream that had seemed within her grasp was nothing short of shameful.

It was a relief, as she and Patrick took the path down the lower burn ten minutes later, to put some of this into words. Patrick knew, as no one else did, her glaring faults and shortcomings, and though he might disapprove of what she did, and was invariably ready to express his opinions without reserve, he wouldn't be surprised at such a confession. Today, however, he seemed prepared to let her off lightly.

'It's always tough to find the best way to help someone who reacts to a crisis in a way totally different from one's own. It may help to remember, though, that you were the person Vanessa knew she could turn to. Just be thankful that you were there for her. Imagine if things had reached this stage with Douglas and you'd been in the States.'

'I know, and I'm glad of it. She couldn't have gone to Phil, that's for sure.' Then, remembering Patrick's still unexplained shortness on that point before, she added hastily, 'I mean, she couldn't very well have stayed with Phil.'

Patrick stared ahead of them down the rocky path, his craggy profile unreadable, making no comment.

'She doesn't seem to have any very close friends on hand either,' Jamie went on after an uncertain minute of silence. 'It's rather a worry to think she doesn't. She likes being with people.'

'I don't think Douglas left a lot of room for friend-ships,' Patrick said. 'He preferred her life to revolve exclusively around his needs and Ryan's.'

Jamie nodded, glad he hadn't jumped down her throat on the unaccountably thorny subject of Phil; this didn't seem a good moment to attempt to sort it out. Her face pinched as she reviewed Vanessa's day-to-day existence in the light of what she now knew. 'But am I going to be able to go on sympathising?' she asked abruptly, her thoughts returning to her original worry. 'I know that sounds awful, but you know me, I get so impatient with her. I really have to make an effort to appreciate how terrifying she finds it to have left home like this, taking so little with her and with no plan, no resources, and no concept of any other way to live.'

'But you're trying to grasp it, that's what matters.' Patrick didn't point out that Jamie could equally well have been describing her own situation. He knew that in her mind she had already faced the inevitable, and was prepared to move on. To her the future might be lonely, altered, difficult even, but it wasn't blank or terrifying, and he silently saluted the courage which she had never realised she possessed.

'What about Ryan, incidentally?' he enquired, when he had listened, concealing his anger, to some of the revelations Vanessa had made, knowing that Jamie needed to talk them out almost as compulsively as Vanessa had. 'Has there been any contact yet?'

'Oh, that's another thing.' Jamie stopped walking to turn to him. 'I meant to tell you. Vanessa's been phoning round his friends, and one of them finally came up with the information that he's gone down to Leeds. But she couldn't get an address, and has no idea what he's doing or how he's surviving, so of course she's in a panic all the time in case he phones home needing help and gets no answer and wonders where she is.'

'Um. Not good.' Patrick's face was grim. For Vanessa, he meant. He couldn't imagine Douglas considerately passing on any messages to his defaulting wife. 'But there's not a lot anyone can do about that one.'

In his view, which he kept to himself, this single factor was more likely to draw Vanessa back to Dunrossie than any other, and he thought a great many things ought to be resolved before she came near that point. 'To revert to Phil for a moment. You have told her what's going on?'

'Vanessa wouldn't let me,' Jamie said quickly. 'No, I knew you wouldn't like it, and I agree with you that we should tell her, but honestly, I can't persuade Vanessa. She thinks Phil would mind too much, and that it's not fair to upset her when there's nothing she can do.'

'But you realise she's going to be desperately hurt to find you've shut her out? You do know how much she minds that?'

'Well, you talk to Vanessa,' Jamie retorted, and Patrick grinned to himself, rather pleased to see a flash of the old temper.

'I will.'

'You don't think it's because Vanessa's considering going back, and if she does Phil need never know?' It was a relief to voice this secret fear.

'Possibly. But she certainly won't say so if that's the case.'

Patrick found Vanessa adamant on the subject. She winced away from the thought of Phil knowing any of this exactly as she would have winced at the prospect of spelling it out to Ryan. In her eyes, Phil wasn't a grown-up, and still needed her protection and care.

'Vanessa, you should give her a chance,' Patrick protested. 'She's not a child any more. On the contrary, I think if you talk to her you'll find you're dealing with a very sympathetic and understanding woman. You seriously underestimate her, believe me.' And always have, he resisted adding. 'At the very least don't you think you should tell her you're here, even if you don't go into explanations? She probably wouldn't want you to in any case. Just don't leave her out.'

'Patrick, I do know my own sister,' Vanessa retorted, a touch of her familiar blinkered certainty reasserting itself. 'It would be terribly unkind to worry her about any of this.'

'Do you see much of Phil?' Jamie asked Patrick curiously, as he was leaving.

'I see her occasionally.' He shot her a look she couldn't interpret. It left her with the odd feeling that she had missed something, and that, in some way she couldn't fathom, he was disappointed in her.

'You're saying we don't know her,' she challenged him, always ready to get an issue out into the open.

'Precisely.' Patrick's voice was cool, but there was an appreciative gleam in his eyes at her tone. 'You've been away too long, so you have some excuse, but Vanessa has been in touch with her on a regular basis for years and still regards her as an immature, ineffectual girl.'

'So how do you know she isn't?' Jamie enquired with interest.

'Because, God help me, I care about the whole lot

of you,' Patrick snapped. Not just you, my brave Jamie.

But at the last moment he turned back. 'Look, I know it's not easy to realise you may have to share your little house indefinitely, but don't give yourself a hard time about minding. You're not being selfish. It did seem the perfect answer for you, after all that's happened, and this isn't quite the same, is it? But hang in there, sweetheart. It'll come right in the end.'

How he longed to be able to make good that promise on his own terms. It seemed desperately hard to him that Jamie, only just struggling clear of the wreckage of her entire world – and no matter how courageous she had been the scars had barely had time to begin to heal – should be asked to shoulder this responsibility so soon. He had so much wanted a period of recuperation for her, at peace in the well-loved surroundings of Calder, creating a new niche for herself there.

He felt thankful at least that Syme, to whom he had spoken himself, was adamant that by the terms of Hal Laidlaw's will Vanessa had every right, provided Phil agreed, to let Jamie keep the cottage. That was one thing Douglas could not take from them.

27

The continued silence from Douglas, which meant also lack of news of Ryan, was not what they had expected, and it was clearly beginning to unnerve Vanessa.

'He's very clever,' Jamie said to Maeve, as together, in pursuit of the overall aim of making Calder appear a loved and cared-for place, they turned out some of the dross that had accumulated in an unused garage. A skip stood permanently in the yard these days, though in the house itself the only work now in hand was the decorating of hall, dining-room and drawing-room. Mr Syme had ruled that employing an efficient contractor, however expensive, would reduce problems and delays, agreeing with Douglas that to sell as soon as possible was the main objective, and he had found a firm which had got on with the job at impressive speed. Even Jamie, who had originally thought they should stick to Grandmother's rule of always employing local labour where one could, had agreed that the builder from Aberfyle, when he finally found himself available, would probably have kept the work going for months.

'Clever how?' Maeve asked, walking a defunct spin drier from its corner by tipping it from side to side.

'Leaving her up in the air, forcing her to make the next move.'

'Wouldn't it have been even more clever to make her think he needed her?' Maeve, growing tired of her slow progress with the drier, wrapped her arms round it and picked it up bodily to carry it outside. 'Wouldn't that lure her back sooner than anything?'

'Hey, hold on, you lunatic, you can't chuck that on by yourself.' Together they swung the drier onto the skip to join a motley crew of ancient and honourable companions. 'But I agree, that is the odd thing. I'd have thought that would be the line he'd take too. Or come up here at every turn to keep the pressure on. But he's more devious than I'd realised.'

'You think he does want her back? He doesn't have someone else?'

Jamie shrugged. 'Who knows? But even if he does my guess is that he needs Vanessa in place as part of the support system. Whether he has another woman somewhere who fulfils other needs – or who doesn't drive him mad with ceaseless gabble and inanities – I wouldn't know. I certainly wouldn't put it past him.'

'Will she go back, do you think?'

Jamie paused, about to check through a box which seemed to contain little but burners from some gas cooker long vanished. 'She's adamant that she won't. And I don't see how she could, after what he did to her.'

'But how does she feel?' Maeve asked wisely, coming to look in the box. 'Jamie, this is nothing but junk. Sling it.'

Jamie, going obediently to the skip, knew she wasn't at all sure of the answer to Maeve's question, though she wasn't ready to say so.

What a boon it had been to have Maeve around during these strangely suspended days. Patrick had had to go back to Blackdykes, to get on with pressing work but also because Naomi hadn't been well. A summer cold, she had insisted, but Jamie could see that Patrick was concerned. She must go down to see her herself soon, but for the moment she felt she couldn't leave Vanessa.

Vanessa's mood was so subdued. She crept about like a bird with a broken wing, pale, her eyes red, her mouth looking as though at any moment weeping might overtake her again. She cried a lot in the night, Jamie knew, though by this stage Jamie didn't go to comfort her. Vanessa had begun to fret about it, insisting that knowing she was ruining Jamie's sleep made her feel even worse, and this Jamie had interpreted as preferring to be left alone. And indeed, little more could be said.

But it was becoming obvious that in fleeing Douglas's violence, in making her statement of outrage by coming to Jamie, Vanessa had had no notion of what might follow this gesture. It seemed incredible to Jamie. Surely if this kind of abuse had been going on for a long time, even though, as Vanessa said, its outward form had usually been less dramatic, and Douglas had not always resorted to inflicting physical pain, surely she would have turned over in her mind other ways of living? Surely, however vaguely, she must have considered her options if she left Douglas, and weighed up any recourses available? At the very least she must have wondered where she would live, what she would live on, and what would happen about Ryan.

Observing Vanessa, however, as the days passed, Jamie began to understand how deeply conditioned she was to expecting someone else to make decisions for her. She was not, and had never been, the initiator. To Jamie, who had accepted her without question in the role of responsible eldest as they grew up and, when Jamie was still in her teens, as the engaged then married woman, capably looking after her household and playing her part in the sort of social life which to Jamie had been utterly remote, this discovery was something of a shock. Certainly Vanessa had always taken her duties seriously, from childhood on, but for the first time Jamie saw that she had only been obeying rules laid down by others, desperately anxious, indeed, that they should be kept. She had never queried them, and when Douglas married her he must have seen her as a girl, decorative, gentle and adoring, who could be moulded as he wished.

Yes, but had he bargained for the wittering, Jamie thought, returning to the mundane with a grin. Anxious as she felt for Vanessa, and full of anger at what had been done to her, day by day, minute by minute, Vanessa was quietly driving her mad. The only thing to do, Jamie reminded herself, as she had a hundred times, was to take each day as it came, and not let herself look forward, appalled, to the prospect of living at such close quarters for any length of time. And again she thought, thank God for Maeve; thank God that with her she could get stuck into the sort of jobs Vanessa wouldn't dream of embarking on.

Where Maeve and Jamie attacked lofts and sheds, drains and fallen wood, Vanessa spent busy clucking hours – apart from shopping, cleaning, cooking, washing and ironing, all of which she had taken over as a matter of course and which she had, probably unconsciously, already shaped into a cast-iron routine – going through linen cupboards and storerooms in the house.

A haze of domestic comfort had spread gradually over the cottage. It wasn't what Jamie had envisaged, but it was hard to combat. How could she protest about flowers appearing everywhere? What was wrong with flowers? And what was wrong with frilly curtains, newly covered cushions, or the chintz covers Vanessa had so cleverly revamped to fit the dingy old chairs? Wasn't she lucky to have the gloomy bathroom turned into a fresh and wholesome place, smelling of expensive scented soap rather than mildew, her bath towel hung over a warm rail instead of slung over a chair whose paint flaked off onto it? Why should she feel resentful every time she went into the newly painted kitchen – anyway, she'd done the painting herself, so what was she complaining about? – to find every object burnished, and a rack of scones cooling on the table, filling the air with the feel-good smell of baking?

Because it's not *me*, she would cry silently. But she knew that, below this surface resentment, what bothered her was not knowing where any of this was heading, which in turn meant that plans for her own future must wait. In practical terms it didn't matter, as she frequently reminded herself. She had enough to live on for the time being. But accustomed as she was to being in control – or believing she was, she would amend with a spurt of bitterness – this deferment of all plans made her restless.

Yet in one way things were progressing at amazing speed. Before the sale of Calder had even appeared in the pages of *Country Life*, the selling agents had notified those of their clients in search of this type of property, and the response had been startling.

'I'd assumed all that would take months,' Jamie said to Maeve. She knew it was illogical to feel hustled by this promising speed, but she saw the quiet weeks alone, adjusting and recharging, being inescapably eroded by events. 'I'd thought getting the house into shape for selling would take much longer, for a start.'

'Well, I suppose if you'd tried to wipe out everything your stepmother had done it might have. But the only big job was the hall, and even there you settled for a compromise.'

'I know. I suppose it was the shock of coming back after so long away, to find the house so altered, that made me think it would be a huge job to restore it to anything like what it used to be. But can you believe that in a matter of weeks, according to Mr Syme, we could actually be showing people round?'

Maeve turned to look at her. 'It makes it a bit real, doesn't it?'

Jamie pulled a face. 'What a lot of ground you've just covered in that simple sentence,' she said, her tone deliberately light. 'But you understand. You always do. Being confronted with the reality of selling, knowing it's so close, does stir up a lot of thoughts. Memories, for a start. Grandmother, and Father when we were small. I feel as though the last chance to picture it as it was is being snatched away before I'm ready. As though, as soon as the first stranger walks into the rooms, takes a view, approves or disapproves, it will be gone for ever.'

'And the buyer, whoever that turns out to be, will affect your life as well.'

'That too. It's happening too fast. And there's always the feeling that I have to get Vanessa sorted out before I can turn my mind to anything else, yet as far as she's concerned I can only sit back and wait. It's not my decision. But she needs time, I do understand that, and I try not to pressure her.'

She needed time herself, but where Vanessa sought support she would have preferred to be alone to do her thinking. With the scope of what Bryden had done accepted, she knew she should examine more honestly than she had till now her own role in their relationship. Had she deliberately ignored the signs; had she invited disaster? And she knew that, even more urgently, she must examine her feelings about being with Patrick again.

She had not known how she would react; indeed there had scarcely been time to think about it, as the news of Zara's death followed so swiftly on her own personal disaster. That Patrick would always be somewhere in the background of her life she had accepted without question, though the contact between them had been minimal for years. Nothing would alter that. I shall always tell him my jokes, she used to phrase it to herself at lonely times, surrounded by people who spoke a different language, her mind turning to him as someone who would always understand – understand not only what she said and what she laughed at, but who she was.

Would she have raced for Calder, for the solace of knowing Patrick would be on hand, if the quite separate reasons for returning had not presented themselves with such remarkable timing? And in what light, exactly, had she seen Patrick, if that was the case? She had been deeply involved in a full and satisfying sexual relationship with another man; a relationship which would have continued for the forseeable future as far as she had been concerned. So how could seeing Patrick again affect her so much? Because with him feelings were on a totally different level, was the answer to that. To talk about him and Bryden in the same breath was not to compare like with like.

Accepting that, did she imagine she could be with him again on the old friendly basis? Could she deal with that? With her life in crisis, hadn't it been natural to turn to him and find in his company everything she wanted? She had been vulnerable, needing the comfort of being with someone who knew her well. How much did her pleasure in being with him stem from that need?

Yet none of this took into account the vital fact. Being with Patrick now, as adults who had lived their separate lives for years, there was a new dimension. She was physically attracted to him in a compelling, unqualified way which she had never known before. And if this feeling was genuine, and not simply another facet of need and loneliness, what questions did that raise? Could she trust herself to remain in his orbit, when to him she was, still and always, merely one of the Laidlaw sisters for whom he felt vaguely responsible?

The question reminded her of their conversation last night, when she had phoned, as he had made her promise to do, to let him know how Vanessa was.

'And what about Phil?' he had asked again, when she had described Vanessa's passive, waiting mood, and released some of her own frustration about it. 'You have talked to her?'

'Vanessa still doesn't want me to.'

'And you think that's fair to Phil?' His tone had warned her that he wasn't going to let it go.

'Be reasonable, Patrick, it's not my decision.'

'Make it your decision. You know perfectly well that you can't keep her in the dark for ever. She and Vanessa see each other every couple of weeks. She'll be phoning Dunrossie, then she'll hear what's going on from Douglas, and I dread to think how he will present events.'

'Yes, OK, I know you're right. But how can I—?'

'Don't be so helpless. I thought you were the one who got a grip of things. Anyway, do you imagine Phil is going to be entirely surprised? Give her some credit. I'll talk to her if you like.'

It was tempting, and Jamie was grateful for the offer, but still felt it had to be Vanessa's choice.

Vanessa, now that they had time to spend together, had at last begun to look beyond her own problems and remember that Jamie's life had also fallen apart. It had been possible for Jamie to talk out some of her sense of rejection, to take a more objective view of what Bryden had done, and even to touch occasionally on memories of their happiness together. It hurt, but it helped her to reaffirm that there had been good times, that she had not been completely deceived.

Perhaps it was this communication and sharing which made up Jamie's mind. Patrick was right; Phil should not be debarred from knowing what was happening. It was too easy to sideline her, and she would have to know in the end. The best plan seemed to ask her to come up to Calder, without telling Vanessa. Or is that the plan which will mean the minimum aggro for me, Jamie mocked herself, imagining the scenes they would go through if she tried to persuade Vanessa first.

When Phil came Jamie was ashamed that she had ever hesitated. She brought with her an enveloping, loving, unquestioning warmth and, as Patrick had hinted, seemed unsurprised at what they told her. Since Jamie had warned Vanessa that Phil was coming only minutes before she was due, there was a certain amount of drama to work through, but Phil took it in her stride. Nor did she waste time on throwing up her hands, merely nodding in silence as she pieced the story together.

But this is about someone striking our sister, dealing her a blow that could have cracked her cheekbone, Jamie found herself silently protesting. This is about bullying and abuse, subjection and intimidation – among us, in our family, between Douglas and Vanessa, beneath the ordered and 'happy' façade of their marriage.

But Phil's concern was with the practical and immediate, and listening to her quiet comments and questions Jamie was forced to realise that her own response, which had boiled down to waiting as patiently as she could for Vanessa to sort herself out, had been shamefully inadequate.

'You must be so worried about Ryan,' Phil said, and Jamie saw that she had gone at once to the core of Vanessa's deepest anxiety. 'Do you want me to find out from Douglas if he's been in touch?'

'Oh, Phil, would you? I can't bear not knowing where he is or how he's managing. Perhaps you could find out if he needs anything. If he wants stuff sent down I'm sure we could manage it somehow. He doesn't need to write to me or anything. I just need to know that he's all right.'

'I'll do my best,' Phil promised.

'But I don't think Douglas will be prepared—'

'I'll deal with Douglas.'

And Jamie, closing her mouth again, felt Vanessa must be as convinced as she was by the assurance.

Yes, but Vanessa wants to be convinced, since reassurance on the subject of Ryan is all-important to her. Why do I feel it, Jamie asked herself. Phil is never the one we turn to for practical help. But have we ever attempted to turn to her? Would this calm willingness to do anything asked of her have been there all the time if we had?

'Do you need more things?' Phil was asking. 'Or is there anything at the house that you want seen to?'

As they went into details about paying Pauline and the man who did a few hours a week in the garden, about a leaking outside tap which should have been attended to, and Vanessa's panic about Douglas's car tax being due, Jamie realised with shame that Vanessa had kept all this from her. Listening to Phil soothing, promising to see to it all, though by this time Douglas must have dealt with most of it, and if he hadn't that was his problem, Jamie realised how impatiently she herself would have responded. Yet these cares lay at the heart of Vanessa's existence, and even to talk about them again was clearly some form of relief.

'I can't imagine how Douglas has been managing for shopping and clean clothes,' she could say at last, secure in Phil's sympathy and patience.

Paying some woman to do it, Jamie thought

dourly. There'd be no problem about finding the cash for that. But she knew that was precisely why Vanessa had gone into none of this with her. This was not about finding answers, but about being able to voice the swarm of anxieties which had tormented her, without fear of being put down.

As Douglas would have put her down; had put her down through the long years. I haven't even begun to help her, Jamie saw, dismayed.

'She never seems to stop thinking about Douglas,' she said to Phil, when Vanessa, clearly feeling better, had trotted off to make tea. 'She says she wouldn't dream of going back, but she still seems totally focused on what he'll do, what he'll say, what he'll decide – as well as worrying about how he's managing for shirts.'

Phil turned her head and gave her a long questioning look. 'It's marriage, isn't it?' she said at last. 'That's what marriage is about.'

How should you know, Jamie thought impatiently, defensive at once.

'But if it's a disaster?' she said, more sharply than she had intended.

Again Phil took her time. 'That's her life,' she said, sounding as though she wasn't sure she should say something so obvious. 'Douglas and Ryan. What else should she think about?'

As Phil was leaving, Jamie, with some muddled idea of making amends, for the way she had regarded her more than anything said or done, offered awkwardly, 'Look, Phil, I really will come down and see you sometime. I'm sorry I haven't been before. It would be good to see where you live, and to know a bit about what you do.'

Again Phil regarded her with the expressionless stare which had always been able to rouse Jamie to instant irritation. Again she seemed to turn over her response with care, as though wishing to be sure she had found the right words to articulate her slow thoughts.

'I think not yet, if you don't mind,' she said at last, with her apologetic smile. 'Not quite yet.'

And away she went in her noisy van, leaving Jamie to head back to the cottage feeling disconcerted and oddly chastened.

28

It was not easy, trying to shape some sort of acceptable life for Vanessa at Calder. The things that drew
Jamie, the associations of the past, the glorious
surroundings of the glen in a summer that had been
mostly good, the tentatively renewed contacts with
old friends and the prospect of new ones, to say
nothing of the pleasure, deeper than all the rest, of
being back in a place where Patrick often came,
meant little to her.

She got on well with Maeve – it would have been
hard not to – but Maeve's offhand approach to the
concerns which governed Vanessa's life, keeping up
appearances, punctuality, observance of rules and
routine, made Vanessa a little apprehensive in her
company. She didn't understand at all about the
basic level of existence Maeve enjoyed in her ram-
shackle hut, her bare tanned thighs, her beer drinking and her broad-brush, relaxed philosophy for
living.

'I don't think she eats proper food at all,' she
worried to Jamie. 'She's going to find it difficult
to get that weight off later on when she wants to. It's
all very well when you're young, you can get away

with it then, but when you get a little older . . . And that hut of hers is terribly damp. Even in summer I shouldn't think her clothes are ever properly aired.'

Jamie didn't think Maeve would even recognise the problems Vanessa brooded over on her behalf, but knew that any attempt to make Vanessa understand an attitude so fundamentally opposed to her own would lead to arguments of the most futile kind. However, she soon saw that the evenings she and Maeve had enjoyed together, taking things as they came, having supper at the cottage after a shared stint in the garden or going back to Maeve's shack, drifting to the pub or dropping in on this house or that about the glen or village to lend or borrow, do some promised job or merely chat, weren't going to happen with Vanessa there.

In the first place, she would have planned dinner, and quite early on would begin making an issue about the time they would eat and whether Maeve was going to join them. And it would be dinner, two courses if not three, warmed rolls with soup, vegetables in vegetable dishes, table properly laid, hot plates. A rite for which it was only fair to scrub up.

More and more items found their way from Zara's kitchen; more and more elaboration crept in. Most frustrating of all, this establishing of rituals, this 'improving' on Jamie's way of doing things, was not only done with love and good intentions, but was snarled up with emotional undercurrents which Jamie knew Vanessa wasn't even aware of.

Need me, need me. It clamoured in the polished

glasses, the flowers, the carefully prepared food. It was the only way in which Vanessa knew how to reach out, to seek to please. Jamie, who had imagined that inherent in Vanessa's flight would be a thankful escape from taking such trouble, an escape from propitiation, was dismayed to find not only that she clung to these things, but that their influence was spreading like fungus over her own new-found freedom. Yet to be ungrateful would wound Vanessa unforgivably. Jamie recognised the trap they were caught in, but couldn't see how to deny Vanessa the sense of purpose which seemed to be the one thing which kept her going.

Vanessa didn't know how to sit back and let life flow by. She was scarcely capable of sitting down with a cup of coffee after a meal. But the worst thing was that she hadn't the faintest idea that her restlessness might be maddening. How could it be anything but nice, she would have asked, baffled, to have your cup refilled, the fire replenished, the window closed as the evening air turned colder, the washing-up done, dried and put away?

Jamie could see how this had spiralled out of control with Douglas. As his impatience and boredom with Vanessa grew, she would have redoubled her efforts, eager, obtuse, hurt by rebuffs but incapable of standing back and working out what was wrong. Although now, after her disclosure that Douglas had reached the point of finding pleasure in abusing her, whether verbally or physically, Jamie no longer muttered to herself, God, I can see how anyone would want to dot her one, she was daily more aware of the blinkered, nervous state Vanessa had got herself into. She needed help as much as Douglas did, Jamie became convinced, but it was impossible to discuss such matters as long as they remained locked in stalemate by Douglas's continuing silence.

Fights flared up over little things. Vanessa liked linen handkerchiefs and napkins, linen sheets and pillowslips, and had even unearthed a couple of what she called Grandmother's 'afternoon tea' tablecloths. She twitched everything away to be washed the moment it was used, and ironed obsessively everything she could lay her hands on, including dishcloths, dusters and the non-iron sheets and duvet covers which Jamie used.

Jamie, fresh from a culture where such absurdities had long been abandoned, would in spite of her resolutions be driven to protest. 'You're just making work for yourself, doing this. What's the point?'

'I like things to look nice,' Vanessa said, complacently unaware that this answer didn't meet the case. 'And really, Jamie, you need a little looking after, you know.'

'I don't, that's just the point. Don't hang this one on me. Why don't you take a good long look at what you spend your time doing, and try to decide what it's about, and what it actually achieves?'

But even as she spoke Jamie knew the answer. Vanessa needed to find her time filled, and if possible filled by looking after someone else. Beyond that she had no function, and the emptiness which such questions would open up was too frightening to contemplate. Better to be occupied, to let the scents of ironing and baking fill your nostrils, to find pleasure in the smooth folds of sheets squared with mathematical precision, put little bowls of flowers by Jamie's bed, never let self-doubt in.

Only in one area, apart from domestic activity and regular visits to Freda when, happily unaware of undercurrents, she felt secure in the certainty of doing her duty, did Vanessa appear at ease, even to be enjoying herself. Louise Erskine had not forgotten her promise to get in touch after the meeting in the pub, and on visits to the sprawling, comfortable house of Nether Fallan Vanessa seemed briefly to revive in an atmosphere she thoroughly understood.

Here there were associations with a past which in retrospect seemed happy. Here, virtually unchanged, was a house she had known well in the past, though in even earlier days she would have gone to the gaunt house on the hill above, where Hugh and his brother had grown up. This was still occupied by Hugh's irascible elderly father, though Vanessa was relieved to find that he had mellowed considerably under the influence of Hugh's cheerful, down-to-earth and gregarious stepmother.

True, both Hugh's exotic first wife, the mother of his teenage daughter Emily, with whom he had had a brief and stormy marriage, and his second wife, the mother of his sons, whom he had dearly loved but who had left him for his best friend, had vanished from the scene, but who better to find in their place than the gentle and welcoming Louise? Even Hugh, who in the past had seemed a slightly daunting person to Vanessa, full of a driving energy and not inclined to suffer fools gladly, seemed more relaxed than she remembered him. He pleased her by dipping into reminiscences of a time Vanessa cherished as the most perfect of her life – the time when, soon after leaving school, she had met Douglas and become engaged to him; a time when everything on her horizon had seemed full of glowing promise.

Jamie, trying not to wish that she had been able to re-establish this friendship on her own terms, was glad to see Vanessa enjoying the contacts with the Erskines. It was a relief to have somewhere to take her where she would relax. Sallies to the local in her company had turned out to be a very different thing from the agreeable evenings spent there with Maeve. Vanessa would sit, uptight and edgy, a glass of orange juice clutched in her hand, ready to be polite and doing her best to join in. She would enter into stilted exchanges with people like Fraser Kerr which reminded Jamie of nothing more nor less than Grandmother taking a kindly interest in her estate workers. 'And do you live in the village itself?' She sounded like the Queen doing a walkabout: 'Have you come far today . . . ?'

Vanessa also annoyed Jamie by visibly having trouble in 'placing' Abby, the friendly, untidy, long-legged girl who had been the Erskine nanny and had married one of the Gask sawmill workers. But Abby – the fact had come up in conversation with Louise, for she never mentioned anything of the sort herself – was the daughter of a high-ranking diplomat, and her soft and cultured voice certainly suggested some such background. It was all very puzzling for Vanessa, after her blind leap from her own established niche, where the parameters were clearly defined and clearly understood.

Her inability to relax in this undemanding, easygoing company, her surreptitious glances at her watch, her refusal to have a second glass of orange juice in case she might have to go to the loo, dreadful to contemplate, invariably drove Jamie to give up and go home early.

All mildly annoying, but though Jamie sounded off more than once to Patrick on this and similar irritants, she did try very hard not to get into arguments with Vanessa over them. She knew it would do no good, and she could imagine the blank denial with which Vanessa would meet any accusation of class consciousness or narrow-mindedness.

Not important in itself, perhaps, but it contributed to Jamie's feeling of not being able to move forward, distanced from much that she had hoped for when she settled into the cottage. Neither Calder in its traditional relation to the glen, counting as its 'neighbours' only the inmates of the other big houses, nor Calder in its graceless isolation during Zara's rule, existed now, and she had looked forward to adapting to a new style, as the Erskines had done. Such concepts were beyond Vanessa, and Jamie made no attempt to discuss them with her, though she believed they mattered.

Work on the cottage had had to be suspended, or had taken a form very different from the one which had so enticed her. Bashing through windows in the south gable with Maeve's breezy help (except, of course, that she would have been helping Maeve) seemed inappropriate with a guest in the house. For in spite of all Vanessa did, a guest she somehow, inescapably, remained. In practical terms, both bedrooms were needed, nor would Jamie have felt she was exactly offering Vanessa the sanctuary she needed if she had surrounded her with the sort of mess and rubble she most hated.

Another point which Jamie did her best to keep in mind was that, technically, she wasn't offering sanctuary at all. Vanessa was still a part owner of the cottage, and had as much right to be there as Jamie herself. Vanessa wouldn't see it in these terms, and wouldn't have dreamt of saying anything even if the thought had occurred to her, but Jamie knew she had no right to mind Vanessa's presence, let alone flatter herself that she was doing the decent thing by providing her with a roof.

But for how long? Setting aside her own needs and wishes, Jamie knew that for Vanessa's sake this question should at least be aired. An insidious acceptance of marking time was developing, a feeling of everything being on hold until some outside force came into play.

This worried Jamie more and more as time passed, and Vanessa gave no sign that she thought any further step should be taken. It seemed inconceivable to Jamie to take no action whatsoever. What was Vanessa waiting for? If she had left Douglas for good, as she insisted she had, then surely the situation should be put on some legal footing? At least, Jamie urged, Vanessa should talk to a solicitor, and get advice about the next step. This would safeguard against jeopardising her future position by giving Douglas the chance to take steps of his own while she hesitated.

At this Vanessa's face would become defensive and unhappy, her eyes unable to meet Jamie's. She would throw out vague ideas about getting a little flat somewhere, though adding at once that wherever she lived there must be not only a room for Ryan but a room where he could have friends to stay. Her thinking seemed so woolly, as though she had that moment plucked her ideas out of the air under pressure, that Jamie was privately horrified.

Vanessa might start by saying, 'I thought perhaps somewhere in Perth. Most of Ryan's friends are there,' then she would at once amend, 'though the shops aren't nearly as good as they used to be. You really have to go to Edinburgh to find anything nice these days.' Or she would produce some other argument so trifling that it was obvious her thinking had never moved beyond the most superficial aspects. She seemed to have no grasp of the financial implications of leaving Douglas, except to say from time to time that it was really very lucky that Calder was being sold.

'But you don't have to depend on that,' Jamie tried to tell her, doing her best to speak temperately, when Vanessa had said this for the third or fourth time.

'Oh, I'm not going to ask Douglas for anything,' Vanessa said quickly. 'I wouldn't dream of doing such a thing.'

'It's not a question of *asking*. You and Douglas own between you everything you have. I'm pretty certain that's the law here now. If you leave him then everything is divided up. But you really should talk to someone, Van, and establish your exact position. You can't sit here ignoring everything for ever. I mean, of course you can be here as long as you like, but all this can't just be left in the air.'

'Yes, you're right. I must say I thought Douglas would have been in touch long before this,' Vanessa said restlessly. As she spoke she got up and crossed the room to adjust one of the curtains so that it exactly matched its mate.

Jamie's jaw dropped at this response, and she watched in stupefaction as Vanessa smoothed the folds of the curtain with evident satisfaction. Was this what really mattered? Jamie closed her eyes as Vanessa came to sit down again. It seemed to help.

'But why does it have to be Douglas who gets in touch?' she asked when she was sure her voice was under control. 'Why don't you get in touch with him, and say you'd like to get things sorted out?'

'It's not up to me. I left him.' And from this

illogical position Vanessa refused to budge. She had made her gesture, an enormous and dramatic one. She had proclaimed, by acting in a way completely alien to her character, that Douglas's behaviour was unacceptable; that she had done her best and could do no more. Then she had looked no further, and seemed incapable of looking further. In her eyes, whatever happened next would be determined by Douglas's reaction.

Jamie was coming to understand, in spite of Vanessa's assertions about never going back, and her talk of finding somewhere to live, that she had been convinced at a much deeper level that Douglas would show that he wanted her. She couldn't imagine him managing without her. That was what it came down to. Douglas had never lifted a finger in the house, and had never been asked to. He had never changed a nappy, ironed a shirt, washed a dish or cooked a meal, and Vanessa's vision of him now, without her to do these things for him, was that he must be living in discomfort and squalor. She wasn't vindictive about this. In fact she didn't like to imagine it at all. It was simply the consequence of the gesture she had made, and it must be only a matter of time before it had its effect.

When the unwelcome truth was forced upon her that in some inexplicable way Douglas was managing very well, the discovery was so painful and destructive that Jamie couldn't bring herself to use it as an argument to take action at last.

For, arranging to meet Phil at Dunrossie – a less

abrasive companion than she would have been, Jamie
had acknowledged, trying not to mind – Vanessa had
driven down to collect more of her belongings.
Douglas, approached by Phil, had raised no objections, a compliance which Jamie, and Patrick when
she discussed it with him, found highly suspect.

It had shaken Vanessa to find the house clean and
orderly and, apart from tiny details which she had
pounced on and made much of to soothe her sore
heart, looking much as it always had. That hurt in
some profound way which it was hard for Jamie to
comprehend, and after this visit Vanessa went
through a night of tears and anguish about the future,
which was more searing to witness even than her
distress when she first arrived.

Jamie, doing her best to grasp the root cause of this
helpless grief, was thankful that one good thing had
come out of the expedition. Phil had made Vanessa,
much against her will, trawl Ryan's room for any
information they could turn up about his friends and,
patiently following up every detail, had finally
tracked down a contact address in Leeds.

Jamie sometimes wished Phil hadn't been quite so
painstaking, as they rushed into a whole new cycle of
need, guilt and racked feelings. Vanessa wrote to
Ryan at once, a long and, Jamie suspected, inadvi-
sedly emotional letter. Ryan didn't reply. Vanessa
sobbed openly about this each day at post time, then
wrote again, more briefly, begging only for the merest assurance that he was well. There was no response.

'If only he'd given me a phone number, but I don't even know the name of the people he's staying with, so I can't try enquiries. Do you think I should just drive down and see him? I must know that he's all right. He's bound to be dreadfully upset about my not being at home. He won't understand at all. He'll think I've deserted him. It might traumatise him, wreck his chances of university for good, wreck his whole future life.'

Jamie winced to think of the rebuff Vanessa would almost certainly meet if she went to Leeds.

'Honestly, I don't think it would be wise to go down,' she said. 'Especially without warning him. Leave it for a day or two. I'll think of something.'

Even at such a moment, she was amused as well as incredulous to find that Vanessa seemed to regard this as some sort of solution. In her place Jamie would have demanded some suggestions at least, and if one was offered that sounded even half feasible would have acted on it without delay. Amusement fading, Jamie pondered, not for the first time, the damage done by a dominating personality working without scruple on a weaker one over a long period of time.

She wrote to Ryan herself. She didn't dress matters up. 'Phone me at 7.00 p.m. on Wednesday, without fail.' She gave the Calder number. At seven o'clock Vanessa would be safely in the toils of dinner. Ryan, Jamie was almost sure, would not defy a direct order from such a source at such a time. However angry she felt about his callousness in ignoring his mother's pleas, she did agree with Vanessa that he must be feeling baffled, excluded, resentful and full of questions and uncertainty.

Ryan phoned, and though the exchange was brief, he determined to give as little as possible away, Jamie unable to bring herself to be very conciliatory, she was at least able to assure him that, apart from Vanessa being at Calder – impossible to enter into her reasons – no major decisions affecting the future had as yet been taken. She extracted a telephone number from him, and made him give her a time when he would be in later that evening, in return for a promise that she wouldn't let Vanessa bombard him with calls night and day.

But he hadn't fought too hard about yielding that number, she decided, going over their halting exchange on her way back to the cottage. He had, in fact, seemed to want contact desperately. She wondered, as she had before, what it must have been like for him day after day, walking the quaking bog which was family life at Dunrossie. No wonder he had taken refuge in glowering silence. No wonder he had fled.

As with so many other things she had been forced to face lately, she realised that she had skimmed the surface here too, accepting Ryan as he presented himself and looking no further. She, whose success in the world of business had largely depended on an acute observation and understanding of people, had been dismally blind in her personal life. It had been time for a crash of some sort. Well, she had crashed.

The contact with Ryan, though Vanessa returned

drowned in tears after talking to him, did remove her principal anxiety as to his whereabouts. But lesser ones took its place. Ryan, it appeared, wasn't staying with a friend. He'd found a job in a garage, rented a room and intended to stay, giving up any plans for university.

'Well, at least he's got a job.' Jamie tried to find some comfort. At least you don't have to worry about him sleeping rough. But you didn't say that sort of thing to Vanessa, who would never be realistic enough to think for herself that *her son* might come to such a pass.

'It's not doing things to cars, though, not learning something useful.' Was that Douglas speaking? 'It's only taking money for petrol.'

The idea that this distinction could be a new source of anxiety made Jamie groan, but she said nothing.

It was impossible to hold her tongue, however, when Vanessa, unable to bear the deadlock any longer, got in touch with Douglas. It wasn't so much the getting in touch that Jamie minded, for it could have been prompted by the sensible determination to reach some decisions. Instead Vanessa, lost and lonely, unable to feel at home in the cottage or to imagine where else she could go, alarmed at the idea of taking responsibility for Ryan and worn down by Douglas's silence, phoned to ask him what he wanted her to do.

29

'How could she be so weak?' Jamie demanded passionately. 'How could she let him treat her as he did, and reach the point where to stay with him was unendurable, and then *ask* him what she should do? It doesn't make sense. It's going back on everything she's said. It makes me so angry I can hardly speak . . .'

Patrick thought that she wasn't doing too badly, ranging up and down his sitting-room at Blackdykes, spilling out her frustration and outrage.

'They met in Pitlochry. For dinner, of course. It would have to be dinner for Douglas, dinner and a decent bottle of something. And she came back in absolute tatters, riddled with guilt and unable to see anything straight any more.'

'Straight as in—?'

'I don't think she could even remember why she'd left him. He'd obviously spent the evening doing just what he's always done in the past, overriding her, dismissing everything she said, telling her she'd got it wrong. She told me so, and yet – it seems incredible – it was as if she didn't relate it to anything that had actually happened. Made no connection.'

Almost as if she had welcomed it, as though being

told what to think, told what she remembered, was so inevitable and familiar that in some strange way it comforted her. That seemed disturbing and somehow perverted to Jamie, and even to Patrick she didn't attempt to put the feeling into words.

Patrick watched her, his face as carefully masked as ever, as she swung away again and went to gaze from the window, where she found little to comfort her in the stark appurtenances of Patrick's trade, the gantry and scaffold, the fork-lift truck, the stock of obdurate stone from which his own obdurate character would wrest the powerful images.

How she hated compromise, Patrick knew. How she herself went all out for things, heart and soul. How well he could understand her difficulty in seeing that an unsatisfactory marriage could hang together for any number of reasons – out of habit and convenience, fear of the unknown, pride, status and the importance of appearances, but also, as he suspected might be the case here, through the insidious hold of a pattern of behaviour. This could become so much part of existence for both partners that they found it virtually impossible to break free of it.

What place did affection, let alone love, have in such a relationship? Yet for certain people this basis of conflict could be almost equally compelling. Was it that some element in each protagonist created the situation in the first place – in this case the compulsion to dominate on the one hand and to be dominated on the other – and in the end neither could do without it? It spoke of weakness, of one kind or another, in both of them (how that would anger Douglas), and Patrick didn't think that Jamie, with her uncompromising and often reckless honesty, could begin to apprehend such a need. It would appal her. For her, a relationship had to be all or nothing, and anger burned in him again to think of how she herself had so recently been betrayed. If that capacity for feeling, that directness, could be for him . . . He dragged his mind away and concentrated on the matter in hand.

'You can only do exactly as you've been doing,' he said quietly, his mind, as always, seeing primarily her position in this, and her pain. 'You can only go on assuring Vanessa of your support, listening to her, giving her time, making her feel safe. She's nowhere near even thinking about plans. In fact, we both know this was never about looking for some new life for herself.'

'But if she was driven to go, like that, after being violently assaulted, rushing out of the house just as she was –' Jamie checked, remembering that it was also true that Vanessa had laid the table for Douglas's breakfast. She didn't think she'd mention that. 'She must have been desperate to escape. She must have thought about it every time there was a row between them. She must have wanted to find some different way of living. Can't you imagine what it must have been like for her, watching every word, spending her days working out ways to please, always terrified Douglas wouldn't be satisfied, never knowing when he was going to explode next . . .'

Patrick waited, not interrupting, letting her pour out her churning revulsion and dismay. He shared both feelings, and had been thankful that he had not run across Cairney recently, not sure he would have been able to contain them had a meeting taken place, but he also knew that Jamie was viewing the situation in terms of how she would behave herself. Vanessa's eroded feeling of self-worth, her dread of facing the mechanics of living alone, without a recognisable label, as it were, in the eyes of her world, were factors very alien to Jamie.

And if Vanessa did stick to her guns, and refuse to go back to Douglas, what in fact would she do? Would she find it beyond her to relinquish her temporary refuge and set up some new life of her own? Would she stay on at Calder, patching together an empty and purposeless existence, sending Ryan food parcels and counting the weeks till he turned up to favour her with a little of his time? Would she nest there, surrounding herself with frills and sponge cakes, pot plants and Flash?

She would drive Jamie mad. It wasn't what Jamie had planned or needed. Impossible to imagine them shaking down into some workable long-term arrangement. Jamie would be off again; he could see it coming. Drawing a hand hard down over his mouth and chin, he wiped all expression from his face.

More years of waiting. Waiting for what, he demanded of himself with sudden rage. He had waited for her to grow up, to get through university, to work out the defiance and wildness which had been the response of her forceful character to a largely unloved childhood. He had waited while she took on the world, carving out her own success, finding her own fulfilment. And, though he had tried to tell himself otherwise, that his reclusive lifestyle was his own choice and that marriage or commitment to any woman was not for him, in fact, unable to help himself, he had gone on waiting even when, though those at home had received few facts, she had appeared to enter at last into a stable relationship.

Then, so startlingly, she had been back, everything that made up her life arbitrarily wiped out, alone, battered and bruised, and for him the feelings and hopes, like the deep currents of a shadowed pool rarely disturbed, had eddied into violent motion.

Well, they would subside again into stillness and shadows, he supposed dourly, though it might take a little time. He had long ago recognised that no other woman was likely to have the mixture of courage and enterprise, laughter and energy – combined with the whippy, active body and the keen, intelligent face he loved – which so drew him. Nor would there be, with any other woman, the long associations of the past, or the sense of close, deep familiarity which he so valued.

No one else had ever come near the hidden, intensely emotional core of his feelings, and no one ever would. But he had grown used to solitude. If Jamie disappeared again, to reshape her life along new lines in some new place, nothing would have fundamentally changed for him, except that, briefly, daz-

zlingly, he had realised that not only was she free, but
that there was a chance that this time she might
remain close at hand. He had thought that time
was for once on his side, and had hoped that gradually, cautiously, he might be able to awaken her to
how he felt about her.

Vanessa's presence at the cottage changed that. He
could hardly grudge her its haven, poor girl, but if
her being there drove Jamie away, as it must do if she
stayed for long, his chance would be gone. Chance
for what? He shifted in his chair, filled with angry
self-disgust. How astounded Jamie would be to know
what he was thinking. And disgusted in her turn. To
her he was no more than an old family friend, in
terms of age roughly comparable to Mr Syme probably, and fulfilling much the same supporting role in
her life.

Jamie drove back up the glen feeling much comforted. Just to be with Patrick put problems into
proportion again. It had been good to see him in his
home setting for once, though he had not offered to
take her over to the workshop to show her whatever
work he was engaged on. There had been the faintest
sense of exclusion in that, though she supposed he
would have shown her if she had asked. To her, his
sculptures were a vital part of him, and it would have
been good to be allowed to come closer to that side of
him, to stand in silence and draw from some emerging image a sense of the inner forces which he kept
so firmly in leash. It would have been interesting too

to trace in powerful three-dimensional form the changes the years had made in him.

How long since she had last been at Blackdykes? She saw again the small well-furnished house, with its aura of permanence and comfort. No clutter, no superfluous objects, whole walls lined with books, every light in the right place, and the essential atmosphere Patrick seemed to create, of things working smoothly in the most practical order. How self-sufficient he was, with the absorption and release of his work to round out his chosen way of living. He didn't need people. Lucky man.

Naomi hadn't seemed quite as warm and welcoming as usual today, though. Jamie's mind went back to her earlier call at Longmuir with a slight check of uncertainty. She had felt something of the sort the last time she had been there. She had stayed away too long, she told herself grimly. She couldn't expect to keep her place in people's lives, particularly if she barely bothered to write to them. Naomi was old, her daily existence narrowing to a set routine, and a visitor who didn't appear on a regular basis no doubt ruffled the even calm she now preferred.

In this way Jamie tried to rationalise away the lingering sense of disapproval, doing her best not to let it remind her of Freda's more blatant rejection.

Patrick could have told her that any chill she had detected in his mother's manner stemmed from a keen disappointment that Jamie had never had the perception to realise how he himself felt about her, or, to Naomi's mind, the basic good sense to return the feeling. Naomi knew she had little time left now to hope for the outcome she had always thought so obvious and desirable. She would have to go leaving her adored son condemned to a lifestyle she saw as unnaturally empty and incomplete, and which she considered sadly wrong for a man of his depths of feeling. Finding it hard to hold her tongue on the subject to Jamie, she had fallen back on a tight-lipped constraint.

It wasn't important, Jamie told herself. It was ridiculous at her age to look for the unreserved welcome she had received as a child. But she knew she did mind. It seemed one more element lying between Patrick and her, reminding her how separate their lives were.

She was glad to remember, as she swung down the curves of the Calder drive (noting with satisfaction the excellent effect of the work she and Maeve had done), that Phil would be with Vanessa. The visit to Naomi had been arranged before Vanessa's meeting with Douglas and the emotional storm it had whipped up, and Jamie, reporting developments to Phil as she now scrupulously and gladly did, had remarked that she disliked inconveniencing Naomi, but didn't see how she could leave Vanessa alone in her present state.

Phil, unexpectedly, had said she could take the day off. She wouldn't have her van, for some reason, but had said she would come to Aberfyle by bus, if Jamie would meet her there.

'Of course I can, but are you sure it isn't a drag for

you?' Jamie had asked. 'It would be perfect if you could come – you're sure to be a lot more sympathetic than I am when she starts beating up on herself – but can't I fetch you? It's no distance, and I don't have to be at Longmuir till lunch-time.'

'No thanks. It's very kind of you, but I'll come on the bus. Ten twenty in the square.' Phil had spoken with the calm firmness Jamie was only just beginning to get used to. Then she had added, more hesitantly, 'I'd been meaning to come and see you about something anyway.'

The words came back to Jamie now. Phil had not been communicative this morning about whatever it was she had wanted to talk about. In fact, she had been noticeably silent, even for her. Whatever was on her mind – surely not a change of heart about the cottage, Jamie wondered with sudden alarm, instantly dismissed, for Phil was unswervingly dependable in such matters – it was lucky she had been free today, and that she and Vanessa had had so many peaceful hours together. Without her. It would have been good for both of them. It was what they were used to, and would have given them the chance to talk properly, one on one. Jamie, bleakly perceptive today, was ready to admit that three-sided conversations between them, in which she was too prone to take a leading role, didn't always work well.

Yet when she went into the sitting-room of the cottage, now in regular use and graced (or marred) by Zara's large television, she was surprised to find the atmosphere not obviously one of calm after storm.

Certainly Vanessa, red-eyed and a little tremulous, gave the impression of having offloaded a good deal of emotional baggage onto the shoulders of her phlegmatic younger sister, but Phil herself, though outwardly unruffled, seemed to Jamie even more stolidly reserved than she had been this morning.

Or had her own arrival cut across their communication? Once more Jamie felt the small chill of being cut off from the true feelings of those around her. It made her sad for a moment, the sense of sibling unity which had so warmed her when she first came back out of her reach. She had lost her place here, by her own actions. That was the truth of it.

Phil, it seemed, had been urging on Vanessa the common-sense course of taking her time, staying where she was, and changing nothing until she was sure of what she wanted. In Phil's eyes, the availability of the cottage precisely when it was needed was a piece of uncomplicated luck. It had never occurred to her for a moment to wonder if Jamie might mind Vanessa's presence there, and this made Jamie feel guilty, and even more out of step with what was going on.

Vanessa, an afternoon of cathartic tears behind her, seemed almost cheerful as she bobbed about bringing in tea. She had made butterfly cakes. Jamie, stupefied, surveyed the neatly arranged plate. How could Vanessa, at this crisis of her life, think of solemnly slicing the top off little round cakes, cutting in half the piece she had removed, filling the hollow with whipped cream, sticking back the bits like wings

and then *adding a cherry*? I'm missing something
here, Jamie thought, accepting a cup of tea. I don't
operate on their level.

'I know you like these,' Vanessa was saying to Phil,
offering her the plate and sounding almost happy,
pleased to have produced a nursery favourite for a
sister well into her thirties who should not, with her
build, be eating cream cakes at all.

Phil helped herself obediently, but her mind
seemed to be elsewhere. She glanced at the clock
more than once as tea progressed, and scarcely
seemed to listen to Vanessa's flow of chatter, though
it was Jamie who had visited them, about Patrick's
latest exhibition, Naomi's increasing difficulty in
getting about and how much she minded not being
able to work in her rock garden.

Has Phil got to go on duty this evening, Jamie
wondered, seeing her look at her watch this time, and
then glance towards the window. How shameful it
was to know so little about the details of her life. With
a rush of compunction, in which there twisted perhaps a thread of need to be involved, to be closer,
induced by her earlier thoughts, Jamie took the
chance to say, when Vanessa was absent replenishing
the teapot, 'Phil, you are going to let me run you
back, aren't you? It's dreadful to let you go by bus,
and it seems all wrong to have no idea of where you
live or—'

To her surprise Phil, her face scarlet, her eyes
almost hunted, darted another look towards the
window and, rattling her plate down anyhow, drop-

ping her knife as she did so, scrambled clumsily to
her feet.

'Jamie, look, I've been wanting to say . . .' she
began, then let the sentence hang, standing with a
look of defeat as Vanessa came back and began
offering tea.

'Wait a minute, Van,' Jamie ordered, frowning,
putting up a hand to ward off more goodies. 'I think
Phil wants to—'

What? What did Phil want, standing there like a
cornered stirk, slow thoughts turning, her cheeks
red, words refusing to come?

'Do sit down, Phil,' Vanessa said, oblivious.
'You're in the way there. And you can't go yet,
you haven't finished your tea. Oh, you've dropped
your knife. Really, you might be six years old again.
I'll get you another.'

'Vanessa, no, don't!' Phil's voice sounded strained,
almost harsh, and she said quickly, 'Thanks, but no,
I don't need one. I just—'

'Goodness, don't say it's time to go for your bus?'
Vanessa exclaimed. 'I'd forgotten all about that, I'm
so sorry. Why didn't you say? What time do you have
to be there? Though to be honest I think it would be
far more sensible to let one of us take you all the way
back. In fact, I don't know why you didn't let Jamie
fetch you this morning. She didn't have to be at
Naomi's till lunch-time, and she could easily have—'

'Van, please, it's not that,' Phil broke in desperately. 'I don't need a lift. I only wanted – I should
have—'

She didn't seem able to muster the words she wanted, and sat down again helplessly.

'Is there something wrong with the van? I should have asked before. I do apologise, Phil,' Vanessa said contritely, 'I've been far too wrapped up in my own troubles today.'

'It's all right.' Phil barely seemed to hear her.

'But what's wrong?' Jamie demanded, concern growing. Has some disaster befallen Phil's life too, and they had taken no notice? I can't bear it if it has, she thought in sudden anguish. I don't want to hear. Then she pulled herself together, ashamed of the impulse to ward off more misery. 'What is it you want to tell us?' she asked quietly.

But Phil, getting up again, didn't answer. Her ear, cocked and attentive, had heard sounds they had missed. She knew before the firm knock sounded that he had come, and she was on her way to the door before either of her sisters moved.

'Phil? What's—?'

'Who can that be?'

Vanessa and Jamie, with a questioning look at each other, came to their feet. Voices in the hall, and then Phil, blushing, doubtful yet half defiant, was coming back in with a man at her heels, a round, broad-chested, young man with very short legs, a navy-and-white striped T-shirt straining round his chunky torso, a head of tiny, baby-soft, ginger corkscrew curls, and a face as scarlet as Phil's own.

He nodded to them affably. 'Not a bad kind of day,' he offered. 'Though we could do with a drop of rain, right enough. Not late, am I?' he enquired of Phil. 'Back of five, you said, and it can't be much past that.'

'Do come in.' Floundering, looking from his face to Phil's, which were on an exact level, Vanessa did her best. 'Have you come to give Phil a lift back? How kind. But won't you have tea while you're here?'

Well done, Vanessa, thought Jamie sincerely. 'Hi, I'm Jamie,' she said, coming forward and holding out her hand.

'Bruce,' said the red-haired man, thrusting out a stubby hand at the end of a short thick arm golden with freckles and ginger hairs. The hand was work-hardened and powerful. He hurt her quite severely.

As his arm returned to his side Phil unexpectedly wrapped both hands round it.

'Bruce is my husband,' she said.

30

How little I had understood. It was the thought that
came to Jamie over and over again in the days that
followed. Arresting and humbling, the realisation
made her open her eyes to a hundred things disre-
garded before, and look at her own life with a new
and ruthless objectivity. The time had come for
decision. She had let events and other people's affairs
influence her for long enough.

The revelation that Phil and Bruce were married
stood out, in retrospect, as the single factor which
made the most impact on her. That and what lay
behind it.

They had been married, it turned out, for almost
two years, and Bruce, though he was only twenty-
five, had a six-year-old daughter. She was called
Rhoda, and she had learning difficulties.

Such a moderate term to describe the reality Phil
had to contend with, Jamie thought, finishing the
boring fiddly part of painting the frame of the new
window, which now transformed the sitting-room
with sun and light from the south. Only the sill to do,
the easy part. But with the thought came a tiny flicker
of dismay that in a matter of minutes it would be

done, the very last bit of work on the cottage. And then what?

She turned back deliberately to Phil's situation. Rhoda was a volatile and unpredictable child, given to raging tantrums. She couldn't keep herself clean and couldn't, or wouldn't, feed herself. She solicited attention with aggression whenever a stranger was present, and was destructive and violent if attention was withheld. Phil loved her and cared for her with apparently effortless patience, somehow juggling the requirements of taking her back and forth to her special school, sharing with Bruce the task of looking after her when she was at home, and at the same time keeping on her demanding job in the residential home – more demanding than Jamie or Vanessa had realised, since she had become assistant matron eighteen months ago.

She, Bruce and Rhoda lived in dark and tiny quarters, formerly a porter's lodge, set in the wall of a narrow, sunless courtyard at the back of the home. Damp and cramped, these rooms were furnished with some of the drabbest furniture, little of which they owned, that Jamie had ever seen. Bruce had done the decorating, covering the walls with busily patterned papers, which presumably they had chosen together, and painting all the woodwork dark green. They were perfectly happy there.

Bruce was handyman-gardener at Burnbrae, though in fact he was unskilled in either role. It had been obvious to Jamie, however, when she began to visit them, refusing to be kept away any longer, that he put a great deal more into the job than mowing the grass, planting out rigid lines of gaudy bedding plants, or having a go at any repair job that cropped up. He was a man of tireless energy and goodwill, bouncing up at the first hint that he was needed, his short legs and small feet endlessly twinkling about the rambling house and grounds, his round red perspiring face always beaming.

Barely able to read and write, and never losing the naivety and innocence which had made him a hapless victim in the rough environment in which he had grown up, he had survived by not recognising that he was victimised. He had no opinion of himself, so why should other people think anything of him? His cheerfulness could not be dented, even during a period in Glasgow when he had lived on the streets, though it was a time he didn't talk about. He had found his way to Muirend by chance, coming up with a van-load of youths he scarcely knew to do a job, which he had supposed meant work. Finding he would be no use to them the others had shoved him out and driven off, and he never saw them again. He didn't have so much as his fare back to Glasgow.

The Job Centre had sent him to Burnbrae House as a fill-in for two weeks. He had never left. Here he found a niche ready-made for him. His good nature, compassion and vast strength could be channelled into caring for the elderly and mostly incapacitated residents. He entered into everything that went on, driving the minibus, listening to grumbles, comforting or rallying, attending every party or celebration (single-handedly shifting the sofas and armchairs in the main lounge as required), lifting and carrying, fixing and mending, producing little treats, and never counting the hours he worked.

When Rhoda was born and he was told she was his, he hadn't for a moment queried the statement, believing that his initiation into embarrassed sex after a Hogmanay street party had represented true love. When Rhoda had been placed in care after the disappearance of her mother soon after she was born, he had visited her with unfailing regularity, taking her absurd presents he couldn't afford, though accepting without question that he couldn't be considered a fit person to look after her. When he and Phil married he had never doubted that making a home for Rhoda was the thing they both wanted most.

It had been something very special for Jamie, this summer, to see Phil with him, and to be welcomed, shyly at first, into their environment. And though it had often been painful, and the guilt for her own heedlessness would remain with her for the rest of her life, it had been good to find the opportunity to talk to Phil at last, and to be told in candid though never accusing terms why Phil had found it simpler to keep the truth from them.

She had been unwilling to let their inevitable criticism, in the guise of concern or however else they intended it, spoil things so important to her, neither Burnbrae and its vulnerable community, with its small-scale concerns and the shifts its straitened finances imposed, nor her love for Bruce and his embattled and disadvantaged small daughter with her profound needs.

Vanessa's reaction, Jamie was obliged to admit, had amply justified Phil's unwillingness to let them come close to what really mattered in her life. Vanessa had trouble with all of it. Though she would have been shocked to be accused of it, she had led such a sheltered life that her whole outlook constituted prejudice. Bruce Howie was the gardener, from a dreadful background, completely uneducated. What could he and Phil possibly have in common? (That she found him physically repellent, that she winced at the whiff of sweat which lingered in his cheap acrylic shirts, that he had a Glasgow accent, slathered tomato ketchup over everything he ate and read the *Sun*, she would not have brought herself to put into words, but Jamie knew these things made her unhappy.) Vanessa overlooked the fact that, in spite of Phil having spent years at an expensive boarding school, she had emerged little better educated than Bruce was. She also failed to see, locked in conventional attitudes as she was, the generosity of spirit and sweetness of temper which Phil and Bruce shared, their instinct to care for others, and their great, quiet happiness together.

Perhaps that was something which Vanessa genuinely couldn't understand. The thought made Jamie's face bleak, as she finished the sill and stepped back to survey her work. Vanessa's values, as she had demonstrated, were fundamentally different. For

Vanessa had gone back to Douglas, and Jamie was finding that very hard to deal with.

He had played her with finesse. He had intended her to come back from the start, because he liked having her in place to make his life smooth and comfortable, and because she was part of his image. It filled him with anger to imagine the perfection of that image marred in the eyes of friends, colleagues and acquaintances. But most of all he wanted her back because she was his, his possession. Irrespective of how he felt about her, he would never let her escape him. Walk away, make her own choices, establish a life independent of him? Never.

He had known precisely how to bring her to heel. He waited. He showed his hand just enough to make it clear that he thought she should be back at Dunrossie, though he never directly asked her to return, and he reiterated at every meeting that no incident like the one which had driven her away would ever occur again.

For after that first dinner in Pitlochry they did meet. Not very often, and always on neutral ground carefully chosen by Douglas, ground where Vanessa was, consciously or not, reminded of the life she had given up — a life of comfort and affluence, where nothing ugly impinged, and where one met people who lived in the same way and observed the same codes of behaviour as oneself. It was not that Vanessa longed for these things, or could have defined them, but being subtly drawn back into that ambience brought home to her, as Douglas meant it to, the impossibility of a single woman, separated or divorced or whatever it came to, taking her place in such a circle. To Vanessa it was unimaginable, for example, for a woman to dine alone in a hotel. It was not that she thought convention frowned on it, it was that the whole scenario seemed alarming. And why would one do it? What enjoyment would there be in venturing alone into the sort of places where Douglas took her? Then she would be ashamed of her inability to think on a more serious level. How much of life, after all, did one spend in hotel dining-rooms? But the dinners with Douglas kept the image before her, and though she didn't recognise that they epitomised the male paying-and-protecting role she was used to, they did become a symbol of all she would lose by leaving.

She knew that to attempt to express such things, especially to Jamie, would be impossible. They would sound pitiful and each example, weighing nothing in itself, could be swept aside by someone so independent and confident. And how, her mind turning forlornly to other images, could she plead that she missed the sunny spaces of her house, her luxurious bathroom, her enormous walk-in wardrobe with its reassuring rows of clothes, its racks of expensive shoes which were as much a delight to handle as to wear? And how, to someone as tough-fibred as Jamie, could she confess her cowardly longing not to have to drive everywhere all the time, but to be safe in the passenger seat of a powerful, quietly purring car, without ever having to wonder whether it would start or what made it go, whether it needed oil or petrol or air in its tyres. The figure of the driver remained indistinct, but was male, of course, and in broad terms well-built and well-dressed, exuding assurance. It made her realise how much she needed the presence of a man in her life, but this was something else she could never admit to Jamie, nor her terror at the idea of entering into a relationship with someone new and unknown. Who, where, how did one begin?

Douglas had continued to pursue his own life without missing a step, denying Vanessa the one thing she yearned for – an indication that he missed her contribution to it. It would have given her power over him, and that he was determined to withhold from her. In his view, service could be bought. The financial crisis which he had exaggerated in order to push along the sale of Calder would never be allowed to impinge on his own comfort. But if you wanted a clean shirt it didn't have to come with devotion and emotional need and longing for praise ironed into it. Shopping and cooking, cleaning and polishing, could be paid for. There might be trifling inconveniences, details less than perfect, a gratifying level of cosseting absent, but there was also a clinical simplicity which had its attractions.

Not for too long though. For Douglas's needs, on a plane quite separate from the practical and domestic, or even the sexual, important as that was, were as deep-rooted as Vanessa's, and here he was scarcely more honest with himself than she was. Perhaps

could not have been, for these needs had their existence in a deeply buried part of him, and had to do
with the stimulus received from control, instilling
fear and, ultimately, inflicting pain. He genuinely
believed what he said when he told Vanessa he would
never strike her again. That he recognised as unacceptable behaviour. Yet still there coiled in him the
need for absolute possession and, though he would
never have used the words, for having her at his
mercy. Another source of deep unspoken anger
which needed assuagement was the fact that Ryan
had escaped him, slithering away without direct
confrontation.

He had let time pass, making no moves to influence
Vanessa except the occasional suggestion that they
should meet 'to discuss things'. He knew that by
leaving her to contemplate the barrenness of a future
alone he would gain his ends more effectively than by
persuasion or pressure. And he had been right.

Vanessa, knowing she couldn't stay at Calder for
ever, and faced with the prospect of life in some
similar cottage, which in her eyes provided no more
than the barest necessities, or alone in some town flat,
struggled to imagine how her days would be filled.
What would there be to do, with only herself to look
after? Join things? What things? A keep-fit group,
perhaps; she needed to lose a little weight. But would
she meet anyone nice there? And would she have to
wear Lycra? Well then, what else? An art class? She
was hopeless at drawing. A reading circle? She would
be too frightened to open her mouth to discuss the

clever books they would doubtless choose, books which never seemed to be about the kind of people Vanessa considered 'normal' and which made her feel desperately inadequate.

The truth was, she would conclude wretchedly, she had no faith in her ability to make friends, as a person on her own, all familiar props stripped away. Though she hadn't always especially liked the people she met through Douglas, she understood in a dim way that they were part of her world, outside which she had no identity, and no inclination to create one for herself.

Inevitably, she began to ask what had been so dreadful about the life she had led. Most of her days had been pleasantly occupied; she had been peacefully alone for much of the time, doing things she was good at and surrounded by objects she enjoyed and prized. Quite apart from the aching need to be somewhere where Ryan, however hurtful his behaviour to her, might eventually reappear (for in her heart she still believed that her cooking, her care, her ceaseless supply of clean clothes must be what he really wanted), and the even deeper need for a recognised role, she would be seized by a nostalgia she wouldn't have dared confess to.

She would find herself longing obsessively for her own kitchen, and all the sophisticated appliances she had taken for granted. How pathetic Jamie would think it, but it was true. Gropingly, unused to examining such ideas, she saw that she had been sheltered, by what these things represented, from the realities of the threatening world beyond Dunrossie – a world of want and violence, drugs and crime, of hurricanes, avalanches, floods and global warming, of ethnic cleansing, genocide, rebellion and war. She had been safe from huge and dreadful issues it was easier not to think about, disasters unstoppable, far away, which happened to other people.

It was Jamie who refused to let her forget her reason for having fled this haven, which, as the days passed and other options looked more and more terrifying, appeared increasingly desirable.

'All right, you say he's promising to behave himself and never touch you again,' Jamie said, during one of the muddled and emotionally exhausting discussions they seemed unable to avoid whenever Vanessa had been with Douglas, 'but there was more to it than that, wasn't there? It wasn't just a couple of occasions when Douglas lost his temper—'

'But I did annoy him. I see that now. You get annoyed with me yourself, you know you do. I can't seem to help—'

'Vanessa, that wasn't the point. Don't get dragged off at a tangent all the time.'

Vanessa, who could rarely think back past the last point made, particularly when she was wrought up as she was now, was silent, though inner protests rose confusedly, making it harder than ever to think clearly. That was so often her difficulty, when fear that she was going to be stupid and not understand yet again prevented her from giving her full attention to what was being said, so starting up the cycle once more.

'It wasn't just about Douglas hitting you, was it?' Jamie persisted, then shook her head in exasperation to see Vanessa instantly resist this bluntness. 'Nor about him bullying and abusing you. No, Van, *listen*. Don't reject the words you don't like. It was about the fact that he liked doing it, waited for his moment, got a kick out of it. You know that's true.'

'I was upset when I said that. In fact, I don't think I ever did say it. You said it, I'm sure you did. I'd never have used such an expression.'

'But it was the reality behind the rest, wasn't it?' Jamie kept her voice calm, refusing to be side-tracked, knowing how fatally inclined Vanessa was to slide away from the unpleasant truth, not even aware she was doing it. Her mind, unused to the logical development of an argument, shied away from anything difficult.

'No, it wasn't like that,' Vanessa protested. 'He was just very tired that night. He'd had awful problems at work, and he was worried about money. He's explained it all to me.' And she fell back on the tried and true clinching argument. 'You don't understand. When you're married and have children you can't just think of yourself. There are always going to be ups and downs, that's inevitable. Of course I was in a state at the time, anyone would have been, but Douglas is really appalled at what he did. Anyway, I expect it was my fault. I must have provoked him . . .'

'Vanessa—' But what was there to say? This was taking them right back to the very beginning again.

And it was then that Vanessa produced her trump card. 'Anyway, he's agreed to go for counselling.'

The panacea of modern times; the strange belief that by making this gesture, and nothing more, all problems will automatically vanish, all cracks be healed.

Vanessa, he'll never do such a thing. Don't you know him? And even if he goes once, to convince you, he'll never change. People don't. We are what we are.

Jamie, recalling this conversation and others like it, released some of her feelings by hammering the lid onto the paint can. Someone would have trouble getting that off. It wasn't likely to be her. And with that thought the imminence of waiting decisions rushed back. She had her own future to face. All the jobs that had occupied her, supervising the work carried out on the big house, clearing and tidying outside with Maeve, getting this house as she wanted it, jobs which had carried her from day to day without too much thought, were finished. Her responsibility was now confined to the cottage itself, and the stretch of river bank newly designated as belonging to it.

They had been stunned by the speed at which things had moved as soon as – or even before – Calder was on the market. From the feeling of the sale being some remote and vaguely visualised event, the new owners hazy unknown figures, they had been swept into the reality, with no interval between putting a first toe into the water and finding themselves swimming hard. Apart from the immediate interest shown in the property, no one had bargained for the persistence of those most attracted, or for the strange involvement which developed, for Jamie at least, in their lives and hopes and their reasons for wanting the place.

Another unforeseen aspect had been the demands of showing them round, not only in terms of time, but of energy and emotion. It had proved impossible to take anyone on the tour of house, buildings, gardens and what remained of the demesne, without on the one hand wanting passionately to do one's best for Calder, and on the other hating to think of it in strange hands.

'Maybe you're the wrong person for the job,' Patrick suggested, only half teasing, one evening when he was resuscitating Jamie with dinner at the Toll-house, after a day when she had shown two would-be buyers round and announced herself exhausted. 'Here, take a slug of this.'

He handed her an American-style martini, and she gasped at her first sip. 'Hey, what are you doing to me? I'm out of the habit.'

'Brace you up. You're pouring out your heart's blood on these people. Bear in mind that most of them will be looking at other properties as well, and even for those who aren't there can only be one buyer.'

'I shall feel guilty about the ones that lose out,' Jamie admitted. 'I know you're right and I'm being ridiculous, but when they tell me their life stories and say Calder is exactly what they've always dreamed of, I want each one to have it.'

'I can see why you're a limp rag,' Patrick mocked, but he was painfully conscious of the implications behind the sale, and it was hard to resist asking Jamie what she intended to do.

He knew how tough she was finding it to accept Vanessa's return to Douglas, and how cut off she felt from her because of it. She hadn't talked about it much, but when she did the same passionate question always came up. 'How could she do that, knowing what he's like? How could she? She can't believe anything will be different.'

'She wants to believe it, as you must see. There's so much in that life she values and depends on. She'd be lost on her own, lost and miserable and frightened. And Douglas has probably learned something. He can't ever have expected her to take off like that.'

'Yes, he's learned he can do what he likes and get away with it,' Jamie said.

Privately Patrick agreed, but he only said gently, 'Jamie, you can't change it. It's what Vanessa chose.'

He was coming up to the glen at every moment he could during this unsettled period, when with each potential purchaser a new set of possibilities took shape, and he saw the strain, though she joked about it, which this put on Jamie. She had had far too much to deal with in recent months, in his opinion.

He had been quietly satisfied to find how whole-heartedly she embraced the fact of Phil's marriage, and how warmly she accepted Bruce. But he had not missed the soul-searching which the uncovering of the secret had produced. Jamie had not been able to ignore, as Vanessa with her different agenda had, what Phil's concealment of such facts said about them.

'How could we have grown so far apart?' Jamie had demanded in shame. 'But I'm the most to blame, buried in my own affairs, arrogant and complacent. Imagine Phil dreading our reaction so much. I still can't bear to think of it. And believing everything was fine in Vanessa's life, cruising along myself, blind as a bat. It terrifies me to think what else I'll miss.'

It terrified Patrick to think of the lengths to which this sense of failure might drive her. But it was no good trying to shield her, as he longed to do. She must, as she had always done, seek out her own answers.

31

At one level, Jamie knew, she had arrived exactly where she wanted to be. She was living in the cottage, alone again, the sale of the big house was going through and she had the funds to build the framework of a new life.

They knew now who would be moving into Calder in a few weeks' time. The half dozen other contenders who had stayed in the race were already faceless and unreal. Very soon a new family would begin to put down roots here, make friends, face crises, work through problems and hopefully find happiness. A family called Adamson. Niall Adamson, who owned a family printing firm which had expanded into computer supplies, proposed to operate mainly from home, leaving day-to-day management to his eldest son. There was another son, a daughter still at school, and an absent older daughter, about whom little was said. Her one-year-old twins, however, were being brought up by their grandparents, so the Calder nurseries would be occupied once more.

'That's why they got your vote, isn't it?' Patrick teased Jamie. 'You're nothing but an old softie.'

'No voting about it, we did as Mr Syme told us,' Jamie retorted. 'Biggest offer, no messing.'

But she knew he understood the pleasure it gave her to think of those rooms, associated with the only sense of real security she had ever known, alive again. She liked what she had seen of this big family, and hoped they would soon come to love Calder.

But there her thoughts jarred, as they did whenever they reached this point. What was her own place in all this? She wasn't needed by either Phil or Vanessa at present, and she no longer had any useful function at Calder. Patrick, as she had in her heart known would be the case, was as remote from her as he had ever been, absorbed in his own life and still with that unalterable aura of belonging to the adult world.

The factor that brought her to a decision did not, however, concern any of these three, nor was it particularly significant in itself.

On a glorious September day when the colours were beginning to turn, the beeches along the drive bronzing, larches the softest yellow still laced with green, she and Maeve took a day off and followed the ridge up to the bare tops above Fallan. As they sat below the summit cairn to have lunch, facing the wide tumble of hills to the west and arguing with cheerful inaccuracy about their names, the new owners of Calder were once more the topic of conversation.

'I know it's only first impressions,' Jamie said, 'and time may uncover all kinds of skeletons, but they do seem an outgoing, friendly crowd. They laugh a lot together. I like that.'

'There's enough of them,' Maeve commented. 'And isn't the eldest son engaged, so no doubt they're all set to breed some more. They need a house the size of Calder. And talking of houses, you might like to know before the news gets around, I'm moving in with Fraser.'

Winded, Jamie turned to gape at her. 'With Fraser?' Maeve, to whom independence was the breath of life? She had had no idea it was even a possibility.

'He's not a bad bloke,' Maeve said easily, with a sideways grin at Jamie's thunderstruck face.

'Of course, I know he's not, but you—'

'Give it a try anyway. No big deal.'

'Maeve, it's great news.' Jamie, shaken by the dismay which had filled her, was ashamed of her lack of warmth. 'I'm delighted for you, truly.' She meant it. When she considered it, she found she had no difficulty in seeing Maeve and Fraser together.

But that evening, up at the bridge beside the empty Toll-house, she faced the assembled facts at last. The toehold to which she was clinging here was tenuous and contrived. On every side people were involved in lives which were full and complete. The rejections of the past, normally kept well buried, came achingly back. Mother, who had belonged to Vanessa, never to her. Freda, who had belonged to Phil, and had taken the greatest satisfaction in making clear at last what she thought of Jamie. Her father, whose favourite she had believed herself to be, allowing Zara to take control of his life and abandoning all interest in his daughters.

And Calder. Good though it had been to remove all trace of Zara, it was now in the hands of strangers. And however important it had seemed to hold on to the cottage, could it be more than a bolt-hole in the background? Was the idea of making a life here, taking whatever makeshift local job she could find, the merest cowardice? She had come here fleeing from disasters she had brought upon herself. Had that been cowardice too? Then where did she fit in? In that empty moment, dusk bringing the first chill breath twining up from the water, the only sound the bustling of the river over its cold stones, it seemed to her that the only place she could lay claim to was the one she had created for herself. Not specifically in Seattle, but in that world. She had given it up too easily. She had allowed Bryden, in destroying the relationship she had so deeply believed in, to strip away everything else she was or had achieved. But need she let him deprive her as well of her capacity to start again, succeed again?

Wasn't it self-indulgence to hide here? Didn't she have some kind of duty to go back and prove herself, and prove that Bryden couldn't so easily write her off? Could it satisfy her to stay in this quiet glen, living on the fringe of other people's lives, clinging to a dream which had never had any real substance?

To go on seeing Patrick on the old footing would be more than she could bear. The warning signs had grown too clear. Why not be honest? Why not admit that the sight of him, the sound of his voice, could change the colour of the day? When he wasn't there her whole self was waiting. It was no way to live. It was weak and wrong. Shattered by what Bryden had done she had used this absurd hope to bolster her up. But enough was enough.

Thank God for the numbness which takes over on a journey, Jamie thought. Had taken over, in fact, as soon as the decision was made. There had been almost no pain in the simple actions needed to unpick the flimsy structure which was all she had managed to build during the short months of summer.

The cottage would stay as it was, to be used by all of them. Phil had said how much Rhoda would love it, which Jamie rather doubted, and that perhaps some of the old folk would enjoy a day there occasionally. Vanessa, never forsaking her blind optimism, had said Ryan could take friends there. Jamie had made no comment on that.

Maeve could have moved in for the winter, she had thought with a twist of ironic amusement. For Maeve, having resisted involvement for so long, had discovered she'd been missing out on something marvellous, and though she was teased about it on every side, made no secret of the improbability of ever needing anyone's spare accommodation again. Nor, Jamie had to accept, did she need Jamie's company. They would always enjoy seeing each other, but never again would there be the lovely sense of time at their disposal, the careless, contented drifting through hours of shared work, talk and laughter. Maeve wouldn't miss her. No good thinking that. Maeve enjoyed what was there, on hand, happening. Keeping in touch was not for Maeve.

Though Phil and Vanessa had both protested about losing Jamie again, she suspected that they were resigned to her going, and had probably expected it. So there had been no resistance to overcome, few arrangements to make. Not so much as a library book to return. The belongings Jamie would need where she was going fitted once more into the single suitcase with which she had run for home. Hoping for what? She winced to remember.

There had been bad moments, and to these she tried to close her mind. She had wandered round the cottage, fingering the few treasures from the past which it had meant so much to reclaim. She had walked the river path, stood on the footbridge under the icy-fingered spray of the falls and stood, for much longer, on the grass outside the Toll-house, blind with tears.

She had said her farewells. To Freda, who stood for the irretrievable past. To the Erskines, who had moved into the different present, and who had been more outspokenly sorry to lose her than anyone else, making her promise to write, to come back soon. She had said goodbye to Naomi, more conscious than ever of the coldness she had glimpsed before, as though Naomi was impatient with all these comings and goings and wanted them done with. Driving away, Jamie had felt she had been written off for good. There had been an odd feeling too of letting Grandmother down, for Naomi in a way represented her. How it had hurt.

And she had said goodbye to Patrick. Had she actually said goodbye, in so many words? She could remember little of that brief, agonising meeting. She had been almost mute, hardly able to remember why she was going. Patrick's face had been grim, his mouth a harsh line. He had not, then or at any other time, attempted to understand her reasons for going, nor had he tried to make her change her mind.

Had she wanted him to? Jamie moved restlessly in her seat, her book unread on her lap, oblivious to the fellow-travellers around her, doing her best to suppress flaying questions and keep the protective numbness in place.

Patrick crossed to the workshop in the misty early light of a sharp autumn morning, shoulders hunched, hands driven deep into his pockets, his face sombre with reluctance to face anything that was part of his normal life. He could hardly bring himself to imagine going on with it, yet if he didn't have that he had nothing.

He went into the chilly, high-ceilinged spaces of the workshop and, flicking on the powerful directional lights, he tasted the dust on the air. In spite of having extractors, dust seemed to exude from every object overnight, and for a moment he hated it and every aspect of his work with an explosive resentment. Even so, driven by habit, he switched on the compressor, hardly aware of its familiar beating sound as it came up to pressure, dragged on his dust-stiffened overalls and steel-toed boots, his mask, clammy with yesterday's condensed breath, and the rest of the protective gear which made him feel, today, encumbered and resistant. Then he stood for long moments to study the work in progress. This was usually the point when the process took over, when other preoccupations fell away. Chalk in hand ready to mark the areas needing attention, he found himself utterly incapable of bringing his mind to bear. He had come here, unable to sleep, because work was the only recourse he had, and it was failing him.

Had he ever, truly, believed that Jamie would stay, or that she could see him as anything other than some remote authoritarian figure, a substitute for the father who had first spoiled and petted her, then ruthlessly shed her when he finally accepted that she could never be the son he had wanted.

But if she had stayed, could he have handled it? His work had suffered drastically since she had been home, that was for sure. A half-smile softened his mouth. No one but Jamie could have had that effect on him; that was also for sure.

The airport concourse seemed a hostile place, full of weaving movement, its too-powerful lights bounced back from pale, diamond-hard surfaces, its atmosphere repellent with the taste of air endlessly re-breathed. Jamie felt trapped, shut away from all that was real or that related to her. Around her strangers pressed forward to their private objectives, driven by invisible anxieties, or, seduced by glitter and the promise of a bargain, headed for the thronged shops. Sound was distorted, and the eddying movement, much of it apparently random, added to Jamie's sense of foreignness. I don't belong here; no human being belongs in this glaringly lit and artificial scene.

It was as though in that single instant all her dubious motives, her dread and loneliness, were washed away by a restoring wave of reason and clarity. What was she doing here indeed? How had she thought for a moment that she could return to that pressured, striving, materialistic world? Bryden's world.

For the first time she saw that even now, right up to this moment, he had held some remnant of power over her. She had wanted, still, to defy him, to show him . . . what? That she could survive what he had done to her? She was showing no one but herself then, for he was long gone, deep in the next scam, gulling the next victim. He probably barely remembered her name.

It was as though, for the first time since learning what he had done and finding her life collapsing around her, she had a choice. She could decide, for herself, where she wanted to be, what she wanted to do, what mattered to her. First of all, then, she must escape this thronged, unreal place, more stifling with every moment that passed. Would there be some kind of shuttle to the city? Where did it leave from? But even as she asked the questions a more effective part of her brain was taking her towards the cab rank.

'Queen Street station, please.'

'Right you are, hen.'

Sitting back, trying to subdue the wild excitement beginning to grip her, Jamie grinned. Never would she have thought such mundane words could sound so good.

'But where are you?'

'Glasgow. About to get on a train to Perth.'

'God, Jamie.' Patrick could hardly speak, hot tears springing to his eyes as he leaned his forehead against the cold acoustic hood of the workshop phone.

'Could you – would you mind meeting me?' Her voice sounded suddenly uncertain, muted, far away.

'Of course I'll meet you.' His voice in turn sounded almost angry, so much trouble was he having in dealing with the shock she had given him.

'I'm sorry to be a—'

'Don't be a fool! Don't be such an unutterable fool. What time does your train get in?'

He thought he had himself well in hand. With great calmness he had unplugged the air grinder, shut down the compressor, locked the workshop, gone to the house to change, light a fire, and make sure he had enough food to give her. He had not allowed himself to leave earlier than necessary, and had driven at his usual speed, and, he hoped, with his usual concentration, to the station. In fact, he realised now, his mood had been quite abnormal, for he had been aware of nothing. Now, seeing her, control, caution and habit cracked apart.

Shaking, his arms crushing her, his head bent over hers, he was aware of tears on his cheeks, a terrible aching in his throat.

'Don't ever, ever do that to me again.'

The moment seemed so extraordinary, so suspended in time, outside every other part of their lives, that to decide whether to go to Blackdykes or to Glen Fallan seemed impossible, outlandish. Their minds weren't ready to see themselves, together, in either setting. Association with anywhere or anyone they knew seemed for the moment an unendurable intrusion.

Safe in the characterless calm of the Station Hotel, they gazed at each other across their locked hands, their eyes tentative, almost afraid, yet both acknowledging that the embrace on the draughty platform had made a statement from which there could be no retreat.

Awkwardly, hardly able to focus on the prosaic interruptions of ordering and coffee arriving, and then refocus on what was happening to them, they began to talk.

'I thought I ought to go back to where I'd made a life before. As though it was something I had to finish. Not to let Bryden take it from me. And then too – I don't know – I seemed to have no particular place here, nowhere where I was needed. I felt kind of extra.'

'Extra.' Patrick let his breath out in a laugh that was almost despair at her obtuseness. 'Extra. What a banal little word to choose.' And yet he was thankful that she had not chosen a word more piercing – unwanted, unneeded, rejected. Those he would have found it hard to take, among the coffee tables and the hushed voices and the doilies and shortbread.

'Phil and Vanessa – their lives are both complete. Even though I was so appalled at Vanessa going back to Douglas, I do begin to understand that for her, awful as it seems, there was almost no choice. And Phil – well, it's great to see her so happy, but she never has a moment to spare, and with Rhoda to look after having someone drop by is probably more trouble than—'

'Jamie.' Patrick gently shook the hand he was holding, wrapped in both his. 'Jamie, hush a minute. You are so wrong. Did you ever try to talk to Vanessa or Phil about this? No, of course you didn't. You just formed your own ideas, set them in concrete and battered on, giving yourself grief in the process as usual. Now, pay close attention to what I'm about to say.'

His eyes were smiling, though he was watching her carefully, and Jamie felt her relief and joy to be with him, at this moment, no matter what came later, well up and nearly choke her. 'I'm listening.'

'Good. Then can't you see that precisely now, for both of them, you are more important than you've ever been? Do you really not grasp how much soul-searching Vanessa still does, how every time Douglas is in a tricky mood, or has a go at her about Ryan, who clearly has no intention of coming home or toeing the line ever again, she's terrified that she's done the wrong thing, and ashamed to think that cowardice drove her back? Don't you think that she needs you, not necessarily seeing you often, but knowing you're *there*. That's the point, Jamie. They've always wanted to have you close by. Cheerful and good-natured as Phil is, you must know that coping with all she has on her hands isn't plain sailing. But, in her case, that's not the issue. What she longs for and has always longed for, is to share things, with both you and Vanessa. She was so thrilled that you liked Bruce, and she looked forward to ordinary family coming and going more than anything. She's been deprived of it for far too long, even if it was by her own choice.'

'Hey, stop kicking me around,' Jamie protested, beginning to laugh at this long and forceful speech. 'I'm feeling fragile, remember. In my mind I've just been halfway across the Atlantic, and have had an emotional experience on a station platform thrown in.'

Patrick laughed, but Jamie saw his eyes change as he looked at her. 'And you thought I didn't want you,' he said, finding his voice would barely make the sounds.

Words, explanations, the pent-up questions and doubts of the years, poured through Jamie's mind. How could she begin to make him understand what he meant to her, how her life pivoted around him?

She was silent, helpless, tears unexpectedly threatening, afraid that, now the moment had come, she would never be able to make all this clear.

'Jamie, don't you see, I had to let you make the mistakes.' Patrick's voice was rueful, but amused too. 'You had to work through so much defiance against a world you felt had never much wanted or needed you. Even now, I had to be prepared to let you go, as long as you felt you still had something to prove. You'd never have been happy otherwise.'

'It was weird, that moment when I realised Bryden was still controlling me,' Jamie said reflectively. 'Or at least influencing my actions. I saw it, and I was free of it. Extraordinary. Expensive too,' she added. 'Cost me an air fare.'

Patrick gave her a fleeting grin, but still waited for what really mattered.

'I thought to you I was – we were – children, the next generation. As though you'd inherited us, long ago, whether you liked it or not, because of the link between our families, and had always felt responsible for us in some way. And then . . .' She paused, head down, taking a grip on his hand which he suspected she wasn't aware of. 'Well, when I was younger, I did hero-worship you, everyone knew that. I was afraid that if I ever tried to tell you how I felt, before I went to the States, even before I went to London for my first job, you'd see it as that and brush it aside.' She looked up at him, unable to go on.

'Jamie, even then? And I always thought you saw me as a father figure, so I was afraid to say how I felt too. I thought you should find someone your own age.'

'What a cliché-ridden pair we were,' Jamie said, but neither of them laughed, filled with a startled, groping wonder to think that the long waiting was over.

'God, the time we've wasted,' Patrick said with sudden anger. But even as he spoke, he knew there could have been no other way for them. Jamie had had to find her own way home.